EMPIRE HIGH

Runaway

IVY SMOAK

To my mom.

Thank you for instilling in me a love for reading.

CHAPTER 1

Friday - 16 years ago

Matt. I squeezed his hand and he squeezed mine back. God I loved him so much. And waking up next to him had quickly become my favorite thing. In a few months, I'd be his wife. Our wedding day couldn't come soon enough. I couldn't wait to be Brooklyn Caldwell. Matt squeezed my hand again. It was the most comforting feeling in the world.

Especially after the crazy nightmare I'd just had. I'd dreamt that I'd played a horrible prank on my evil half-sister Isabella. Matt had been furious with me. And I could see why. Isabella had fallen through the ceiling in my nightmare. The prank had gone way too far. *Such a crazy dream.*

But then I felt a sharp pain in my side. I winced. And everything suddenly felt…wrong. Like the room was spinning. I felt like I was going to be sick.

This didn't feel like the bed I shared with Matt. The mattress was hard and the sheets were thin and itchy.

The room didn't smell like him either. It didn't smell like anything at all.

And that was most certainly not Matt's hand holding mine. It was all wrong.

I opened my eyes and had to blink because the room was blindingly white. My dad was sitting next to me holding my hand. His eyes were closed and he was in a wheelchair, his arm attached to an IV in the corner. For just a second I was alarmed by how sickly he looked. For just a second…I was worried about him. Which was ironic.

Because he certainly wasn't worried about me. He didn't give a shit about me.

It felt like my heart stopped beating. None of it was a dream.

No.

Never.

Nunca.

Tears started welling in my eyes. The prank had happened. Matt did hate me. He'd left me. He'd called me a liar and just walked away. He didn't answer any of my calls or texts. He just…ignored my existence. Just like he had when we'd first met. Like I meant nothing to him. My chest ached. Like my heart was ripping in two. *Matthew Caldwell hates me.*

And yet…none of that was the worst thing. The monster sitting next to my bed topped everything else. And I needed to get the hell away from him.

I pulled my hand out of my dad's grip.

That startled him awake. "You're awake, princess," he said, his voice hoarse and groggy.

I was not his princess. That was his name for my evil half-sister. And I wanted no part in it. I wanted no part of this family. "Don't call me that." My voice sounded even hoarser than his. I looked down at the IV that was attached to my wrist and tried to pull it out.

"What are you doing?" He reached out to stop me.

"Don't touch me!" My stomach rolled as I sat up. I was definitely about to be sick.

"Princess, calm down. You need to rest."

I pulled out the IV and grabbed my wrist as the blood dribbled down my arm. I needed to get out of this room. I needed to get away from the man that called himself my father. *That sick fuck.*

"Brooklyn, you need to calm down," he said more forcefully.

"You stole…you stole my…" It was like my mind was all jumbled. Everything was blurry as I tried to climb out of bed. And my side hurt so damn much. When I pushed myself off the bed, I fell to my knees. My foot hit the metal pole the IV was attached to, and it fell to the ground with a clang.

"Brooklyn, stop." He reached out for me again.

I cringed when he put his hands on my shoulders. *Ow.* I grabbed my stomach. I wasn't going to be sick. I was just in pain because my dad had tried to kill me.

"Shit," my dad mumbled.

Something in the room started beeping like crazy.

And Dr. Wilson rushed in. "What on earth is going on in here? Did she fall out of bed?"

"She's hysterical," my dad said. "Do something!"

Hysterical? I'm not hysterical. He was the crazy one, not me. "Help me," I croaked and grabbed Dr. Wilson's pant leg.

Dr. Wilson stared down at me like I'd lost my mind. Like I was a feral animal he wanted to kick away. Why was he looking at me like that? I was asking him for help. Begging him to save me from this hell. Did he not realize what had just happened?

"I didn't agree to this," I said. "I didn't. Let me go. Please let me go. Let me out of here." It felt like air wasn't reaching my lungs fast enough. I choked on my own breath.

Dr. Wilson glanced at my dad and then back at me.

"Please get me out of here. I don't want to be here anymore." Not in this room. Not near my dad. Not in this house. Not in this fucking state.

"Did you give her too many painkillers?" my dad asked.

"I…" Dr. Wilson's voice trailed off. "I don't know. Did you see her take more medication?"

I'm not high! But Dr. Wilson's statement made me realize that he was not here to help me. He was part of the reason I was in pain. He'd performed the surgery. It wasn't just my dad. Dr. Wilson was a monster too. I couldn't be here. I needed to get away from both of them. I tried to get up but fell back down.

"Brooklyn, try to take a deep breath for me," my dad said. "I think you're just having a panic attack."

Fuck him for using that against me. I trusted him. And now he was trying to make me feel insane. "I'm not," I gasped. Maybe I was. But deep breathing wasn't going to help. I needed to get out of this haunted apartment.

"I'll take you wherever you want to go," my dad said. "Where do you want to go, princess?"

Stop calling me that. I wasn't his princess. I wanted nothing to do with him. "Please just let me go." I tried to push myself up off the floor but the pain was blinding. The room started to spin. The door seemed like it was a million miles away. If I could just…

"We'll get you back to your bedroom, alright?" my dad said. "Please take a deep breath."

"No. I don't want to be here anymore. Please." I felt the tears streaming down my cheeks.

He lowered his eyebrows. "Okay. We'll get you out of here, if that's what you want. Just tell me where you want to go."

I wanted to go to Matt's. Desperately. But he no longer wanted me there. He'd made that pretty clear after our fight. And my best friend, Kennedy, was mad at me too. I had nowhere to go. But I needed out of this room. Out of this house. Out of this life. I couldn't do this anymore. Everything hurt.

"Just tell me where, princess."

I wasn't his fucking princess. "As far away as possible from you."

His face fell. "Brooklyn, what's going on?"

"You stole my fucking kidney, you psychopath!" I tried to stand up again but the room was spinning too fast.

"No. No," he said more sternly. "Princess, I…"

"Don't princess me! I'm not your princess! Don't pretend for a second that you care about me. You just used me for spare parts."

"You signed the contract. You agreed…"

"I didn't read the contract! You're supposed to be my dad. You're supposed to love me. How could you do this? How could you do this to me?" I couldn't be sure because I was crying so hard, but I swore I saw tears in his eyes too.

"I'm sorry," he said. "I thought you knew. I never would have…"

"Stop lying. For once in your life, stop lying to me."

He just stared at me. "Brooklyn, I swear…"

I didn't believe a word he said.

"We talked about it several times."

What the hell was he talking about? He'd never told me he was about to steal my kidney! "Please just let me leave. Please let me out of here."

He nodded. "Okay." He reached out like he was going to help me up.

I grimaced. "Please. If you care about me at all." My whole body shook with my tears. Everything fucking hurt. But I was pretty sure my heart hurt most of all. None of it had been a dream. Which meant Matt hated me. He thought I was the monster. Not my dad or Isabella, but…me. "Please," I sobbed.

"Okay. Honestly, I think this is for the best," he said. "This was what I wanted all along. I'm glad you're finally seeing reason." He nodded to Dr. Wilson.

I felt something pinch my arm and looked up a second too late to see Dr. Wilson injecting me with something.

The room grew even blurrier.

"Shh," my dad whispered, gently patting my shoulder.

Get away from me.

He'd tricked me.

He'd used me.

He'd never actually loved me. No one loved me.

All my father had ever wanted me for was my kidney. He'd sought me out just to use me. An illegitimate kid with no other purpose. Someone to use and cast aside just like everyone else in my life had. I had nothing. And no one.

"Go back to sleep," my father whispered. "Everything's fine."

Nothing was fine. I tried to move away from him, but my body wasn't listening to me. It was like it had just…given up.

"What did you give me?" At first I wasn't sure he heard me, because my lips felt weird. But he finally responded.

"It's just a mild sedative so you can get your rest. I'll take care of all the arrangements. I'll get you somewhere safe. A fresh start, princess."

I didn't want whatever his version of safe was. And I didn't want to sleep. I wanted the pain to stop. I just wanted…everything to stop. It hurt too fucking much.

CHAPTER 2

Friday

I was in a white room. I wasn't sure where. Despite the machines everywhere, it didn't look like a hospital room. Just a normal bedroom. If something so sterile could be considered normal.

I'd woken up here a few minutes ago. Or maybe it was a few hours.

At least my body worked now. I curled up in a ball and stared at the white wall. It looked like one of the blank canvases I'd given to Matt yesterday. A Thanksgiving Day present. Or at least, I thought it had been yesterday. I had no idea what day it was anymore.

All I knew was that the painting set I'd given Matt was stupid.

I'd been stupid. About all of it.

I'd thought he had my back.

I'd thought he loved me.

The white wall blurred in front of me as the tears clouded my vision.

I'd loved him. I'd loved him so much. And he…he'd left me alone with my dad and half-sister. Matt knew I was scared of Isabella. He knew what kind of man my dad was. And he had left me in their clutches. And now I was God knows where and missing a fucking kidney. What kind of fiancé left the supposed love of his life in the hands of the devil himself?

Not one I believed in.

I hated Matthew freaking Caldwell.

But I loved him a lot more than I hated him right now. I loved him so much it hurt.

I pulled my knees tighter to my chest. I felt foolish. For the first time in a long time, I'd let my guard down. I'd let another person into my life knowing that I'd end up here again. All alone.

Was he thinking about me now?

Was Kennedy?

Did either of them know what my dad had just done?

Did they even care?

And where the hell was I?

I tried to remember what my dad had said to me as I was waking up from surgery. He said he'd take me somewhere safe. But he didn't understand that he was the one I wanted to get away from. I'd never be safe with him. He'd probably steal my liver next.

And I certainly didn't want to be here in this white empty room all by myself. With a beeping monitor in the corner, telling me my heart was still working. I didn't believe it. It couldn't possibly still be beating.

Maybe this really was all a dream. But I never remembered a dream physically hurting this damned much.

I looked down at the hospital gown I was wearing. I didn't remember putting it on. Which meant someone else had put it on me. Like I was some doll that could be played with.

Fuck everyone.

I pushed the thin fabric to the side and stared down at a bandage on my stomach. I pulled the fabric back into place. All I was good for was donating organs.

Because I was a liar. A bad friend. A bad fiancé. A bad niece. I felt the tears falling down my cheeks again.

Maybe everyone was right. Maybe I was just like Isabella.

Yeah, I wasn't sure how the machine in the corner was beeping. Because my heart wasn't working properly anymore.

I pulled my knees back up to my chest and my left hand caught my eye. *No.*

My engagement ring was gone. *What?* I looked around the bed. I pushed the blankets and sheets aside. I moved the pillow. Where was my ring? My heart started beating faster, the monitor in the corner going frantic. This ring meant the world to Matt. I couldn't lose it. He already hated me. I could beg him for forgiveness for the prank. But he wouldn't forgive me for this. I tossed the pillow onto the ground. It had to be here somewhere. I shoved the sheets off the bed until it was just me sitting on the mattress surrounded by nothing.

Had Matt been here? Had he taken my ring? I stared at the bare spot on my finger. If he'd been here, I didn't remember any of it. I knew we'd had a fight. I wished I could take back the damage I'd done. And I knew that wasn't possible. But I could at least try to fix it.

I just kept staring at the bare spot on my finger. What if Matt didn't want me to fix it though? What if he didn't want to be an *us* anymore? I felt the tears rolling down my cheeks. What if this was the end?

I only had myself to blame. I'd hung out with the Hunter brothers when Matt had specifically told me not to. It didn't matter that I had good intentions of fixing his friendship with them. I'd hoped for the best, but I should have expected the worst. The worst tended to follow me around like a black cloud. Or else I wouldn't be sitting in this empty room, on this empty bed, recovering from my dad stealing my fucking kidney.

I was bad luck.

Cursed.

I was a Pruitt.

No.

I was a freaking Sanders. And Sanders didn't give up. Not like this. Matt would forgive me. He had to. And he'd help keep me safe from my dad. I just needed to figure out a way out of this room. I grimaced as I pulled the IV out of the back of my hand. I climbed off the bed. *Ow.* I clutched my stomach as I made my way over to the door. But when I tried to turn the knob...it didn't budge. He'd locked me in here? What the hell? I had to get out of here. But I didn't bang on the door. It would just alert everyone.

There was a window in the room. If I could just climb out... I took another step and had to double over from the pain.

Damn it. I couldn't stay here. I was a sitting duck for whenever my father decided he needed another organ. I took another step forward. It felt like someone was ripping my stomach in two.

"What are you doing out of bed?" A nurse rushed into the room.

"I need to leave."

"You need to lie down."

I tried to move away from her but she stepped in front of me.

She pushed a button by my bed and two big male nurses came into the room. One was holding a syringe.

No, not again. "Get away from me." I wanted to scream and throw things, but my knees were weak. I was seconds away from collapsing, but they stabbed me with the syringe anyway.

Everything was blurry as they got me back in bed.

"Try to rest," the first nurse said.

I looked back down at the empty spot on my finger where the ring Matt had given me had been. I'd thought I had it all figured out. I'd thought I'd be a Caldwell and live happily ever after.

But I'd always be a Pruitt.

CHAPTER 3

Saturday

I was in a new room now. One without a window. My dad must have been worried I'd try to escape again. So he was keeping me prisoner in a windowless cage.

But I didn't have any visitors. None of the nurses told me anyone was trying to reach me. Which meant my dad didn't really have anything to worry about. Where would I go? Kennedy hated me. Isabella was trying to kill me. My friend Felix was in jail because of me. I looked down at where my ring once sat. Matt didn't love me anymore.

I had nowhere to go.

And I was tired.

I closed my eyes tight, wishing I could wake up from this hell.

Everything hurt. Every single inch of my body. But nothing hurt as much as my heart. It felt like it was shattered in a million tiny pieces.

I closed my eyes tighter.

I was familiar with this feeling. I'd felt the same way when my mom passed away. And I'd felt it again when I lost Uncle Jim.

It felt like…loss. Unsurmountable loss. I felt my tears trail down the sides of my face, falling into my hair.

I couldn't do this again. I just wanted to let go. Matt and Kennedy's words swirled around in my head.

"You're just like Isabella."

"My life isn't a fucking fairytale like yours, Brooklyn."

"I guess we're both liars."

I'm a monster. A whimper escaped my throat.

RUNAWAY

Why couldn't it all be a dream? Why couldn't I wake up?

CHAPTER 4

Monday

"You need to eat," the nurse said as she set down another tray of food beside the one I hadn't touched from this afternoon.

I didn't bother responding. I'd already told her several times that I wasn't hungry. A hunger strike probably was a good move at this point. But that wasn't why I left all my food untouched. I just…wasn't hungry. Not when my stomach was so twisted up inside.

She wrote something down in a notebook.

Screw you too. "Can I please have my phone now?"

"We've already been over this. You don't have a phone."

I hated this bitch. "Then can I please use your phone? Or the house phone? Or the phone wherever we are?"

"That's just not a possibility. Now make sure you eat every bite."

If I'd still had the IV cord I would have tried to strangle her with it. "Please," I said.

"See you in the morning." She hurried away, ignoring my very reasonable request.

All I ever saw were her and the two big nurses who liked to inject me with something whenever I misbehaved. Which I'd stopped doing, for the record. All I did was sit here all day. I eyed the food on the tray and then turned away from it.

Each day that went by made me more and more hopeless.

I sighed and stared at the white wall.

Kennedy had been right. For just a few seconds I'd had everything. My life had seemed like a fairytale. But it had all been a façade. Kennedy was the one that had everything. Everything that I'd lost. She had a loving mother. Someone who was always on her side. An unconditional kind of love I'd never have again. I just wanted to go back home to Delaware. I wanted another chance to do everything differently.

My life was no fairytale. Which meant Matthew Caldwell wasn't my knight in shining armor. He wasn't going to show up and save me. He'd always been good at not showing up when I needed him most.

CHAPTER 5

Wednesday

Please, Matt. I'm sorry. Don't leave me here. All I could feel was the wetness on my cheeks.

I closed my eyes, praying to a God I didn't believe in that this was all a terrible dream. I begged him to let me wake up from it.

But there was no waking up.

The scar on my stomach and the ring missing from my finger were both permanent reminders.

I'm sorry I lied, Matt. I'm so sorry. Please save me.

CHAPTER 6

Thursday

I was mad at Matt for leaving me at the Pruitts' apartment when he knew they were dangerous. I was mad at him for not answering my calls before the surgery. And I was mad at him for not having my back.

What was he even upset about, anyway?

Isabella was the worst. No, she probably didn't deserve to be covered in pudding. But it was funny.

Or was he upset about my hanging out with James and Rob? I was trying to fix his friendship. Was he jealous? Was that it? Because that was ridiculous. I loved him and only him. He knew that. And just thinking about him being mad at me made me furious at him.

I'd apologized to him immediately. And his response? That I belonged with the crazy Pruitts. That I was officially one of them. And that stung. I'd always thought he'd seen me for me. That my new last name didn't define me. He'd been lying to me the whole time. All he saw when he looked at me was my last name.

But just because I was mad didn't mean I stopped loving him. My anger didn't take away all the good memories we'd shared. And that we'd share again as soon as I got out of my cage.

I was going to fix us. All I needed to do was get out of here. I sat up when the nurse came in with my food.

She sighed as she saw my previous untouched plate.

"I need to talk to my dad."

"Your father is a very busy man. You know this."

He hadn't been busy a few days ago when he stole my kidney. And shouldn't he have been recovering too? Probably in some fancy recovery center where they didn't lock their patients in their rooms. If he had time to do all that, he certainly had time to talk to me on the freaking phone. "Please. Could you just call him and tell him I need to speak with him? Tell him it's urgent."

"And what exactly is urgent?"

The fact that you're keeping me locked up in here. Although, I was pretty sure she was following my father's orders. "It's a private matter."

"I see. Well, I'm under strict instruction to not bother him with anything unimportant."

"It is important." I was pretty sure him kidnapping me was illegal. Locking me up here? Stealing organs from me? It was very important. And he couldn't hide from me forever in his apartment, even if there were a million rooms to hide in.

"If you relay it to me, I'll make sure he receives a message about it. But today's not a good day."

I just gaped at her. Not a good day? He couldn't even bother to take a message from me? Seriously? My kidney had saved his life. He at least owed me a conversation. "It's just a quick phone call."

"All the arrangements had to be made immediately. Can you imagine how exhausted he is after the surgery and all that?" Her eyes grew round like she'd said too much.

"All...what?" I asked.

"If you'll excuse me."

"What arrangements?"

She hurried to the door.

"Wait!" I yelled. "You can't keep me here!" I jumped off the bed, but she pulled the door closed before I could make a run for it. "Let me out!" I yelled at the top of my lungs. "Someone help me!"

But there was no answer.

I banged on the door. "Can anyone hear me?"

No response.

I banged on the door harder. "Someone please help me!"

But there was no response.

"Someone help me," I sobbed and let my body fall to the floor. I slammed my palm against the door. "Please." I let my forehead rest against the door as I continued to hit it with my palms. Someone out there had to have a heart. *Please.*

***

I was being lifted into the air. Someone was cradling me in their arms. I blinked but the room was pitch black.

They set me down on my bed.

"Brooklyn?" said a deep voice. A voice I recognized.

"Miller!" I wanted to hug him and cry and scream for joy all at once. I'd needed a familiar face desperately. And it was like my prayers had been answered.

"Shhh. I'm not supposed to be in here."

I pushed myself up into a seated position. "Miller, you have to get me out of here." I tried to climb back off the bed but he put his hand down on my thigh.

"I can't." His voice broke. "I'm sorry, Brooklyn, I can't."

I swallowed hard. "What do you mean? I never gave my dad permission to do this. He can't keep me locked up here. I want to go home. Please, you have to get me out of here." I reached out for him in the darkness. He hissed when my hand collided with his shoulder. It sounded like he was holding back a cry of pain.

Tears started welling in my eyes. There was only one reason why Miller would make that noise. And even though I couldn't see his face in the darkness, I knew. I swallowed hard. "What did he do to you?" My dad had taught Miller a lesson recently. And he was only just finally healing. What had my father done to him now?

"I'm fine," he said. "I'm more concerned about you. I thought I heard you yelling earlier. But I had to wait to sneak in. Are you in pain?"

He was always way more concerned about me than himself.

"Just tell me where it hurts," he said.

I was in pain. But not from my surgery. My chest ached every day. My heart was breaking. I couldn't eat. I couldn't sleep. "Everywhere."

He reached out and ran his fingers through my hair. "I'm going to go get the nurse, okay? She can give you something."

"No. Please don't leave me."

"I'm not even supposed to be in here."

"Please. Don't go." I caught his hand before he had a chance to flee. And I felt it. I felt what I always felt when I was around him. This undeniable sense of comfort. And it had been so long since I felt safe that I started to cry.

"Brooklyn." His voice cracked.

"Please just stay. For just another minute."

He squeezed my hand.

And even though he had to leave…he stayed. Because he cared about me. Because Miller did have my back.

"Just another minute," I mumbled. I was finally tired. And a little hungry. It was like his hand in mine had restored me somehow. And I hoped to God he wouldn't let go.

CHAPTER 7

Friday

When I woke up, Miller was no longer sitting by my bed. And I had the strangest feeling that I'd imagined the whole thing. Just so I could finally sleep. I remembered all the times I'd snuck into Miller's room at night when I was living with my dad. I couldn't sleep in my room there. But I could always fall asleep in his arms. And he had always let me.

I looked down at my hand that he'd been holding. If it was a dream…why had I dreamt of Miller instead of Matt? It was easy to fall asleep in Matt's arms too. He was there for me after my uncle died. He'd held me as I cried. But he'd never been there for me when I was scared.

I pulled my knees into my chest. Last night wasn't a dream. If it was…certainly I would have dreamt of Matt. And besides, if it had actually happened…that meant Miller was here. Wherever here was. Which meant he might come back tonight to check on me. It was the only hope I had to hang on to.

***

I had no idea what time it was. Not having a window in my room was driving me crazy. Or maybe I was already crazy…and that's why I was locked up in here.

I sighed and stared at the door. The nurse had already been by with breakfast and lunch, so she'd be by with dinner eventually. Not that I wanted any of it. I just wanted it to be nighttime again and for Miller to walk through that door.

So I waited.

And waited.

The food came and went.

I kept staring at the door, wishing for Miller to walk through it.

But Miller didn't come.

Eventually, I switched the lights off.

I was just beginning to think I really had imagined him coming when the door creaked open.

I sat up in my bed. "Miller?"

"Shhh," he whispered as he closed the door.

I breathed a sigh of relief. He was real. He was here. And I had a million questions for him. "Where are we? Is this a hospital or some recovery center or something? Did my dad hurt you again? Did you know he was going to take my kidney? Is that why you seemed surprised when I signed the contract? Where is my dad? Has he stolen other people's organs? The nurse mentioned him making arrangements for something. What was she talking about?"

"Move over, kid," he said without answering any of my questions.

I hated when he called me that. But I slid to the edge of my bed and smiled as he climbed in beside me. He lay down, resting his head next to mine. The warmth radiating off his body comforted me.

"You're shaking," he said, looping an arm across me. "Are you cold?"

I didn't realize I had been shaking. But I immediately stopped when he put his arm around me. He was doing that thing again…where being close to him was making me relaxed and sleepy. But I couldn't believe I'd just fallen asleep last night when I needed answers. I wasn't going to make the same mistake again. "You didn't answer any of my questions."

"I told you to read the whole contract. How do you think I got stuck in a job I can't get out of?"

He'd tried to warn me. And I was too foolish to listen. "Yeah. You did try to warn me."

"This is so fucked up." He sighed. "I'm so sorry he did this to you."

"What did he do to you?"

There was a long stretch of silence. "It's not im-portant, Brooklyn."

It was to me. I reached up and touched his face in the darkness.

He cringed.

"Turn the light on."

"It's late," he said. "How about you try to get some rest?"

"I can't possibly sleep right now. Please, just tell me why he hurt you. It's not like me being in danger this time was in any way your fault. It was his."

"Mr. Pruitt is coming down here tomorrow. He can answer all of your questions."

"Down here? Where are we?"

"Tomorrow, kid."

I slowly exhaled. It was nice to have a familiar face, even if I couldn't actually see him. But he was being pur-posely evasive right now. "But…"

"All you need to know is that you're safe here. No one knows we're here except for the nurses, Mr. Pruitt, and me."

"What about Matt?" I immediately regretted asking the question. I felt Miller's arm tense around me.

"Try to get some rest, okay?" He moved to get off my bed.

"Wait." I caught his arm. "Please don't go. I won't ask any more questions. Just…please stay the night." It was a selfish thing to ask. Miller was already hurt. And if my dad caught him in here sleeping on my bed? I didn't know what my crazy father would do.

But it didn't seem like Miller cared, because he lay back down.

We were both quiet for a moment.

"I'm sorry," I said. "About what my father did to you."

"You don't have to apologize for his actions. You're not him."

I swallowed hard.

"Does it still hurt?" he asked.

I was barely paying attention. I was focused on the fact that he just said I wasn't like my father. I'd been desperate to hear those words ever since Matt said the opposite. I slid closer to him on the bed. For a second I paused, waiting to see what he would do. But he didn't try to leave again. He just lay there. So I moved closer again and rested my head on his chest.

His heartbeat was so steady. And soothing. I closed my eyes.

Miller reached down and lightly touched my stomach. "You didn't answer my question."

"You didn't answer any of mine either."

He laughed. "Please. Put my mind at ease."

"It doesn't hurt as much when you're here." And that included my heart. When I was alone in this room all I could think about was it breaking in two. But when Miller was holding me? It was a lot easier to feel whole again.

"You're going to be the death of me, Brooklyn." His hand moved to my back, holding me closer to him.

I knew that meant that he cared. But I hated the phrase. I'd already experienced enough death. Miller saying it gave me a new goal though. I wasn't just going to get out of here. I was going to get Miller out of here too. He said that there was no way out of my dad's business. But I'd find a way. I owed him at least that. And thinking about saving him instead of myself made me feel a little stronger. Or maybe it was just his arms around me that gave me hope.

CHAPTER 8

Saturday

This morning the nurse told me that it was Saturday. I'd been here for over a week. My dad had left me here alone to…what? Give me a chance to get over the fact that he was a kidney thief? Spoiler alert…it wasn't working. If anything, that just pissed me off even more. I was never going to get over this. He'd pretended to care about me for months just so he could get an organ. He could not speak to me for the rest of my life and it wouldn't be long enough. Honestly, I was hoping that was his plan. He'd gotten what he needed from me. So now he could just let me go. He would come today and say goodbye. Cast me away for good. Unless he needed another organ.

I couldn't wait to get out of here. Today he'd come and I'd tell him I was fine. That we were all good. No hard feelings. But it was time to part ways. I'd be professional and composed about it. I just wanted to put this all behind me.

The door opened. I sat up in bed to greet my dad but…it was just the nurse again.

She looked at my untouched food and sighed. "I'm going to have to suggest to your father that we send you to a rehab facility next."

"What? Why?" I didn't want to go from one prison to the next.

"You have anorexic tendencies."

Anorexic tendencies? That was a weird way to put the fact that I was too thoroughly depressed to find food appetizing. "I'm just depressed that my dad stole my kidney."

"Well, we can get a psychologist to come in and speak with you then. There's pills for such things."

The last thing I wanted was to take prescription pills I didn't need. I wouldn't put it past my father to meddle with them and try to kill me or something. "I'm fine."

"Then eat."

"I'm not hungry."

"Well, then I have no choice but to put your IV back in. You're going to starve to death at this rate."

I grabbed my wrist. It hurt from the two times I'd ripped the IV out. And I freaking hated being attached to an IV. It made me feel like I was on a leash. I picked up the spoon and ate a few bites of applesauce to appease her.

"Good girl."

Bite me. "When is my dad getting here?"

She stared at me. "Who told you that your father was coming here?"

Crap. I wasn't trying to get Miller in trouble. "I just figured if he refused to take my calls it was because he wanted to plead his case for harvesting organs in person."

She glared at me. "Your father is paying an arm and a leg for you to be here. You should at least be grateful for his generosity."

Excuse me? She couldn't be serious. There was something wrong with this lady's head. "I wouldn't need him to be paying for any of this if he hadn't stolen my kidney. If anyone is generous it's me." And honestly I was a little concerned about my missing kidney. If my dad had kidney issues, it might be hereditary or something. I might need an extra kidney a few years down the road and I wouldn't freaking have an extra one now. *Asshole.*

She just shook her head.

"So when is he coming?"

"He's a very busy man." She lifted up my untouched tray from breakfast. "Now finish eating your lunch."

Did that mean he wasn't coming at all? What the hell? But before I could ask, she hurried out of the room. I was starting to hate that woman more than I hated my father. And that was really saying something.

I stared at the ceiling and tried to practice what I'd say to my father if he did end up coming today. Or if I ever saw him again. I needed to remember to stay calm and composed even though I could feel rage pulsing through my veins. It was easy to stay calm though. Because my anger eventually boiled over to sadness. An endless loop of anger and despair.

It was Saturday. Which meant my fight with Matt happened nine days ago. *Nine.* And as far as I could tell, he'd just let me go. I rolled over and stared at the blank wall. I willed myself to not look at my left hand, where my engagement ring once sat. Because every time I looked at it, I started to cry.

The last voicemail I'd left Matt had been horrible. I'd called him a hypocrite. I'd said awful things. And I played those hateful words on repeat as I lay here in this hospital bed. I missed him. Desperately. And each day that passed made it seem like he didn't miss me at all. How could I be reduced to so little in his mind when he was still my everything?

I quickly wiped away the tears on my cheeks. Maybe I did need to talk to a therapist. These mood swings made me feel like I was insane. It reminded me of when I went to the nurse at Empire High and she suggested I go see the school counselor. My uncle had just died and I was struggling. Honestly, I was *still* struggling. Some days it felt hard to breathe. It was like every time I thought my life was going to be okay again…something terrible happened.

Something awful and irreversible. And I was so tired of waking up all alone in my misery.

There was a knock on the door.

I quickly sat up. It was definitely too early for dinner. Which meant…

"Princess," my dad said. He was in one of his normal suits, and if it wasn't for the cane he was leaning on…there would be no way to know he'd just had surgery. He looked healthy and the smile on his face made it appear that he was happy too. Great. He was the exact opposite of me. And just like that…I got angry again.

"Please don't call me that," I said. "That's your nickname for Isabella. And I'm not Isabella."

His smile faltered. "Of course you're not. You're my angel." He sat down on the edge of my bed.

"An angel would have willingly given you a kidney. You had to steal mine."

His smile disappeared completely. "Brooklyn, you have to understand…I thought you knew. I never would have…"

"Bullshit."

"Language," he warned.

He wasn't allowed to be a kidney thief one minute and a good parent the next. "Fuck you!" Wow, this conversation was not going at all how I'd planned.

For just a second he looked ghostly pale. But he quickly recovered. "We've already been over this. You signed the contract and…"

"Dad! How can you not see my side on this? You gave me the world's longest contract to sign. I couldn't possibly have read all the fine print. And we never talked about it."

"We did discuss it. I tried to talk to you about it at the diner that day I picked you up during lunch. Remember?"

What? I shook my head. "We were talking about me getting on birth control. Which was super awkward and I wish you'd stop…" *Oh. Wait.* I tried to remember the conversation. It had been super weird. And it had ended with him talking about staying in front of the issue. About getting it over with as soon as possible. Had he switched the conversation halfway through to talking about the weird kidney thing without me realizing it? "Wait…were you worried I would get pregnant and wouldn't be able to do the surgery? Is that why you kept talking about it?"

"Yes, I told you that."

"You didn't tell me that! I had no idea what you were talking about!"

"Brooklyn, I even gave you an out. I told you if you weren't comfortable talking about it with me, then maybe you weren't ready to do the transplant."

"I thought you were talking about birth control and sex the entire time!"

"Oh. What a misunderstanding." He patted my shin.

"You even said I could see Dr. Wilson about getting on birth control. I know you did. I…"

"Good heavens no. Dr. Wilson is a specialist dealing with my kidney problems. He's not an OBGYN."

How could I have misunderstood everything so horribly?

"But I do appreciate you going through with it."

"I was forced into it. It doesn't matter that our discussion was a misunderstanding. You still tricked me. You sought me out after 16 years of ignoring my existence. All because you needed a kidney!" I slid away from him on the bed so he couldn't touch me. "You made me believe that you loved me!"

"I do love you."

"What's the point of lying now? Do you need my liver too?"

"Brooklyn. I love you so much. And I hate to admit it, but I never sought you out. I never even knew you existed. Your uncle's lawyer came to me. Because I'm your legal guardian. Do you really think I wouldn't have found you sooner if I'd known you were out there?"

"Yeah, which goes back to the whole thing with how you wanted my mom to abort me. Don't sit there and pretend you give a shit about me, Dad." I put a scathing emphasis on his name.

He pulled his eyebrows together. "I loved your mother. I still love your mother even though she's gone. I made some terrible mistakes when I was younger. Trust me, I don't need you to remind me. But I never sought you out because I needed a kidney transplant. It was a happy coincidence that you fell into my lap. And yes, of course I thought about it when I found out you were alive…"

"Which is why you were so overly protective of me. And concerned about my health. And why you wouldn't let me live in a bad part of town with Kennedy and her mom."

He shook his head. "That wasn't why I brought you into my home. It had nothing to do with that. I love you because you're a piece of me and I will do anything in my power to keep you safe."

"By cutting me open?"

"I thought you were giving me your kidney willingly. Because I'm your father. Because we were a match. Because you're wonderful."

I shook my head. "I'm not an idiot. All those tests you ran on me that first day when you locked me in that apartment? You were testing me to see if I was a match right away. Don't sit there and lie and pretend that wasn't the first thing running through your head."

"No." He stood up. "You know what the first thing I thought when I found out about you? I was ecstatic. I've regretted leaving your mother every single day since she left New York."

I couldn't even look at him. He was lying. He was a dirty fucking liar.

"And when I met you? All I could think about was how much you looked like your mother. And it was hard to look at you."

I remembered being shoved in the back of his car. He'd acted distant and aloof. Had he really been struggling to look at me?

"And I knew that as soon as I brought you into my home that my life as I knew it would be over. The life I'd chosen over a life with your mom. And I did it anyway. Because I love you."

I just stared at him. I didn't know what to say.

"I didn't think of the transplant at all. My whole world was turned upside down. I called Dr. Wilson because I saw where you were living and I figured you hadn't seen a proper doctor in years. And yes, I wanted a paternity test. But as soon as I saw you...I knew. I knew you were my blood. Dr. Wilson ran the extra tests without me even knowing it. Apparently he assumed the worst of me too." He stood up and ran his fingers through his hair. He looked completely distraught.

But I couldn't tell if it was all an act or if he was being sincere. I wanted to believe him. Because he was standing there telling me he loved me. And I didn't have anyone left in my life that loved me.

"Please don't cry, angel."

I tried to wipe away my tears. "If you had just asked me…I would have said yes. I don't want to lose you too."

"I'm so sorry."

I would have given anything to save my mom. My heart was so broken when she died. I'd remembered thinking that if my heart was going to break anyway…that I wished I had given it to her to save her. I never thought I could keep going. But here I was. My heart was still beating. Still broken, but still beating. I wished my mom was here right now. She was so good at reading people. She'd know if my dad was telling the truth. I stared at his face. She'd loved him once. She trusted him once.

But so had I. He'd betrayed her trust and now he'd betrayed mine. I looked down at my lap. The last words I'd said to Matt were hateful. I'd pushed him away. I couldn't afford to push my dad away too. I wiped away the rest of my tears and stared at him. "Are you feeling better?"

He smiled. "A million times better, thanks to you. I feel like a new man." He took a deep breath. "But we need to talk about you and the fact that you haven't been eating."

That nurse was such a traitor. I'd eaten some applesauce! "I was upset. With you. Why would you just leave me here without any connection to you or the outside world for over a week? I've been going crazy. And have you seen my ring? Did Dr. Wilson take it off before the surgery?" That was what I'd been hoping. That Matt didn't come take it back while I was unconscious. That it was just missing. A missing ring was better than one that had been taken back.

"About that. We have something we need to discuss."

I pressed my lips together. "Did Matt…did he…" my voice trailed off. "Did he break up with me?"

My dad reached out and grabbed my hand. "It's over, yes."

What? "But…I need to talk to him. Can I borrow your cell phone? If I could just explain…"

"It's going to be a little hard to explain. Actually, it's going to be impossible. Matthew thinks you're dead."

CHAPTER 9

Saturday

Matt thought I was…dead? I just stared at my dad. I must have misheard him. "Sorry, what did you say?"

"I said that Matthew Caldwell thinks you're dead. He believes you died during surgery. So unfortunately you can't call him. That would be confusing for the poor boy."

"What do you mean he thinks I'm dead?" I touched my chest like I needed the affirmation that I was alive. "I'm fine."

"Of course. But everyone except for myself, the nurses at this facility, and your bodyguard believe you to be dead. I've been planning this for quite some time and was going to discuss it with you. But after the surgery last week you said you wanted to leave the city. So I expedited everything. And here we are."

"I don't want everyone to think I'm dead. I need to talk to Matt. And I need to fix things with Kennedy and Felix…"

"I think everything is fixed. Felix is out of jail and all charges have been dropped. He'll be allowed to go back to Empire High. And as for Kennedy and Matthew…they seemed awfully sad at your funeral. So I'm sure whatever misunderstandings you had with them were laid to rest at your tombstone."

"How could I have a funeral? I'm right here!"

"It was on Wednesday. A fake funeral is actually an excellent and underutilized way to see who your real friends are. You had quite the attendance. You should be flattered." He patted my shin.

"I don't care about who attended my fake funeral. I don't want to be fake dead. I want…"

"There is no other option, angel. Isabella has been threatening some rather…awful things. I found some plans hidden under her mattress." He shivered, just thinking about whatever her plans had been. "It's better if you disappear for a while. We'll see if everything calms down after she graduates in the spring. Or maybe we'll be safe and wait five years until she graduates from college as well. She'll mature immensely in her college years. Certainly she won't be jealous of you then."

I didn't think Isabella hated me because she was jealous. I was pretty sure she hated me and wanted to kill me because she was legit psychotic. "So you told everyone I was dead and had a fake funeral for me, all to make sure Isabella is happy? Dad! We talked about this. I shouldn't have to change my life when she's the crazy one. You need to lock her up. Not me."

"I'm doing what I need to do to keep you safe."

"I'm not an animal! You can't keep me in a cage for five years while I wait for my half-sister to stop being murdery!"

He stood, ignoring me. "I'm sorry, but the arrangements have already been made."

"Then unmake them. I'm not going to pretend to be dead."

"You said you wanted to disappear, and there's no going back."

I'd never used those words. I'd said I wanted to leave. I wanted to be away from *him*. "You can't do this…"

"It's done." He glanced down at his watch like this conversation was boring him.

"You can't just leave me here."

"I'm not leaving you here. As soon as you're fully recovered we'll be moving you to a secure location. You'll have a bodyguard protecting you at all times. I've made all the necessary arrangements. You'll have no contact with the outside world, other than me. You'll finally be safe."

Safety and isolation were two very different things. "Please don't do this."

"Brooklyn, I'm not doing this *to* you. I'm doing it *for* you."

For me? God, and just like that I was pissed again. *For me?* Was he kidding? I said I wanted to get away from *him* after the surgery. Not be trapped in a life with only him in it. "I don't want anything from you."

He lowered his eyebrows and lightly touched the side of his stomach like he was in pain.

Was he trying to get out of this conversation by playing the "I'm in pain" card? Maybe a normal daughter would be concerned about the fact that her father was standing in front of her with a cane. But...not me. I wasn't concerned about his health at all. Besides, he'd be fine. He had my kidney after all. The sympathy card wasn't working on me.

I opened my mouth and then closed it again when no words came out. He was telling me I had to stay in this room for as long as he deemed fit. This room without windows, where I didn't know if it was day or night.

All I knew was that...I was terrified of my father. One minute he was caring. And the next he was telling me I was trapped with no way out. I wanted to slap him across the face. But I didn't dare. Instead I just blinked at him. He'd pacified me with his explanation of the kidney debacle. But keeping me locked up here? There was no explanation I would accept for that. I wished I was brave enough to knee him right in the crotch and make a run for it. "Please just let me go, Dad." I hated that I'd just called him that. I wanted to throw up.

He lowered his eyebrows. "Let you go? Brooklyn, I'm protecting you."

"By keeping me locked up?"

"You're not locked up. You're in a hospital recovering from surgery."

The door's locked, you psychopath. I'd checked countless times. "So you stole my kidney, told everyone I know and love that I'm dead, and now you expect me to just roll over and be your prisoner?"

He sighed. "Of course not. And just for the record, I love you. I love you so much that I moved mountains to keep you safe. And as for the kidney stealing thing, would you please stop saying that out loud? That sounds terrible."

"It *is* terrible."

"No, it's an excellent lesson, don't you think? Always read the fine print. Speaking of lessons, I've hired a great tutor for you once you resume your school year. It's virtual of course. We can't let anyone else see you."

It wasn't an excellent lesson at all. What he'd done had to be illegal. I was a minor. I couldn't sign my kidney away even if I wanted to. And why was he changing the subject? "I'm not doing virtual learning. I'm going back to Empire High."

"No. You're not. You're not stepping foot back in New York City until I tell you it's safe."

"That's not fair…"

"Not fair? Life isn't fair, Brooklyn. If life was fair I'd still be with your mother. We would have raised you together. We would have had everything."

I swallowed hard. He didn't need to tell me life wasn't fair. But we had a really different picture of what our lives would be like if life was fair. Because I wasn't picturing him in mine at all. I was picturing my mom still alive and just the two of us back in Delaware. Happy and carefree and whole.

"You have to let me go. Please, Dad. I can't stay here. I can't."

He shook his head. "It's too late."

"No it's not. Just undo whatever you did. Say it was a prank or something. And we can all laugh about it in a few years."

"You don't know Isabella like I do. You need to stay dead, or you'll actually be dead. Do you understand me? I'm protecting you. I'm doing the best job I can under impossible circumstances. So you will stay here for as long as I say you'll stay here. And you'll have no contact with the outside world, other than with me. Do I make myself clear?"

I could feel the tears spilling down my cheeks. My father was usually kind to me when he wasn't snatching organs. But I'd seen him mad like this before. Like the anger was oozing out of him. He was probably seconds away from breaking his cane in half.

I'd lost this argument. Because I was too scared of him to continue it. But it didn't matter. None of it mattered. I wasn't staying here. I'd figure a way to get out. And I'd run to Matt. I'd tell him I was sorry. I'd apologize to Kennedy too. I'd apologize to everyone.

Because I didn't want to be dead. I didn't want to be forgotten. I didn't want to start over again. My dad couldn't erase my existence as easily as he wanted. Because the dead had to agree to stay dead. And I didn't agree to any of it.

CHAPTER 10

Saturday

I didn't say a word as Miller let himself in that night. I'd had hours to think about what my dad had told me. Hours to try and think of a way out of this mess. But it was a little hard to think of a way out when it felt like my brain had stopped working. Maybe the nurse was right. Maybe I was slowly killing myself by not eating.

"Are you awake?" Miller asked.

I didn't turn to him. "I'm dead. How can I be awake?"

He laughed and the bed dipped as he sat down next to me. "So your dad told you everything?"

"He said my funeral was well attended. Apparently I should be happy about that." I turned to face Miller, but I couldn't see him in the dark. "Can you turn the light on?"

He didn't respond.

"Miller, please let me see your face."

"You wouldn't recognize me even if the lights were on."

I swallowed hard. "Why did my dad do this to you?"

"He wanted it to look like I'd disobeyed his orders. Like I crossed him for the last time."

"But you said there was no out in my dad's line of work. Why would any of his staff believe he just got you beat up and then fired you?"

"Because he beat me until it looked like I was dead. You're not the only one who just disappeared, kid."

I sat up in bed. *No.* "But what about your family? You took this job in part to pay off your dad's debts. Isn't your dad going to…"

"Going to what? If my father cared about me at all he never would have let me take this job. I don't have anyone in my corner. It's just me. It's been just me for a long time."

"I'm in your corner."

He didn't respond.

I reached out and gently touched the side of his cheek. It felt swollen. And it felt like there were stitches on his jawline. My dad said that Miller was one of the only people that knew I was actually alive. "Why did my dad ask you to disappear with me?"

"Because he knew I'd be willing to do it."

Willing to get beat up within an inch of his life? Willing to pretend to be dead? Willing to give up his whole life in New York? There was only one reason my dad would think someone was willing to do all that. I let my hand fall from his face. My dad had told me to stop sneaking down to the lower floor. He'd had cameras watching me all the time. But he made it seem like he didn't know I was sneaking down to see Miller. Why had he pretended not to know?

I had a sinking feeling in my stomach. My dad said he'd been planning my fake death for a while. He must have known he'd need to send at least one bodyguard with me. Why not the one closest to my heart? "How did my dad know that you'd be willing to come with me?"

"It's late. You should probably get some sleep."

"Miller." I grabbed his hand.

He sighed. "You really don't want to know the specifics. But he knew you were sneaking down to my room at night. He knew there was something going on between us. He must have known the whole time. I think he enjoyed beating the shit out of me for touching something that belonged to him. His words. Not mine."

I put my hand over my mouth. Miller never pursued me. I was the one who kept showing up at his door. He'd tried to tell me to stay away. But I…couldn't. He'd been my salvation when I lived with the Pruitts. He'd given me hope that my new life wouldn't be awful. He'd helped me hold on.

And he'd never touched me inappropriately. He was always a complete gentleman. It was only ever stolen kisses between us when we thought no one was looking. If my dad wanted to beat someone up for touching me, he was beating up the wrong guy. Matt was the only boy that had ever touched me. I'd given him everything.

I didn't even know what to say. I just shook my head. "I'm so sorry, Miller." It felt like my heart was breaking all over again. "We need to get out of here as soon as possible. I was thinking that if we…"

"I can't run away, Brooklyn. Your father made it very clear that he had a three-strike policy. I already have two. Because even though your dad was grateful that I said I'd come with you, he took it as a confession for what was going on between us. The beating me up wasn't just for show to the rest of the staff. That was my second strike."

"What happens if you get a third?" I knew the answer. But I still felt compelled to ask. I needed to hear him say it. I needed to remember just how dangerous my dad was.

Miller didn't respond though.

I slid my hand into his and squeezed it. "Please just say it. I know my dad's a horrible man."

"I'm lucky to even be alive right now after what happened at homecoming. Your father doesn't usually give out any strikes. It's either you do it the right way or you end up six feet under. Which is where I'll be if I don't follow his orders one more time."

"And what are his orders?" I was pretty sure I knew the answer to that already too.

"To protect you."

I wished I could see his face in the darkness. "And that's it?"

He slid his hand out of mind. "And to not lay a finger on you."

Oh. I swallowed hard. "You already broke that last one."

"Which is why I should probably go." He stood up but I didn't hear him walking toward the door.

I wanted to ask him to stay. But I couldn't. This wasn't a game. This was life or death. "I wish my dad left off that last part."

"Me too."

I'd hurt Miller. I'd chosen Matt over him. And yet…here he was. "You don't have to hold me as I cry myself to sleep. I've never wanted anyone's pity."

"That's not why I held you last night. I never stopped liking you, Brooklyn. You stopped liking me."

"I never stopped liking you." But I loved Matt. I loved him with every fiber of my being. He consumed me. But I never stopped liking Miller. "All I want to do is ask you to stay the night again. I don't want you to get in trouble though."

"I have a really hard time walking away from you when I know you're hurting."

"I'm okay, Miller. I'm going to be okay."

"That didn't sound convincing at all."

I laughed. The noise sounded strange in my throat. And I realized I hadn't laughed since Isabella fell through the ceiling. And for some reason tears were falling down my cheeks. I was suddenly happy that we were in a dark room. I didn't know what else to say. Because I was seconds away from begging him to stay. I cleared my throat. "So it'll just be you and me somewhere after this. No nurses or anything. And no communication with the outside world."

"And a virtual tutor," he said.

Right. One that wasn't allowed to see my face. "Completely isolated."

"That's going to make it even harder not to touch you."

It felt like there was a knife in my chest. I missed Matt. Desperately. So why did I so badly want Miller to climb back into my bed? Why did everything hurt so damned much? I tried to wipe away my tears undetected, but I stupidly let out a sniffle.

"The thought of being alone with me makes you cry?" His voice was soft.

"No, it's not that. It's that I don't want you to go. I want you to stay all night. I want you to hold me and tell me everything's going to be okay. But I shouldn't want that. Because I'm engaged to someone else. Was engaged. I need to talk to Matt." I hated how much I was crying. "I'm so confused."

"It's okay." He climbed back into my bed and pulled me against his chest. "Like you said…you're going to be okay."

"But you didn't believe me when I said it."

"I'm saying it now though. And it's kind of my job to make sure it comes true."

Miller was too good to be true. I wanted to hold him close because I knew better than anyone that I never got to feel content for long. I just needed a few minutes to feel like I wasn't falling apart.

We were both silent. Because he knew he shouldn't be in my bed. And I knew I shouldn't have started crying to make him feel obligated. But I was pretty sure neither of us wanted to move. He didn't even care that I'd just soaked the front of his shirt with my tears. We just…stayed completely still.

"You said I wouldn't want to know the specifics of the conversation you had with my dad," I said, keeping my head resting on his chest. "But I do want to know. Can you tell me the whole story?"

"Brooklyn…"

"Please. I need to know what happened."

He ran his thumb beneath my eye to help wipe away my tears. "He told me his plan to make you disappear. He asked if I wanted to be the one to go with you. And he let me know that he'd have to make it look like I'd died too. He told me upfront that he would make a scene about it in front of the rest of the staff."

"You said yes even though you knew he'd hurt you?"

"It didn't matter. I wasn't going to trust your life in the hands of someone else. I didn't even hesitate. I said yes."

Miller was the most selfless person I knew. He'd agreed to go with me right away? "And then what?"

"He said, 'Right answer. Or else you'd be dead.' And I didn't know what he meant. But he made it pretty clear as a few of his thugs beat the shit out of me. I'm not sure which part of it was for show and what was real. But he seemed pissed." He stopped talking like he was lost in his thoughts.

I wasn't sure I wanted to know what else my dad said to him. Or how badly he'd been hurt. It was bad or else he'd turn the lights on. "And then what?"

He started absentmindedly drawing little circles on my back with his fingers. "They knocked me out. I woke up here too. End of story."

"Why does that not seem like the end of the story?" It seemed like he'd skipped a whole lot of important details.

"Well, not the end exactly. How could it possibly be the end? If anything it feels like a new beginning."

That wasn't at all what I expected him to say. "Being trapped here with me feels like a new beginning?"

"Being far away from Mr. Pruitt definitely feels like a fresh start. I never thought I'd ever get to leave that apartment."

Right. That made sense.

"And if I could choose anyone to be stranded with…it would be you."

My chest ached a little less when he said that. It shouldn't have. But I'd be lying if I said I felt nothing. I'd meant what I said earlier. I'd never stopped liking him. How could I possibly?

"It's okay," he said. "You don't have to say it back. I know you're thinking about Matt."

I didn't want to talk about Matt right now. I couldn't even think about him without feeling paralyzed. What was he doing right now? Was he missing me? Was he grieving me? "I'm glad you're here too, Miller. I don't know what I'd do without you."

He held me a little closer.

"So you don't regret agreeing to my dad's crazy plan?" I asked.

"No. And not just because apparently he would have killed me if I'd said no. I know you're not happy about being locked up here. But he showed me one of Isabella's plans he found. It was…horrifying."

"What was it?"

"I'm not going to give you nightmares too."

I laughed. "It gave you nightmares?"

"I think it even gave Mr. Pruitt nightmares."

Wow. I couldn't even imagine what horrible thing she was plotting. But it must have been terrible. Especially if it was in retaliation to the pudding prank. "So you're happy to be here. Does that mean you really don't want to create a plan to get away from my dad for good?"

"I'm not in any condition to make some grand escape plan right now. And I don't think you are either. Rumor has it that you haven't been eating."

"I don't like the food here." That wasn't exactly true. I'd only ever tried the applesauce. But it was kind of blah.

"Hm. You gotta eat though."

"Maybe I'm on a hunger strike," I said.

"And how is that working out for you?"

I slowly exhaled. I would have said that no one had noticed. But that evil nurse had noticed and snitched to my dad. And Miller had clearly noticed too. "No one seems to care."

He ran his fingers through my hair. "I care."

I know. I snuggled into his chest and yawned. "You should probably go before you accidentally fall asleep in here and get caught with your arms around me."

He laughed. "Just go to sleep, kid. Let me worry about that."

CHAPTER 11

Sunday

The door opened and I held my breath. I'd left the light on this time, hoping that when Miller came I'd be able to sneak a glance at him.

But all I saw was his arm reach in and hit the lights. And then he ducked into my room without me being able to see him again.

"Miller, please. I just want to see you. You're the only other human I'm allowed to see besides Evil Nurse."

"Trust me, I look like a monster."

"Evil Nurse isn't so pretty either."

He laughed at my nickname for the nurse and sat down on the edge of my bed. "Here." He shoved a bowl in my general direction and I almost dropped it.

"I'm not hungry."

"But I brought your favorite. Mint chocolate chip."

He brought me ice cream? It was the truth that I wasn't hungry. But he'd brought me ice cream. It would have been rude to not eat a little. I lifted up the spoon and took a huge bite. *Mmm.* "So freaking good."

He didn't respond, but I could tell he was smiling.

"Wait. Why do you get ice cream and all I get is oatmeal and applesauce?" I took another bite. And another. Suddenly I was starving. Exclusively for ice cream apparently.

"Because Mr. Pruitt isn't concerned about my diet."

"Ugh. My dad and his stupid rules." I'd skimmed through that part of the contract with his strict clean eating rules. You only live once. And what was living without ice cream? And who put consent for organ donations and foods not allowed in the house in the same contract? My father was insane. We didn't need to talk about that though. We both already knew it. Besides, I had something I was dying to talk to him about. "So I was thinking…"

"If this is about your escape plan, I told you. I can't."

"But just hear me out. People get new identities on TV shows all the time. How hard could it really be to change our names and hide from my dad? Besides, Evil Nurse is pretty tiny. I think I could take her. And you have a room somewhere in this place too, right? Where is it? And are you locked in too?"

"I'm not a flight risk, so no, I'm not locked in. And I'm down the hall, last door on the right."

"Great. So I'll take down Evil Nurse and then come get you. I'm assuming you're not in a windowless hellhole? So we can climb out your window…"

"I can't."

"But if we…"

He climbed off the bed.

"Miller, wait! I'm sorry. Please don't leave…"

But instead of leaving he switched on the lights.

Oh my God. It felt like all the air left my lungs. He was wearing a long-sleeved T-shirt and a pair of sweatpants. There wasn't much of his skin showing. But his face and neck… He wasn't just covered in bruises. His right eye was swollen shut. And there was a huge bandage on the other side of his face, covering what must have been a pretty deep cut. There were exposed stitches underneath his swollen eye. And just so many bruises. I put my hand up to my mouth.

"This isn't even the worst of it. I'd take my shirt off and show you, but my shoulder is busted up pretty badly.

Evil Nurse has to help me get dressed. It hurts to even move. I can't scale a building right now. I can barely walk."

"I'm sorry." I didn't know what else I could say. He looked like that because of me. Because of my father. And he'd willingly agreed to it to keep me safe.

"You have nothing to apologize for. It wasn't your fault."

"It was my fault. All of this is my fault."

"It's not, Brooklyn. I got myself in this mess all on my own."

I looked down at my lap. "Right," I said. Our situation certainly was a mess. I was so happy he was here with me. But surely he wished he was anywhere else.

"Hey. Look at me."

I slowly lifted my head.

"I wasn't saying being here with you was a mess. That's not what I meant. I chose to be here. I just meant foolishly taking a job with Mr. Pruitt in the first place. I'm happy that I'm here with you. I meant what I said yesterday."

He couldn't possibly mean that. How could he be happy stuck with me in this prison? I looked back up at him and he was smiling. He looked so sincere. "You really believe it's a new beginning?"

He nodded.

It was hard to believe in a new beginning when my heart was back in NYC with Matt. But...he couldn't help me escape right now. Or maybe ever. We'd have to be positive Mr. Pruitt would never find him again. Or else...the unthinkable would happen. I couldn't even imagine being the reason that Miller stopped breathing.

I climbed off my bed and walked over to him. I needed to see what else my father had done to him. Because it was all my fault. I grabbed the hem of his shirt.

"Brooklyn, don't." He caught my hand.

"You said you're not supposed to touch me. That doesn't mean I can't touch you." I had not meant for that to sound so suggestive. But I knew how it came out when his Adam's apple slowly rose and fell as he stared down at me.

I was frozen in place with him staring at me like that. If I'd thought my words were suggestive…his eyes on me were just as suggestive.

"Okay." I wasn't exactly sure what I was saying okay too. *Okay I won't touch you? Okay I'm going to? Okay that was awkward yet somehow not awkward at all?*

We continued to just stare at each other.

I needed to break the tension. "Maybe we can discuss this all again when you can dress yourself?"

He smiled and then winced.

"I'm so sorry." And without trying to second guess myself, I did what I wanted to do. I stood up on my tip-toes and kissed his cheek where there miraculously weren't any stitches or bruises. "Thank you for not leaving me all alone, Miller. Thank you for coming with me. I owe you everything." I hugged him, trying hard not to put too much pressure anywhere on his body. I couldn't believe the last few nights he'd held me in his arms as I fell asleep. That must have been incredibly painful for him.

"I'm just doing my job," he said.

"We both know that isn't true. Pretending to die and take care of a member of the family was definitely not in your hiring agreement."

"It certainly was in the contract I signed. Mr. Pruitt's contracts are very thorough."

"Well, either way, bringing said member of the family ice cream wasn't in it." I took a step back from him before I did something awkward and kissed his cheek again.

"And it's melting. Come on, back to bed with you." He hit the lights.

I was happy he turned them off again because looking at him made me want to cry. And not just because of the damage to his face. But because I could see that his feelings for me hadn't changed. He still looked at me the same way he did when I crawled in his bed back at my dad's apartment. Before I chose Matt. Before Matt chose me back. My ring was gone, but that didn't make me feel any less engaged.

And when Miller looked at me like that? Like he wanted me to touch him? I was worried that maybe a little piece of me wanted that too.

CHAPTER 12

Wednesday

"Your wish came true," Evil Nurse said.

I was busy staring at the ceiling so I didn't bother turning toward her. She had no idea what I was wishing each night when I went to bed. I was wishing my heart would stop aching. Because I was thinking about Matt even though Miller was the one holding me. Or maybe I was thinking a little too much about Miller. Which wasn't fair. No, Matt hadn't come to rescue me like I'd hoped. But how could he? He thought I was dead.

"Are you not even going to take the phone?" she asked.

I finally turned toward her. She was holding a cell phone out to me. I immediately sat up in bed and tried to grab it.

She pulled away at the last second.

What kind of cruel joke was this?

"Your father is on the line. You will take his call and then hand the phone back. Do we understand each other?"

No. No we did not. I was most definitely going to try to call Matt. But instead of confessing the truth, I just nodded my head.

She handed the phone over and stood there staring at me, her arms crossed in front of her chest.

A little privacy would have been nice. I pulled the phone to my ear. "Hello?"

"How are you feeling, angel?"

So we were back to pretending I'd willingly saved him? *Great.* "I'm all better. So I was thinking. Since you and Miller both know I'm alive…couldn't we tell like…two more people? I think Matt and Kennedy deserve to know where I am. They can keep a secret. If you'd just let me explain to them…"

"I'm not calling to negotiate. I'm calling to let you know you'll be moving to the secure location tomorrow. Miller will be escorting you there. You'll find everything you need once you arrive. Your virtual classes will start on Monday. Everything is all set up for your new life."

I swallowed hard. I didn't want a new life. And even though I didn't know my father very well, I could tell by his tone that he was serious about not negotiating. "So it'll just be me and Miller?"

"I'll visit when I can get away. Don't worry, angel."

I tried to think if I could actually do this. Be good and stay put for the rest of the school year. Just until Isabella was off to college. It wasn't that far away. Six months until she graduated from Empire High. It would keep Miller safe if I just…accepted my fate. But what was Matt doing? Was he falling apart too? It wasn't right to let him mourn me when I was right here still breathing.

"I can't do this to Matt. Dad, please. You have to let me speak to Matt. You have to."

"Once it's safe…"

"So just until Isabella goes off to college?"

"Or five years or so. We'll see."

He'd said that before. But I was hoping he was joking. I could already see six months turning into a year. A year turning into five. And five turning into forever.

I thought about how strong my feelings for Matt were. He felt the same way about me. I knew he did. "What if you tell him he has to move far away with me? If you told him the circumstances, he'd come with me. He's not just some random guy I was dating. We're engaged. He loves me." I'd follow that boy anywhere in the world. He'd follow me too.

"For a young man in mourning, he certainly seemed eager to have the ring back."

I swallowed hard. "What?"

"The first thing he said to me when he found out you were dead was if he could have it back. Because he still wants to get married one day."

"You're lying."

"Why would I lie about that? He was never good enough for you. I tried to warn you. It's better for you to know the truth now than to find out years later."

I shook my head. There were a million reasons why my dad would lie to me. The first of which was that he was trying to control me right now. What better way to control me than to tell me I left no one and nothing behind. That he was the only one who cared about me. Well…fuck that. "I don't believe you."

"Do you see the ring on your finger?"

I didn't bother to look down. I knew what was missing. My hand felt lighter. It bothered me every day. I clenched my hand into a fist. But now it somehow felt heavier too. Like there was some truth in my dad's words. My whole body suddenly felt heavier. Like the ground was about to collapse beneath me and swallow me whole.

"You're lying," I said again. But tears were streaming down my cheeks now. I didn't want to believe him. It couldn't possibly be true. He'd put the smallest ounce of doubt there though. And it felt like it was strangling me. "Please, I need to speak with him. Please."

"I love you. I'll do everything in my power to protect you. And I'm glad that this is protecting you from that boy. He never would have been worthy of you."

It wasn't about being worthy. It wasn't about worth at all. Matthew Caldwell made me feel…loved. He made me feel whole. He'd promised me forever. I'd promised it back. Matt was my home. My heart. My everything. The tears streamed down my cheeks even faster.

"I'll visit as soon as I can."

"Wait. Did…did Matt say anything at my funeral?" My dad said that a funeral for the living was a great way to see who truly cared about you. Surely Matt had said something beautiful. Surely he was as devastated as me right now. He had to be.

"I asked him to make a speech. He declined."

What? How could Matt say nothing at all? He was my fiancé. Our forever had been cut short. How could he have no words? The doubt was definitely strangling me now. I could barely breathe.

"He said he'd said everything he needed to when he last saw you."

My father's words stabbed me in the chest like a knife and twisted. I gasped for air.

"I need to go," he said. "I'll visit you as soon as I can. I love you, angel." He hung up before I could even respond.

My plan had been to try to sneak in a call to Matt. But…I couldn't breathe. I dropped the phone on the bed and turned away from the nurse.

She said something, but I ignored her.

I lay back down and curled into a ball. My whole body shook as I cried. Matt had nothing to say because he'd said all he needed to already? I'd never forget his last words to me. He'd called me a liar. I sobbed harder. He'd called me a liar and walked away. He left me. He left me and now I was one kidney short and locked up. And he had nothing else to fucking say?

I'd given Matt my whole heart. He'd promised not to break it. But I guess ripping it out and throwing it into oncoming traffic wasn't technically breaking it. It was just stealing it and getting it run over.

Fuck you, Matthew Caldwell.

CHAPTER 13

Thursday

"Stop looking at me like that," Miller said as he stared out the windshield.

We were driving down I-95 at exactly the speed limit. Apparently the last thing my dad wanted was for us to be pulled over and recognized by a cop. That would ruin his plans of keeping me dead.

But I wasn't staring at Miller because I wanted him to put his foot down a little harder on the gas. And how did he even know I was staring at him? The big sunglasses I was wearing for a disguise made it a little hard to tell where my eyes were trained. "Looking at you how?"

He glanced at me for a second and then put his eyes on the road again.

"I'm not looking at you in any way."

"Sure."

"I wasn't."

"I know that look," he said. "You want me to turn around and go back to New York."

Honestly, I had no idea what I wanted. My head was as confused as my heart. The things my dad had told me about Matt... They could easily be lies. My father was manipulative. But...what if he was telling the truth? Matt had been mad at me. Furious, really. What if he was just relieved that I was gone? I was glad I was wearing sunglasses, because I knew my eyes were puffy from crying.

I didn't want to think about any of that right now though. I was happy to be out of my windowless room. I had no idea where we were going, but anything would be better than that. Especially because it would be just me and Miller. I'd had quite enough of Evil Nurse. "That's not what I was thinking."

"Then what are you thinking?" he asked.

His baseball cap was pulled down low. But nothing could hide the bruises all over his face, his black eye, the stitches, or the big bandage on his cheek. I still wanted to see the rest of him. I needed to know what damage I'd caused. Miller's hoodie and jeans were covering the rest of him though. He usually wore freshly pressed suits. I hadn't seen him in casual clothes since I used to creep down to his room at night. He would always greet me in sweatpants and no shirt. It was a look I'd grown quite fond of. "I was thinking that I like your outfit."

"You mean my disguise?"

"It's hardly a disguise. I feel like this outfit is a lot more you than the suits my dad requires you to wear."

He didn't respond.

"I was also thinking that your face looks painful."

He laughed. "I'm fine."

I never believed anyone when they said that. Because I said it a lot. And I was never telling the truth. I was happy that he was laughing though. "And maybe I was also thinking a little bit about the fact that this would be the perfect opportunity to get as far away from my father as possible. Maybe we should head west? I've never seen the Pacific Ocean. We could be runaways together."

"As fun as it would be to go all Bonnie and Clyde with you…there's a tracker on the car. And on my phone. If we don't show up at the destination within two hours he'll have everyone looking for us. You'll need a better plan than to just turn right instead of left."

"Then let's stop at the next rest stop and hotwire a car. Toss your cell phone into the back of someone's truck or something. Let it be a wild goose chase for them tracking your phone. Meanwhile we'll be long gone."

"Not a bad plan. Do you know how to hotwire a car?"

"No. Don't you?"

He laughed. "Why would I know how to do that?"

"Because you're all…you."

"What is that supposed to mean?"

"You have that bad boy air of danger vibe about you. Certainly you've stolen a car before."

He just shook his head and kept driving.

"But can we stop at the next rest stop anyway? I need to pee."

"Well that just makes it sound like you're going to run away from me."

"I would never do that." It was one thing I could definitely promise. He had to keep me safe…or else. Which meant I couldn't just ditch him. Besides, I didn't want to. What would I do out here in the middle of nowhere with no money and no phone? It would be like when Isabella stranded me all over again. Sure, this time I would have clothes on. But I wouldn't have James' hotel room to run to. I had no one to run to. Everyone hated me.

I continued to stare at Miller. "But seriously…I need to go. Like now."

"The next rest stop isn't for another 15 miles. Can you hold it until then?"

Really, that far? "No, I don't think so. Can't we just take this exit?" Surely there was a gas station near the exit.

Miller hit his turn signal and merged over to the exit lane. "Hopefully we can find a fast-food place or something." He took the exit and there was…nothing but farmland. Mile after mile after mile of nothingness. No fast-food places, or restaurants, or gas stations.

I started drumming my fingers on my thigh. "Can we turn around? There's nothing out here. We can backtrack to that other rest stop." But I wasn't actually sure I could hold it until then.

Miller did a quick U-turn to retrace our path…but it quickly became apparent that we'd made a wrong turn somewhere.

God, I was going to literally pee my pants.

"Let's play a game," he said.

If he was trying to distract me, this was not going to work. I just groaned.

"I spy with my little eye…something brown."

"The millions of dead corn stalks in the middle of no-where?"

"Bingo," he said with a laugh. "Your turn."

"I spy with my little eye no toilets anywhere."

"Wow, that's not how you play. I'll go again. I spy with my little eye…um…something else brown."

"Your eyes?"

He looked over at me with his dark brown eyes. There was a smile playing on the corner of his lips. "No."

"Don't look so cocky. I wasn't checking you out. There's just literally nothing out here. This is the worst game ever. Can't we just knock on someone's door and ask if we can use their bathroom?"

"No. That would be super weird."

"Weirder than me peeing in the passenger's seat? My bladder is literally about to explode here."

He laughed.

"It's not funny!"

"We can't knock on a stranger's door. No one's sup-posed to see you."

Fair point. Not that I was totally opposed to being alive again. "But seriously, Miller, I can't hold it much longer."

He started driving a little faster. There was no way we were going in the right direction.

I started humming to myself. *Damn it.* I was legit going to pee my pants.

Miller pulled over to the side of the road. "Go ahead."

I looked out the window at the rows and rows of corn stalks. Um…what? "I can't pee on the side of the road! I'll be arrested!"

"Well don't just drop your pants right on the side of the road. Hide behind some of the corn stalks. Be discreet about it. I'll keep lookout." He reached across me and opened up my door. "Go."

But… God. I didn't exactly have any other options. "But there's no toilet paper." It was my last line of defense. I couldn't pee on someone's farmland. There was zero way this was happening.

"Use this." He pulled off his hoodie and tossed it at me.

Um…what now? "You want me to use your hoodie as toilet paper? That's a bit extreme. Don't you have something…smaller?"

He shrugged.

Okay, fine. This was happening. I didn't have time to overthink it or I'd pee myself. I stumbled out of the car with his hoodie in my hand and ran through the corn stalks until I was a safe distance away from the road and any prying eyes. I dropped my pants and squatted down just in time to not pee all over myself.

I sighed. I felt so much better. But I really wished I'd had a pen and paper to try to leave a note to the farmhands that I was being kidnapped and needed help. And then I started laughing. I started laughing and I couldn't stop. What the fuck was my life?

I was about to wipe with Miller's hoodie, but then thought better of it. The corn stalks were dry and sad. I was pretty sure they were harvested in the summer, not the fall. So I looked around and grabbed a leaf. I quickly wiped and pulled up my pants.

Whenever I saw Matt again we could laugh about this. I was pretty sure he'd find it hilarious. Rob definitely would. God, I really missed my friends. The cool autumn wind blew and I pulled Miller's hoodie on.

Part of me wanted to turn around and just keep running through the corn stalks. To get as far away from my dad as possible. I looked off into the distance at the woods. But I'd never do that to Miller. I shook my head and retreated back to the SUV.

Miller eyed me as I climbed back in the car.

"What?"

"Did you…use that to wipe and then put it on?"

I started laughing again. "No. I was resourceful."

He started laughing too. "I have no idea what you mean by that. Did you wipe with an ear of corn?"

"No." I lightly shoved his shoulder.

He winced and I pulled back.

"I'm so sorry. I…" *Oh my God.* He was only wearing a t-shirt now. There were deep cuts and bruises all over his arms.

"It's okay. It was worth seeing you laugh."

I forced a smile back onto my face.

He cleared his throat. "I called your dad and got directions. We should probably get back on the road."

"Here, let me give this back…" I started to pull off his hoodie but he caught my arm.

"No, keep it. I'm overheated. And it looks better on you anyway."

Before I could respond, he pulled the car back on the road.

I was happy he wasn't hiding his scars from me anymore. I was even happier that the smell of his cologne was on the hoodie. I felt myself sinking into my seat, surrounded by the warmth of the hoodie. It was like a big Miller hug.

"Are you sniffing my hoodie?" he asked.

"What? No." I pulled the front of it down, away from my face.

We were both quiet for a long time. We eventually pulled back onto I-95, driving down the highway.

"I missed you too, you know," he finally said, breaking the silence.

I looked over at him. His eyes were still trained on the road. I guess wanting to smell his cologne probably was confession enough on my side. I slid my hand onto the center console. I wasn't sure what I was reaching for. A peace offering? Was I just desperate for physical comfort in the form of his hand? Or was it more?

He slid his hand into mine.

I stared down at his hand. It wasn't mine to hold. And yet…I didn't want to let go.

CHAPTER 14

Thursday

"Hey." Miller lightly touched my shoulder. "We're here."

I yawned and slowly opened my eyes. The combination of his warm hoodie and his comforting scent all around me must have put me right to sleep. I blinked and looked out the window. "Holy shit." I was expecting some kind of old wooden cabin in the middle of nowhere. Not...*this*. I unbuckled my seatbelt and climbed out of the car.

The sound of waves crashing in the distance soothed my soul. And the smell of salty air. And the call of the seagulls. I used to go to the beach all the time with my mom. Every summer until she got sick. I swallowed hard.

"No so bad, huh?"

When my mom and I used to walk along the beach, we would take turns pointing to the big beach houses lining the coast, saying which ones we'd own when we were older. It was a stupid game. But I was young and naïve. I didn't know that she'd almost had it all. Or that she didn't have enough life left to chase any more dreams.

And now that I was standing here staring at one of the monstrosities? I wanted to laugh. I wanted to cry. I just...wanted my mom back. I blinked fast, hoping I could keep my tears at bay.

I turned to look at Miller. "This is where we're staying?"

"Yup." He closed my car door and locked it. "Welcome home." He started walking up the drive.

I quickly followed him. "Wait. You can't be serious. I thought we were supposed to be in hiding. Not on vacation."

Milled laughed. "The busy season is over. I'm sure your dad will move us before summer starts. The beach is pretty deserted right now though." He unlocked the front door and held it open for me.

I couldn't even believe it when I walked across the threshold. It was decorated just like a beach house should be. Blue and turquoise paintings and accents everywhere that matched the color of the ocean, beige walls the color of sand, and so many seashells. There were seashells *everywhere*. Paintings of seashells on the walls and actual seashells in glass lamps and on the coffee table. It was elegant and somehow cozy at the same time. Which was not the vibe I'd been expecting. "There's no way this place belongs to my father."

"No. He's renting it."

I walked over to the glass windows lining the back of the house, and looked out at the deserted beach. The view was beautiful. And I...hated it.

I knew what my father was up to. He was trying to get his way. He didn't send me to the middle of nowhere to sulk. He sent me to a beautiful location in the hopes that I'd be content and leave my old life behind.

There was just one problem with that. It didn't matter how cozy a place was. You couldn't just make a place a home without loved ones. My house with my mom was a home. Uncle Jim's apartment was a home. Kennedy's place was a home. Matt's house, at least the kitchen, felt like home. I could picture the Caldwell kitchen so easily, bustling and full of life. Tears ran down my cheeks, blurring the perfect view.

Here? In this beautiful location? I stared out at the beach. A house wasn't a home unless you were with the people you loved. And this wasn't a home at all. Matt was my home.

I closed my eyes, trying to blot out the view that was meant to manipulate me.

Was that why my dad had asked Miller to be my babysitter? Because he knew we used to be close? He thought if he put me in this dream vacation home with a cute boy I'd just…roll over? He didn't know me very well at all. And he may have been able to cast my mom aside like she meant nothing. But I wasn't as coldhearted as my old man. I couldn't just erase Matt from my mind and move on. He was everything to me.

My loyalty couldn't be bought. My father greatly underestimated my willpower. I wasn't going to stop asking to talk to Matt. I'd never stop.

Miller's cell phone rang. I turned toward the kitchen to see him answer it.

He locked eyes with me. "Yes, we arrived safely." He nodded and walked over to the fridge. "Looks like we're all set for a while. Yeah, there's instructions too." He pulled out a casserole dish.

So Miller was my bodyguard. My driver. And my personal chef? Yeah, there was no way this shit had been in his original contract. I was grateful that he was here with me. I was. But…he shouldn't have been. This wasn't fair to him. He should be allowed to quit and do whatever the hell he wanted. I knew he was saving up for college. Would he ever be allowed to go?

Miller walked over to me and handed me the cell phone. "He wants to speak with you."

I took the phone, even though I had no desire to speak with my father. "Yes?" I said.

"How do you like your new place?"

"It's…" I didn't really know how to describe it. It was lovely. And suffocating. "It's…cold."

"Ah, get Miller to turn up the temperature a few degrees."

That was not at all what I meant. But I didn't expect my dad to understand. He basically lived in a haunted mausoleum. "Can I speak to Matt now?"

"Angel, try to settle in. We'll discuss everything again soon, alright? But in the meantime, enjoy yourself."

"It's hard to enjoy yourself when you're a hostage."

"Do you really feel like you're a hostage? Look out the window. Your mother loved the beach. I was hoping you loved it too."

I swallowed hard. God, he wasn't supposed to have sweet memories of my mom to use against me. "I do love the beach."

"Ah. I knew it. Have a good long weekend. I'm excited to hear all about your classes on Monday. Goodnight, angel." He hung up before I could respond.

"Dinner will be ready in about an hour," Miller said.

I handed him his phone back. There was no point in trying to call Matt. Miller wouldn't let me. And I wouldn't want him to even if he would allow it. I wasn't going to get him hurt again.

"Want to explore a bit? I think your room…"

"Let's explore outside instead." I opened up one of the sliding glass doors and walked out onto the deck. I didn't care what my prison looked like. If it was up to me, I'd be outside the whole time. It had been years since I'd been to the beach now. I walked down into the sand, not caring about my sneakers being filled with sand that would be nearly impossible to get out. I tried to remember the last time I'd been to the beach with my mom. But I couldn't place it. I hated that. That memories of her faded more with each passing day.

"What are you thinking?" Miller asked as he stepped up beside me to watch the ocean waves.

"That I miss my mom."

He didn't say anything. He always had been a good listener. But I could tell from the way that he was staring at me that he felt bad. Like he wished he could take my pain way.

I started walking and he walked beside me. It was comforting to have him here. But it was in the back of my head the whole time that he had to be. He was walking with me because he was supposed to protect me.

I cleared my throat. "My dad sent us here because my mom loved the beach. She and I used to dream of living in a place like this one day." I looked back toward the house, but we'd walked so far that I couldn't even see it. "And now that I am? I just feel...claustrophobic."

"I have a few ideas on how we could fix that."

"How?"

"Come with me." He put his hand out.

I slid my hand into his and he pulled me back toward the beach house.

I trusted him. I think that was part of the problem. I trusted Miller with my life. But I didn't trust my father at all. And I didn't know whether Miller was more loyal to me or to my dad.

Either way, it felt like my heart was breaking again. I'd always dreamed of walking hand in hand with a boy at the beach. Matt and I had planned to come to the beach on our honeymoon. It was what I was looking forward to the most about all of it. Being Mr. and Mrs. Caldwell snuggled up in the sand.

I gripped Miller's hand a little tighter and hoped he knew how grateful I was for him. I knew he was here to protect me. It wasn't his fault that I didn't want or need it. I just wanted to be free.

"Crap, I forgot about the food," Miller said. "It's probably burning in the oven." He started jogging on the beach, pulling me with him. His stride was so much longer than mine that I was practically sprinting.

And I couldn't help but laugh.

I felt free with Miller. Maybe he was right. Maybe this was a fresh start. A new beginning.

***

We'd salvaged the lasagna by scraping off the burnt top layer. But it still had a charred flavor to it. It was hard not to laugh at Miller's cooking. He couldn't even heat up a premade lasagna.

"Stop laughing at me," he said and kicked my foot. "You're the one that kept walking and walking and made us miss the timer."

"This is not my fault," I said and picked at the mess with my fork. "But I'll cook tomorrow."

"There's a bunch of prepared things already in the fridge. I'll bring a phone timer next time."

"It's not a big deal. Besides, we don't need to just re-heat stuff. For all my father's stalking, he didn't realize that I'm a great cook. Probably because he never asked." He never asked a lot of things. He'd only been concerned that my kidney was a match.

"Well, I assume you're at least better than me."

So true. I took a bite and chewed it slowly. Really...why was it so chewy?

"Don't make that face. I tried my best."

I laughed. "Sorry, it's delicious."

He rolled his eyes and we both gravitated toward looking at the ocean.

Miller had brought down a bunch of blankets and pillows to the beach. He'd made us a kind of fort on the sand. He'd made good on his promise. It was hard to feel claustrophobic out here. But even with all the extra blankets and layers, it was still getting cold.

I set my plate down. "Should we head back inside?"

"What? No. We're sleeping out here." He lay back, putting his arms behind his head, and stared up at the stars.

"But it's freezing." I ducked lower into his hoodie.

"Don't act like you're afraid to steal my warmth, kid."

"You're seriously going to sleep out here?"

He continued to stare up at the sky. "Isn't that what you wanted? To be outside?"

It was what I wanted. But I wasn't exactly used to hearing the word "yes" recently. I smiled as I lay down beside him, snuggling into his side. He was right. It was warm when we were together. He was practically a space heater.

I stared up at the sky too.

"Make a wish," he said.

And for some reason, as I stared into his eyes, I couldn't wish for the thing I truly wanted. The thing I thought I wanted. Matt. How could I wish for someone else when Miller was here with me? It felt like a betrayal. So instead I wished to find a way for Miller to be free. Free from this mess he was in. Free from me.

As soon as I made the wish, I wished I could take it back. I didn't want Miller to leave me. Because then my whole world would be cold.

CHAPTER 15

2 Weeks Later - Saturday

I picked up my pace as I jogged farther away from the beach house. Miller and I had a good routine going. We both exercised in the morning. I'd go for a long and very slow jog and he'd use the gym at the house. Then I'd cook us breakfast.

I had classes online during the week. And I'd convinced him to sign up for some online college courses too. So during the day we both were focused on our studies. We'd eat a quick lunch in front of our computers. And after we were done for the day, we'd take a long walk on the beach until our stomachs started to growl.

Miller was not a great cook. But he was letting me teach him. Our nights were my favorite. It just felt…normal. Playing house. But that's all it was. A game we were playing until we were both set free.

Soon I hoped I'd be able to run again instead of the weird slow jog I was currently doing. I kept telling myself that once I was fully recovered from the surgery, everything would be better. Running always made me feel sane. And it was one of the only things I was holding on to. Because as each day passed, the clearer it became that Matt wasn't coming for me. I stopped and stared out at the water. One week from today we were supposed to get married. I had been so excited for December 22nd. And now whenever I thought about it, there was a pit in my stomach, growing by the second.

I knew in my gut that the 22nd would come and go. Just like every other day here. Nothing special would happen. Nothing at all. I wrapped my arms around myself as I watched the waves crash. Yeah, I really missed running.

***

I slowly made my way back up to the house. But when I saw a second SUV parked in the driveaway, I hurried up the steps on the deck. For just a second I thought maybe Matt had come for me. It was silly. But there was this hope in my chest. And it felt like my heart was full again. For just one second.

Because of course it wasn't Matt. It was my dad standing in the middle of the kitchen with a scowl on his face.

"You're supposed to stay with Miller at all times," he said. "So you can imagine my surprise when I came into the house and you weren't here. Where were you?"

No greeting. No, "Hello daughter who I'm keeping a prisoner. How are you feeling about your fate now?"

My dad turned his scowl toward Miller.

Miller scratched the back of his neck. He was only just healing from his last injuries. The last thing I needed was for him to get in trouble.

"It's my fault," I said. "I like to run alone. I insisted on it, actually."

"Run? You're not supposed to be running. You're still healing." He walked toward me, putting most of his weight on the cane in his hand. "How are you feeling?"

I used to think it was sweet when he was concerned about my health. Now I was just suspicious about what organ he was going to harvest next. "I'm feeling a lot better. And I'm not really running. It's a super slow jog. More of a walk really."

"Good." He nodded. "It's good to take things slowly. How do you like your new home? Do you have everything you need?"

It's not a home. And of course I didn't have everything I needed. I needed Matt. But my father didn't seem to care about that. "I like the beach."

He smiled. "It's chilly out there. You should wear another layer."

I got overheated on my runs. The hoodie I was wearing was plenty warm. "Next time," I said, not caring that it was a lie. All my father knew were lies anyway.

"Very well. And how are your classes?"

"Fine."

"I saw that you got a B on your first Algebra 2 test. Better take more time studying than jogging, yes?"

Of course he got a copy of my grades. He knew everything I did. Every move I made. Every B I got instead of an A. I just nodded. I would have been getting straight As if I hadn't just had my whole life uprooted. But my dad wouldn't care about that argument. I wasn't even sure why my grades mattered. If my dad had his way, I'd be stuck here for years. That meant no going back to Empire High. No college. None of it mattered. Nothing mattered anymore. I looked down at my wet, sandy shoes. In my excitement, I'd forgotten to take them off. Now there was a trail of sand through the house. I felt tears welling in my eyes. I didn't care about the fucking sand. I cared about everything else.

My dad gently touched the bottom of my chin. "Angel, what's wrong?"

"My wedding's next week."

He started to shake his head.

"Dad, please. Let me talk to Matt. He deserves to know the truth…"

"I didn't want to have to do this." He snapped his fingers at Miller. "Briefcase."

Miller grabbed my dad's briefcase off the kitchen counter and brought it over to us.

My dad sat down on the couch and opened up the briefcase on his lap. He looked up at me. "You'll want to sit."

I had no idea what he meant by that. But I was tired from my jog. I'd noticed that recently. That even a little exercise made me sleepy. I wasn't sure if it was because my body was healing or if I was deeply depressed. Probably a combination of the two. If it was up to me, I'd just lay on the beach all day staring at the water. Yeah, I was probably depressed.

But the last thing I wanted was to tell my dad that. He'd pump me full of drugs. He'd numb me. And I didn't want to be numb. I remembered getting sick after drinking too much. I'd told my uncle it felt nice to be numb for even just a little. He told me that was no way to live. I didn't get many moments with him. But I held on to that one tight. I didn't need drugs or anything else. I just needed to feel this. Feel this and work through it.

"Really, you need to sit," my father said.

I hadn't realized I'd just been staring at him. I sat down and looked at the envelope he pulled out of his briefcase.

"I'm sorry," he said.

I just stared at him.

He nodded toward the envelope.

I slowly undid the clasps and pulled out the contents. A stack of images. Pictures of Felix and Kennedy laughing outside Empire High. Felix was out of prison. And they both looked happy. I flipped to the next picture of them a little closer together. Were they dating now? That's what Kennedy had wanted. I swallowed hard. Was that what my father was trying to show me? That my best friends were happier now that I was dead? I looked up at him.

"Keep looking," my dad said.

I flipped to the next picture. It was of Matt and his friends. All the Untouchables back together. It looked like it had been taken in Matt's backyard. I didn't know how my father had gotten these pictures. But Matt was smiling with his friends. They all looked…so happy. Except for James. James usually had a frown on his face. But that was normal for him. The important thing about the photo was that they were all hanging out again.

Photo after photo after photo of the four of them looking happy. They were back to being best friends again. Since I was gone.

I swallowed hard as I came to the last photo.

Of Matt.

His arm slung around some girl I didn't recognize.

"What is this?" I said, staring down at the picture of Matt. The girl beside him disappeared. All I could see was Matt's face.

"To show you that everyone's moved on, angel. And it's time for you too."

"He hasn't moved on."

My dad pointed to the girl. "I'm pretty sure they're dating."

"No." I shook my head. "I don't believe you. I don't believe any of this." I shoved the photos into his arms.

"Angel…"

"Don't angel me! I'm not an angel!"

"Brooklyn." He reached out to me.

"What are you trying to do to me?" Tears started streaming down my cheeks. "Are you trying to break me?"

"Of course not. I just want you to know that it's okay to be happy without the people you left behind."

"I didn't leave them behind! You took them from me. You stole my life!" I started sobbing.

My dad put the pictures back down on the couch and stood. He tried to hug me but I stepped back.

"I don't know what you're doing. But trying to prove to me that everyone I love is happier without me? What is wrong with you?"

"I'm trying to show you the truth."

"They're snapshots. This doesn't mean they don't miss me. And one picture of Matt with some random girl doesn't mean he stopped loving me!"

"I think it's best if I leave these here for you to look through when you're not acting hysterical." He turned to leave.

Hysterical? God, he hadn't seen hysterical. "Just because my mom didn't choose you doesn't mean true love doesn't exist."

He turned back to me. "That boy never loved you. And your supposed friends? They're happier that you're dead. Believe the pictures or not. But I'm the only one who still loves you."

"This isn't love." I gestured between us. "You're torturing me."

"I'm saving you."

"No. Saving me isn't keeping me locked up. Saving me is getting Isabella help. She needs help, Dad. And keeping me here isn't helping her. It's enabling her."

He shook his head. "All I've ever done was help you. I pulled you out of the slums. I gave you everything…"

"I didn't ask for any of this!"

"We're not having his conversation while you're hot-headed."

"God, and where the hell do you think I inherited that from? It certainly wasn't my mom."

"I brought a Christmas tree and some decorations. I cleared my whole weekend so we could celebrate early."

What? That was the worst segue in the history of segues.

He pointed over to a tree in the corner that I hadn't noticed. "How about we calm down and have a nice day full of family and cheer?"

"Bite me." I wasn't celebrating an early Christmas with this asshole. He was right. Christmas was for family and cheer. I had none of either. And I had no desire to celebrate Christmas a week and a half early just so he could celebrate the holiday on the right day with his legitimate family.

He sighed and looked at his watch. "Well, if that's how you feel, I guess I should get going then."

I certainly wasn't going to protest. If he stayed much longer I might do something that made me deserve to be locked up.

"Merry Christmas, Brooklyn." He shook his head and walked away from me. His cane echoing in the empty house each time it hit the floor.

As soon as the door closed, I thought I would break. I thought I'd fall to my knees and cry the rest of the day. But I just felt…nothing. I was numb, even though that was the feeling I was trying to avoid.

"Brooklyn?" Miller said as he approached me. "Are you…"

"I'm fine. It's fine." I wiped the remaining tears from my face. "I'm sorry that you had to see that."

He didn't respond.

"Let me clean up the sand I tracked through the house. Then I'll make breakfast." My voice cracked on the last word.

Instead of moving out of my way, Miller pulled me into a hug.

And I started crying. Big, chest shaking wails escaped my throat. I barely even recognized the noises as coming from me. I couldn't breathe. "I'm sorry," I said again, even though I didn't exactly know what I was apologizing for. "I'm sorry."

He just held me. He let me fall apart in his arms. He let me soak the front of his shirt with tears and snot. And he didn't let go.

Why was I even crying? I was pissed at my dad. I didn't believe a word out of his mouth. None of it. But the pictures? Kennedy was happy. Felix was happy. Matt…he looked happy. Happy without me.

I was drowning. Every day it felt harder and harder to come up for air. And Matt was hanging out with his friends. Hanging out with other girls. Smiling. Laughing. Living. And I was dying. Slowly dying missing him.

"Take a deep breath," Miller said as he ran his fingers through my hair.

I knew I was just having a panic attack. I knew it and yet…it didn't feel like that. It felt like my life was ending. And a part of me wanted it to. My heart hurt. My whole body ached.

"Breathe, kid."

But I didn't. I just kept sobbing. And I clutched Miller like he was my lifeline.

CHAPTER 16

1 Week Later - Saturday

Miller cleared his throat.

I'd felt him staring at me from the deck for a long time. Or else he'd been watching the sunset too. And the stars light up the sky. I wasn't sure he was brave enough to venture out to the beach to talk to me. Not after he saw how crazy I'd acted last weekend when I snapped at my dad. Or how cold I'd been this week. I felt like getting close to him was a betrayal to Matt. So I was pushing him away. And now I felt more isolated than ever.

"Do you want to come inside?" Miller asked.

"No." My teeth chattered. I thought he'd walk away, but instead he sat down next to me.

"Do you want to talk about it?"

I didn't look at him. I couldn't look at him. I just kept staring out at the ocean. "What's there to talk about?"

"Everything." He sighed when I didn't respond. "Any-thing."

I sniffed. What did he want me to say? I was supposed to get married today. I should be smashing cake in Matt's face right about now. No, it was probably later than that. He'd probably be whisking me away in a limo to the air-port. We'd be lounging on a warm beach somewhere by morning. Enjoying life.

Instead…I was dead. There would be no "I dos." No promises of forever. Our forever had been cut short be-cause my dad was a monster. And so was I.

I kept coming back to that. Maybe if I hadn't betrayed Matt's trust, he'd be looking for me. Maybe we'd still be saying "I do" in front of all our family and friends. Instead…he hated me. I was dead and forgotten.

Miller cleared his throat. "The first thing I ever heard about the two of you was that you were broken up. I asked you what he did. And you said it was because of what he didn't do."

"Yeah. I remember." Matt used to treat me like a dirty little secret. But he'd changed.

"I know you're upset. But…"

"Miller, I really don't need to hear a whole speech about how Matt doesn't deserve me or wherever this is going. I chose to be with him forever. We deserved each other. Because we're an us."

"I wasn't going to say you deserve better than Matt. Not at all. I was going to say that this situation has nothing to do with what he didn't do. I wasn't sure if you were out here upset with him for not trying to come rescue you from this mess. But how can he rescue you if he doesn't know you're still alive?"

I sniffed.

"I think he would have shown up if he knew you were out there somewhere. I truly believe that."

I tried to blink away my tears. That was kind of him to say. Especially because he didn't exactly like Matt. After all, I'd chosen Matt over him. None of it mattered though. I'd had a week to think about the pictures my father had shown me. And Matt wasn't missing me. "You didn't see the pictures."

"Actually I did. Maybe you didn't." He pulled one out of his pocket and handed it to me. And then he turned on a flashlight, spotlighting the picture so I could see it.

It was the one of Matt with his arm draped about some other girl's shoulders. "He's smiling," I said.

"Is he though?"

I wiped the tears out of my eyes. Matt most definitely was smiling. But I knew him. And now that I was looking at it closer...something was off. Yes, he was smiling. But it didn't reach his eyes. His eyes looked...haunted. Sad. Tired.

Exactly the way I'm sure my eyes looked.

Miller made me laugh sometimes too. I snuggled into his side when I needed comfort too. But I'm sure my eyes looked as vacant as Matt's. I swallowed hard. "He misses me."

"Of course he misses you. You're easy to miss."

I sniffled. There was this hope in my chest. This small thread of hope I could hang on to. Maybe Matt was looking at the stars tonight too. Missing me. Wishing we were together again. When I first saw the picture, I didn't want to believe he'd moved on. I freaked out. But what if he hadn't?

"Come on," Miller said and switched off the flashlight. "It's freezing out here. Let's go inside."

I shook my head. "I can't."

"It's too cold."

"Please, Miller. I just...I need to be out here tonight. I can't be in there. I need to know that he's out there somewhere looking at the same sky as me. Wishing that we were getting married too. I just need...I need this."

"Okay." He put his hand down on my shoulder and squeezed it. "I'll be right inside if you need anything."

"Actually, could I have the flashlight back?"

He handed it to me. "I know today was supposed to be the best day of your life. And I'm sorry it was one of the worst instead."

I turned the flashlight back on and stared down at Matt's face in the photograph. I hadn't asked for this. I never wanted to die and fade away. And Matt wouldn't let that happen. I felt terrible for doubting him. Terrible for letting my father's lie creep under my skin.

Matt loved me.

He was out there. Thinking about what today could have been too. I traced his smile with my fingertip. I'd find my way back to him if it was the last thing I did.

CHAPTER 17

Tuesday - Christmas

Miller knocked on my bedroom door.

I groaned and rolled over. I didn't want to face today. The 22nd had been hard enough. But this would be my first Christmas without my mom. I thought I'd be spending it with Matt in the Bahamas. Two newlyweds having fun on the beach. The holiday would have been easier to swallow that way. But here in this house? No, I wasn't going to face today. I'd already planned to tell Miller I was sick and had to stay in bed all day.

Miller slowly opened the door. "Merry Christmas."

I opened my eyes and couldn't help but smile. He was wearing a Santa hat and carrying a steaming cup of something.

"What are you wearing?" I asked.

"Just bringing some Christmas cheer." He walked into the room and handed me the mug.

I looked down at the marshmallows floating on the top. "Hot chocolate for breakfast?"

"It's Christmas. What else would we have for breakfast?"

I laughed. "Oh, I don't know…" I pictured Christmas with my mom. "Monkey bread and eggs and fresh fruit and so much candy from our stockings." I took a sip of the hot chocolate. Honestly, this was pretty great too.

He laughed. "Well, as we both know…I'm not that great of a cook. But…I think you'll like what's waiting for you in the kitchen."

"What?"

"You'll have to get up and see." He grabbed the hot chocolate mug out of my hands.

Well, now I was too curious to not climb out of bed. Plus, it seemed like I had to or else he wouldn't give me my hot chocolate back. And I didn't feel like cooking, so that was probably the only thing I would get to eat all day. I shoved my feet into a pair of fuzzy slippers and followed him down the stairs. My feet froze on the last step.

Miller had transformed the whole first floor into something straight out of a Christmas movie. There was thick, green garland draped all over, covered in red ornaments and white Christmas lights. There was fake snow, candy canes, and the tree I'd ignored in the corner was fully decorated. It looked like a Christmas elf had broken into the house overnight and gone totally ham.

"What is all this?" I asked.

"I thought maybe we both needed a little Christmas spirit. Are you hungry?" He gestured toward the kitchen counter that was filled with everything my mom would make. The fresh fruit, the monkey bread, and scrambled eggs.

"But...how? How did you know?"

"You told me once. One of those times we chatted the night away in my bed."

I remembered now. One of the nights I'd crawled into his bed back at my dad's apartment. I always worried I rambled on and on. I wouldn't have blamed him for not listening. I was...very talkative in his bed for some reason. Probably because when I was talking it was easier to keep my hands to myself. I shook my head and smiled up at him.

"I can guarantee it won't taste as good as your mom's..."

"Are you kidding?" I ran into the kitchen. "Besides, it's the thought that counts." I piled my plate high with everything, being careful to pick away a few burnt pieces of monkey bread. "Really, how did you even know what monkey bread was? No one ever knows." I put a big chunk of the sugary goodness in my mouth and practically groaned.

He smiled. "I just looked it up. It's basically cinnamon rolls."

"Only a million times better. This is fantastic." Sure, it wasn't quite the same. And he'd definitely forgotten to salt and pepper the eggs. But I was so overwhelmed by his sweetness that I almost burst into tears.

"And wait for it." He grabbed a remote and hit a button. Christmas music flooded into the room. "May I have this dance?" He bowed and put his hand out for me.

I'd told him dancing around the kitchen with my mom was one of my favorite memories of her. But she and I had never done it on Christmas. We were too busy eating too many sweets and opening presents. But I had a feeling this was going to be a new favorite tradition of mine. I took his hand and laughed as he spun me in a circle.

Honestly, I never thought I could be happy again. But it was really hard not to smile as Miller dipped me low in the kitchen. He was about as good at dancing as he was at cooking. And I kind of loved that.

"There's also a freaking ton of presents for you to open from your dad."

I looked over at the pile of presents surrounding the tree. "I'd rather keep doing this."

He smiled down at me as he attempted some dance move I couldn't quite describe.

I started laughing.

This place felt a lot more like a home today. "I'm sorry I've been pushing you away. I just…"

"It's okay. I get it."

I shook my head as I looked up at him. It wasn't okay. I'd acted like I was in total isolation. Which wasn't true. Not in the slightest. I had a great friend right here with me. No one had ever had my back the way Miller had. At least since my mom. I owed him everything and….*crap*. "Oh my gosh, Miller. I'm so sorry. I didn't get you anything."

He smiled down at me. "This right here is all I wanted." He reached out and lightly brushed my bottom lip with his thumb. "Your smile."

"Merry Christmas, Miller."

His hand slid to the back of my neck as he looked down at me. For just a second, I thought he was going to kiss me. But instead he just smiled and dipped me to the music again. "Merry Christmas, kid."

CHAPTER 18

4 Months Later - Sunday

I wrung out my hair and stared at the new shade in the mirror. I refused to go fully brunette. I didn't want to look anything like Isabella, and I was scared if my hair matched hers that I might see her in my reflection. Instead my hair was now a mousey brown. And I'd cut it to right above my shoulders. I didn't look anything like myself.

It was funny. I'd been trying to come up with the perfect plan to escape from my dad over the past few months. I thought that a change like this would have been my own idea. But my father was waiting in the living room for me to come out and show him my new look.

He'd wanted to move Miller and me for the summer. And I told him I wasn't starting over again. I vehemently refused. He'd slowly been giving in more and more to me over the past few months. And after a lot of persuasion, he finally agreed to let us stay here as long as I didn't look like myself anymore.

Which was easy. I didn't feel like myself anymore. And now? I looked at the stranger staring back at me. I'd lost a lot of weight. My cheeks looked hollow. And now my hair was completely different. No one would recognize me. I barely recognized myself.

I walked out of the bathroom and down the hall.

My father set the newspaper down that he'd been reading. "That'll do," he said.

I sat down next to him on the couch. "So we can stay?"

He nodded.

I smiled, but resisted hugging him. I preferred to keep my distance from my father. Yes, he was being nice right this moment. But that could easily change. And I still didn't trust him.

"No talking to strangers though, alright?"

"Stranger danger," I said. "Got it."

He laughed. "Exactly. So you're excited to spend the summer here?"

I wouldn't use the word excited. But Miller and I had kind of made this place our home despite the fact that it was our cage. I didn't want to talk about my summer plans though. All I was going to do this summer was go for runs and dream of another life.

I cleared my throat. "You said you'd think about talking to Matt." I'd brought it up enough times that I was pretty sure he was close to caving on this too. My dad and I had come to a mutual understanding. I wouldn't throw a fit when he came. And he'd be nicer to me. Sometimes it was really hard not to want to scream at him though.

"I did." He pulled out his phone. "I want you to be happy. And safe. That's all I want."

So…was that a yes or a no? I just stared at him.

"I gave this a lot of thought. And you're right. Now that the dust has settled, maybe it'll be okay."

My heart started racing. "I can talk to him?"

My dad cleared his throat. "Sorry, I should have made myself more clear. *I'll* speak to him. Or…I'll try to." He handed me the phone.

I looked down at the screen. I recognized Matt's number. My father had sent him a text. He said he had something important to discuss with Matt.

And Matt hadn't responded.

He'd said nothing at all in response.

That knife that had slowly eased from my chest over the past few months was back. Slowly twisting. I wanted to pretend it was because Matt didn't know who was texting him. But my dad had said it was Mr. Pruitt. It reminded me of when my dad told me that Matt had said nothing at all at my fake funeral. Like I'd been completely erased from his mind. Like I meant nothing.

"Can you text him again?" I asked. "Maybe he didn't see it?"

"I'll try again soon." He took the phone back and put it in his pocket.

My dad was a liar. I knew that. And yet...that was Matt's number. Matt hadn't responded. Wouldn't he be desperate for news about me? I felt desperate every day. Although, maybe a little less now than I had at first.

I felt comfortable here with Miller. And safe, just like my dad wanted me to be. It was why I didn't want to move to a new place. It was why I'd cut and dyed my hair to pacify him. I liked it here. Which I'd never expected to. I liked waking up to the sound of crashing waves and seagulls. I liked seeing Miller's smiling face every morning. I felt...less empty now than I had when we'd first arrived.

And for some reason that made me feel guilty. I wasn't supposed to feel less empty. I was supposed to be trying to escape. And I was worried my father's accounts of back home were messing with my head. There was definitely something I'd been thinking about over and over again. "Those pictures you showed me before Christmas. Are you sure they were...current?" Maybe they were old. They could have easily been taken before I moved to New York. Kennedy had a crush on Felix. It made sense for the two of them to look close in the pictures. And the Untouchables had all been friends before I messed everything up too. And Matt had hooked up with a lot of girls. I knew that.

"I'm not trying to hurt you. I wouldn't show you fake pictures."

I nodded. I didn't want to believe him. But I kind of did. "I thought Matt looked sad in the one with that girl." The picture was burning a hole in my pocket right now. Well, half of it. I'd torn off the side with the random girl and thrown it out. But I kept the picture of Matt with me at all times. Because some days I needed to see the sadness in his eyes too. It made me feel less alone.

"I have more if you want to see what everyone is up to."

I wanted to be strong enough to turn down his offer. But I wasn't. I was eager for more information. I wanted to hear and see everything I could. I missed my friends. I missed Matt. My father was the only interaction I had with the outside world. I'd take whatever he could give me.

He pulled out a new manilla envelope and handed it to me.

I hated every picture. Because maybe I was making it up…but Matt looked less sad. Less tired. Less…empty. I knew I'd just thought the same thing about myself. I was a total hypocrite. But at the same time, I wasn't sure I looked any less sad or depressed. I still wore that pain like a mask. Partially to protect my heart. Partially to keep Miller in the friend zone. I was definitely still sad.

But…I smiled more now than I did at first. Miller was great at making me laugh. Every night since Christmas, while we cooked together, Miller turned the volume way up and we danced. I had fun with him. Could I really be mad at Matt for having fun too?

I paused halfway through the pictures, on one of Matt cozied up to a new girl.

I'd been cozying up to Miller too. On nights when it was hard to breathe, I climbed into his bed uninvited. And he held me without saying a word. Miller was my rock.

I'd be a hypocrite for being upset with Matt.

But I also knew what kind of man Matt was before he met me. He slept around a lot. He'd hooked up with practically the whole cheerleading team. Was he doing that now?

Yes, I'd cozied up to Miller. But I hadn't once kissed him. I'd been loyal to Matt. He was my fiancé. Did Matt remember that? Did he remember me?

I loved Matt. I wanted him to be happy. But it stung that he was so happy without me by his side.

"Are you sure you want me to try to reach out again, angel?"

I nodded. Even if it was just to know Matt had moved on. I needed to know. I needed to know everything.

I looked out the sliding glass doors at Miller. He was out on the deck reading. He loved nonfiction books. I joked around with him about it. I preferred fiction because I loved living someone else's life for even just a little bit. Miller never acted like he needed an escape though. He was just happy here. With me.

I kept him at arm's length because I'd made promises to Matt. It wasn't fair to Miller. I knew that. Would everything change if Matt had moved on? Would I want more with Miller?

Yes.

I didn't even have to think about it. There were lots of nights I wished he'd kiss me. But I knew he wouldn't. Because I filled the silence with stories about Matt. I'd put him so far into the friend zone that there was no wiggle room.

If Matt had truly forgotten all about me though? Yeah, I'd want more with Miller. And I felt guilty for even thinking about it.

Not that it mattered. I'd never do anything with Miller until I was able to talk to Matt again. I'd made Matt a promise. And a few months didn't erase my feelings for him. It just made him feel farther away. Miller was close. That was all it was. And that's probably what was going on with the different girls in pictures with Matt. He was just trying to not drown.

"There is one other thing," my dad said. "I wasn't sure whether to wait to tell you or not…but it's important to keep you updated on the situation back home. I need you to know that I'm not putting Isabella above you. I'm going to send her away. For a while."

I stared at him. "Like this?" At a beach house somewhere with no contact with the outside world?

"No. Not like this." He sighed. "A psych ward. I don't want to get your hopes up. But…I'm going to monitor her progress. I'm not making any promises. But I'm trying."

That was definitely trying. I'd been begging him to make her go away instead of me. "Thank you."

"Like I said, I don't want you to get your hopes up. It's just a first step."

I nodded. But my hopes were a little up. In the back of my head I was thinking that if Isabella was locked up I could be free. But that wasn't what my dad had said. I think he wanted her to get better before he released me. And I wasn't a big believer in Isabella ever getting better. Her wanting to kill me probably wasn't something that could be undone. I wasn't sure there were enough psychologists in the world to untangle her mess of a mind. Too bad there wasn't a little pill that made you not a serial killer. So yeah…my hopes had been up for a second. But it was pointless. My dad wouldn't let me leave if I wasn't safe. And I truly believed that I wouldn't be safe until Isabella took her last breath.

"I need to get back to the city." My father stood up. "Unless there's something else you need?"

"No. I'm good."

He kissed the side of my forehead. "See you again soon, angel."

I watched him walk away. He no longer needed his cane. He looked healthy and happy. I knew I should hate him for keeping me here. But it was hard to hate him when he was being nice to me. For a long time I wished him dead. I was glad he wasn't now. I was glad I'd helped save him. He was the only family I had. And even though he was going about this situation all wrong…he was trying. It wasn't his fault that he was a bad parent. Before I showed up he'd only had a psychotic daughter. If I was Isabella's parent, surely I'd be a monster too.

I sat back down on the couch once the front door closed. It was tempting to go out on the deck with Miller. But I was still eager for more information. And I'd only been through half the pictures.

I loved seeing Kennedy and Felix happy. It was hard to tell from the pictures if they were just friends or something more. But their smiles were real. I'd hated how I left things with Kennedy. She had been my best friend. I'd betrayed her trust. And I wished I had one more chance to explain. I was just trying to help. I tried not to get teary-eyed as I saw her smiling and laughing. I was happy for her.

I flipped through a few more and my hands froze.

I'd wanted more information.

I'd wanted answers.

And there they were.

Matt wasn't smiling at the camera in this one. He was too busy making out with some girl with brunette hair. It wasn't Isabella. But it didn't really matter. What mattered was that it wasn't me. It wasn't me and it looked a lot more like Isabella than it did me. I didn't know what that meant. But I knew what him kissing someone else meant.

He'd moved on.

I shook my head and flipped to another picture. Another one of him and the random girl in a full-on make-out session. I didn't care that there were red Solo cups everywhere. There was no amount of alcohol I could drink that would make me cheat on Matt.

I tried to take a deep breath.

He thinks you're dead.

It was a good argument for his actions. But at the same time…he'd promised me the rest of his firsts. But he'd just had another first kiss with someone new. Were the promises he made to me really so easy to forget? Was I that easy to forget?

I stared at the picture.

Apparently I was.

He thinks you're dead.

There was just one problem with that. I wasn't dead. And my heart was broken.

***

Sometimes when I ran, I'd stop really far away from the beach house and scream at the top of my lungs. I'd scream as loud as I possibly could. But that's when the beach was isolated. It was busier now. Someone might hear me scream and ask questions. And questions would lead to me having to move to another safehouse.

So instead of screaming, I just ran farther and farther. I ran until my legs hurt. Until I couldn't run anymore. Until I collapsed in the sand and cried.

It hurt to think of what a life without Matt would be like.

Like this? Running until my lungs and legs gave out? A life filled with pain? That's what life felt like without him. I'd been holding on to a hope that no longer existed.

He'd forgotten about me.

And the only thing that kept me going was thinking that he hadn't.

It felt like he'd actually cut out a piece of my heart. And the life was slowly draining out of me.

Miller collapsed on the sand beside me. He always followed me on my runs, keeping his distance. He had to. I knew he saw me scream out my frustrations. But he never approached me when I screamed. I was surprised he approached me now.

"I saw the pictures," he said. "Do you want to talk about it?"

"There's nothing to talk about. He forgot about me." I hated the tears that stung my eyes. I shouldn't be crying over a boy that was happy I was dead.

"I'm sure he didn't. I know it's hard to put yourself in his shoes, but imagine how he must be feeling." He ran his hand up and down my back, soothing me. He was good at that. Calming me down. He made it easier to breathe.

"I know how he's feeling," I said. "He's feeling like he's horny and wants to bang some rando."

Miller laughed. "Maybe. Or he's in pain and missing you too. And just trying to find some semblance of happiness in the chaos."

"Why are you always defending him? Why don't you throw him under the bus? You don't even like him."

"I don't. But you do."

I shook my head. "You should be telling me how terrible he is. How you and I are a better fit. How he moved on and so should I." I regretted the words as soon as I said them. I didn't want Miller to try to win me over. Not when my heart was broken. Not when I didn't know what was real and what wasn't. My head and my heart were confused. I didn't know what I wanted. All I knew was that I was fucking pissed. I was pissed at everyone and everything.

His hand fell from my back. "You made your choice last fall. And I'm doing my best to respect that."

What if I didn't want him to respect my decision? What if I wanted to climb on top of him in bed instead of curling into his side? I deserved to find happiness in the chaos too. And what if I was just being an idiot and I'd chosen wrong last fall? I'd made a lot of terrible decisions back in New York. Maybe Matt was one of them.

"I saw the way you looked at him," Miller said. "You didn't look at me like that."

"Like what?"

"Like you couldn't live without him."

"He seems to be living perfectly fine without me," I said.

"And what about you? How are you doing without him?"

"I'm doing great. I'm living it up at a beach house with a hot guy." I stared at him. *Fuck Matt*. I was done. "But I'd be doing a lot better if we were more than friends."

He raised his eyebrow. "You're in a destructive mood today."

"Wouldn't you be?"

He slowly stood up and brushed the sand off the back of his shorts. "Maybe. I don't know. I don't have anyone missing me back home."

Me either. But I knew what he meant. He'd left nothing behind. "Well, I can think of a few ways we could both feel better." I didn't even know what I meant by that. Part of me wanted to walk into the ocean and drown. The other part of me wanted to jump on top of Miller and make out with him right in the sand.

"You'd regret it."

I wasn't sure if he was thinking about the make-out session or the drowning thing. "I wouldn't regret kissing you." I'd kissed him before. I liked kissing him. I loved kissing him. Miller was a fantastic kisser. And it wasn't like I hadn't been thinking about it. Of course I had. Unlike my dad's nickname for me, I wasn't an angel. But I hadn't acted on it. Because I was fucking engaged.

"Well, I'd regret it," he said.

Ouch. I probably deserved that though. He was right. I was in a very destructive mood today. It was like I was asking to be hurt. Maybe I just needed a little push to walk into that water and keep going until it was impossible to turn around. Because a part of me wanted that. It already felt like I was drowning. Why not actually drown?

"You can't be angry with me right now," he said. "You know how I feel about you."

I shook my head.

He grabbed my chin and forced me to look at him. "Ask me to kiss you again when you're not pissed off at the world. Ask me when you mean it. I'm not doing this again as a substitute for what you really want. Ask me when I'm your first choice." He let his fingers fall from my chin. "And then I'll say yes."

My heart was racing. And it wasn't because I was out of breath from my run anymore. I wanted to ask him again right now. Because he was looking at me like he wanted to kiss me. But...I'd seen him look at me like that a lot since we'd been shacked up together. I'm sure I'd looked at him the same way.

We were friends right now for a reason. Because a friend was all I needed. Right?

I wasn't looking at him like a friend anymore though. I felt betrayed. I felt empty. I felt…like I'd made the wrong choice last fall. I'd messed up. Miller was patient. And kind. And gorgeous. I even found the small scar on his cheek beautiful. He was amazing.

I loved Miller. And I'd been slowly falling in love with him.

And I hated myself. I hated myself for being a hypocrite.

I was in love with two people at the same time. And only one of them was staring back at me. I couldn't tell him I was all in when half my heart was with Matt though. So instead, I just nodded.

"Race you back?" Miller said.

"I have a better idea." I looked around to make sure the beach down here was clear and pulled off my sweaty shirt.

Miller just stared at me.

"I bet the water feels amazing right now."

He shook his head. "I bet it's freezing."

"There's only one way to find out." I kicked off my shoes and pulled down my spandex shorts.

"What are you doing?"

I pretended like I was about to take my sports bra off.

"I swear if you take that off, I won't be able to control myself."

I laughed, even though I knew he was serious. "Are you going to join me?" I really was feeling destructive. But for the first time in months I also felt alive.

He shook his head as I slowly backed into the water.

"I dare you," I said.

He rolled his eyes.

"I'm going to need someone to keep me warm if it's cold."

He shook his head.

I turned around and ran into the water. He was right. It was fucking freezing. I dove into a wave and came up for air. When I turned around Miller was gone. For a second I frowned but then he came up out of the water too.

"You win," I said. "It's freaking freezing in here."

He pulled me close.

I wrapped my legs around him in the water and held him tight. And I breathed easily for the first time since I'd seen the pictures. I loved Matt. But I didn't remember feeling this close to him. There was something about the way Miller and I fit. From the second we met…I felt like we were equals. With Matt I never felt good enough.

I rested my chin on Miller's shoulder and breathed him in. It was selfish of me to do this. And yet…I couldn't stop.

His breath was warm in my ear.

I waited for him to say something.

Instead, he kissed me behind my ear. And then the side of my neck. It didn't feel at all like a friendship kiss to me. It felt amazing.

Fuck.

It wasn't allowed to feel amazing. I put my forehead against his. I wanted to kiss him. But I couldn't. I needed to talk to Matt. I needed to get out of here so I could figure out what the hell was going on. I needed an escape plan.

CHAPTER 19

1 Month Later - Friday

Miller's skin was bronze from the summer sun. And I had a hard time not staring at his six-pack. It wasn't my fault. He was sweating because we were running. And his abs were practically glistening. I was pretty sure I was about to do something stupid if I stayed this close to him.

It was hard not to be this close to him though. Ever since I'd had a meltdown on the beach a month ago, he started running with me instead of trailing behind to make sure I was safe.

I didn't mind it. I liked looking at him. I just needed to make sure I didn't touch him. And it was getting harder and harder. We did everything together, especially in the summer since neither of us had online classes. It gave me barely any time alone. And I needed time alone to plot out our perfect escape plan.

I stopped and put my hands on my knees, pretending to be completely out of breath. "Go ahead. I need a minute."

But instead of continuing on down the beach, he plopped down in the sand. "I have a confession to make."

"And what is your confession?" I couldn't help smiling when he was smiling. His good mood was contagious.

"You're going to find it very shocking."

"Oh, I'm going to be scandalized?" I asked and put my hand to my chest, feigning shock.

He laughed. "Probably. Drumroll."

I just stared at him.

"Don't make me give myself my own drumroll, kid."

I wanted to roll my eyes. But I was actually having fun playing along with whatever ridiculous confession this was. I patted my thighs, giving him a perfect drumroll.

"I hate running!" he yelled at the top of his lungs, like the truth was just bursting out of him.

I started laughing.

"God, it feels good to admit that."

"That was hardly a scandalous confession." I sat down next to him. "You really don't have to come with me on my runs."

"Actually I do." He leaned back in the sand and stared up at the clouds.

"You're going to be completely covered in sand now. It's going to stick to all your sweat."

"Oh. Like this?" He rolled over so he basically looked like a sugar-coated doughnut.

"Miller what are you doing?!" I couldn't stop laughing. "You're never going to be able to get all that sand off. It's going to be all over our house for weeks."

"Our house," he said. "I kinda like the sound of that."

My smile faltered. I kept doing this. Flirting with him by accident. It happened so often that I wasn't even sure it was by accident anymore. But he was very good at distracting me when my smiles faded.

He tickled my side and I screamed and rolled over. He kept tickling me until I'd turned every which way, getting completely covered in sand. And then he grabbed my hands and pinned them over my head so I couldn't squirm away anymore.

We were both breathing hard from our laughter. And the laughter in the air had been replaced with something a lot heavier. His body pressed firmly against mine. I'd been trying to avoid exactly this. And I was starting to wonder why. Matt had moved on pretty easily. *Stop.* Why did I always think of Matt when I knew he wasn't thinking about me? I wanted to be brave and kiss Miller. I could easily close the distance. I swallowed hard. But I wasn't ready to tell him he was my first choice. I wasn't even sure I knew how to make a logical decision anymore.

"Now you're going to track sand all over our house," he said. "What were you thinking?"

I looked down at my stomach. I'd been just as sweaty as him and now we were matching sugar-covered doughnuts. "Damn it." I really loved the beach. But I hated that no matter what we did the sand refused to stay outside.

He laughed. "Don't sweat it. It's definitely my turn to sweep."

"I've never seen you pick up a broom."

"Which is how I know it's my turn." He smiled down at me. "Come on, we better go rinse off," he said and pulled away from me. He kicked off his socks and shoes. "You coming?" he asked.

"Yeah. I just need a minute."

I watched him run into the water.

I took a deep breath. I needed a minute to calm down. My heart was beating too quickly. It was like I could feel it hammering against my ribcage. I wanted to think it was because I had just run for miles. But it wasn't that. Miller made my heart race. When he was close. When he was far away. Whenever I thought about him really.

My stomach twisted in knots. Was Matt staring at some new girl the way I was staring at Miller? Probably. Most definitely.

I closed my eyes for a minute.

But Matt thought I was dead.

I needed to see him. I needed to clear my head somehow. But that was a little hard to do. Because when I opened my eyes, Miller was standing above me.

I screamed as he lifted me over his shoulder. "Put me down!"

Instead of listening to my very reasonable request, he sprinted back into the water, carrying me with him.

"It's freezing!" I screamed as he pulled me down into the cold water.

He laughed as I splashed water in his face. "Sorry, but I couldn't let you track all that sand into the house."

I gave him an exaggerated scowl. "I'm still wearing my running shoes."

"I'll buy you a new pair. Besides, it might be kinda fun to run barefoot on the sand. It's probably better for your feet."

"My feet are fine, thank you very much. And you just confessed that you hate running. I don't trust your running advice at all."

"Fair point. Do you want to swim back?"

"No. It's a little hard to swim in sneakers." We weren't in very far, so my sneakers were awkwardly sinking in the wet sand beneath me. Swimming would be impossible.

"You're really not letting up on the sneaker thing, huh? Don't you have like a million pairs of shoes in your room?"

Yeah, there were tons of shoes and clothes in my closet. But I barely spent any time in my room. I spent way more time in his. Or out here.

It was strange. I knew my dad was keeping me in a well thought out cage. But it was hard to feel that way when I was out here. I felt…free. Especially when I was next to Miller.

I was pretty sure it was what my father wanted.

To keep me in a cage willingly.

"It's not a big deal," Miller said and lightly touched the side of my face. "Like I said, I'll buy you a new pair. But to make up for it…we can head back to the house however you want. Swim, run, crawl…"

I laughed. It was going to be a squishy walk back in these shoes. "I have a better idea."

"That look of pure evil on your face… What are you going to make me do?"

I smiled up at him. "Nonsense. I'm not the evil sister. But I am going to demand a piggyback ride."

"Done." He turned around and I climbed onto his back.

We laughed the whole way home. Especially when he kept threatening to roll us in the sand. He slowly walked up the stairs of the deck and pretended like he was going to open the sliding glass doors and walk right inside.

"What are you doing? You need to rinse off your feet!"

"They're not even that sandy."

So maybe he wasn't pretending like he was about to open the door. "The outside shower is right there." I pointed to the side of the deck.

"I'll sweep. I swear."

"It's going to get everywhere. Miller…"

He somehow managed to open the sliding glass door while battling me. I started laughing because he really was ridiculous. Or maybe I was ridiculous. I didn't even know anymore.

"Stop," I laughed and tried to wrap my leg around his arm even though it was too late. He'd already taken the inevitable first sandy step. "All is lost!"

He started laughing even harder.

Someone cleared their throat.

Miller and I both froze. My dad was standing in the middle of the living room.

"Dad." My voice died in my throat when I saw his expression.

My father's face was…cold. Hard. Terrifying. "What are you doing?" he said.

I wasn't sure which one of us he was talking to. I slid off Miller's back. "I got my shoes wet. Miller carried me back so I wouldn't get them all sandy too." But I didn't really know how to explain away our little wrassle back there. I knew how that probably looked. It looked exactly like it was. Like Miller and I were flirting. Being handsy. It looked like we were more than friends. Which was strictly against my dad's rules. I smiled at Miller. "Thank you, bodyguard," I said formally. "That'll be all. Away with you." *Away with you?* What the hell was I even saying? Miller was my bodyguard. Not a houseboy.

Miller cleared his throat. "Yes, ma'am. And I'll sweep this mess up immediately."

"Good. Make it snappy." Seriously, what was I saying? I turned back to my dad. Our little display did not seem to pacify him at all. I tried to think of another strategy. "Hey, Dad." I walked over to hug him but he held up his hand.

"You're soaked. Go change. We have a lot to discuss."

I nodded. *Fuck.* I really hoped I didn't just get Miller in trouble. I kicked off my wet shoes and ran up to my room to change as quickly as possible. I didn't bother to rinse the saltwater off my skin. I threw on a t-shirt and shorts and ran back down the stairs.

Miller and my father were talking heatedly in the living room. I watched in horror as my father pulled a gun out of the back of his belt and lifted it toward Miller.

"Stop!" I screamed as I ran down the rest of the steps. "Don't hurt Miller." I stepped in front of him and put out my hands, as if that would somehow protect us from being shot. "He's done nothing wrong!"

My father ignored me and proceeded to reach around me and…hand Miller the gun.

Miller didn't make eye contact with me. He just slid the gun into his waistband.

I looked back and forth between them. "What's going on?"

"There's been a little hiccup in my plans. I told Isabella the news that she was going away to get help. But she thinks the only reason she's going is because you're still alive. She's convinced you're out there somewhere. I tried to tell her otherwise. But I don't know if she listened. The security at the institute she's going to is good. But I'm worried it's not as good as my own. She's heading there on Monday. And I just wanted to make sure you'll be safe just in case she…gets out. And finds you. And tries something. Or maybe even tries something before she arrives at the institute."

"She thinks I'm alive?"

My dad nodded.

That was bad. Really bad. And yet…I wasn't even really concerned about that. I was concerned about the fact that this afternoon could have gone very differently. My dad was a violent man. He easily could have shot Miller a few minutes ago. He wouldn't have even blinked an eye. And it would have been all my fault.

"So no more leaving the house until I say otherwise."

What? No. I needed to be outside. This house was stifling. The only reason I wanted to stay here instead of going to someplace new was because I got to be outside all the time. "But…"

"No buts. There's a treadmill in the gym. You don't need to leave for anything."

Except my sanity. "She won't recognize me. I cut and dyed my hair."

He shook his head. "You have no idea what you're up against here. You will not step foot out of this house. Do I make myself clear?" His voice was so icy. He hadn't been this angry with me since before Christmas. Before I started playing nice.

I swallowed hard. "Yes." He'd made himself perfectly clear. My cage had just gotten significantly smaller.

"Look at me."

I hadn't even realized my eyes had gravitated to the floor. I looked back up at him.

"And if I ever see something like I saw this afternoon between the two of you again? We will be having a serious *discussion*."

But he didn't say the word discussion normally. He'd basically just confessed that he'd murder Miller if he saw him touching me again. I clenched my hands into fists and glared at him. God, what I would give to be able to punch him square in the nose.

"I don't have time to stay today. I just needed to make sure you were both briefed on the situation." He pulled out his wallet and handed me a credit card. "Buy yourself a new pair of sneakers. And anything else at all you need."

I looked down at the credit card. It wasn't my name. I looked back up at him.

"It's untraceable."

Untraceable. To everyone? I wondered if that meant including him. I had an idea running through my head. Isabella was insane. I knew that. We weren't safe here. But not because of Isabella. Because of my dad.

Miller hadn't followed my father's rules. Because I hadn't let him. I climbed into his bed almost every night. I made him feel obligated to hug me and hold me, even though my heart was confused. I was going to get him killed.

I needed to get us out of here. I needed to fix this. "Thanks," I said and gripped the credit card a little tighter. I was pretty sure I'd just found our out.

CHAPTER 20

2 Months Later - Monday

My hands were shaking as I walked into the kitchen. Miller was cooking us dinner tonight. He'd actually gotten really good at it over the last few months.

"Miller?"

He turned toward me, the smile on his face faltering. "What's wrong?"

"Don't be mad."

He left his post at the stove. "What's going on? Did Little Dicky call?"

I wanted to laugh. We'd started referring to my dad as Little Dicky. The fact that lots of Richard's went by the nickname Dick was strange enough on its own. But then we'd started laughing one night agreeing to call him Dick from now on. And it somehow tumbled into Little Dicky. It made thinking about my father a lot easier when I referred to him that way. And for some reason we both found it hilarious. We'd needed more lighthearted moments these past couple months when we weren't allowed to step foot outside. "No. I mean, yes, he did. But it's not about that."

I handed him the envelope. "I did something. You're probably not going to like it. But just…give me a chance to explain, okay?" He'd been incredibly patient with me. I went from snuggling him in the ocean one minute to barely talking to him the next. I loved him. And I hated myself. I was just so freaking confused. All I knew was that we couldn't stay here. Neither of us. "Open it."

He pulled out the passport with a fake name. A debit card linked to a bank account with the same name on it. And a set of keys.

"What is this?"

"Remember that credit card my dad got me a few months ago? I've been working with someone online to pull money into a secure account. For you. For your fresh start."

He lowered his eyebrows.

"You told me you preferred lakes over oceans. I pointed to the keys. There's a cute little place right by a lake that you own now. It's…it's perfectly you. You'll be happy there. And no one will find you…"

"Are you crazy? Brooklyn, we can't leave."

I pressed my lips together. There wasn't a *we* in this. "You said my dad was coming down this weekend. That gives you a whole week to get a head start."

"You didn't say we."

The way he was staring at me made my heart break all over again. I was a fragment of the person I used to be. I was confused. And broken. And in pain. Whenever my dad came by, he brought more pictures of Matt and my friends being happy without me. He claimed to have texted Matt a few more times, telling him they needed to talk. He said he was willing to tell Matt the truth if that would make me happy. But apparently Matt had never texted him back.

My dad also told me that Isabella was still safely locked up in a psych ward. Even though he'd tried to scare me half to death by saying she might escape. He was just trying to scare me. He was just trying to keep me locked up here forever. Literally now. I hadn't gotten to leave the beach house in months. I was trapped here. And I couldn't breathe anymore. It was like my father was trying to break me. Break my spirit. Break any hope I had of a normal life one day. He just wanted me to obey him.

So I'd decided that I didn't believe a word that came out of my father's mouth. Maybe I was in denial. But I was calling my father's bluff. If he said it was okay for Matt to know…I'd tell him myself. In person. Maybe I was being naïve. I'd seen the pictures. But…what if they were old? What if nothing was as it seemed? I couldn't keep going like this. I had to get to the bottom of it all before my heart exploded. I needed answers. If I was going to move forward, I just needed to know.

Isabella wasn't a threat as long as she was locked up. And Matt was good at keeping secrets. If he still wanted me…if he still loved me…I'd just stay camped out in his house instead of here. The Caldwells wouldn't care. His mother was one of the sweetest people I'd ever met. I knew they'd welcome me back with open arms.

"This isn't a good idea," Miller said. "We've talked about this."

"And you said I needed a better plan. This plan is flawless. You'll be safe. You'll be free."

He looked down at the keys in his hand. "Brooklyn, Matt thinks you're dead. It's been nine months. Are you sure you've thought of all the possibilities here?"

"You said it yourself. This isn't about what Matt didn't do this time. He doesn't know I'm alive. If he knew…he would have come. He wouldn't have kissed anyone else. I believe that. I have to."

"What if your father has been telling the truth?"

I shook my head. "He's not."

"But what if he is?"

I swallowed hard. "Then I'll deal with that when the time comes. I have to go see Matt. I feel like I'm slowly dying here without him."

Miller looked away from me, out toward the beach.

"I didn't mean it that way," I said and grabbed his hand. "You being here with me has been the only thing keeping me going." He had to know that. He'd kept me alive over the past several months. I loved him. I loved him so much that going in opposite directions physically pained me. But how could I move forward with Miller if I didn't know whether or not Matt had moved on?

"So you want me to just…disappear?"

"Isn't that the only way for you to get away from my dad?"

"Yeah. But it takes me away from you too." He stared at me the same way he always did. Like I was his whole world.

But he wasn't mine. And I couldn't do this to him anymore. He'd become my best friend. The person I literally leaned on when things were hard. I loved him. Fiercely. I was pretty sure I was in love with him. But I'd been faithful to Matt. I needed to go back to him. I needed to speak with him. We were still engaged. It didn't matter that my ring was missing. I was Matt's. And he was mine. Even though I wasn't even sure he had my whole heart anymore.

"Is this really what you want?" Miller asked.

"Yes." *No. I don't know.*

He closed his fist around the keys. It looked like he was going to walk away. Which was what I wanted. But instead he shook his head. "Those first few months, I knew you thought about him when I held you. I'm not an idiot, Brooklyn. I knew that. And I hear you. I know you want me to walk out that door. But is that your head or your heart talking? I know you're trying to make good on promises you made to Matt. But I don't know how you can stand here and say that you still think about him when I hold you now. Not after everything we've been through the past few months. You have feelings for me. I don't know how you can want me to walk out that door and never see me again. I don't believe it."

"Miller…"

"I love you, Brooklyn. I've always loved you. If you want to run away from your dad? If that's what you need to be happy? Then fine. Run away with me."

It wasn't that simple. "I promised Matt forever."

Miller shook his head. "Not all promises are meant to be kept."

Honestly it wasn't even about that now. I knew Matt had probably broken his promises to me, no matter how badly I wanted to believe in him. But he thought I was dead. Miller had said that himself. "You told me to ask you to kiss me when I was ready to put you first."

His Adam's apple rose and fell.

"I can't do that until Matt knows the truth. I need to see for myself that he's moved on. I can't move on until I know for sure."

"So you want me to go to this new house. And…wait. You want me to wait and see if Matt chooses you back? I'm here right now saying I choose you."

I stood up on my tiptoes and kissed his cheek. "I have to do this. I don't know how else to explain it. He has a piece of my heart. I either need to give him the rest of it or get it back. I need it back. My heart can only break so many times before it stops working completely. It's broken. It hurts. I hurt all the time."

He cradled my face in his hands. "Okay." He let go of my face and pressed one of the keys into my palm. "I'll be waiting for you, Brooklyn."

CHAPTER 21

Monday

Miller was gone. I watched him drive away in the rental car I'd gotten him. He didn't know it yet, but there was a lot of money in that bank account. More money than either of us could imagine in our wildest dreams.

Money meant nothing to me. I'd never wanted to be thrust into the world of the elite. But I knew Miller needed it. He had dreams bigger than just me and him. I knew he did. He had to. That was the only way I could do what I needed to do.

I pulled my backpack over my shoulder. There were only a few things I was bringing with me. Some stuff that my mom had left me. A few pictures of Matt. And the notes Matt had left me. I read through them sometimes. Trying to remember when my life was simpler. Which was silly. Because at the time I'd never thought it was simpler. Everything back then had seemed so messy and so important.

But the only important things were life and death. And I needed Matt to know I wasn't dead. I owed him that.

Rereading some of those notes had kept me going. Matt's last words to me had been…cruel. Not that I blamed him. Mine had been cruel too. But his notes? His notes reminded me of what we had. Reminded me of what we could still be. *Maybe.* They also reminded me of when he'd kept our relationship a secret. He had a bad habit of not being able to put me first. *Stop.*

He thinks you're dead. Yes, I was upset that he'd kissed someone new. But maybe he was just coping. Maybe he was still missing me too. The feeling hadn't faded away for me. It got less intense. But it was still there. This nagging ache. I needed to see him. Talk to him. Explain everything. That didn't make pushing Miller away any easier though.

It was strange watching Miller drive away. I felt the same way I had when I noticed the engagement ring missing from my finger. And I wasn't sure what that meant, besides that I was a freaking mess.

I looked back at the kitchen, remembering Miller dancing with me every night as we cooked. I smiled. He was a terrible dancer. And a wonderful person. I sighed. I never thought I'd be sad to leave my prison. I was finally free. But I barely felt alive. One of my happiest memories was of Miller surprising me Christmas morning. And I don't just mean since moving here. I mean of all my memories. That was an amazing day. Dancing nonstop on Christmas morning was something I wanted to do every year. A new tradition. And yet…I was about to drive in the opposite direction of Miller.

He was gone.

I'd watched him drive away.

He left.

I was used to people leaving me. But never because I pushed them away. I didn't have to lose Miller. I could go after him. I had the key to his new house in one pocket and the picture of Matt in the other. And I was torn.

I felt paralyzed.

I didn't want to make this choice.

It wasn't even supposed to be one.

Matt was my fiancé, even if he didn't realize it was still true. And Miller was quickly becoming my whole world. It wasn't just because I was isolated with him, which was something I thought about regularly. That definitely wasn't it. I'd given him a piece of my heart last fall when I moved in with my dad. I'd always been drawn to Miller.

And I'd always been drawn to Matt.

God, what was I doing?

I walked out of the beach house and closed the door. I was going crazy. Matt was my future. He was my everything. There was no choice here. I promised Matt forever. I gave him my heart. I'd be married to him if my father hadn't ruined everything. And I wouldn't have regretted it for a second. I needed to go to him. His arms were the ones I belonged in. It was him. I'd made a choice last fall. It was Matt.

I left the note for my father beside Miller's abandoned cell phone. I'd thought long and hard about what to say to my dad. Beg him not to freak out? Tell him I was sorry for leaving? Ask him not to worry because I'd be fine on my own?

Nope, none of that. I went with the two-middle-fingers-in-the-air version instead. My eyes scanned the note, making sure it was what I wanted to say as my parting words to father dearest. Little Dicky himself.

Richard,

I'm not a pawn. And I'm done being played. Don't look for me. And don't look for Miller.

I swear to God, if I find out you did anything to him I will never forgive you. You'll be dead to me. Buried in the grave next to my fake one.

If you wanted to keep me safe, you should have looked for me 16 years ago. You should have used your resources to save my mom. But you didn't. You found me when you needed me. But I never needed you.

I didn't sign it. He'd know it was from me, unless he had some other illegitimate children locked up somewhere. My heart was torn between Miller and Matt. But I wasn't confused about my dad at all. He could pretend to be nice all he wanted. He could pretend what happened last fall was a misunderstanding. But I hated him. He'd ruined my life. He'd put me in a terrible position. Fathers weren't supposed to do that. But that was the whole problem. I didn't have a father.

I took a deep breath and left the beach house. I climbed into my rental car and drove away. And when I pulled onto the interstate, I was very aware that I might be following my head instead of my heart. I was going back to New York. Back to Matt. Back to where I was supposed to be.

It was the first decision I'd gotten to make for myself in months. And apparently I'd gotten really bad at making my own choices. My stomach was twisted in knots. Each mile closer to Matt made me feel like I was betraying Miller. But I had the odd sense that I'd feel the same way if I was driving toward Miller instead. I'd feel guilty for not driving toward Matt. I had to do this. I needed answers.

I took a deep breath. I tried to remember what it felt like to fall asleep in Matt's arms. I remembered feeling whole. Content. Optimistic. He'd pieced me back together after my mom died. After my uncle died.

But so had Miller. Miller had also been there for me when Matt didn't have my back. Miller let me hang out with him when I was scared of my dad. And he'd held me together for the past nine months.

I hadn't even known Matt nine months.

I slowly breathed in and out. None of the particulars mattered. The truth was that Miller held me tight every night. And I dreamed of Matt. I dreamed of Matt coming to save me.

But that was the thing. I hadn't really needed him to save me. I just needed him to not forget. That wasn't asking too much.

Matt still loved me. I felt it in my bones. Because I still loved him too.

I was making the right choice. And I was proud of myself. I was going to New York. And I was going to live happily ever after with the first boy I ever fell in love with.

CHAPTER 22

Monday

I rolled down the windows of the car, happy to have the fresh air in my hair. When my dad told me I couldn't go outside anymore, Miller had been wonderful about letting me open a window to let the breeze in. As long as we were watching the window at all times. Which meant not at night, which made it hard to sleep.

After all, one never knew when Isabella might crawl through the window with a machete. I wouldn't put it past her. She had killed a cute dog and painted a threat in Matt's room with the little guy's blood. She was crazy. I truly hoped she was getting the help she needed. But I wasn't going to wait around for her to be sane. That could be a lifetime.

Maybe that's why my stomach twisted into more knots the closer I drove toward NYC. I didn't know where the institute Isabella was staying was located. And it felt like I was driving toward danger just as much as it felt like I was driving home.

It was possible that Isabella was already out. My dad hadn't visited in a couple weeks. And I had a suspicion he wasn't going to make her miss her first semester of college. So…she could be free. Out there thinking I was alive.

I tried to shake away the thought. I didn't look like myself. I didn't even feel like myself anymore. And I didn't want to waste another second of my life thinking about Isabella.

I wondered if Miller had reached his new place yet. Did he like it? I'd spent a lot of time searching for what I thought would make him happy. That's what I wanted. For him to be happy. It's all I wanted. Miller deserved the whole world.

I smiled as the breeze went through my hair. It reminded me of running on the beach with Miller. It was strange. I'd spent the fall, winter, spring, and summer with Miller. I'd only ever spent one fall with Matt. The summer breeze didn't remind me of Matt at all. And it was weird that something that didn't remind me of him could make me so happy.

I knew Miller in every season. I loved him in every season.

Stop.

God, what was I doing?

I wanted to turn the car around. I wanted to press down on the gas harder to get to Matt faster. I didn't know what I wanted at all.

I took the first exit I could and pulled into the rest stop. I wished my mom was here. She'd know what to do. She always had the best advice. And she hadn't lived long enough for me to ask her advice about boys.

But I knew her well enough to know what she'd suggest at this moment. *Ice cream.* I smiled. Yup, she definitely would have recommended ice cream. Ice cream was a cure-all at our house. I climbed out of the car and wandered into the rest stop. I kept my sunglasses on. My hair was still nothing like it used to be, but I wanted to make sure no one recognized me. I wouldn't put it past Isabella to run me off the side of the highway and kill me road rage style.

I ordered some mint chocolate chip ice cream and sat down in a plastic seat, as far away from anyone else as possible. I picked up my spoon and was just about to take a bite when my stomach twisted further into knots.

Miller would have suggested ice cream too. Whenever I was upset, it was like he knew I needed a bowl of mint chocolate chip ice cream. He kept the freezer stocked full of it. Did Matt even know I liked mint chocolate chip ice cream? I couldn't remember. Why couldn't I remember? It suddenly seemed like a very important thing he should know about me.

And now I was sitting here wondering if I was craving ice cream because my mom would have suggested it or because Miller would have.

I missed my mom.

I stared into my bowl. I missed Miller too.

And I wasn't hungry anymore. I set the bowl down on the table.

Maybe I shouldn't be going to Matt or Miller. When Miller first drove me to the beach house, I'd told him we should head west instead. I'd always wanted to touch the Pacific Ocean. I wondered if it was the same as the beaches here. The same salty smell in the air. I could just drive away from all of this. Start over completely. I had a new passport in the car. A new identity. A fresh start where no one knew me.

But...I didn't really want to disappear. I loved the life I'd made with Matt. And I loved the life I had with Miller. I didn't want to start over. I just didn't know where I wanted to keep going.

I sat in the rest stop until my ice cream melted. I was frozen. I was frozen in time. It was like I'd stopped living. Which was a crime in and of itself. I knew better than that. Life was short. And I knew why I was frozen.

I needed to see Matt. I dumped my melted ice cream and headed back out to my car. I couldn't move forward until I had answers. I'd made up my mind about this. And I was only second guessing everything because I didn't know what I wanted to see. Matt mourning me? Matt being happy? Even though that last one felt like a knife in my heart, I still wanted that for him. I just wanted him to be happy.

Just like I wanted Miller to be happy.

It was time to rip the Band-Aid off. I needed to know the truth. I needed Matt to know the truth. I couldn't run away from this. Or hide on the west coast because I was scared.

I pulled back onto I-95. I was a Sanders. And Sanderses were brave. My mom was brave as she faced death. My uncle was brave too. And if they were brave facing the unknown, I could be brave facing the unknown too. *I'm a Sanders. Not a Pruitt.*

***

I parked the car down the street from Matt's, right in front of James and Rob's place. I wasn't sure why. Maybe it was because I was scared about what I was about to see. And if I needed a pick me up, Rob could make me laugh. Or James could sit with me while I cried. I wondered if they really were all friends again. I also wondered why I was thinking about the Hunters at all. I was here for Matt.

I didn't need Rob to make me laugh. Or to drown in sorrow with James. I needed Matt. My heart was racing so hard in my chest that it actually hurt.

Now that I was parked here, staring at his house down the street, I knew I'd made the right decision. This place had become my home. I never thought I would fit into his world…but I did. We fit. It was as simple as that.

I pulled on a baseball cap to hide my identity even more. I checked my reflection in the mirror. Sunglasses, a hat, and hair that wasn't mine. No one would know. And Isabella was locked up. *Probably.* I was fine.

But what if she really was out? It wouldn't be out of the question for her to be in one of the houses on this street. She was friends with the Untouchables. *Kind of.* She could easily be staring at me from the Hunter's mansion.

Before I could talk myself out of it, I climbed out of the car. I kept my eyes trained on the ground, hoping no one would try to talk to me. Not that there was anything to worry about. The neighborhood seemed deserted. School was going to start up in a couple weeks. I wondered if everyone was on vacation. Maybe all these people had houses in the Hamptons like my dad. They were off vacationing. Living life. Not remembering the girl who died last fall.

I stopped on the street outside Matt's house. There weren't any cars in the driveway, but that wasn't unusual. They had a five-car garage. I stared at the gargoyles on either side of the front steps. I remembered how haunting they'd looked the first time I came here. But I actually thought they were kind of cute now. The house didn't look nearly as menacing. Maybe I'd just lost my mind. I didn't find the beach house menacing either. It had been my prison and I…kind of liked it. I didn't know what menacing was anymore.

I tried to shake away the thought. I didn't need to be second guessing myself anymore. I'd made my choice. I was here. For Matt. I stood up a little straighter. This was my home. This was where I belonged.

I looked up at the second story. Was Matt in his room? Was he thinking of me?

My heart started racing even more at the thought. I remembered our first kiss in the auditorium. The one he stole. I thought about how he'd sung to me on the homecoming float. I could almost smell his cinnamon exhales.

And just like that…I wasn't scared anymore. I was excited. I was so excited to see him. I hurried up the long driveway and up the front steps.

I knocked before I lost my nerve. There were a million thoughts circling around in my head. The first being that I probably should have thought of what to say. If his butler answered, should I pretend to be a salesperson or something? Or confess everything to him so he'd let me in? What if Matt's mom answered? Would she recognize me? God, I missed her hugs. And I could really use a hug right now.

Or maybe Mason would answer and pick me up and twirl me around in a big hug. Or maybe Matt himself would answer. My heart beat even faster. It felt like it was going to explode out of my chest. I'd dreamt of being reunited with him. Countless times.

He'd be upset at first. Then relieved. Then he'd be on me. I imagined him not even being able to wait to have me again. Pressing my back against the door.

But I didn't have to think about any of their reactions. Because no one answered the door. I lifted the heavy knocker and knocked again.

No answer.

Damn it. They were probably off vacationing somewhere extravagant. Not thinking about me at all. *Stop.* I knocked again.

No answer.

But I heard…laughter? Maybe? From somewhere. I tried to peer into one of the big windows, but the curtains were drawn tight.

I heard the noise again.

Oh. The Caldwells had a pool. They were probably all out back hanging out and relaxing. I remembered seeing the closed pool, looking forward to the summer when it would open.

I made my way back down the front steps and across the lawn. Even though I'd missed a lot of seasons with Matt, I had dreamt of a lot of them. All of them. I'd dreamt of our fairytale wedding in the winter. Lazy spring days when he didn't have football practice. And summer fun in his backyard in the pool. I'd wanted all those things. I'd been looking forward to all of it with him.

I heard another laugh. It was like I was walking back into happiness. And each step I took…I knew it was right. This was the right choice.

I'd made Matt promises for a reason. When I reached the side of the house I started running. I wanted back in his arms. Back in his heart. Back in his life. It felt like I was falling in love all over again.

And I almost did fall when I reached the backyard. I certainly froze.

Because Matt was there. With a girl. They were too close.

She moaned and her fingers tightened on his shoulder.

I ducked behind a bush. *No. No, no, no.* That wasn't…they were just…it couldn't be. I peered out from my hiding spot.

Matt pulled her hair so she'd tilt her head back. For just a second I thought it was Isabella. It was like all I could focus on was her dark hair. Maybe because I couldn't even believe the rest of what was happening. I blinked. But the scene in front of me didn't stop. Matt didn't push her away and say he was engaged. He didn't stop her at all. Or more accurately…he didn't stop himself. Because he was the one initiating this. He was the one with his hands all over her. His lips all over someone that wasn't me.

I watched him kiss her neck. I watched his hands wander to her breasts. I heard her moans. I listened to her beg for more. I listened to him groan.

This wasn't happening. It couldn't be. I blinked. Again. And again. Trying to rid the image from my eyes.

But they just kept going.

"Matt," she moaned. "Oh, God, yes, Matt!"

He buried his face in her breasts.

I was going to be sick. I remembered when he kissed my neck like that. Touched me like that. Groaned like that when he was inside of me.

I was definitely falling. But not back in love. I was just…falling. And no one was there to catch me when I landed anymore.

I closed my eyes tight. And as their moaning got louder I covered my ears. I felt my body trembling. I heard myself crying. But I wasn't worried about them hearing me. They were being plenty loud enough.

How could he touch her like that?

Kiss her like that?

Fuck her?

She wasn't me.

She's not…me.

I wasn't sure how long I sat in the dirt crying. But eventually I thought the sounds had stopped. I peered back out from the bush.

The girl was sitting on the edge of the pool now, splashing water at Matt.

Matt was still in the pool, smiling up at her. And I wasn't close enough to know for sure. But I was pretty sure that was a real smile. And it was real when he kissed her ankle. And slowly traced his lips up her thigh. And pulled her back into the water to her screams of protests. It was all real. The kiss they shared was real.

The pictures my father showed me weren't fake. And they weren't even the worst of it.

Which meant…my dad was telling the truth.

All the Untouchables were friends again.

Kennedy and Felix were happy.

And Matt? He really hadn't said a word at my funeral.

The knife in my chest twisted.

He really had asked for my ring back.

The knife twisted again.

He really had moved on.

The knife tore my heart in two.

It was all true.

All of it.

I sat here staring at him, missing him, hating him, loving him. I never knew I could feel so alone when I wasn't. But watching Matt with that girl? I'd never felt more alone in my life. Like my solitude was strangling me.

I watched her kiss away his laughter. My replacement. A better version, really. She wasn't Isabella. She looked oddly familiar, but I couldn't place it. Maybe she'd gone to Empire High. I had no idea. All I knew was that she was prettier than me. And had bigger breasts. Her bathing suit was expensive. She clearly fit better into his world than I did. Not that it was a competition. Matt certainly seemed to prefer her.

He thought I was dead.

And he'd moved on. I felt the tears streaming down my cheeks.

I wanted to be happy for him. But it was like he'd just forgotten me. Had he ever hurt as much as I did? Did he even care that I was gone?

He'd said things to me that I didn't think would be easily transferable to someone else. But was anything he said ever true?

Screw him.

Screw his new girlfriend.

I hoped they were happy together. I hoped they had a winter wedding and a honeymoon at the beach. I hoped they had four kids and spent summers out by the pool. I hoped they lived happily ever after. *My happily ever after.* I felt like it had been stolen from me. Like Matt had stolen my dreams and put in a substitute.

How could he be so okay when I was gone?

How?

Fucking how?

I started choking on my sobs.

Well, fine. He could have my happily ever after with someone new. I didn't want it anymore. Not with Matt. Not here. I didn't want any of it.

But…I didn't move. I just kept staring at him betraying me.

He was supposed to wait for me.

I'd waited for him. I'd wait a lifetime for him.

I'd had temptation and I didn't give in. He'd given in. Who knew how many times. And despite what he said, he was the liar. Not me. I meant every promise I'd made to him. I meant it. I was here because I loved him. When did he stop loving me?

Was it after the pudding prank?

Was he relieved I was dead?

How could he be? I still fucking loved him.

I wiped the tears off my cheeks.

Good for him. He never had to hurt like I did. He never had to suffer. Because he was Empire High's golden boy. He got everything he wanted handed to him on a silver platter. And he didn't want me anymore. Maybe he never did. That's how it felt. Like he never cared at all.

I heard her start moaning again.

Again? Seriously? They'd just banged. I couldn't look. I couldn't listen.

Yes, I'd been torn for the last nine months. But I'd kept Miller at arm's length. Because I couldn't move on so easily. My feelings for Matt had been real. I loved him. I loved that boy so much it hurt. It really fucking hurt right now. Like I couldn't breathe. *I can't breathe.*

It had been a while since I'd had a panic attack.

Because Miller made me feel safe.

There was no need to panic when he was by my side.

But now? I had nothing. And no one. *I have no one.* I'd put all my faith in Matt. All of it. But he was perfectly okay with me being gone. Blissful even. Fucking some random girl in his pool without a care in the world.

I should have walked out of those bushes and fucking slapped him. Confronted him for not keeping his promises to me. But what was the point? There was nothing he could say to fix this. Nothing.

I needed out of this yard. Out of this city.

Matt thought I was dead. And he was happy with that. And even though I was mad at him...I did want him to be happy. Of course I did. Because I still fucking loved him. He was happy without me. So it was better than I stayed dead. It's what he wanted.

I pushed myself up off the ground. And I ran. I ran away and I didn't look back. My tears blurred my vision.

I didn't even know where I was going. I couldn't think about anything but getting away from him.

He didn't want me.

He'd moved on.

He thinks you're dead.

But what did that matter? Based on the pictures my dad showed me, he hadn't even mourned at all. He was happy I was gone. Blissfully happy with someone new.

RUNAWAY

I stopped running when I realized I was standing beneath James' treehouse. I looked both ways to make sure no one was looking and climbed up the ladder. I slowly peeked my head inside to see if it was empty. The coast was clear. So I climbed up the rest of the way.

I curled into a ball and cried.

I cried until my lung hurt.

And my whole body was exhausted.

I hated that I was mad. It was selfish. I told myself I wanted Matt to be happy. But maybe he was right about me the whole time…I was a liar. Because I was fucking pissed that he was so happy without me.

I hated him.

I loved him.

And I cried because I hated myself. I hated myself for wanting him to be miserable. But if he'd just waited…

Stop.

It didn't matter. He hadn't waited. I couldn't undo what he'd done. And I wasn't going to mess up his life any more than I had.

I sniffed and sat up. I stared at the photos tacked to the wall.

All the Untouchables smiling and happy.

They were happy again now. My dad had shown me pictures. He'd shown pictures of Kennedy and Felix happy too. Everyone was happier with me gone. Happier that I was dead.

I hadn't wanted to believe it.

But I did now.

Everyone's glad you're dead.

Everyone was better off without me.

I needed to get out of this treehouse before someone saw me. The last thing I needed was to be recognized and make everyone miserable again.

I took a deep breath. *Matt doesn't want you anymore. He doesn't love you anymore. You need to leave.*

But my body didn't crawl back out of the treehouse. Instead I moved closer to the wall of pictures. I found one of Matt smiling at the camera. He was younger in it. He looked so happy. It was before he met me. Before I messed up his life.

Yeah, I needed to leave. And this time I'd leave it all behind. I'd leave and never come back. Ever again.

It hurt to think of what life would be like without him. But he was already living his life without me. I had to let him go. I had to let him be happy.

I was dead to Matthew Caldwell. I traced my fingertips across the picture of his perfect face. And he was dead to me too.

CHAPTER 23

Monday

I pressed my foot down harder on the gas. But it didn't matter how fast I drove. I couldn't get the scene of Matt in the pool out of my head. It just kept playing on repeat.

Who was that girl?

How was I so easily replaced?

I actually felt…dead.

I wanted to be back on the beach screaming at the ocean at the top of my lungs. But I wasn't at the beach. I'd left that life behind. Just because I'd held on to some stupid hope.

I drove as fast as I could away from Matt. And out of the city that had only ever caused me pain.

My music blared and for a long time I felt numb. Until suddenly I didn't anymore. I pulled over to the side of the road and screamed at the top of my lungs in my car. And screamed and screamed. Until my voice was hoarse and the tears had dried on my cheeks.

I thought about just abandoning my car and running off into the woods. I could just run until my legs gave out. Until I couldn't breathe. I couldn't do this anymore. It hurt too much. Every time I thought I overcame something, I kept getting knocked back down. I couldn't keep doing this. I just wanted to…

What?

I stared at the woods.

Did I want to die? Was that really what I wanted? My body was running on empty right now. I wasn't thinking clearly. I knew that. And yet the running until I died in the middle of the woods option felt like my best one. Literally running from the pain. Running until I couldn't run anymore.

Everyone already thought I was dead. I put my head down on the steering wheel and started to cry again. I didn't want to be dead. I just wanted to stop hurting so much.

It would hurt less the farther away I got from Matt. It would. I had to believe that. I lifted my head and pulled back out onto the highway. I drove farther and farther, waiting for my chest to stop hurting.

Matt and I were over. We'd been over for nine months. What had I been thinking? He was a player. Of course he was going to move on. Maybe he did love me back then. But love was fleeting for some people.

I didn't even know where I was driving. I just…drove. It was like my body was working without my mind.

And when I pulled into the cemetery, I wasn't at all surprised this was where it had taken me. I climbed out of the car and walked through the cemetery until I reached my mother's grave. And then my body gave out. It was like it had gotten me to this point and couldn't function anymore.

"Mom," I croaked. My voice was hoarse from screaming and crying. "Mom." I lay down on top of her grave and somehow managed to cry even more. "Mom I'm so tired. I don't know how to keep going."

She didn't respond. Of course she didn't. She was dead. And it wasn't lost on me that even though she was dead I still loved her fiercely. Whereas when Matt thought I was dead he filled his days with other women.

"I fucked everything up," I said into the silence. "Everything. I'm just so tired."

I tried to picture her smile. Her voice. Her laughter.

But every day that passed without her made it harder for me to remember.

"I miss you so much."

Silence.

"I thought I found a new family." I thought about how accepting all the Caldwells had been. They'd embraced me like I was one of them. "I thought I had a home again."

Silence.

"Why didn't you tell me about my dad? Why didn't you let me visit Uncle Jim more when I was little? Why did you keep a whole part of your life a secret from me?"

Silence.

"I was stronger than you realized. I could have handled the truth. I needed the truth from you."

Silence.

I wasn't sure why, but I was mad at her too. I was mad at her for leaving me all alone, knowing that the vultures were circling. Knowing I might wind up with my dad. Knowing I'd have no one. But I didn't want to be mad. I just wanted to...I stared at the grass. I don't know what I wanted. A piece of me wished I would actually stop breathing. That I'd die right here. Everyone else already thought I was dead.

"I'm sorry," I said. "I'm not mad at you. I'm mad at myself."

Silence.

"Does it stop hurting? Loving someone and them not choosing you back?"

Silence.

But my mom had lived through this pain. My father had chosen Isabella's mom instead of mine. My mom had loved him. And she'd spent the rest of her life alone.

Matt chose someone else. And I didn't want to spend the rest of my life missing someone who wasn't missing me.

I pulled my knees into my chest. "Matt made missing you easier. He made breathing easier. And I don't know what I'm going to do without him."

I pictured Miller waiting for me at his new house. It would be easy to go to him. To tell him I was choosing him. But it would be a lie. This didn't feel like a choice. This decision wasn't in my hands.

Maybe I should have confronted Matt. Instead, I'd hid. Why hadn't I come out? He might have been happy to see me.

But he already looked happy.

I lay here missing Matt. Missing Miller. Missing my mom. "What am I going to do?"

Silence.

I wasn't even sure why I thought she'd be able to give me good advice here. She had terrible taste in men. My father was the worst.

"Please tell me it stops hurting." I wasn't even sure what I wanted to stop hurting. My heart? My head? All I wanted to do was climb in my car and drive to Miller. But it wouldn't be fair to him. I couldn't go there unless I knew for sure he was what I wanted. And right now my heart was broken.

I closed my eyes. I thought coming here would make me feel closer to my mom. But it didn't. She felt…dead. The cold, hard ground felt nothing like a hug from my mother. But I couldn't move. I didn't have anywhere to go.

I pictured dancing with her in our yellow kitchen.

I pictured dancing with Matt in our Halloween costumes.

I pictured dancing with Miller on Christmas morning with his silly Santa hat.

I'd had so much love in my life and I'd lost it all.

I was cursed.

But then my mom's words came back to me. Words I'd heard her say all the time. The best thing I'd ever learned from her. *Time is precious. Don't waste it.*

How had I forgotten that? My mom's life had been cut short. And I refused to waste a second of mine. I'd been wasting mine for nine months, letting myself be held captive. What was I doing?

I exhaled slowly. Or maybe I hadn't been wasting it at all. Maybe I'd been falling in love with Miller. Slowly going from friends to more. The kind of love that was strong. And lasting. And real.

Honestly it was hard to know what was real at this point. I just needed some time to myself. Time to grieve my mother's loss on my own. And my uncle's loss. And losing Matt too. I needed to sort through this mess in my head before I figured out what I truly wanted. But right now I just wanted to lay here and talk to my mom.

"I have a lot to catch you up on," I said.

Silence.

"I fell in love with a boy who was way out of my league. And for a little while he loved me too."

CHAPTER 24

Thursday

The Pacific Ocean was colder than the Atlantic. And it didn't smell the same at all. I couldn't really explain it, but it was all wrong.

I was hoping standing here would give me clarity. But all it did was make me miss the beach house. Or was it Miller I missed? It was both. It was definitely both.

The more days that passed, the more I realized that I kind of loved the cage my father had put me in. I loved my routine there. I loved running on the beach with Miller and the lazy days swimming in the ocean. I loved reading next to him, sprawled out on the couch. And I loved dancing with him as we cooked. I loved my cage.

And I didn't know what that said about me.

I needed to figure out how to be happy without being in isolation.

I wasn't really sure I knew how to be happy on my own.

I needed to learn what it meant to be…me. Because I wasn't dead. I was here, breathing, staring at an ocean I hated.

But it was still the beach. I'd loved being at the beach with Miller. I needed to see if I liked it on my own just as much. I needed to figure out my shit.

I sat down in the sand and stared at the crashing waves in the distance.

I needed clarity.

But right now everything just hurt.

CHAPTER 25

3 Months Later - Thursday

I liked waiting tables. I observed happy couples and families on vacation. They reminded me that happiness was possible. And I needed that reminder most days.

But the best part? Patrons treated me like I was invisible. And I liked being invisible. When I'd first stepped foot into Empire High, I was completely invisible to the other students. I kind of wondered what would have happened if I'd stayed that way. If I'd never stared at Matt. If I'd never made my way onto Isabella's shit list. Would I still be going there? Would I be happier?

I shook away the thought. I was perfectly fine here. I'd come to the conclusion that happiness was just a bonus in life. Living was the real gift. And I was living. I didn't need to smile and laugh all the time. I just didn't. I'd take being invisible-and-okay over visible-and-in-pain any day. And I felt pretty okay here.

I refilled one tables' drinks. They didn't even look up to thank me. Which was fine. The less people that bothered to look me in the eye, the better. Isabella was probably off at some prestigious college now. Hopefully she wasn't thinking at all about me. But…it was better to be safe.

Especially because my hair dye was slowly fading away. My hair was past my shoulders again. I wanted to keep my identity a secret. But I also wanted to be me again.

I grabbed two plates full of pancakes and eggs and set them down on one of the tables I was waiting. "Anything else I can get for you?"

"Nope," the man said, without making eye contact.

It was rude. And perfect. "Enjoy." I hurried away and looked up at the clock. Only twenty more minutes until my shift ended. I worked the breakfast shift. At first I hated it. Because it meant that I had to run in the hot summer sun in the afternoon. But now that it was fall? My schedule was perfect. The cool breeze coming off the ocean was perfect for a midday run.

I had a great routine. Wake up. Get my free breakfast included with my work. Do my shift. Run. Jump around in the freezing cold water for a bit. Head to my second job. Come back and cook while dancing alone. Then read until I fell asleep. Rinse. Repeat.

I didn't have a phone. Or a computer. I didn't want to be tempted to look up anything about anyone I knew. One because it would possibly lead to my dad tracking me down. And two because I didn't want to know what anyone was up to. They were all happier without me. I didn't need the reminder. I was slowly learning how to be happy by myself.

The last couple whose check I had to close out kept me ten minutes late. When they finally left I hurried over to the table. $2? *Fuck.* It didn't matter. It was money. And I didn't have much of it. I'd set Miller up with unlimited funds. But I hadn't set myself up with anything at all. I'd been heading to Matt. I didn't think I'd need any money. But that quickly changed when I found myself out here.

I pocketed my tip and unwound my apron from my waist.

"A few of us are going out for drinks tonight," Amelia, one of the other waitresses, said. "You should come this time."

She always offered. And I always declined. I wasn't out here to get close to anyone else. Besides, even though my fake ID said I was 21, I wasn't. The last thing I needed was to wind up in jail. And yet...for the first time I wanted to say yes.

I'd started smiling more recently.

I'd started feeling more like myself.

This place was supposed to be my home. How bad would it be to put down some roots? "I can't tonight," I said. "I have another job. But maybe another night?" I'd have to look to see when my next day off was.

"When does your other shift end?"

"Usually 8 or 9."

"Oh. Well, that works fine. We never go out until 10 anyway. Let's do it! Come on, it's going to be so much fun."

10 seemed pretty late. Especially since we all showed up here at 6 am. But...maybe it would be fun. "Sure," I said. Even though I wasn't sure at all.

"Did you hear that, Heidi?" She turned to her friend. "Jane wants to go out with us tonight."

It was weird when people called me that. I'd picked the most common name possible when I got my fake ID. Jane fit the bill.

Heidi beamed at me. "Finally! Oh, there's that new club that just opened down the street. Barracuda. We can all go together. I'll text you the details. What's your number?"

"I actually don't have a cell phone," I said.

She stared at me like I was an alien. But she quickly re-covered. "That's fine. We can just meet there. How about at 10:30?"

It was 10:30 now? God, I was going to be so tired to-morrow. But I found myself nodding. "Yeah, I'll see you guys there." I wasn't sure what the hell I was doing. I'd heard about Barracuda from some patrons. Everyone seemed to think it was the new hot spot. But I kind of liked curling up in bed with a book pretty early.

Who knew though. Maybe clubbing was my new thing. I was here to try new things. To figure out what I wanted.

I waved goodbye to them and hurried back to my place. I was renting an apartment a few blocks from the beach. If you could even call it an apartment. It was practi-cally the size of a closet. But I didn't care. What mattered was that there was a big window that let plenty of fresh air in. No, it wasn't the same beach air as the east coast. But it was still fresh air.

I changed into my running clothes and headed back to the beach. I started running along the sand, dodging the water that came up on the shore. One wave crashed harder than I expected and splashed my thigh. I laughed and looked over at…nothing. For a second I thought Miller was beside me and would find humor in what had just happened.

I did that sometimes. Forgot where I was. Forgot that I was alone. I tried to shake away the feeling. But it didn't elude me that when I was happy I thought of Miller. We'd run together on the beach so much that sometimes it felt like he was here with me.

The water on my thigh made me shiver. This water was getting colder by the day. I picked up my pace. Thanksgiving was a few weeks away.

Thinking about Matt's words from last Thanksgiving hurt less every day. I felt bad about how we'd ended. But I'd untangled the last words he'd spoken to me. I used to believe them. I used to believe I was awful.

I didn't believe that now. I believed I made mistakes. But I was always trying my best. And he couldn't see that. Because he never saw the best in me.

I didn't dream about Matt as frequently now.

Slowly the pain had eased in my chest. And even though this beach was different, I think being here had helped. All alone. I looked out at the water. Yeah, the beach here definitely wasn't the same as the one on the east coast. There were more weed shops than ice cream shops. They had it all backward here. I was an east coast girl. And yet…I stayed. I felt like I couldn't figure out who I was without some semblance of a home. This was my home now.

But it sure felt empty.

Tonight I was trying something new though. With people I could only really classify as acquaintances. I couldn't exactly trust anyone here. For all I knew someone was a spy for my dad or Isabella. It was honestly a little weird that I hadn't heard from my dad. Yes, I'd had a good escape plan. But he had a lot of resources. And yet…nothing. Maybe he was happier without me around too. Everyone else seemed to be.

I wondered if Miller was happier too. Probably.

I turned my head like I'd see him running alongside me. It was like images of Miller haunted me. More and more every day.

It was strange that I thought about Matt less. And Miller more. It was probably because I didn't need to wonder if Matt was missing me. He most certainly was not. But was Miller missing me?

Did he think about me when he went for runs? Or when he cooked? Did he even do either of those things anymore? He hadn't exactly loved those activities before he knew me.

He was probably sitting on his dock right now, staring at the lake. It's why I'd picked the place for him. It just looked so serene. Kind of like how the beach house felt. I looked out at the Pacific Ocean. This wasn't nearly as serene.

I started running faster, as if I could run away from the constant Miller loop in my head. But that was the thing. People weren't forgettable to me. I wasn't Matt.

***

I was down on my hands and knees scrubbing the bathroom floor. My second job was as a maid. I was just as invisible cleaning as I was serving food. But I liked this job more than my first. I liked using my hands and the muscles in my arms to scrub things. I liked taking a step back and seeing the visible difference. Like I was making an actual difference, even if I was invisible.

My uncle had been the janitor at Empire High. I knew people made fun of him behind his back for picking up after them all day. But this was hard work. Good work. And it wasn't beneath me. It was in my blood.

I felt closer to him when I was working.

Like a little piece of him was here with me.

I plopped the sponge in the bucket and sat back on the floor. I remembered being on the bathroom floor in my uncle's small apartment. I'd gotten sick after drinking too much. He'd been there to help me through it. He'd cared about me. He'd had my back. I didn't realize how rare of a quality that was. And I missed him.

It was one of the reasons why thinking about Miller a lot didn't make me run back to him. Because I thought of

Uncle Jim a lot too. And my mom. I loved them all. Of course I thought about them.

The only difference was that Miller was still alive. It wasn't the same. I could go be with him. We could be happy together. I knew that deep down. And yet…I didn't run back to him.

I didn't know if I could promise someone else forever right now. I honestly wasn't sure I ever could. So I needed to stay here. I needed to stay here and figure out what I really wanted. Because if I ever saw Miller again, it had to be because I really wanted him. And only him. Forever.

I pulled the sponge back out of the bucket and got back to work.

But there was a nagging thought in the back of my head now. I was okay with just being okay. I was fine with my conclusion that happiness was just a bonus. And yet…I'd been happy with Miller. Even in a cage I was happier with him than I was right now. I was free and…fine.

I knew for a fact that the last time I truly smiled, it had been with him. The last time I really laughed? The belly aching kind? It was with Miller.

Was our situation perfect? No. We weren't even allowed to leave the house the last couple months we were together. But…I still smiled and laughed.

I could remember it clearly.

I could barely remember laughing with Matt anymore. And honestly looking back at our relationship? He may have made me cry a lot more than he made me laugh. I shed so many tears over that boy. I still shed tears over him. When he did make an appearance in my dreams, I'd wake up devastated. Like I'd just lost him all over again. It was still hard to believe that he'd moved on so easily. That I was truly so forgettable. But…I guess I was.

I wondered if Miller was okay with me gone too? If he was happily kissing some other girl. If he never really loved me either.

Those were the questions that made me stay here. Yes, I was trying to figure out what I wanted. But I think I was mostly scared that Miller had moved on easily too.

And my heart couldn't take that.

I scrubbed the floor harder. Trying to rid the annoying thoughts from my mind.

I could have fun on my own. I was going to have fun tonight. With new friends. I nodded to myself as I scrubbed harder. I could be happy here on my own.

CHAPTER 26

Thursday

I stopped by a Goodwill on the way home from work. It took a little while, but I found something passable as chic on a budget.

I pulled on the summer dress and stared at my reflection in the chipped mirror in my bathroom. It wasn't the right season for a summer dress, but I didn't really care about that. I did care that it was a little shorter than I meant for it to be though. My legs were still tanned from summer and toned from my runs. And I didn't want anyone staring at them. Or staring at me in general. I used to catch Miller staring at my legs sometimes. When we were curled up on the couch at night reading. I'd look up from my book and catch him staring at me. Although…I guess I'd been staring at him too.

I quickly pulled off the dress and tossed it on my bed. I didn't want someone other than Miller staring at me. My chest suddenly hurt. I tried to rub away the pain as I pulled my worn jeans out of the hamper. They were casual and probably not at all what other people would be wearing at Barracuda. But I didn't really care what other people were doing. I was going because I loved dancing. I would have been dancing right now as I cooked dinner anyway. At least this way I was socializing. I grabbed a clean tank top and my outfit was complete.

Before leaving, I pulled my hair up into a ponytail. Dancing with your hair down was for amateurs. My hair was more dirty blonde than brown now. I was pretty sure in a few weeks it would just be blonde again. It was going to be nice to look in the mirror and see myself again. Although my hollow cheeks kind of gave away that I wasn't the same Brooklyn anymore.

I loved cooking, and I cooked dinner every night. But I couldn't afford much. I ate a ton of food every morning at the diner because it was free. At night I usually made boxed pasta with a jarred sauce. Or peanut butter and jelly. That wasn't much to dance about. Which was fine, because I was usually pretty tired after cleaning things all afternoon. I was tired right now. My bed was calling to me. But I wasn't one to back out of plans. That felt as bad as backing out of a promise. And I wasn't Matt.

I decided to walk down the beach instead of the street. I rolled up the bottom of my jeans so they wouldn't get wet and held my Keds in my hand. It had been a long time since I'd worn my favorite shoes. They used to make me feel close to my mom. But now they were just a reminder of everything I'd lost. Her. My uncle. Matt.

They were still the cutest shoes I owned though. And they were perfect for dancing. I saw the neon lights of Barracuda and made my way up off the beach.

Heidi and Amelia were standing outside the club. There was a line stretched around the side of the building. They spotted me walking up from the beach and waved.

They were both in tiny dresses and heels so high I didn't know how they weren't falling over. And both of them had their hair down. Amateurs. How were they going to dance in those shoes? And their hair was going to get all sweaty on the back of their necks.

They were staring at me like I was the amateur though as I kicked the sand off my feet and pulled on my Keds. I unrolled the bottom of my jeans, even though I knew that wasn't why they were shocked by my outfit. Their stares reminded me of how Isabella looked at me. Like I didn't fit in. Like I would never belong.

"How are you guys?" I said.

I half expected them to ditch me.

Instead, Heidi smiled and looped her arm through mine. "Ready for the time of our lives."

"Ready to make all the guys drool," Amelia said and grabbed my hand and pulled us toward the doors.

"Don't we have to go to the back of the line?" I asked.

"Psh. No. They'll let us in. We're hot."

As we got closer to the doors, I realized that most of the people in line were men. Or couples. And Amelia was right. The bouncer lifted the red rope and let us in without blinking an eye. Well, he may have blinked a couple times at my ID.

I tried to stand up a little straighter. *Please just let me in.* I didn't want to make a scene. I wasn't even going to drink. I tended to make bad decisions when I drank.

The bouncer looked back and forth between me and my ID one more time and then handed it back. I breathed a sigh of relief and hurried through the doors behind Amelia and Heidi.

The music was *loud*. Ground shaking loud. The last party I'd been to had been at Matt's house on Halloween. Barracuda wasn't nearly as glamorous as that.

It was all neon lights flashing and sweaty bodies pressed too close. It smelled like stale liquor. It was horrible. And for some reason…I loved it. Because it was dark. And loud. And I could keep being invisible.

Heidi pulled me over to a table and ordered a round of drinks.

"I'm good!" I yelled at her over the music.

"You're about to be."

"I don't drink."

"It's just one shot," she said as the waiter dropped off our drinks. "Come on. It's our first night out together."

"Let's make it a night to remember," Amelia said and lifted her shot glass.

God, I really hated shots. I had mistakenly thought such a small glass couldn't possibly affect me that much. I had been very wrong. But it had been a long time since I'd hung out with friends. Or had a drink. I was older now. Certainly I could hold my liquor better. "A night to remember," I said and lifted up my shot glass too. We all clinked them together and I downed it. *Ugh*. I still hated the taste of whatever that was.

The waiter brought by a second round of shots.

"No way," I said.

"I didn't order them," Heidi said and held up her hands innocently.

But I didn't believe her.

"They're from the gentlemen over there," the waiter said and nodded to a nearby table.

I turned around to see several guys staring at us. One smiled and lifted up a matching shot glass. I quickly turned back around.

Heidi pushed a shot over to me.

"I'm good," I said.

"You can't pass up free drinks! It's a crime! Besides, they definitely sent them over because they're checking out how amazing your ass looks in those jeans!"

What? I turned to look down at my butt. *Fuck*. My ass did look really good in these. *I should have worn the dress…* I glanced up at the table and now all the guys were staring at me staring at my own ass. *Crap*. I quickly turned back around. I was sure my face was bright red. But it was dark…so…no one knew. Except me. I grabbed another shot and downed it.

I was just about to ask Heidi and Amelia to dance when a few of the guys from the other table wandered over.

"You ladies want to dance?" One of them asked.

"We most certainly do," Heidi said. "Thanks for the drinks!"

"No problem." The guy that had asked us to dance put his hand on my hip. His touch felt like fire. It was all wrong. Just like the air was wrong here. And the ocean was wrong.

"Tonight just got a whole lot better," he whispered in my ear.

"Sorry," Heidi said. "I meant we do want to dance. But not with you guys." She grabbed my hand and pulled me away from them before I even knew what was happening. The three of us disappeared into the crowd, away from the guys.

"You okay?" she said. "It looked like you were about to pass out!"

I laughed. Because I didn't know what else to do. I'd felt sick when he touched me. And I wasn't even sure why. *Because he's not Miller.* The nagging thought appeared out of nowhere and stuck. I liked dancing with Miller. Not some stranger at a seedy club. "I'm fine!" I yelled over the music, even though I was anything but. "Let's dance!"

Amelia threw her hands in the air and then started to shimmy.

I laughed and started dancing too. The beat seemed to turn up around us and we all started singing along to the music. Heidi and Amelia were hilarious. They copied each other's moves, each trying to make them more sexual than the other. It was impossible not to laugh.

I'd almost forgotten how it felt to be happy.

My body moved to the music. My heart beat along with the bass. It really had been a long time since I'd felt this good.

This was what living was.

Laughing.

Dancing.

Feeling empty. *Damn it, not that last thing!* I looked up at the strobe lights. I did feel that way, though. I felt empty. That was why I usually filled all my spare time with reading. So my thoughts couldn't wander and stick to annoying things. Why couldn't I just focus on dancing? Why were my thoughts so loud? Maybe it was the alcohol making my thoughts louder. I wanted to scream "shut up" at the top of my lungs.

Someone grabbed my waist from behind and kissed the side of my neck.

I remembered Miller kissing my neck like that. I closed my eyes for a second. It felt like he was here with me. And I'm pretty sure I smiled harder than I had in months. I didn't feel empty when Miller was with me.

I moved my hips with his. It felt like dancing with a ghost. I wanted to cling to him. I didn't want him to disappear again. I wanted to be locked up in a cage with him again. I wanted to go back to this summer. I wanted to let him kiss me. I wanted to let him in. I wanted to undo what I'd done.

He'd crept into my dreams at night. Slowly and steadily until I woke up most mornings panting. I pictured being curled up with him at the beach house. I pictured being brave enough to kiss him. And I pictured way more than that.

I was too tightly wound. I hadn't been with anyone since Matt. And yet…I wasn't dreaming about Matt. I ached for Miller. I wanted him in the sand. In the ocean water. In the bed. On the fucking floor. I didn't care where we were. I just wanted him. It was like my subconscious knew exactly what I wanted. And apparently I wanted to spread my legs for Miller. Like I was starving for him. Like I needed him back.

But then he kissed my neck again.

My eyes snapped open. It wasn't Miller. And I liked it a hell of a lot better when Miller did it. I pushed the guy off of me.

"Come on, we're just dancing," the guy said.

But I didn't like being touched. Not by him. I thought about being curled up next to Miller in bed. Our limbs intertwined. I liked being touched by Miller. In real life and in my dreams.

The guy reached out for me again.

I took a step back.

"Don't be a bitch," the guy said. "We bought you drinks."

I turned to Heidi and Amelia for help but they'd disappeared somewhere in the crowd.

The guy pulled me back toward him.

Panic rose in my chest. I didn't like being touched. And I hated when people thought they could use me. Matt used me to make him happy for one season. My dad used me for a kidney. Everyone just used me.

The guy leaned down to kiss my neck again.

I didn't want his lips on me. I didn't want him anywhere near me. So I did the first thing that popped in my head…I kneed him hard right in the balls. I have no idea why. He wasn't being that aggressive. I could have just walked away. But I really fucking hated being touched. It reminded me of being cut open. I didn't like when people touched me without permission. I hated it.

"What the fuck is wrong with you?" he yelled.

I don't know? Everything? I took a step back from him and then started running. I pushed my way through people dancing. I ran out of the club and took a deep breath of the stupid air that wasn't quite right. Nothing was right.

I ran down onto the beach. I didn't care that my Keds were getting sandy or wet. I didn't care about anything at all. Or maybe I cared about everything a little too much.

I stared at the water and yelled as loud as I could. I screamed at the top of my lungs, just like I used to back at the beach house. But I wasn't screaming because I was trapped now. I was screaming because I wasn't. I wasn't trapped. And I wanted to be trapped with Miller.

I was sick.

There was something wrong with my head.

My father had ruined me.

I screamed even louder.

CHAPTER 27

1 Month Later - Monday

I was pretty sure I knew what I needed to do. But I needed just a minute to sit with my thoughts. I stared out at the ocean and closed my eyes. The problem was, I could never clear my head. I thought about Miller constantly. Obsessively. I pictured him alone, missing me. I pictured him happy with someone else. The only constant was that I was picturing him. He was always in my head. Always on my mind.

I'd become complacent here for a while. I'd thought happiness was some bonus thing that some people got. But that was such bullshit.

I hated drinking. It made my head spin and my limbs feel heavy. But a month ago when I went out with Heidi and Amelia, I'd gotten clarity. The clarity I had been searching for. I wanted to be dancing with Miller. I wanted to keep dancing with Miller for the rest of my life. I wanted to be happy. It wasn't a bonus thing. Happiness was living. It was the only thing that mattered at all.

But even though I'd come to that conclusion, I'd stayed here. As if time would change my mind. It hadn't. My thoughts had settled. And now it was time to say goodbye.

The cold December breeze should have made me shiver. But I just stood there staring at the water. This was it. I was going to leave today. I had to.

I'd tried the living on my own thing. I'd given it a chance. And I'd come to the conclusion that I didn't want to be alone anymore. I wasn't happy here. I hadn't been happy since I'd driven away from Miller.

Yes, I probably was sick in the head. No one should like being imprisoned. But I'd trade everything to go back to that beach house. I wished I'd chosen him. I'm pretty sure I let him go because he was too good to be true.

We'd been playing house. But somewhere over those months, I'd stopped pretending. It was real for me.

I pulled the picture of Matt out of my jeans pocket and stared down at his smiling face. A year ago today, we were supposed to be married. Last year, I'd been devasted. But this year?

Memories had a strange way of shifting around once something bad happened. Every day that passed made it harder for me to remember the good. I pictured Matt angry and disappointed at me more than I pictured him happy with me. And I pictured him with that brunette more than I pictured him with me. Something was probably wrong with my head. But several months of remembering the worst?

I stared out at the crashing waves. Of course I was still sad. I'd wanted to marry Matt when he'd asked. I had. I'd meant what I said when I promised him forever. But I'd also made promises to myself. I refused to let life pass me by in a meaningless blur. I wanted to start living again. And living missing someone else was no way to live. It took me a while to figure out the mess in my head. But I'd always known that my promises to myself were a lot more important than promises to someone else. Because I was the only one that was ever going to put myself first. I didn't need another kidney to be stolen to learn that lesson.

Matt didn't love me. I believe he had at one point, but he didn't now. My heart hurt less every day I let that sink in. We weren't an everlasting love. We weren't. And this December 22nd hurt a lot less than the last. This one just felt…empty and meaningless. In a way I was relieved. It would have been a mistake to walk down the aisle when Matthew Caldwell's love was fleeting. I'd dodged a bullet. At least, that's what I liked to tell myself. It was for the best. And the more I told myself that, the more I believed it.

We may have never even made it to our one-year anniversary. Even if we were together, we may have drifted apart. So no, I wasn't devasted as I stared out at the ocean. I was just disappointed in myself for forgetting the most valuable lesson I'd ever learned…to not take a single day for granted. What was the point of thinking of what could have been? Matt and I hadn't happened. And we never would.

Today I was actually thinking more about Christmas than a wedding that never happened. Specifically, last Christmas when Miller had surprised me by cooking all my favorite things. I remembered his ridiculous Santa hat and how we'd laughed and danced all morning. It was perfect. He was perfect. He'd dipped me low to the music and I should have kissed him right there. I should have. But…I hadn't.

It wasn't necessarily a mistake. I was trying my best to be loyal. But if I knew what I did now…I would have put my happiness first. I knew that now.

I looked back down at the picture in my hand. When I stared at Matt's face…all I saw was a teenage kid. A kid who didn't know what forever meant. It wasn't his fault. We were both dumb kids. But I didn't want some boy with empty promises. I wanted a man who knew exactly what he wanted. I wanted Miller.

I knew it without a doubt in my mind. I dreamed of waking up next to him. Of running along the beach with him in the summer. Of raking leaves and jumping into them in the fall. Of hot cocoa mornings in the winter. And curling up and reading with him in the spring, with him sniffling because of his adorable spring allergies. I missed him so much it hurt. And it hurt every day even more.

I was happy I came here to give myself time. I did grow here. I grew stronger. I grew up.

My hair was blonde again. My cheeks were still hollow, but my appetite was back. I was healthy. And I knew how to be happy.

I just hoped I wasn't too late. I let the breeze lift Matt's picture out of my hand. It danced in the wind and landed in the ocean, where a wave crashed down on it.

Please don't let me be too late.

CHAPTER 28
Thursday - Christmas

Christmas music played on the car radio and a light snow had started to fall. It had been four months since I watched Miller drive away from the beach house. He'd asked me to come with him. He told me he loved me. He asked me to choose him.

And I didn't. I let him walk away. That last look in his eye haunted my dreams. I didn't want to live a life of regret. But I did regret not going with him. I was pretty sure I'd regretted it every day I'd been on the west coast. The beach wasn't the same without him. Life wasn't the same without him. I knew that now. But what if I'd realized it too late?

I hit my blinker and took the exit off the highway. The snow was starting to fall faster now, and I hoped that I'd make it to Miller's place before it became impossible to drive.

I also hoped that Miller was still at the lake house I'd arranged for him to go to.

What if he wasn't?

Or what if he was and he'd moved on?

My dad had shown me pictures of Matt kissing other girls only a few months after I had "died." Would Miller move on that quickly too?

I hadn't stayed away to test him. I'd stayed away to figure out what I wanted. To make sure I was doing the right thing for me.

But I knew it was possible that Miller had found someone that was a better fit for him during that time. I'd abandoned him for months. And I knew I was replaceable. I'd seen it happen before.

Honestly, this whole thing was crazy. I was about to show up at Miller's on Christmas morning and confess my love for him. Yeah, it was completely nuts. I'd told him I was choosing Matt. I didn't even know how old Miller was. Hell, I didn't even know his first name. But I did know that I was in love with him.

I'd felt this way once before. With Matt. I wasn't discounting my first love. That had been real for me. And I'd dreamed of Christmases with Matt. I'd thought we'd spend every Christmas for the rest of our lives together. I'd wanted that. It was all I wanted. Until...it wasn't. I thought a part of me would want to head to New York when I started driving. But I didn't. I'd mourned that loss for months. It was almost like Matt was dead. Like I had to let him go. A piece of me would always love that boy. Always. It was love, I knew that. I loved him. But it was past tense. He'd moved on. He didn't love me anymore. And I couldn't afford to keep missing a boy who didn't miss me back.

Because this feeling I was feeling now? I was in love again. And of course it was different. But it wasn't any less. If anything, the feelings I had now were more all-consuming. It was scary how much my heart craved Miller. Especially because I knew how easily he could reject me.

What if it took me just a little too long to figure out I wanted him back?

What if I was too late?

The snow started falling harder. I leaned forward, straining my eyes to see through the fast pace of the windshield wipers and snowfall. It was so hard to see that I almost missed the next turn.

I slowed down so I wouldn't miss his driveway. 2761. I looked down at my map even though I knew his address by heart. There had been so many times when I thought about writing a letter to him. Letting him know I was safe and missing him. But I was worried about the paper trail. And more worried that I couldn't trust myself with his response. Or lack of response. It had kept me away longer than necessary. The unknown was terrifying.

I turned onto his driveaway and slowly made my way down the long path.

My tires skidded a little as I hit the brakes. I'd made it just in time before the roads became impassable.

As soon as I turned the car off, I shivered. I hadn't packed any winter clothes. I hadn't needed any in California. All I had was a raggedy old hoodie barely keeping me warm. I was wearing the same jeans that I now knew hugged my butt. And my Keds that were a little stained from sandy nights on the beach.

I was just…me. Several months ago, that had been good enough for Miller. But I wasn't sure if it was enough now.

I sat in my car for a minute, watching the snow fall slowly in front of his house. It was exactly how I'd pictured his home. I'd chosen it mostly for the isolated location…acres and acres that belonged only to him. But also because the house reminded me of our beach house. It was smaller, but decked out in all the same beautiful features. It was like a miniature version plopped down in the middle of the woods. Because one person didn't need that much space. Or…two people. *Maybe*. I swallowed hard.

I knew it would be beautiful in the summer. And the fall. And the winter and spring. It was picturesque. Was he in there with a cup of hot chocolate and a roaring fire? Was he curled up with someone new?

Panic was rising in my throat. If he turned me away...I had no idea where I would go. I had less than $50 to my name and no backup plan. And it was Christmas morning. This was a terrible idea.

But also the best idea.

Because it was Christmas. And I was hoping for a Christmas miracle. I hadn't gotten him a present last year. But I came prepared this year. It was the reason why I only had $50 in my pocket. I'd wrapped the gift painfully slowly in a parking lot a few days ago. There was a huge red bow on top. It was festive. And I hoped he'd love it.

Even if he turned me away, I wanted him to have this. I wanted him to have a piece of me. Because he'd always have my heart.

I climbed out of the car with my present in tow. My Keds skidded a little in the snow and I was shivering when I reached his front door. I swallowed hard and rang the bell.

I forgot how quiet it was when it snowed. All I could hear in the silence was my own heart beating. Faster and faster. Usually I found the snow peaceful and serene. But when there was no answer...the silence felt heavy.

I knocked this time instead of ringing the bell.

Still no answer.

I looked across the lawn. It was like déjà vu. Was he around back? With another woman? My heart started racing faster in the silence.

No, he had to be inside. I put my present down on the front step and knocked harder.

No answer.

I peered into the window. There was a roaring fire in the fireplace. And a Christmas tree in the corner. Actually, it was decorated a lot like Miller had decorated the beach house last Christmas. It looked homey. It looked like my home. With him. But he was nowhere in sight.

The beautiful cozy room started to blur. I quickly wiped the tears from my cheeks. How had I fucked everything up so badly? I'd missed him for months and I'd stayed away. I'd walked away from him. It was too late. He'd never take me back now. How could he possibly still want me?

An unhappy person wouldn't have decorated for Christmas. He was happy. He was happy without me. Of course he was. My stomach twisted in knots.

I thought I heard a noise. I moved away from the window and stared at the side of the house. Was that noise from the backyard? I could feel more tears welling in my eyes. I didn't want to go back there. I didn't want to see him with someone new.

And yet…I'd come all this way. I needed to know. My shoes crunched in the freshly fallen snow as I made my way around the side of the house.

The snow was falling so fast now that it was hard to see very far into the distance. If he was with another woman, I couldn't tell. Hell, if he was even in his backyard at all, I couldn't tell.

"Miller?" I called out.

There was no response. The wind picked up and made the snow dance all around me. I knew from the pictures that the lake was a little farther down. My sneakers slid in the snow again as I wandered down toward the lake. It was almost impossible to see now but…my feet froze.

It wasn't anything like the scene I'd walked into at Matt's house in the summer.

Miller was all alone. He was standing there with his back to me, staring out at the frozen lake. His hands were stuffed into his pockets and he was wearing the same Santa hat he had worn last year. But for some reason, it looked sad and deflated this year. Like all the magic and worn off.

He dropped his head like he was looking at the ground. Like the weight of the world was too heavy.

I knew that feeling. And for just a second, I watched him. Did he look that sad because of me? Because he missed me too?

I shivered. My hoodie was soaked from the snow. But I was pretty sure I was shaking because I was nervous. And excited. But mostly nervous. I willed my feet to keep moving. And when my right foot crunched a branch, Miller spun around.

I don't know what I was expecting. A hug? A greeting? *Something.*

But he blinked and just stared at me…like he was imagining I was there.

I'd fucked everything up. I knew that. And all I wanted to do was apologize. I wanted him to know how much I'd missed him. How my body craved his touch. How I wanted to be his and only his. That I was ready to put him first.

We were still several feet away from each other. But he didn't approach me. I felt my stomach twist further into knots. He couldn't turn me away. I needed him. I loved him.

"Miller…" my voice cracked.

And it was like he snapped out of his daze. "Brooklyn?"

I didn't respond. I just ran down to him, closing the distance between us. And I lunged into his arms.

He caught me, grabbing my ass as my legs straddled his waist.

We both just stared at each other as he held me. Like this was some kind of dream. And I knew it then. That he'd dreamed of this too. That he'd ached for me too. That he needed me too. He didn't need to say it.

But I had a million things I needed to say to him. Right now there was only one thing I needed him to know though. "I'm not pissed off at the world anymore." I stared into his eyes. "You're not a substitute for what I really want. You are what I really want. You're my first choice. And I'm asking you to kiss me."

His eyes gravitated to my lips and then back to my eyes. "I'm dreaming."

I smiled. "No. I love you and only you, Miller. I'm in love with you…"

He silenced me with a kiss. And it wasn't at all how I remembered his kisses to be. It was like he was devouring me. I had no idea if it was because I hadn't been kissed in over a year. Or if because his feelings had grown too. But these weren't sweet lazy kisses in the middle of the night. He kissed me like he was starving for me. And I kissed him back the same way. Because I'd been dying to kiss him for longer than I should have been. Back at the beach house. Last Christmas morning. I'd wanted him then. I'd always wanted him.

My fingers slid to the back of his neck as I deepened the kiss. I accidentally bit down on his lower lip as my teeth chattered in the cold. I needed more of his lips. More of his tongue. More everything.

"You're soaked," he said and lifted his mouth from mine way too soon. "Why aren't you wearing a coat?"

I didn't want to talk about where I'd been. I just wanted him to kiss me again. I pulled his face back down to mine and he groaned in my mouth.

He started carrying me somewhere, but I wasn't paying attention. All I knew was that I needed more. I didn't want to ever stop kissing him. Holding him. Feeling his hands on me.

Suddenly I wasn't shivering anymore. I heard him kick the door closed with his foot, but I didn't stop kissing him.

He leaned forward, lowering us down onto the couch. And then his lips fell from mine.

"I'll find you a change of clothes," he said. "Give me a sec."

Before I could protest, he was walking out of the room.

My hoodie was heavy from the wet snow. I pulled it off over my head and dropped it on the floor. My tank top underneath was soaked too.

I looked at the hallway Miller had disappeared down.

I'd only ever slept with one boy. I'd made the wrong choice last year. And it was about time I fixed that. I wanted to forget all the pain. I needed him to help me forget. And I'd dreamt so much of having Miller that I knew I couldn't wait another second. I was sick of dreaming. I wanted him.

I pulled off my wet tank top, kicked off my shoes, and somehow managed to peel my soaked jeans down my thighs. I was standing in the middle of his living room in just my underwear.

It was forward.

I swallowed hard.

It's what I wanted. *Him*. I'd been dreaming of another Christmas with him. Another Christmas just like this. Where we spent the day tangled up together. I moved to stand in front of the fireplace. The warmth from the flames drew me even closer.

"Brooklyn?"

I turned around to face him.

His eyes traveled down to the tops of my exposed cleavage and down to the lace of my panties. His Adam's apple rose and then fell. "There's a bathroom at the end of the hall."

I took a step toward him and took the clothes out of his hand. "I have a better idea." I dropped the clothes on the floor and draped my hands behind his neck.

"You're still shivering." His hands settled on my hips.

Was I? I didn't feel cold. I just felt...alive. Like my dreams were morphing into reality. "Then maybe you should warm me up."

"I'm not even supposed to be touching you." But his thumbs had hooked under the waistband of my panties, like he was dying to lower them. Dying to touch me.

And God, I wanted him to touch me. "We're free now. We can do whatever we want." I stared at him, daring him to make the first move.

"And what do you want?" His eyes searched mine. Like I held all the power here. But I didn't. I was already too far gone.

"You. I want you."

CHAPTER 29

Thursday

He grabbed the back of my neck and pulled my lips back to his. It's like those were the exact words he needed to hear. I'd say them to him forever. *You. I want you. You, you, you. I want you, Miller.*

I wasn't even sure how it happened, but we fell to the rug in front of the fire. Him pressed on top of me.

It was like the months apart made it impossible to be close enough to him. My fingers slid under his shirt, tracing the contours of his abs. I remembered staring at him as we ran together. I'd been desperate to touch him even then.

He leaned back and pulled his shirt off. And then his mouth was back on mine. He was devouring me again. Just like he had outside when I asked him to kiss me.

I reached down and felt his erection through his jeans.

He groaned into my mouth.

He didn't stop me as I unbuttoned and unzipped his pants. God, I couldn't get close enough. I needed his skin against mine. I needed him inside of me. I needed to remember what it felt like to be loved. But before I could reach into his boxers, he moved.

He kissed down my stomach and nipped my inner thigh with his teeth.

Oh, fuck. I wanted this. I wanted all of this. But right now? If I didn't have him inside of me, I was going to explode. "Miller, please."

He pulled my panties down and pressed his lips to my clit.

It wasn't what I was asking for, but oh my fucking God. I felt my hips thrust up to meet his mouth. His tongue greedily stroked me. Faster and faster. He swirled around my wetness, practically grinding his face against my pussy.

I'd never experienced anything so hot in my life.

My fingers dug into his hair as his nose rubbed against my clit.

Yes. Just like that.

He moved his mouth back to my clit as he thrust his fingers inside of me. And his throat made this guttural noise, like I was the most delicious thing he'd ever tasted. Like he could never get enough.

And I broke.

My legs shook and my back arched as I pulled him closer. God I couldn't get close enough to him.

I'd touched myself while thinking about him. I'd envisioned this moment. But this felt a million times better.

He placed one last slow stroke against my pussy and then kissed back up my stomach.

He stopped when he was eye level with me, putting his weight on his hands. "You came back to me." He grabbed the center of my bra and pulled down, letting my breasts free. He groaned again.

My heart was racing so fast. I didn't have any words. My mind was scrambled from what he'd just done.

"What am I going to do with you, Brooklyn Sanders?"

I felt tears welling in my eyes. I loved that he didn't call me a Pruitt. He didn't think I was a monster. He never had.

He pushed my thighs farther apart, spreading me for him. "You have no idea how long I've dreamt of his moment," he said. His thumb brushed across my clit again. "I've been hoping you'd come. But…I didn't actually think you would." He pulled away. "I don't even have a condom."

Screw me. I wanted to tell him it was okay to not use one. But I wasn't on birth control. I'd been about to get on it but got my kidney stolen instead.

He sighed and dropped down next to me on the rug.

I saw his erection straining against his jeans.

"You said you dreamt of this moment," I said. "So you've dreamt of me coming back for a long time? Or of fucking me?"

He turned toward me. He reached out and pushed a strand of hair out of my face. "Both."

"For how long?"

He didn't respond, but his fingers stayed on me. Gently sliding down my neck and massaging my shoulder.

"Did you want to fuck me back when I used to sneak down into your room?"

His Adam's apple rose and then fell. "Yes."

"Did you ever touch yourself when you thought of me?"

"Brooklyn…"

"Did you?"

"Yes." He paused for a moment. "I jerked off to the thought of you. More than I'd like to admit. Usually at night before I knew you'd crawl into my bed. So I wouldn't do something stupid."

I got that. He wasn't supposed to be sleeping in the same bed as me. Let alone touching me. "What was I doing when you thought about me?"

He continued to massage my shoulder. But there was a heat in his gaze that wasn't there a moment ago. "I liked you on your knees. Begging me."

I swallowed hard.

"I liked picturing your lips around my cock."

Jesus. But honestly, I felt a lot like doing that now. He'd been better than my dreams. I wanted to be better than his too. I slowly sat up and shifted my weight to my knees. "I want you."

"Brooklyn you don't have to…"

"I need you. Please." I wasn't above begging for what I wanted. I'd already undone his pants. So I reached forward and shoved his boxers down. He was rock hard. I wanted him in every way. I'd actually dreamed of this too. Of him being mad at me for taking so long to come back to him. I pictured him shoving his cock down my throat. He'd wanted to punish me for making him wait. I'd touched myself to that very image.

I leaned down and licked his tip.

"Fuck."

I didn't bother teasing him anymore. I took his whole length into my mouth. All the way to the back of my throat.

He buried his fingers in my hair.

Each groan from his mouth made me tighten my lips and move faster.

I'd dreamed of this too. My lips around his cock. I'd dreamed of it when I shouldn't have. And something about knowing he'd thought about us like this too…I felt sexy. I felt desired.

And I felt super hot. Like way overheated. And I wasn't sure if it was because of the fire or because I was desperate for his touch again. Not even having a hug in the past several months made me feel like I was starving. I wanted his hands, his mouth, anything he'd give me. I tightened my lips again.

He came in my mouth. Shot after shot. It was sweeter than I expected it to be. And I drank him down.

He just stared at me. "What the hell have you been doing the past few months?"

I laughed and lay down next to him. "Tons of prostitution."

He lightly slapped my ass.

"No." I put my head on his chest. "I've been missing you. Dreaming of that. Dreaming of you."

He pulled me closer and pressed a kiss on the side of my forehead.

***

I hadn't realized I'd fallen asleep. I opened my eyes and yawned. For a second I had no idea where I was. I sat up in the bed and looked around.

I thought I'd dreamt of him again.

But I was here.

I breathed in Miller's familiar scent as I ran my fingers across his comforter. He must have carried me in here once I fell asleep in front of the fire.

He was real. This was real. And…it was Christmas. I didn't want to sleep the whole day away. I jumped out of bed and hopped around, the wooden floor cold on my bare feet. My clothes weren't anywhere in sight, so I opened up Miller's drawers to find something. All I could find that might work were a pair of sweatpants with a drawstring at the waist and a t-shirt that was way too big. It was not at all a cute outfit. But Miller had never cared about what I looked like.

I wandered out into the hall, glad that the pants were too big so that I was stepping on them instead of the cold floor. Miller was sitting on the couch reading. He heard me and lifted his head.

"Hey," Miller said.

"Hey." I sat down next to him.

We both just stared at each other. I think there was a lot we needed to say, but neither of us wanted to say it.

Instead of speaking, he placed his book down, grabbed my hand, and pulled me onto his lap.

I sighed and leaned my forehead against his. "Merry Christmas."

He pulled his head back from mine and traced my lower lip with his thumb. "Where have you been, kid?"

I groaned. "You can't call me that anymore. I'm an adult. And it's weird because we just did that thing."

His hands fell to my waist. "What thing?"

I stared at him.

He raised his left eyebrow at me.

I laughed. "*The* thing." Why was I being so weird? I tried to crawl off his lap, but his fingers tightened on my hips.

"Tell me what we did." He lightly kissed my jawline and up to my ear. "Tell me I didn't dream that." He nipped at my earlobe.

God. My fingers tightened on his shoulders and I'm pretty sure I moaned. It wasn't my fault. The whole no human contact for months thing was really messing with me. I knew what he wanted. He wanted me to say those dirty words. It reminded me of when Matt had asked me to tell him what I wanted. And I'd said I wanted him to poke me in the pants. Which was mortifying. And juvenile. I wanted Miller to know I was old enough to want these things with him.

"You didn't dream it," I said as he nipped my ear again. I accidentally started grinding against him and he hissed in my ear. I really liked that noise. "I recall giving you really amazing Christmas morning head. You're welcome, by the way."

"I recall returning the favor."

"Hmm did you? I don't remember that."

He kissed behind my ear again and then pulled back, feigning a shocked expression. "You don't remember? I must not have done a good enough job then."

I squealed as he shifted on the couch, tossing me on my back.

"Miller you don't have to…"

He pulled my sweatpants down and slid a finger inside of me.

I should have been embarrassed about how wet I was. But I wasn't embarrassed at all. How could I be when he groaned by just touching me?

"Do you remember now?" he asked, sliding another finger inside of me.

God. I lifted my hips and he pushed them back down with his free hand.

His fingers slowed down. "Did you dream of me too, Brooklyn?"

What was he doing? The slow pace was driving me insane.

"How long have you wanted me to touch you like this?" His thumb traced slow circles on my clit.

I moaned.

"Tell me you thought of us too." He moved his fingers even slower.

Fuck.

"When you crawled into my bed at night? Right after I'd jacked off thinking about you? Did you want me then?"

"Yes," I panted.

"Did you want me to fuck you with my fingers? Did you want me to eat your delicious pussy?"

Jesus. "Yes," I moaned.

"How long have you wanted that?"

"Forever."

He laughed.

God. I couldn't be mad at him for laughing. I was so fucking close. So fucking…*oh God. Yes.* I felt myself clench around his fingers.

The guttural noise that escaped his throat made the sensation a hundred times better.

I'd come imagining this before. The real thing was better. So much freaking better. Miller seemed to like handing out orgasms. I was just about to beg for more when his fingers fell from my skin.

I opened my eyes and he was sitting on the floor, staring up at me on the couch.

"These look better on you," he said and lifted the sweatpants back in place.

Despite what we'd just done…he looked…distant. "Not accurate. They look amazing on you."

He leaned forward, resting his chin in his hand as he stared at me. "This was the best Christmas present I could possibly ask for."

"Then why do you look so sad?"

He continued staring into my eyes. "I don't want to be your backup plan, kid."

"You're not."

He sighed and turned away from me, staring at the fire. "You deflected the question before. Have you been with him this whole time?"

"Miller…"

"Have you?"

I swallowed hard. "No."

He didn't respond. He just continued to stare at the fire.

I slid off the couch to sit next to him. I didn't want to talk about what happened with Matt right now. I just wanted to enjoy being with Miller. And it was Christmas.

We could go into more details some other day. "I was in California trying to figure out what I wanted. End of story."

He looked down at me. "You were gone for months, Brooklyn."

"I had a lot of stuff to figure out." I smiled, hoping it would make him smile too.

It did not.

I needed to diffuse the tension in the room. "Come on," I said and held out my hand to him. "You owe me about a thousand dances."

That finally made him smile. He grabbed my hand and let me help him up. "A thousand dances, huh? That could take a lifetime."

"That's kind of what I'm hoping."

CHAPTER 30

Thursday

Miller turned up the music as I put the monkey bread in the oven.

"I can't believe you had all the ingredients." It was really quite shocking given that Miller's kitchen wasn't stocked very well. But I didn't need a fancy turkey feast for Christmas dinner. I'd always loved breakfast for dinner. And the fact that he had all the ingredients for my favorite Christmas staple... It meant that he'd hoped I'd come. That he was longing for me too. And I couldn't wipe the smile off my face.

"Of course I had the ingredients. Just in case." He pulled me in close and dipped me to the music.

I laughed as he pulled me back up. There was a funny song about reindeer blasting through the speakers, but I was glad we were slow dancing. It was like I couldn't get close enough to him. I was starved for his touch. I wanted to hold him and stare at him and kiss his lips constantly. And this time, I didn't want to mess anything up. "I want to get this right."

"What do you mean *this*?" He pushed some hair away from his eyes.

"Us." I reached up and put my fingers through his hair. He used to always keep it shaved close to his skull. But he must have let it grow out over the past several months. It looked good on him. But it also looked like the hair in his eyes annoyed him a bit. "Do you want me to give you a haircut?"

He laughed. "You're changing the subject again."

I hadn't even realized I was doing that. I sighed and put my head on his shoulder as we swayed slowly to the music. "I want to get us right this time. I'm sorry I ever let you walk away." This wasn't coming out right. "I mean, I'm sorry I pushed you away. I'm just…sorry."

"I'm sorry too."

I pulled back. "What are you sorry for?"

"Asking you to come with me when I knew you needed closure. Not letting you have your space to figure it out. I wasn't trying to pressure you. It was hard for me. Watching you fall for someone else. Watching you choose someone else. Watching you miss someone else."

It was hard for me too. Missing Matt. I blinked fast, trying to keep the images of him pushed to the back of my mind where they belonged. I was here with Miller. I was present with him. I was choosing him. "I missed you when I was in California. Desperately."

He smiled. "I missed you too." His hands slid to my ass.

I laughed. "You seem to like my butt in these pants."

He looked down at the baggy sweatpants. "I like you in anything, Brooklyn."

I pushed my fingers through his hair again. "I like you in anything too. And nothing."

He smiled down at me.

"If I confess something, do you promise you won't think I'm weird?"

"Well…how weird is it?"

I ran my fingers down to the back of his neck. I'd had a lot of time to ponder this. And I wasn't sure what it said about me. But it was the truth. I was so tired of hiding from the truth. "As soon as I was free…I wished I was back in my cage."

"Is that what you felt like? That you were in a cage?"

"At the time, yes."

He pressed his lips together.

I wasn't sure what I was expecting him to say. I'd basically just told him I'd felt trapped with him. But that wasn't how I'd meant it. "I guess I needed to leave it to know how much I liked it."

He raised his eyebrow. "Are you talking about liking me or the beach house?"

"Both I guess. Mostly you." I smiled up at him even though I was suddenly sad. "I think I just felt guilty being happy there with you. It was like I was torturing myself. Even though I'm pretty sure I had everything I ever wanted right in front of me. Think about how much fun we could have had if I'd just given in to temptation."

"I still had fun with you, kid."

I stuck my tongue out at him.

He laughed and lifted me up so that I was sitting on the edge of the counter. He stood between my legs. The height from the counter made us eye level. I felt…balanced. Even. Like I was staring back at my equal. I'd never really felt that way with Matt. He never meant to…but he made me feel lesser. Even once I got my new last name, I still wasn't good enough for him. But with Miller? I breathed in his exhales as we just stared at each other. I'd never felt such a…rush. I'd been so blind.

I leaned forward and lightly pressed my lips against his.

But he didn't kiss me back.

He shifted so that his face was a few inches from mine. "We're still in a cage. Running from your dad makes it hard to have a normal life."

"Who cares about Little Dicky?"

Miller smiled and then shook his head. "I do if it means you can't live the life you want."

"I just told you…I don't mind being in a cage with you. I picked this place because I knew you'd love it. But I knew I'd love it too. I want this life with you. Winter nights curled up in front of the fire with hot chocolate. Spring nights on the back porch looking out at the lake. Summer nights…"

He pressed his lips back to mine. But the kiss was fleeting again. "Have you heard from him at all?"

"My dad?" I shook my head.

"Me either. It's weird, right? That he hasn't tried to find either of us?"

"I had a flawless plan."

"It was a decent plan. But you used your dad's money."

"Yeah. It wasn't traceable though. The guy online said…"

"And how much did you know about that random guy you found online?"

I shrugged. Not much. But he'd gotten me the passports. He'd gotten Miller this house. He'd made sure to have a bank account set up for Miller… I lost my train of thought when I looked down and saw a hole in the knee of the sweatpants. I thought about how the pantry was barely stocked with any food. And Miller had chastised me for not wearing a jacket, but the one he'd been wearing looked like it was threadbare.

I looked over at the Christmas tree. There were lights but no ornaments. And I had no way of knowing, but I bet he cut it down himself from somewhere in the yard. The Christmas magic in the air made me think everything here was perfect. A perfect Christmas scene that I'd walked right into. But was it?

Miller cleared his throat and tried to step back. "I should probably start making some eggs.

I caught his hand. "Have you not been using the money in your account?"

"I don't want any of that money, Brooklyn."

"But…it's yours."

He laughed. "No, it's not mine. If anything it's yours." He walked over toward the fridge and opened it.

How could he not use that money? I'd gotten it for him. To make sure he could have whatever life he wanted.

I slid off the counter as he cracked some eggs into a very old looking pan. "You don't think you earned that money for all the shit my dad put you through?"

He didn't respond.

"My dad clearly doesn't miss it. He hasn't come after either of us."

"I don't need it," Miller said.

"What about your online classes?"

"I finished the fall semester. And I'll pick the classes back up when again when I save up some money."

"But you have the money just sitting there…"

"I'll save up soon enough. Probably by next fall. The following spring at the latest."

I didn't expect to come here and have my first fight with him. But this was ridiculous. The money was for him. I'd gotten it for him. "Saving up what money? You can't get a job. You need like legal forms for that and stuff."

"I'm getting paid under the table at a local restaurant."

"You're a waiter?" We were on opposite sides of the country doing exactly the same thing. Except he was the one with a fat bank account. He didn't have to rely on crappy tips and pinching pennies.

"No." He pulled out the monkey bread right before the timer went off. And then he plated the eggs and handed me one of the plates. "I'm a line cook."

I was about to laugh. Miller was not a great cook. And yet…the eggs on my plate were perfectly scrambled. They weren't even a little burnt. I looked back up at Miller. "You're a cook?"

"Don't act so surprised. I had a pretty good teacher."

I opened my mouth and then closed it again. I wasn't pissed anymore. I was…kind of impressed. Had he been practicing cooking this whole time? I scooped some monkey bread out of the pan and sat down on a stool at the kitchen island. The eggs were delicious. The bread too. "You can cook now."

He laughed. "I had to learn how to do it on my own eventually. Someone left me to my own devices."

I lightly shoved his shoulder. "Are you kidding me? I left you with millions of dollars!"

He blinked. "What?"

"Did you not even look at the account?"

"No. Did you just say there were millions of dollars in the account? Millions with an s?"

I laughed. "Yeah."

"Huh. How about that." He started to eat.

"That's all you have to say? Huh? Are you going to use it now?"

"Nah. I have everything I need."

What? "But…"

"I have everything I need, Brooklyn." He grabbed my hand on the counter. "Really. Everything I need is right here."

Me. I was everything he needed.

"Now eat before I start thinking you hate my cooking."

I laughed and took a bite of monkey bread. It was so much better than last Christmas. I watched him as he took a bite of eggs. Last Christmas had been amazing. But this Christmas? Hands down, it was my favorite yet.

***

We were sitting right in front of the fire, our limbs tangled.

"How old are you?" I asked. "And don't say 'older than you.' You've given me that answer before."

He laughed. "Did I say that?"

"Yes you did. Now answer the question."

He pushed his hair off his forehead. It was almost like he was nervous to tell me. "I'm 23."

"Hmm." Yup, I was right. Miller wasn't a boy who had no idea what he wanted. He was a man. And 23 wasn't that much older than me at all. Ever since my mom got sick, I felt like I was aging double time. According to that logic, I was pretty much in my twenties too now. And I wasn't just some kid confused about what I wanted. I knew I wanted him. "So I guess you were 22 when we first met?"

"Yeah."

"Your 'older than you' response back then was a little pompous then, don't you think?"

"I just didn't want you to get any wrong ideas."

"What kind of wrong ideas?"

"Oh…I don't know. I didn't want you to think that you could climb into my bed. Or kiss me. Or anything like that."

I laughed. "Well, that backfired pretty hard."

"You're very persuasive." He hooked my leg over him.

"Am I?" I sat up so I was straddling him. "That's good, because I really want to know your first name."

He laughed, but didn't tell me what it was.

"So…what is it?"

"Nope."

"Nope is not a name." I stared down at him. He'd stopped making eye contact with me. If anything he looked more nervous about this than the age thing. "Why won't you tell me?"

"Because I like when you call me Miller."

"I promise I'll still call you Miller. Honestly, it would be hard to stop calling you that at this point. Just like you have a hard time not calling me kid."

"How about you just keep calling me Miller and I won't call you kid anymore."

"No deal. Tell me your first name."

"I don't like my first name. And you won't like it either."

"I like everything about you."

He laughed. "You won't like this."

"Oh come on." I leaned forward, knowing perfectly well I was grinding against him. "Knowing your first name is all I want for Christmas."

"I thought that *that thing* we did earlier was your Christmas present." He put *that thing* in air quotes.

"Ha. Ha. Very funny. If anything that was more of a present to you."

"Is that right?"

"Miller." I grabbed his hands and moved them to either side of his face, holding him down. "Tell me your name right now."

His Adam's apple slowly rose and then fell.

"Stop looking at me like that. You're distracting me. I need to know your first name."

"Then don't pin me down like you're about to devour me."

"I'm not going to release you until you spill it. And stop trying to distract me!" He'd just shifted beneath me and I could feel his erection. "You're not playing fair. Just tell me!"

It didn't look like he was planning on playing fair at all.

CHAPTER 31

Thursday

"Miller, just tell me your name." I needed a confession from him stat. Because I was pretty sure we were only a few seconds away from being naked again.

"Miller is my name."

"You're being ridiculous. Just tell me."

He groaned. "Why does it matter?"

"Because I'm dreaming of a future with you. And I always imagined I'd know the first name of the person I wanted to spend the rest of my life with."

His eyes dropped to my lips. "The rest of your life, huh?"

"If you tell me your name."

He just kept staring at my lips, like he was daring me to kiss him instead of continuing this discussion.

"It's important to me. Please."

He sighed and his eyes met mine again. "Fine. But I can't undo it once you know. And you might never look at me the same."

"How could it possibly be that bad?"

He groaned and closed his eyes. And then he squinted at me like he didn't really want to see my reaction. "It's…Richard."

Oh. *Oh.* "Richard?" Like my dad? I almost laughed because I thought he was kidding. But he wasn't looking at me like he was kidding around.

"Yeah Richard. As in…the same as your father's name."

I laughed. "Yeah I got that. Little Dicky."

"Fuck, don't call me that. You've seen my dick."

"Big Dicky?"

"You promised you'd keep calling me Miller," he said with a laugh.

"I can't believe your name is Richard. That's so weird."

"Whatever, kid."

"Don't kid me!" I tickled his side.

"Don't Little or Big Dicky me!" He flipped me over and retaliated to my tickle attack with what I can only describe as a tickle onslaught.

"Stop! I can't breathe!" I said through my laughter. "Stop it, Big Dicky!"

He tickled me harder. And right when I was about to protest again he captured my laughter with a kiss. A kiss like the one we'd shared outside. Like he was starving for me. It was the weirdest sensation, kissing and laughing. Like somehow my joy extended into him and his transferred to me. I couldn't remember ever feeling this happy. Or this desperate for someone's touch.

Fuck. How could I go from laughing so hard one minute to being so completely aroused the next? I wrapped my legs around his waist as he deepened the kiss.

"God, Brooklyn." He put his forehead against mine. "If it wasn't snowing so hard. And it wasn't Christmas. I'd be out there buying a huge box of condoms."

It made me laugh. Thinking about the huge box of condoms my uncle had bought me when he thought I was being promiscuous made me laugh even harder. I hadn't been. At the time I hadn't needed them at all. But thinking about my uncle gifting me the box made me remember something really important. "Oh my God. I have something for you."

"Wait you have a condom?"

"No. I wish. But I have a present for you." I'd left it outside on the front step this whole time. In the middle of a huge snowstorm. There was no way it wasn't completely ruined. *Crap.*

Miller didn't move to let me up.

"Big Dicky, I need to get up."

He sighed. "Seriously, don't call me that, kid."

It was the perfect time to strike a deal with him. I'd stop calling him Big Dicky or Richard. And he'd stop calling me kid. But honestly? I kind of liked when he called me kid. It was weird, I know, but it reminded me of when my uncle called me kiddo. And I knew it was just something Miller said because he was looking out for me. Because he loved me. And I'd be sad if he never called me that again. "Okay. You look a lot more like a Miller. No matter how big your dick is."

He laughed and climbed off of me. "You're free."

"Come with me." I grabbed his hand and pulled him to his feet. I figured the box would be in disarray. Frozen. Or melted. Or…something not quite right. I wanted him to see it before I picked it up and it fell apart.

"Where are we going?" he asked.

I grabbed the doorknob and opened the door.

A big gust of wind came into the house, scattering snowflakes everywhere. He pulled me into his chest so I wouldn't get wet again. There was a foot of snow on his front porch. And the present was nowhere in sight. *Shit.*

"It's a freaking blizzard out there," Miller said and went to close the door.

"Wait. Your present is somewhere under all that snow."

He looked down at me. "Where?"

"I don't know," I said with a laugh. "But I have to find it. I spent pretty much all my money on it and since we're not using our enormous savings account…I don't want to waste anything."

"You're not going to use the money either?"

"Not if you don't want to." I crouched down in front of the door and started moving snow around, searching aimlessly for the box.

"Let me get us some gloves at least," Miller said. He disappeared from behind me.

Please be okay. I moved more snow out of the way. I didn't want to pop back into Miller's life again empty handed. And not give him a present two Christmases in a row. I know he said all he needed was me. But…I wanted him to know how much I appreciated him. And I'd spent a lot of time thinking about this gift.

"Here," Miller said and handed me a pair of gloves.

He knelt down next to me and started searching in the snow too. "Was it to the left or the right…"

I laughed and pulled on the gloves. "I don't remember. I was panicking because you didn't answer the door."

"Why were you panicking?"

"I thought you were…" my voice trailed off.

He stopped searching and looked over at me. "You thought I was what? Taking a dump or something?"

"No," I said with a laugh. "I thought maybe you were busy with someone new."

He smiled. "Didn't even cross my mind."

I shook my head and kept searching. "Well, I don't believe that. Surely there's someone out there that isn't such a mess."

"Hey." He grabbed my hand. "I don't want someone else. All I've been doing is thinking about you. Wondering where you were. If you were safe. If you were happy. Dreaming of you." He looked back at the snow.

"I dreamed about you too. All the time. It was weird having seen pictures of this house." I started digging in the snow again. "It was easy to picture you here being happy."

"I wasn't happy without you."

"Me either." Talking to Miller was so…easy. There was never any second guessing what he said. He just told me the truth. And it was easy to be honest with him. "And you already know that some of my dreams about you were quite sinful," I said.

He laughed. "Certainly not as sinful as mine."

I would have been distracted by his comment, but my hands finally collided with something hard. "Ah! I found it!" I pulled the box out from under the snow. The silver foil wrapping paper looked fine, maybe just a little frosty. But the big red bow on top looked a little sad. I hoped everything wasn't soaked inside. "Merry Christmas, Miller." I handed it to him.

He helped me to my feet as I closed the door. "We should probably change," he said.

"Nope. Not until you open that before it melts."

"Before it melts?" He just stared at me. "What is it?"

I pulled off my gloves and rubbed my frozen fingers together. "Just open it." But he was right, I was cold. And if the frozen box was any indication, everything inside was plenty cold. "We can open it in front of the fire."

Miller pulled off his wet hoodie as we sat down on the floor right in front of the fireplace.

I sighed as I stared at his abs. I remembered him rolling around in the sand, laughing. I should have kissed him right then. When we both looked like sugar doughnuts. All my memories of the beach house were tarnished because of how stubborn I had been. I'd pushed him away every time he got close. And I wondered if he thought I'd do that again now.

"You okay?" he asked.

"What? Yeah." I shook my head. "I was just…you gave me a perfect Christmas last year."

The corner of his mouth ticked up.

"And I want this to be your perfect Christmas this year."

"It already has been."

"Hopefully it's about to be even better." I tapped on the top of the box and it felt like mush between my fingers. "Ew, gross. It's ruined."

"It's just a box. Who cares what's on the outside."

I smiled. I wasn't even sure he meant for that to affect me in the way it did. But I was really happy he cared about what was on the inside. That he liked me for me. I'd been so torn up about being a Sanders or a Pruitt or a Caldwell. Thinking about the Caldwell last name felt like a punch in the gut. I swallowed hard and tried to shove the feeling away. None of that mattered. I was just a Sanders now.

Miller untied the soggy red bow and somehow managed to get the mush wrapping paper off. He lifted the lid off the box and I could have cried. Because somehow everything inside seemed fine.

He picked up the oversized mugs. Brooklyn and Miller were written on them. Although, if I'd known his name was Richard I totally would have put Little Dicky on his mug. There was also hot chocolate and mini marshmallows. The perfect things for a cold winter night.

There was a picnic blanket and a cooler for spring picnics.

He laughed when he lifted up the bright yellow swim trunks. I knew they were way too loud for him. But I also hoped that he'd laugh just like he had when he saw them. And they reminded me of the time we'd spent at the beach house.

There was also a set of bowls with our names on them too. They were the perfect size for ice cream. Which we'd started sharing last fall. It was the first time we'd really bonded. Over a bowl of ice cream. "Open the cooler," I said.

He opened the cooler and lifted up the pint of mint chocolate chip ice cream.

I reached out and was happy it was still frozen. Although, now that I thought about it that should have been the least of my concerns. The snow outside was probably just as cold as a freezer. "I got things for every season. The hot chocolate mugs for winter. The picnic blanket for spring. The swim trunks for summer. And the ice cream bowls for fall."

He didn't ask why the ice cream was for fall. He just looked up with a smile on his face. Because he knew.

Memories had a strange way of fading. But it was weird with Miller. Like for some reason all the ones with him were brighter. More clear. Like I was hyper focused on every moment we'd ever shared.

I waited for him to say something…but he didn't.

"I wanted you to know that I've loved every season with you. And I want to keep spending every season with you. And I don't care if we're in NYC, or the beach, or here. I mean, I'd prefer to stay here." He still didn't say anything, so I kept rambling. "I think maybe the whole time I actually picked out the perfect place for us. Not just you. But us together. And I want to stay. If you'll have me."

He looked back down at the ice cream container in his hand.

"I know I hurt you. And I can't really explain away what I did. All I can say is that I was broken. But…I took that time away to heal. And I know what I want. I want you and only you. And I know that we're hiding out from my dad. But I don't think this place will feel like a cage. I think everywhere I am with you just feels like…home."

He still didn't say anything.

"I know I said I'd rather be in a cage with you than anywhere without you. But…I think I had it all wrong. My mind has been so twisted about my feelings of the beach house. I loved being there with you. I had some of the best days of my life there. And I think I was trying to convince myself that I was sick in the head for thinking that. How could I possibly be happy locked up? But I wasn't locked up. I had my best friend there with me."

He cleared his throat. "You want some ice cream?" He stood up.

What? "Miller." I stood up and grabbed his hand. "I'm sorry. Did I do something wrong? I…" my voice trailed off when I saw that there were tears welling in his eyes.

I'd seen him this emotional once before. When I told him I was choosing Matt the first time. I swallowed hard. "Miller?"

He exhaled slowly. "Do you really want to stay? You want to use all these things with me? You want to live here even though you can't use your real name outside these walls?"

"Of course. All that matters is that we're together."

"You already broke me once, Brooklyn."

I blinked away the tears in my eyes. "I know. I don't think there's anything I can say to undo what I've done. But…I'm here. I'm choosing you."

"I want to believe you. I really do. But if you stay and then decide that Matt is…"

"Matt and I are over." The words were final. And I felt them. Matt was happy. I deserved to be happy too. "I'm not going to walk away from us. I promise." I was good at keeping my promises. A lot better than Matt was. And I wouldn't break this one. As soon as I'd jumped in Miller's arms outside this morning, it felt like my heart had started beating again. Yes, Matt used to make me feel alive. Before he was happy that I was dead. But now? Miller made me feel everything. "I promise," I said again. I stood up on my tiptoes and kissed him.

"Don't break me again," he said against my lips.

I wouldn't. I knew how easily hearts could break. And I'd never do that again. "Nunca." I kissed him again. "I love you."

And when he kissed me instead of saying it back...I realized that he hadn't said it yet. He had back at the beach house. He'd told me he loved me. He'd asked me to choose him. And I hadn't.

I loved him. I knew that now. I'd given my heart time to heal. I'd taken the time I needed. But maybe he needed more time.

That was okay. I wasn't going anywhere.

CHAPTER 32

Friday

I slowly opened my eyes. My head was on Miller's chest and he was breathing softly. Each rise and fall of his chest made me smile more. I couldn't imagine being any happier. Although…there was something I wanted to do. Well, two things. But the first thing had to wait until the snowplow came through and we could go to the store. Which left the second thing.

"Miller, wake up." I kissed his cheek. "It's a snow day."

He groaned.

"Come on." I lightly slapped his butt and sat up. I couldn't even remember the last time I'd gotten to play in the snow. Sometime before my mom had gotten sick.

I climbed out of bed and opened up my backpack, knowing full well that I didn't have anything warm enough for the snow. Miller had wandered out to my car to grab it last night. He'd come back with his teeth chattering. If we weren't going to touch my dad's money, then I was going to need to get a job as soon as the snow cleared. Miller needed a warmer winter jacket. And I needed one too.

I started rummaging through his drawers. I found another pair of sweatpants and layered them with the ones I'd borrowed yesterday.

"What are you doing?" Miller said with a laugh. He was sitting up in bed rubbing his eyes.

"It's a snow day."

"So you've said."

"Which means we're going out and playing in the snow." I tossed a pair of sweatpants at him.

"It's freezing out there."

"It won't be cold when we're running around." I pulled on one of his sweatshirts.

"We need to get you some appropriate clothes."

I laughed. "What I need is for you to get your big butt outside."

He just sat in bed, smiling at me.

"Come on!" I hurried out of the room. I figured I only had 30 minutes tops before I was completely frozen. But that was still 30 minutes of fun.

It took us a little time to be able to walk outside. We pushed the snow away from the back door. But once we cleared a small path, we realized that it hadn't snowed quite as much as we thought. It had just drifted against the house. There was only about half a foot of beautiful white snow. I ventured out, ignoring how cold my sneakers were in the snow. It was the perfect amount of snow to...*oof.* A snowball hit me right in the back. "Hey!" I turned toward Miller just as he threw another snowball right at my stomach. Oh, it was on. "You are so dead."

He laughed as I ran after him. But he wasn't running very fast. It was almost like he wanted me to reach him. I jumped onto his back.

He pretended to lose his balance and toppled us both onto the ground. And I had no idea how he did it, but I somehow wound up on top of him, staring down at his smiling face.

He started to make snow angels even though my entire weight was pressing down on him.

It was just like how he'd acted at the beach. Playful and fun. But instead of sand all over him, it was snow.

"I love you." The words just kept spilling out of me. Like I had no control over them.

He stopped making snow angels and grabbed both sides of my face with his snow-covered gloves. He kissed me. He kissed me like he loved me.

But…he still didn't say it back.

After everything we'd been through…I got it. I did. And yet…did his feelings change? Matt's feelings had changed… *Stop.*

Just like I wasn't sure why I kept repeatedly telling him I loved him, I had no idea why I grabbed a handful of snow and stuffed it down his hoodie.

He yelped.

But I was already off him and running down to the lake.

"New rule!" he yelled after me. "No snow under our clothes!"

"There's no rules in this house!" I tapped the frozen lake with my toe. It seemed solid enough. I stepped onto it and my feet slipped. I landed with a thud on my butt. *Ow.*

Miller slid onto the ice next to me but stayed gracefully on his feet. "No rules in this house, huh?" He put his hand out for me.

I grabbed it and pulled him down on top of me.

He laughed and caught himself so he didn't smush me. "So our home is a lawless one?"

"Yes." God, I loved when he was on top of me like this. It made me forget that we were in the snow in very inappropriate snow clothes. I didn't even feel cold. Hell, it made me forget I was outside at all. And all I wanted to do was wrap my legs around his waist.

"So you wouldn't mind if I…I don't know…did this?" He picked up a big handful of snow and I dodged it right before he tried to shove it right in my face.

IVY SMOAK

I squealed and tried to stand up on the ice, but slipped again. I tried to crawl away on my hands and knees.

But he grabbed me from behind, pulling me against him.

And I was instantly turned on. Him behind me like that. Holding me around the waist, my ass tight to the front of him. I stayed completely still.

"Lawless," he said, one gloved hand slid to my hip, holding me in place. "That's what you want?"

I swallowed hard. "Yes."

"So you wouldn't mind if I did this?" He pushed my double layers of sweatpants down, exposing my ass to the cold.

"No rules," I said. "So why would I mind?" I heard his glove drop to the ground.

"What about this?" He cupped my ass in his hand.

I moaned. "That hardly feels lawless. This backyard is private. No one can see us. Who cares if my butt is out?"

"You're right. No one's watching." His fingers slipped between my legs, this cold thumb brushing against my clit. "How about this?" His voice sounded tight.

I moaned. I was really liking lawless Miller.

His index finger slid inside of me. "Fuck, you're so warm."

I laughed, because it was a ridiculous thing to say. "Warm, really? That's very sexy pillow talk."

"Does it look like we're snuggled up in bed right now? And you just shoved snow down my shirt. I'm fucking freezing." He moved his finger faster, making me lose my train of thought for a moment.

"So is this supposed to teach me some kind of lesson about not putting snow down your clothes? Because I'm learning quite the opposite."

"Fair point." His fingers stopped.

Damn it, why had I said that? I didn't want him to stop.

"This is probably a better lesson." He grabbed a handful of snow and shoved it right against where his fingers had been.

"What the hell!" I shrieked. "You're going to give my naughty bits frostbite!" I tried to wriggle out of his grip, but he was still holding me to him.

"That was your punishment. But I think you've learned your lesson. How about I warm you up?" He flipped me over, cradling my ass in his hands so I wouldn't touch the ice.

I was freezing, but something about the fire in his gaze made me stop moving. He slowly lowered his mouth to the snow he'd just shoved between my legs. He thrust his tongue inside of me, pushing some of the snow with it.

I screamed. "It's so cold! Miller…" but my voice trailed off. Because it suddenly wasn't cold anymore. All I could feel was his hot tongue between my thighs, lapping up the snow off my skin. Replacing the feeling of cold with unbelievable warmth.

One of his hands still had a glove on it, so when he pulled me even closer to his face, the rough material scratched my skin. It burned. It felt amazing. I didn't even know how to describe…

He thrust his tongue even further.

"Miller." I grabbed the top of his hat to pull him closer. But it wasn't necessary. He was licking me like he was eating his favorite flavor of water ice. I'd thought last night had been hot. But this? I was seconds away from coming and he'd barely even started.

He groaned like he couldn't get enough. Like he'd never get enough of me.

I felt my thighs tightening around him.

"I love the taste of you."

It wasn't the confession of love I'd been waiting to hear. But it was good enough right now.

He brushed the tip of his nose against my clit as he thrust his tongue even deeper inside of me.

"Miller!" I felt myself pulsing around his tongue. *Fuck.* My fingers dug into the back of his neck as he kept swirling his tongue inside of me. I never wanted him to stop. I never wanted this moment to end. I'd be happy to spend eternity right on this ice with him. Even in the freezing cold there was nowhere else I'd rather be.

He groaned and placed one last stroke against me before lifting his face from my skin. He pulled my sweatpants back up and wiped the wetness off his chin. "Did you learn your lesson?"

I moved to my knees and grabbed the waistband of his pants. "Yes. But it's only fair that now I get to cover you in ice and lick you like a popsicle."

"Yeah…" he caught my hand before I reached into his sweatpants. "Guys don't work like that. It's cold. So he's not having it."

"Really? Even after what we just did?"

He raised his eyebrow at me. "I would never lie about such things."

I pulled the waistband of his sweatpants anyway and peered inside. "Hey there, Little Dicky."

"You're so dead." He started to make a snowball.

I scrambled to my feet. "I call a truce!"

He didn't stop making his snowball, so I started to run, my feet skidding along the ice.

"Brooklyn wait!"

I ran faster, my feet finally adjust to the sleek ice.

"Stop!" he yelled. He sounded really upset.

Probably because he couldn't reach me with his snowball. I took another step and I heard the ice crack. I froze, but my feet skidded farther. The sickening sound of the ice cracking echoed around me.

"Don't move," Miller said.

Some cold water started coming through the cracks, soaking my sneakers. I wasn't fucking going anywhere.

"I've got you," Miller said calmly as he took a step on the cracking ice. The sound grew worse. "Shit." His feet froze. "I need you to get down on your hands and knees, Brooklyn."

"What?"

"I've got you, okay? But I need you to get down on all fours. I need you to trust me."

I didn't even hesitate to follow his instructions this time. Of course I trusted him. I got down on my knees, not caring about the cold water biting my skin.

"Crawl toward me, okay. Really slowly."

"I can't." My heart was pounding against my ribcage. *I can't.*

"Look at me, kid."

I slowly looked up from the ice and into his eyes.

"Just crawl toward me really slowly. I'm right here. Just look at me. You're going to be okay."

I moved slowly, the ice making terrible cracking noises the whole time. I was almost at him when there was a loud crack. My feet went into the freezing cold water first. And then my whole body slid backward. "Miller!" I screamed at the top of my lungs.

I wasn't even sure how he reached me, but he grabbed my hands and pulled me out of the freezing cold water right before I slipped under the ice.

My heart was pounding as I clung to him. "You saved me." My whole body was wet and shivering. But his arms were so comforting. It was like my heart instantly stopped pounding so fast when he held me like this.

He didn't respond. He just held me tightly.

"You saved me," I said again.

He still didn't respond.

I didn't know how he got us safely off the ice. But before I even know it, we were back inside. It didn't matter that there was a roaring fire though. I was still shivering.

He carried me into the bathroom and turned on the showerhead before setting me down on my feet. "Get in there."

I didn't want him to leave me. "Can't we warm up by the fire together?"

"Get in the water before you get frostbite."

Didn't he see that he was the one shaking now, not me? "Then come with me." I grabbed his hand.

He cursed under his breath and pulled off his wet clothes, before pushing me backward into the shower. I was still fully dressed, but the hot water felt like flames against my skin. He helped me get all my layers off, pushing them into a heap in the corner. If anything, I was too hot now. But Miller was still shaking.

I put my hand on his chest. He felt perfectly warm. "You're not cold anymore," I said. "Why are you shaking?"

He ran his fingers through his wet hair, and he looked up at the showerhead. "I almost lost you."

"But you didn't. You saved me." I grabbed both sides of his face and tilted his head back down to me so I could look into his eyes. "I'm okay." I stood up on my tiptoes and kissed him. "I'm okay," I whispered against his lips.

"I only just got you back," he said.

"I'm not going anywhere." I left a trail of kisses across his jawline and down the side of his neck. "I promise."

He sighed and pulled me against his chest.

We just held each other as the hot water fell on us. I hugged him until he slowly stopped shaking, the adrenaline slowly melting away. And as the cold and adrenaline left his limbs, something else slowly grew to attention. Well, not that slowly. His hardness was pressing against my stomach pretty quickly.

I looked up at him. "He's not cold anymore."

"No." But Miller didn't let go of me. He held me tighter if anything.

But it kind of seemed like a distraction might do him some good. I reached down and wrapped my hand around his length.

"Brooklyn, you don't have to…" his voice trailed off and he groaned as I stroked him up and down with my hand.

I knew I didn't have to. I wanted to. I wanted him to forget about what just happened. It had taken me a year to remember how important living in the moment was. There were no more what-ifs. We were both here. Together.

I dropped to my knees and blinked up at him through the water falling around us.

He'd saved me. He was always saving me. How many nights had I waited for Matt to save me? I had no idea why I was even thinking about Matt. I wanted him to be gone from my memory. I wanted him out. I was so tired of thoughts of him pulling me into sadness. I just wanted to be happy. Right here with Miller. He was the one that showed up. He was the one saving me. And I loved him. I really fucking loved him.

He reached down and pushed some wet hair out of my face. His thumb gently tracing the outline of my lips. "You're so beautiful."

I wrapped my lips around this thumb and sucked.

He groaned, his cock growing even more.

I licked the pad of his thumb as he stared down at me. He didn't look like he was in shock anymore. He looked like he was as desperate for me as I was for him.

I stopped sucking on his thumb and wrapped my lips around his cock instead.

He groaned and put his hand on the tiled wall.

I shoved him into the back of my throat before I could confess my love for him again. I didn't want to not hear it back. I just wanted…him.

And I really needed to stop calling him Little Dicky. Especially since I could barely get my lips around this massive thing. Even when he was flaccid outside he was big. Miller was all man. And all mine.

I slid my lips down his shaft until he hit the back of my throat again.

"Fuck," he groaned as one of his hands slid to the back of my neck.

I knew I wasn't exactly great at this. I hadn't had much practice. So I was glad when his hand started guiding me. I was glad that he took what he needed from me. I wanted to give him everything.

I was surprised when he pulled back. And even more surprised as he started to stroke himself as he stared down at me. His first shot of cum hit my chest. I thought he might close his eyes, but he didn't. He was staring at me with so much heat in his gaze. The second shot hit my stomach. And the third landed right between my breasts. I was drenched in him. Like he'd just claimed me. I'd never experienced anything sexier in my whole life.

His chest was rising and falling fast. And then he closed his eyes and tilted his head to the ceiling.

I slowly stood up. "What's wrong?"

He groaned. "Nothing. I'm trying to tell my dick to calm down so I don't fuck you right now."

I laughed. "That wasn't enough for him? I'm covered in your skeet."

He looked back down at me and the corner of his mouth ticked up. "You like being covered in my cum?"

I ran my finger through the skeet on my chest. "It's a little sticky."

He grabbed a bar of soap and lightly pushed me so that I was back under the shower's stream. "I can help with that." But his soapy hands only seemed interested in cleaning my breasts.

I laughed. "You're doing a terrible job."

"Where else do you need to be cleaned?"

I ran his hand down my chest and stomach, stopping right where I was craving him most. "I'm very dirty right here."

"Is that so?" He lightly pushed me backward until my back hit the cold tile. "I dreamt about this too," he whispered in my ear. "Watching my skeet drip down your tits. You begging me for more."

My fingers tangled into his hair. "I do want more."

His thumb gently swirled around my clit. "I'll give you more tomorrow." He stepped back under the water and started soaping up.

"What?"

He ran his soapy hand over his length as he stared at me. "I have to work in the morning. I'll swing by the store tomorrow before I come home."

Oh. *Oh.* There was a lot I loved about what he'd just said. The store meant condoms. And he referred to this place we were sharing as home.

He slowly rinsed the shampoo out of his hair. "I'm going to go whip us up some hot chocolate. Just come out whenever you're properly warmed up."

"Okay," I said, even though I was already too warm if anything.

He smiled. "Okay then."

I stared at his ass as he left the shower. I swear, every inch of him was pure muscley perfection. I bit my lip as he wrapped a towel around his waist. Seriously, he had no business looking that good in just a towel. I desperately wanted him right now. But I'd waited this long, I could wait one more day. It would be a first for us.

A first.

My stomach twisted into knots.

"I'll be all your firsts, Brooklyn." I could hear Matt's voice in my head.

Get out of my head. I stepped back under the water. Matt had no business being in my head anymore. Our promises to each other meant nothing. Yes, I'd already shared this first with the wrong boy.

Matt was my first. But he wasn't my last. Miller would be my last everything. And I'd make sure tomorrow night was perfect.

CHAPTER 33

Saturday

"I'll be back soon," Miller whispered and kissed my forehead.

"Hm?" My eyes slowly opened. Miller was fully dressed, his threadbare winter coat and all.

I slowly sat up in bed. "Should I drive you to work? That way I can use the car to explore and look for a job today."

"No."

I laughed. "What do you mean no? I want to see what's around here. And I need a job to pull my weight."

"I'd rather show you around myself. All you need to do today is sign up for online classes so you can start on Monday. Unless you're already signed up?"

I had most definitely not been taking stupid high school classes online while I was in California. Was it that obvious? "I'm not taking two more years of dumb online classes. I'll just take the GED test."

"Pretty sure 17-year-olds have to take high school classes. Isn't the GED thing for adults?"

I pressed my lips together. "I am an adult. Besides, I'm not even Brooklyn anymore. I'm Jane. And Jane is 21. Which means Jane can take the GED."

Miller raised his eyebrow at me. "Whatever you want to do. But focus on that instead of thinking about getting a job. I've got us." He leaned down and pressed a kiss against my lips. "I'll be back sometime after lunch."

"Okay." I watched him walk out of the bedroom and then I glanced at the alarm clock. It was only 6 am. It was tempting to go back to sleep, but I was feeling restless. I guess I needed to figure out how to take that test online. Or maybe I could take it at the local high school. I pulled on a few layers of Miller's clothes and wandered out into the hall.

There was a wooden desk in the living room with a laptop on it. I sat down and pressed the power button. A box popped up, prompting me for the password.

Crap. Miller had forgotten to tell me the password to his computer. I took a few guesses. His birthday? *No.* My birthday? *No.* What was I supposed to do all day?

I leaned back in the chair, looking around the room.

I had too much pent-up energy. What I really wanted to do was go for a run. But that wasn't exactly a possibility with all the snow.

I stood up and peered out the window. Yup, it was definitely still too snowy. I stepped back and looked around the living room. I wanted tonight to be perfect. Miller was a very organized person. But he wasn't a huge believer in sweeping. I knew exactly what I could do today.

After searching a few closets I found some cleaning supplies. Most people probably wished there was a mop. But I actually preferred mopping with a sponge and my hands. I wasn't sure why. I grabbed the big bucket in the corner and rolled up the sleeves of Miller's hoodie I was borrowing. He'd come home and be so surprised with all I'd gotten done.

***

I'd dusted, swept, mopped, and scrubbed until my arms were sore. I'd cleaned everywhere important. The only places I hadn't gotten to were the two spare bedrooms. Miller never exactly told me to make myself feel like I was at home. But I was pretty sure it was implied when I said I was staying for good.

I wiped my sleeve against the glass of the picture flame and placed it on the end of the mantle. The stone fireplace was beautiful, and I was well aware that my cheap picture frame didn't quite belong. But it was my favorite picture of my mom and me. We were dancing around our yellow kitchen, cheesing at the camera. She was so full of life.

The kitchen timer started going off. I stepped away from the picture before I could get emotional. I hurried into the kitchen and opened the oven. Miller's pantry was scarce. But he had plenty of flour and sugar. There were eggs in the fridge too. It had been a really long time since I'd baked something. I'd been trying to cut back on sweets around my uncle because I was worried about his weight. I'd been worried I'd lose him too.

My hand paused around the spatula. It was weird when I was alone. Like the sadness had nowhere to go but right to my heart. If I stayed busy, it was easy to keep my demons at bay. That's probably why I was fond of having two jobs, not zero.

But the smell of fresh cookies made me shake the thought away. Miller would be home any minute. And I wanted him to walk into a clean house with freshly baked cookies.

I pulled out the tray and moved the cookies to a cooling rack.

I turned off the oven and just stood there, fidgeting with my hands. Now that it was after lunch, I was nervous. Did he mean like…right after lunch? Or more like 3 o'clock? Or maybe after lunch meant right before dinner. Would he be back by 5?

God, I was a nervous wreck. And it had nothing to do with not knowing the exact time he was coming back. Yesterday he'd told me he'd stop by the store after work.

The store meant condoms. And condoms meant we'd be having sex.

Maybe I wasn't nervous at all. I think I was just excited. I'd always had a bad time differentiating between the two. I needed to check my makeup again.

I hurried back into the bedroom and walked into the bathroom. I'd put on mascara earlier, just in case he was coming home early. But that was pretty much the only makeup I ever wore. My face was tanned from the sun. And the mascara made my eyes pop.

But I didn't exactly look sexy. I looked down at my outfit. And by that I mean…Miller's outfit. I was wearing one of his sweatshirts and a pair of his sweatpants. All my clothes were ridiculously cold for this weather. But there had to be something sexier than this.

I started rummaging through Miller's drawers. Maybe I could find one of his old dress shirts he used to wear for work. Wearing just that and my underwear was sexy, right? That was a thing girls did in movies. They made it work.

But I couldn't find any of his dress shirts. All I could find was a warm flannel button-up. Surely it looked amazing on him. But the sexy lumberjack vibe wasn't exactly what I was going for. Anything was better than what I was wearing though. This was our first time. It was supposed to be special.

I pulled off the hoodie and sweatpants and put on the flannel shirt. I kept the top unbuttoned and turned to the mirror.

Okay, I don't know what shirts these girls were wearing in movies…but their men must not have been as big as Miller. I was drowning in this thing. *Maybe if I put my hair up…*

I pulled my hair into a high ponytail. *No.* I pulled out a few strands to frame my face. Now I just looked like a messy lumberjack.

I heard the front door open.

Shit.

"Brooklyn! I'm home!"

There wasn't any time to change out of the messy lumberjack getup. It was what it was. I ran out of the room, hopping on the cold floor. I looked ridiculous anyway, so I should have put on a pair of socks…

I slowed down at I reached the living room. I lifted my head and tried to walk out in a sexy strut. But my feet were freezing. And I'm pretty sure it was more of an unsexy hobble.

Miller smiled when he saw me. "What are you wearing?"

Oh God, this wasn't sexy at all. *Improvise.* I leaned against the kitchen counter and popped my hip out. Not that he could tell because I was drowning in his shirt. *I should have just answered the door in my underwear!* Too late now.

"Aren't your feet cold?"

I looked down at my bare feet. "Yes," I said with a laugh. "I'm trying to be sexy but I totally flubbed it. And my feet are so freaking cold."

"Hm." He grabbed me around the waist and lifted me onto the counter so my feet were no longer on the cold floor. "Well, you've succeeded."

I laughed. "Yeah right."

"I had no idea I was coming home to a sexy, frozen lumberjack."

I laughed harder. "I'm so sorry. I totally ruined the mood."

"What mood?"

"The you just bought a huge box of condoms mood?"

The corner of his mouth ticked up. "This morning it seemed like you might like a little tour of the town. I haven't stopped by the store yet. I was hoping you'd come with me." He lifted up a cookie and took a bite. "These are amazing. And it looks awesome in here. Did you clean?"

"Yes. So back to the important thing we were just talking about. You want me to come with you to buy a box of condoms?"

"Unless you want to stay here."

I didn't actually want to purchase condoms. But he'd probably be doing that. And I really did want to go exploring. "No, I'll come."

"How about you go change into something a little less sexy and we can get going."

"I feel like you're making fun of me."

"I'm not." He caught my hip before I could slide off the counter. "If I knew you'd be waiting for me like this I would have stopped by the store first. Trust me."

I leaned forward and placed a kiss on his lips. "You're way too nice to me." I tried to slide off the counter again, but he kept my hips locked in place.

"I'm serious, Brooklyn. Greet me like this again tomorrow and I'll show you how serious I am." He didn't look like he was joking around now.

I swallowed hard. He seriously wanted to go out and about right now? Because I was pretty sure we'd both rather stay in. But...condoms. I really wanted those condoms. "Then I'll dress like this again tomorrow."

This time he let me slide off the counter. I quickly changed into my one pair of jeans and pulled on his hoodie again.

We drove slowly in the snow. But it only took a few minutes to reach the local Main Street. There were still lights streaming down the sidewalks from Christmas. And even though they weren't lit up for the night yet, it still looked festive and quaint.

Miller opened up my door and held his hand out for me. He kept his hand wrapped around mine as we walked down the sidewalk.

"This place is cuter than the pictures," I said.

"It's really creepy that you stalked everything so thoroughly before you bought this place. I'm trying to show you something new and you already know it."

I laughed. "I wanted to make sure you'd be happy."

He looked down at me. "I wasn't happy until you came back."

I smiled up at him.

He stopped in the middle of the sidewalk and kissed me. Without a care in the world that there were other residents of this little town milling about. We were invisible here. Just the way I liked it. I pulled back. "So where are those condoms?"

He laughed. "Come with me." He grabbed my hand and led me past the cutest little shops. There was a bakery with a pink exterior, a toy shop where kids were staring in the windows, a newspaper stand, a little pub. We stopped outside a local convenience store. The bell jingled as we walked in and the person at the register waved to us.

"People here are so friendly," I said. "It's the exact opposite of New York. I love it."

"Just be mindful. A small town means gossip."

"You think the sweet old man at the register is dying to find out our true identities?"

Miller stopped in front of the condoms. "Maybe."

I looked around to make sure no one was near us. "We have to purchase some other random stuff. Not just *these*. It's going to look like we're sex fiends. Talk about small town gossip."

Miller laughed. "We don't need anything else. Now take your pick."

"What? No. You take your pick."

"You're the one that wants them," he said.

I just stared at him. "You don't want to use one?" I whispered at him. "We can barely afford to feed ourselves, let alone a little monster."

He laughed. "A monster?"

"It'll feel like a monster if you accidentally knock me up." I pulled a random box off the shelf. "How about these?"

"They're neon."

"Little Dicky will like them. He's very retro and loves clubbing."

Miller laughed even though the expression on his face was one of pure shock. "What the heck happened to promising not to call me that?" He grabbed the box of neon goodness and put it back on the shelf.

"I promised not to call *you* that. Not *him*." I wiggled my eyebrows as I looked down at his crotch.

"Whatever you want, kid."

I stuck my tongue out at him.

Instead of sticking his tongue out at me, he captured mine in a kiss. His fingers gripped the back of my neck, pulling me closer. It was exactly how I'd been hoping he'd kiss me when he came home earlier. It was the same way he kissed me right before he'd touch me. Like he was desperate for me.

He groaned and pulled back. "Would you just pick out a box already so we can go home?"

I blinked up at him innocently. "What about touring the town?"

"I'd much rather tour you."

His eyes wandered back to my mouth.

I swallowed hard. God, I loved when he looked at me like that. I turned back to the condoms and grabbed a box of very normal looking ones that were on sale.

"Much better choice," he said. "Let's get out of here."

"But we should buy something else so we don't look…"

"Like sex fiends? I'm minutes away from fucking you in this store. That would make it look a little worse, don't you think?"

"You wouldn't dare."

He paused in the aisle, and slowly backed me up until my butt hit one of the shelves. "Do you want to bet?"

Kind of. Not because I thought he wouldn't. But because I thought he might. And I'd really been looking forward to this moment. The last thing we needed was to get arrested though. I ducked under his arm and hurried up to the register.

As I suspected, the old man looked shocked by my purchase. Especially when Miller came up and put his arm around my shoulders. It was like he was trying to embarrass me. Or torture me. Or something. But it wasn't working. Because he'd turned me on so much back in that aisle that all I could think about was getting home.

I grabbed the bag and raced out of the store. I wasn't nervous anymore. Just excited.

CHAPTER 34

Saturday

"You didn't seem nearly as mortified about buying condoms as I thought you would," Miller said.

"Were you trying to mortify me?"

He shrugged as he unlocked the car.

"What does that shrug mean?"

He climbed into the car, ignoring my questions.

I climbed in too. "Seriously, what does that shrug mean?"

"I'm just trying to make sure you're ready for this step."

"And buying condoms without being embarrassed is some kind of test to make sure I'm ready to have sex?"

He didn't respond.

"I'm not a virgin, Miller."

For a second he just looked…surprised. And then he shook his head. "Okay." He turned his attention to the windshield and put the car into drive. He pulled out onto the road without another word.

Wait. He thought I was a virgin? I stared at him as we drove home in silence. I wasn't sure what I was supposed to say to fix this. I wasn't a virgin. I couldn't exactly undo what I'd already done.

Miller pulled the car into park outside our house. But neither of us moved.

"I was engaged," I said. It was the only thing I could think of to say.

"I know."

"Then why are you surprised about this?"

"I'm not."

"You're acting surprised."

"I'm not surprised. I'm pissed." He stepped out of the car and slammed the door.

I scrambled out of the car. "You're not allowed to be pissed at me about this. You knew I was with Matt. You knew…"

"I'm allowed to be upset about whatever I want to be upset about."

"There's nothing to be upset about. I'm sure you've been with plenty of other women and I'm not mad at you."

"I can be mad that you gave your virginity to some rich prick that was undeserving."

"I can't undo what I did. But I'm choosing you now."

"Are you? Because you refuse to talk about what happened with Matt when you went to New York. What were you doing in California? I was sitting here like an idiot for months waiting for you to show up and I have no idea what you were doing."

"Missing you."

He shook his head. "If you really missed me you would have shown up ages ago."

"Miller…"

"I'm going for a walk. I just need a second to cool off." He turned and walked away.

God, I really hated when people walked away from me. I leaned down, picked up a wad of snow, and threw it at his back. "No."

He slowly turned back around. "No?"

"No." I threw another snowball at him, this one hitting his chest.

"You're being very immature right now."

Me? "And you're being a dick."

He lowered his eyebrows.

"I'm sorry I had sex with Matt. But he's the only other person that I've been with. And you don't get to walk away from this conversation."

He walked back over to me. "I'm not walking away. I'm trying to calm down because you won't tell me about all the holes in your story."

"I was trying to figure things out."

"What happened in New York? Why did you go to California?"

Why was he choosing right this second to talk about this again? I looked away from him. "I didn't have sex with Matt, if that's what you're worried about. He was too busy having sex with someone else." I felt tears welling in my eyes. I quickly blinked them away. The last thing I needed was to cry over that boy one more time. "I saw what I needed to see and I left. It's freezing out here. Let's go inside."

"You didn't talk to him?" He caught my hand to stop me.

"No." I pulled my hand out of his grip and ran up the front steps. Yes, I knew I was the one walking away right now. And fine, I was being immature. But I didn't want to cry about this in front of Miller. I let myself inside.

Miller closed the door behind me. "Why didn't you talk to him?"

"He was busy screwing someone new in his pool. It didn't look like he was in the mood for visitors. And it certainly didn't look like he was missing me." *Damn it, I was going to cry.* Stupid Matthew Caldwell always made me cry. I blinked faster.

"I'm sorry." Miller grabbed both sides of my face, wiping his thumbs beneath my tear-stained eyes.

"No you're not."

"Yes I am. I just want you to be happy. I respected your choice back then. And I did my best to respect it while we were at the beach too. I even told you to have hope because Matt thought you were dead."

"I know." I knew that. I didn't even know why we were fighting right now. None of that mattered. "I would have come right to you, but I went to California because I was hurting. It wasn't fair to ask you to wait anymore. But I just needed time."

"Okay. I get that. I just thought…it was driving me crazy not knowing what happened with Matt."

"Nothing. Absolutely nothing. And I'm here now because I can look you right in the eye and tell you that I love you. I'm choosing you. I'm in love with you…"

He silenced me with a kiss. Not one of his normal sweet morning kisses. Or his ravenous kisses. He was kissing me like he was still angry with me. And as much as I loved when he kissed me, I just wanted to fix this.

"I hate when you're mad at me," I said between kisses.

"I'm not mad at you." He pulled back and ran his hand down his face.

"You seem mad."

"I'm not." He turned away from me.

"Miller, please just talk to me. I told you what happened. Now you know. But you still seem upset."

"Because it should have been me. You should have chosen me. I should have been your first time. I should have been all your firsts. I never would have played with your heart. I never would have hurt you."

I swallowed hard. "I know." I did know that. I'd loved Matt. Or at least, I thought I had at the time. But the more time I spent away from him, the less I knew if my feelings for him had been real. How could they have been when his feelings for me had been so fleeting? Each day that passed made me realize it more and more. "I made the wrong choice back in New York. But I'm here now."

I wrapped my hands behind Miller's neck. "And you can't be my first. But you can be my last."

Instead of kissing me passionately, he placed a gentle kiss on my forehead. "I'm not walking away from this conversation. But I need to grab some wood for the fire. It's freezing in here."

"Okay."

I bit my lip as he headed back outside. I knew he said he wasn't walking away from the conversation. But he was literally walking out of the house. The front door closed and I looked down at the bag in my hand. I put the condoms down on the kitchen counter. God, Matt was even ruining my life from hundreds of miles away.

Today was supposed to be perfect. And I'd messed everything up. Of course Miller needed to know what happened with Matt before our relationship went any further. There were holes in my story. He deserved to know all of it.

I sat down on the couch in front of the fireplace with no fire. So…I'd tell him everything.

***

"I know you wanted to see the Pacific Ocean. Was it everything you hoped it would be?" Miller ran his hand up and down my back, making patterns with his fingers.

He'd sat patiently with me the whole time I was talking. Just listening. He really was the best listener.

"No. I hated it."

"Because you didn't have any money? If this is about the money in that account…"

"It's not." I'd told him about working two jobs and barely having enough money to pay rent. But that wasn't why I hated it. I wasn't scared of hard work. "I hated every second of it because you weren't there. I was at a beach but it wasn't *our* beach. It smelled wrong. And I missed waking up to you every morning."

"Hmm."

"Hmm? Did you miss me too?" I looked up at him.

"Yes. I kept myself busy working. But no matter what I did, you'd always pop up in my mind. Like I couldn't get rid of you."

I laughed. "Were you trying to get rid of me?"

"No. But I was worried you wouldn't come back to me."

I swallowed hard. I think in my heart I knew I always would come back to him. I just wanted to be in one piece before I showed up on his doorstep. "I was always going to come back. Although, I was worried I'd be too late."

"I wasn't going anywhere."

Matt had. I pushed the thought away.

Miller cleared his throat. "I know you said you're okay. But you still cry when you talk about him."

"Because I hate him."

Miller laughed. "Maybe. Maybe not. Either way, I think maybe just because you were ready to have sex with Matt, doesn't necessarily mean you're ready to have sex with me."

I looked up at him. "Is this about the size of Little Dicky that goes oddly against his name?"

He laughed. "No. I'll make sure you're properly warmed up for me. I just meant…I don't mind taking things slowly with you."

"It's a little too late for that, don't you think?"

"We could put the brakes on things."

"No thanks."

He laughed. "No thanks?"

"I reject your proposal." I moved so I was straddling him. "In fact, I'd much rather put my foot down on the accelerator."

He reached up and tucked a loose strand of hair behind my ear. "Maybe when we can have a discussion about Matt and you don't cry."

"My heart isn't broken anymore."

"I think it still is, kid."

I didn't want him to be right. I didn't want Matt to be stuck in my head. I was here because I wanted to be. I was choosing Miller. I loved Miller. And yet…I did still cry when I talked about Matt. As much as I wanted to say that my heart was healed, it still hurt sometimes. "I don't want to go back to being just friends."

"Were we ever just friends?"

No. No, we definitely weren't. "I think we should still do hand stuff. Oh and can you keep doing that thing with your mouth?"

He laughed. "That's the opposite of putting the brakes on."

"Miller, you can't expect me to sleep in the same bed with you and not want more now that I know what more feels like."

"I'll sleep on the couch."

Now I really did want to cry.

"Just until you figure things out." He kissed my forehead. "I don't want you to be thinking about Matt when I'm fucking you." The sweet gesture of a kiss on the forehead combined with his naughty words had my heart racing.

God, why had I cried talking about Matt? I could be under Miller right now enjoying my life. Matt was certainly out there enjoying his. Why was he ruining mine? *Matthew freaking Caldwell.*

CHAPTER 35

Wednesday - New Year's Eve

I was trying to respect Miller's wishes, I really was. But the bed was cold without him. And I knew his back was bothering him from sleeping on the couch. When I told him I didn't mind sleeping on the couch he wouldn't hear of it. *Stubborn ass.*

And just like that I was thinking about how good his ass looked in his gray sweatpants. I was a big fan of his gray sweatpants.

Enough was enough. I'd given it three whole days of us being "friends." I didn't want to be friends with him. I wanted to move forward. I wanted to live. I wanted him to love me back.

In the grand scheme of things, I knew that three days wasn't exactly very long. But Miller and I had been toeing over this friendship line for over a year now. And now that we'd crossed the line…I couldn't go back. I didn't want to.

Besides, it was New Year's Eve. I wanted to spend every second of tonight with him. Including sleeping with him. In both senses of the phrase.

My New Year's resolution was to stop letting Matt haunt my thoughts. And the new year was going to start with a bang. Literally.

I stared at my reflection in the mirror. I didn't bring any warm clothes with me, so I was wearing the spring dress I'd almost worn back in California. Before I chickened out and went with jeans on a night out with my coworkers. When I'd dreamed that I was dancing with

Miller instead of some seedy guy at that nightclub. I'd wanted Miller then. And I wanted him now.

I wished I had something shimmery or sparkly or anything a little more New Year's Eve. But this would have to do. Besides, last time I'd put it on, I hated how short it was. This time? My legs were still tanned and toned from my runs on the beach. And it wouldn't be the first time I caught Miller staring at my legs. I wanted him to take one look at me and not be able to remain "just friends." Or whatever we were.

Yes, sometimes thoughts of Matt still came out of nowhere, hitting me like a ton of bricks. But Matt and I had never spent a New Year's Eve together. Miller and I had. Last year he was very professional and we watched the ball drop without kissing, toasting the new year with sparkling apple cider.

This year I hoped he was anything but professional. I wanted a New Year's kiss. Because this year I wasn't making a resolution to find the courage to flee and find Matt. I'd found all the courage I needed. I was here. With Miller. I'd lost so much over the past couple years. I'd lost so much that I never thought I could keep going. But here I was. Exactly where I wanted to be. And despite what Miller thought, I wasn't broken. I wasn't torn in two directions.

My mind was clear. This year, all I wanted was him.

The tires of his car crunched in the snow outside.

My heart started racing as I left the bedroom. Miller had gone out this afternoon to pick up a few ingredients for the lasagna he was making. The sauce was already simmering on the stove. And the extra heat made my summery dress almost bearable in the cold.

I stood in front of the door and waited for him.

I started wringing my hands together. What if he still told me no? What if he pushed me away again? I bit the inside of my lip. What if he secretly loved sleeping on the couch and didn't want to share a bed with me? Hell, what if he didn't even like me here in his house? What if he kicked me out? I was spiraling. But he was taking forever to come inside…

Miller opened the door. He was holding a grocery bag in one hand and was balancing some logs for the fire under his other arm. He closed the door with his elbow and then froze when he saw me standing there.

I wasn't dressed like a frumpy lumberjack today. I'd made sure of that. I didn't care how cold I was. I'd be warm enough as soon as he wrapped his strong arms around me. "Happy New Year's Eve!" I said.

He cleared his throat. "You look beautiful, Brooklyn." His eyes trailed down my legs.

It was like his gaze made me feel on fire. Yeah, I definitely wasn't cold anymore. "Thank you." I had a whole speech planned out. But my mind was as frozen as Miller's feet. "Here, let me take that." I grabbed the grocery bag out of his hand and hurried into the kitchen. *Pull yourself together!* The worst that could happen was that he'd reject me. And then I'd just try again some other day once more time had passed.

I put the remaining ingredients for the lasagna in the fridge. God, I hated wasting time. *Then what the hell are you doing in the kitchen?* I took a deep breath and closed the fridge door.

Miller was standing in front of the fire holding his hands out to warm them by the flames.

I've got this.

I walked back over to him. I had this scene in my head. But I had no idea if it would play out. Either way, I needed to get this off my chest.

"I think that maybe sometimes I'll always cry when I think of Matt. It feels like I lost him. The way I lost my mom and uncle." I swallowed hard.

Miller looked up from the fire.

I couldn't tell what he was thinking. Usually I could read him pretty well, but not today. I took a deep breath. "He thinks I'm dead. And he feels…dead to me too. I don't really know how to explain it." Damn it, this wasn't coming out right. I stared into the fire instead of at Miller's face. "What I'm trying to say is that I would never go back to him. He's as good as dead to me. I was mourning what could have been. And I have no idea why. I'm not a what-could-have-been kind of person."

I glanced at Miller out of the corner of my eye. I could read him now. He looked…sad. Sad for me. But I didn't want his pity. I just wanted him to understand.

I turned to face him. "I'm over Matt. I'm not standing here with a broken heart."

Miller lifted his hand and touched the side of my face. His hands were warm from the fire. But that wasn't the reason why it felt like I was melting into him. "Then why do you look so sad?"

"I'm not sad." I pressed my lips together. "I'm scared."

He moved closer to me. "What are you scared of?"

"Everyone I've ever loved…leaves me."

"Brooklyn." He put his other hand on the side of my face, cradling my head in his palms. "I would never leave you."

"But what if I'm bad luck?"

He smiled down at me. "You're not bad luck, kid."

I rolled my eyes.

He groaned.

I laughed. "What was that noise for?"

"It does something to me when you roll your eyes at me."

I swallowed hard. "Well, good."

He raised his eyebrow. "Good?"

"Yeah good. Because I just told you that I'm not broken." I stared into his eyes. "I'm standing here with a heart that wants you. I'm here because I love you. Because I want you. And you're the only person I'm thinking about. I swear." I swallowed hard and grabbed the condom I'd hidden in my bra. "And I think it's about time we both let ourselves be happy." I placed the condom in his palm.

For a second he just stared at me.

Please, Miller. Want me back. Want me for me. Believe in me.

Then his fist closed around my hand and he backed me up against the stone fireplace. His hand caught my hip, holding me firmly in place.

Fuck.

"You're everything, Brooklyn."

Something about the way he said it made me want to cry. Not everything to *him*. Just…everything.

"I don't know if you're not broken. But if this is what you want, I trust you."

"This is what I want."

His Adam's apple rose and then fell as he stared at me.

"You're who I want, Miller. I want you. I want this. And I don't want to waste another second of us not being an us."

He grabbed my ass and lifted me so that my legs were wrapped around his waist. "Not another second huh?"

I laughed.

He captured my laughter with his kiss.

I grabbed the back of his neck, deepening the kiss. *Finally.* I buried my fingers in his hair. "I hated being just friends with you," I said between kisses.

"I told you we were never just friends." He bit my lower lip.

I moaned.

He pushed my skirt up, brushing his fingers across my clit through the thin fabric of my panties. "All I want to do is fuck you right here."

Finally. "Then do it." *God, please do it.*

"Not today."

Not today? What the actual hell was wrong with him? "But I just told you…" my words died away when he kissed me again. Slower than before.

He pulled me away from the wall and leaned down, placing me on the rug in front of the fireplace. "I'm going to do what I wanted to do when you showed up on Christmas."

I propped myself up on my elbows as I stared up at him. "And what did you want to do to me on Christmas?" He had to be talking about making love to me right? Instead of fucking? That had to be it. And I wanted him to say the words. I needed to hear him say it back.

He didn't say a word as he pulled off his shirt and leaned back over me to capture another kiss.

"I love you," I said, grabbing both sides of his face.

He kissed the side of my jaw instead of responding.

"I love you," I said again just in case he hadn't heard me the first time.

He pushed the dress strap off my shoulder and placed a kiss in the empty spot.

He couldn't make love to me without actually saying the words first. This was ridiculous. "Why won't you say it back?"

"Say what back?" he asked as he slid my dress up my hips.

"I've told you I loved you dozens of times and you've never said it back."

The corner of his mouth ticked up as he looked down up at me. "Of course I've said it back."

"No. You haven't."

"I haven't?"

I laughed. "No."

He slowly pulled my panties down my thighs and off my legs. And then he leaned down and kissed the inside of my shin.

God, he was distracting me again.

"I'm pretty sure I've said it," he said, slowly kissing up my leg.

He was exasperating. "I swear you haven't."

"I guess I should fix that then." He kissed the inside of my thigh and locked eyes with me. "I love you."

I swallowed hard. His gaze was so intense that I could barely breathe.

He kissed farther up my thigh. "I love you." He kissed me higher still. "I love you." His eyes stayed trained on mine the whole time. And I'd never seen anything sexier in my whole life.

"I love you." He placed a kiss on my hipbone as he pushed my dress up higher. "I love you." He kissed my ribcage.

I pulled my dress the rest of the way off as he un-hooked my bra. "I love you." His tongue swirled around my nipple.

Jesus. I grabbed the back of his head. I wasn't sure what was hotter. Him saying he loved me or what he was doing to me...*God.* He tugged on my nipple with his teeth.

"I love you," he said and kissed my clavicle, moving slowly over top of me until we were eye level. "I'm madly in love with you. And I have been for a really long time. You're sure I never told you?"

I laughed. "No, you hadn't."

He ran the tip of his nose down the length of mine. "I love you, Brooklyn."

"I love you too." I wasn't sure how he got me from laughing one minute to almost crying the next. "So much. And I swear if you tease me anymore I'm going to explode."

I watched him slowly rip open the foil and slide the condom over his cock.

He leaned over top of me, pausing instead of sliding into me. "You have no idea how many times I've dreamed of you looking up at me like this."

He didn't have to explain. I was pretty sure there were stars in my eyes whenever I looked at him. And I'd been dreaming of this moment too. I couldn't even count how many times I woke up panting in California after dreaming of him.

"I love you." He shifted forward, slowly sliding into me. Inch by sweet inch.

I'd almost forgotten how good this felt. How had I ever believed that I could just live the rest of my life without being loved again? It felt really fucking amazing to be loved. I'd barely remembered what it was like.

Miller's kiss was possessive. His tongue somehow mimicking what he was doing inside of me. It was like his mouth was fucking me as his body made love to me. Like he needed to show how crazy he was about me while showing how much he loved me at the same time. He was showing way more restraint than me.

As if he knew what I was thinking, he thrust into me harder.

Fuck. I raked my fingers through his hair. I loved his hair short. But it was really nice having something to grab onto as he picked up his pace.

He hitched my leg up, changing the angle and I moaned.

"God I love that sound." He moved faster. Thrusting into me harder.

If this was how Miller made love, I couldn't wait to see what his definition of fucking was. My fingers ran down the muscles of his strong back, pulling him closer.

I was used to him smelling like sunshine and salty water. And before that like some expensive cologne. But I preferred this smell most. He smelled like snowflakes and a wood-burning fire. He smelled like he was mine.

He buried his face between my tits, kissing them the same way he'd kissed my lips. Like he was devouring every inch of me.

All mine.

One of his hands left my waist and his thumb found my clit.

"Miller," I moaned. "I'm gonna…"

And he squeezed it. Way harder than I thought he would.

My fingers dug into the skin of his back as I started to pulse around him.

"Fuck," he groaned. He rode out his release with my own. Until we were both still, panting, staring at each other.

But the look on his face wasn't what I was expecting. He didn't look sated and relaxed. He looked…devastatingly sad. He slowly pulled out of me.

His eyes searched mine. "Did I hurt you?"

"What? No. That was perfect."

He was quiet for a moment. "Then why are you're crying?"

I reached up and felt the wetness on my cheeks. "I…" I hadn't realized I had been. "I don't know. I feel…overwhelmed."

He lowered his eyebrows.

"In a good way. You're overwhelming. I feel…amazing." I turned to the fire burning beside us. "Like I can feel everything more. The fire seems warmer. And the carpet softer." I turned back to him. "I feel really, overwhelmingly…loved."

He pulled me closer and I rested my head on his chest.

I listened to his steady heartbeat. It had been a really long time since I'd felt this connected to someone. I traced Miller's abs with my index finger as I tried to blink away the rest of my tears.

I did feel overwhelmingly loved.

But there was a small piece of me that felt sad. A small piece that I didn't want to acknowledge. A small piece that I needed to let go of. Matt had taken this first. Not taken. I'd given it to him willingly. But I'd given it to him thinking he'd also be my last.

I closed my eyes and breathed in Miller's familiar smell. Maybe he was more right than I wanted to admit. Maybe I was still broken. Maybe I'd always be broken.

For the past year I thought my future was Matt. He'd wanted to give me the whole world. But the more distance there was between us, the more I realized he meant *his* world. And I didn't want his world. I never had.

I wanted to be snuggled up on a winter's night in a cozy lake house. I'd meant what I'd said to Miller. It was like I was in mourning for a love I'd lost. A love that was dead. I no longer loved Matt. And I hated that I was thinking about him right now while my limbs were tangled with Miller's.

I lifted my head and stared down at him. "Thank you for being so patient with me. I know I'm a mess."

He reached out and lightly brushed my remaining tears away with his thumbs. "You're worth waiting for, Brooklyn."

I swallowed hard. Miller had waited for me. Matt hadn't. And I was pretty sure it was as simple as that. I was choosing to be with a man who thought I was worth waiting for. I'd been searching for love in all the wrong places. When it had been right beside me the whole time.

I ran my fingers down the side of his neck. His skin was softer than I imagined it would be. Everything about him was so much more than I expected. "I'm sorry it took me so long to find my way back to you."

"I'm just glad you came back."

I lifted my leg around his waist and moved so that I was straddling him. "Happy New Year's Eve."

His hands settled on my hips. "It's going to be a good year."

"Oh yeah?" I smiled down at him.

"Yeah."

I laughed as he flipped us, my back hitting the soft carpet. I just knew that we were going to start the new year with a big bang. Or a whole bunch of bangs. God, I couldn't wait for him to be inside of me again.

CHAPTER 36

Wednesday

Miller popped open the bottle of what he claimed was super cheap champagne. But I didn't care. I just cared that we were drinking it together.

He handed me a mug full of it. Somehow this was even better than a champagne flute. I laughed as he lifted up his mug for a toast.

"To us," he said. "And to the best year ever."

I smiled. "I couldn't have said it better myself." I tapped my mug against his and took a sip. The chill of the champagne made me shiver.

Miller cleared his throat. "I need to show you something. But I need you to promise not to be upset."

I lowered my mug. "Is it something bad?"

"No. I…well…it's good. I think. Just come with me."

That somehow sounded very not good. But I took his hand when he offered me his. He pulled me to my feet and down the hall. He opened one of the spare bedroom doors that I hadn't cleaned the other day. I expected it to be empty. But it was full of boxes.

"What is all this stuff?" I asked and looked up at him.

Miller dropped my hand and scratched the back of his neck. "Just some of your old things."

"My things?" *What?* When he didn't offer any more information I stepped into the room and opened one of the unmarked boxes.

There were some of the clothes I'd gotten from my dad for Christmas last year. I hadn't wanted them then. But this year I was actually happy to see them. The warm sweaters and leggings and fuzzy socks were calling to me now. I was still wearing my summery dress and really didn't have anything weather-appropriate here. Well, until now.

But…why were they here? I looked over my shoulder at Miller. Had he gone back to the beach house? I was happy this stuff was here since we weren't going to dip into my dad's money. But…really…why was this stuff here?

Miller looked very guilty.

I swallowed hard. And I was afraid it was so much worse than him going back to the beach house. "You've talked to my dad?"

"What? No." He finally stepped into the room. "Of course not."

"Then why do you have all this stuff?" I looked around at the other boxes. I opened one and it had some of Miller's nice suits in it. There was even a winter coat. I lifted it up. He was wearing a threadbare jacket to work every day. "What the hell?"

"I went back."

My heart was racing fast. "Okay." I didn't know what else to say. So…my dad had called him or something? What the heck was going on?

He stepped farther into the room and took the coat out of my hand. He tossed it back in the box and sighed. "I can't afford to buy you new clothes right now. I'm working my way up…but I…" his voice trailed off. "I don't want you to be cold."

"That does not answer my question. Did you go back to talk to my dad?"

"No." He took a deep breath, his exhale even slower. "When you gave me those keys and a new identity and told me to leave." He shook his head. "I drove for about fifteen minutes before I realized I was being stupid and turned the car around."

I just stared at him.

"I didn't want to leave you. I went back. For you."

Oh, Miller.

"But you were gone." He cleared his throat. "I was too late. But I thought maybe when you showed up at the lake house that you might want all your stuff. If you showed up. And your father wasn't going to be down until the weekend. So I got all the rest of it for you."

"All of it?" I looked around at the boxes. That must have taken him forever.

"Your clothes. Your computer. I made sure there wasn't any tracking on it. All of it. I should have told you sooner but…I was kind of embarrassed."

"Because you went back for me?" I blinked away the tears in my eyes. "I don't think that's embarrassing. I think that's the most romantic thing I've ever heard." And he must have only been a few minutes too late. We must have just missed each other.

"I never should have left you alone. I should have offered to drive you wherever you wanted to go. I just…I missed you so damn much…"

I grabbed both sides of his face and kissed him. He knew I missed him. I'd told him so many times. I felt his smile against my lips.

"Does that mean you forgive me?" he asked.

I laughed. "Forgive you? There's nothing to forgive. I'm actually really happy these clothes are here." I walked back over to the boxes and lifted up a soft white sweater that I'd never worn before. I pulled it over my dress, not caring about how silly I looked. *So much better.* A pair of big fuzzy socks were next, but as soon as I pulled them on it was way too ridiculous. I needed pants. I quickly changed out of my dress so that I was wearing my sweater, leggings, and the cute fuzzy socks. I instantly felt warmer.

Miller was smiling at me. I wasn't sure if it was because of the fuzzy socks looking adorable or because of the mini-striptease. Probably the latter.

I put my hand on my hip. "But I also can't afford to buy you warmer clothes and I don't want you to be cold either."

He lowered his eyebrows. "I'm not wearing that stuff."

"Why not?"

"Because I bought it with his money."

I stared at him. "I hate to break it to you Miller, but this house was bought with my dad's money too."

"Technically it was a gift from you…"

"Technically you're the most stubborn person I've ever met." I wrapped my arms behind his neck. "Wear the clothes. Or I'm dipping into the money in our account."

"You wouldn't." It was probably supposed to be threatening but he was smiling now.

"I would. So wear the clothes. Besides, you earned that money. I was a terribly difficult assignment."

He laughed. "No. You were easy. I mean…I got you exactly where I wanted you."

I couldn't help but laugh. "So it was your plan all along for us to run away together?" I gently traced the scar beneath his eye. There was no way either of us could have planned winding up here together. But I was so happy it happened.

"It was a very devious plan."

"Sure." I was smiling so hard it hurt.

He pulled me closer, his arms wrapping around me. "What's your New Year's resolution?" he asked.

I stared into his eyes. "To live in the moment."

He smiled.

"What about you?"

He tucked a loose strand of hair behind my ear. "To make sure you know each and every day that you made the right choice."

I wasn't sure if it was because of the cozy sweater or his words, but my heart felt warm and fuzzy. Maybe it was the champagne bubbles in my system. "Oh, I made the right choice."

He leaned down to kiss me but I pulled away.

"Did you hear that? I asked.

"Hear what?"

"They're counting down!" I grabbed his hand and pulled him out into the hallway.

We laughed as we ran into the family room to watch the ball drop in Times Square.

Miller held me tight as the announcer counted down.

"Ten. Nine. Eight."

My heart was hammering in my chest.

"Seven. Six."

I meant what I'd told Miller. I was going to start living in the moment.

"Five. Four."

Which meant letting go of my past. For real.

"Three. Two."

The pain of losing my mom. My uncle. Matt. I wasn't meant to live broken. I was meant to have a full happy life. Just like they all had. And if mine was cut short too? I didn't want to regret not living enough of it.

"One."

I looked up at Miller. "Happy New Year!"

"Happy New Year, kid." He picked me up and twirled me around.

I laughed and wrapped my legs around his waist to prevent him from accidentally tossing me.

His hands slid to my ass as we sealed the New Year with a kiss.

It was a promise of forever.

And I kept my promises to people that kept theirs.

CHAPTER 37

5 Months Later - Saturday

Miller looked like a Greek God in his yellow swim trunks. He swore they were ridiculous. I swore I loved them. So he wore them even though he didn't like them. For me.

I stood on my tiptoes like I was about to kiss him. But instead I stopped a fraction of an inch from his lips. "Race you to the water," I whispered and then started running for it.

I laughed as Miller chased me down the dock.

He definitely could have caught up to me. But I think he was curious if I'd actually go in. He'd hung out with rich snobs in the city too. Which meant girls who didn't want to get their hair wet. But I wasn't the kind of girl to lounge around tanning my skin on a hot summer's day. Had he forgotten our last summer together? It felt like a lifetime ago that we'd been locked up in that beach house.

It was strange. We were still stuck in hiding. But I'd never felt more free. More alive.

"Cannonball!" I yelled when I reached the end of the dock. I jumped, pulling my knees in and made the biggest splash I could.

When I came up for air, I just caught him mimicking me. But he made a much bigger splash.

I was laughing when he came up and grabbed me around the waist.

"You were right," I said. "The water is freezing."

"I tried to warn you."

I wrapped my legs around his waist. "I don't think I've ever been this happy. Cold water and all."

"Me either."

"You saved me." I dropped my forehead to his.

"You scared me half to death that day you fell through the ice."

Oh. Right. "Yeah, that. But also just…in general." I owed him everything.

He stared into my eyes. "What do you mean?"

"You were right. I think I was still a little broken when I showed up on Christmas. But now? I wake up smiling every morning. Because of you." I watched his perfect smile spread across his face. "I really can't imagine being any happier."

"Well, I actually have some news."

"Does that mean good or bad news? Like…I'm about to be happier? Or less happy?"

He laughed. "Happier I hope."

"Okay. Hit me with it."

"Remember that batch of cookies you made last week?"

"Mhm."

"I took a dozen of them into the restaurant. The owner was so impressed that she wants to hire you to do all our desserts. The current dessert menu was very limited. So you can pretty much make whatever you want."

"Are you serious?"

"Yeah. You can make everything here. And then just sell them to her."

"That's amazing!"

"Yeah?"

"Of course!" I placed a big kiss against his lips.

"I was a little worried that you were unhappy when we were talking about you getting a job over the summer a few weeks ago. I thought this could be a compromise."

It was true. We'd had a little tiff about that. But he was right. It was safer the less I left home. And he'd gotten a raise a couple months ago. We were doing okay. I was a little restless with the idea of having the whole summer off though. I'd ended up taking online classes instead of going right for my GED. It wasn't exactly a normal high school experience. But it was as normal as I could get. And I didn't want to miss out on normal things just because I'd chosen an abnormal path.

School took up a lot of my time during the winter and spring. But now I was a little bored. I'd started a garden out back but apparently I was bad with plants. I'd read online that you could sing to them and Miller had made fun of me on more than one occasion when he caught me signing to the dying tomato plants.

"This is going to be perfect," I said. "I can bake whatever I want all day? That sounds like my dream job."

He smiled at me. "It's definitely a dream for me. I love your cookies."

I kissed the tip of his nose. "I love you."

His hands slid to my ass. "I love you."

"This is perfect. You're perfect." I leaned forward and rested my head on his shoulder.

For a long time we just stood in the water like that. Wrapped up in each other. The sun beating down on my shoulders made the chill from the water disappear. Miller's hot breath on the side of my neck helped too.

"You know," Miller said. "There is one good thing about these hideous swim trunks."

"Just one good thing? You know you shouldn't say such hateful things about a gift."

"I'm trying to tell you the benefits."

I laughed. "And what are the benefits?"

"They have pockets."

"Oh, very nice." I made a mental note that Miller was a fan of pockets. I learned something new about him every day. I smiled down at him.

"It's more what's in the pocket that's nice."

I laughed as I reached down and put my hand in his pocket. *Oh my.* "There is something very hard in your pocket, good sir."

He laughed. "Other pocket."

"I kind of like this one." I wrapped my hand around his length. I really liked the surprise in this pocket.

"Other pocket," he whispered into my ear.

I reluctantly reached into the pocket on his left side instead. "There's nothing in there," I whispered back.

He laughed. "Sorry, the other pocket."

"Geez, how many pockets are there?"

"I told you these swim trunks were ridiculous."

I laughed.

"But I meant my back pocket."

"Miller are you trying to make me grab your butt? All you had to do was ask." I slid my hand into his back pocket and felt the foil packet. *Oh.* I pulled it out. "You thought ahead. I was just thinking about how much more fun this would be if you were inside of me."

"Were you?"

"Always."

He put his hand on the side of my face. "You're insatiable."

"No. Just a bored housewife." As soon as the words left my mouth I flushed. "I mean…house person. Just like a person who stays in a house. A woman in a house."

"Right." The corner of his mouth ticked up.

"Stop it."

"Stop what?"

"Internally laughing at me." I unwound my legs from around his waist and tried to swim away.

But he caught my ankle, pulling me back. My head dipped under water. When I broke the water's surface I dunked him back.

And then somehow we started a splashing fight. I was totally winning until he cheated and dunked me again. I tried to swim away again but he caught me around the waist. "Miller!" I screamed.

He pulled me to his chest.

I was completely out of breath. And so was he, his chest rising and falling. And suddenly all I could think about was him fucking me. I buried my fingers into his long hair and kissed him.

He kissed me back, frantically pushing down my bikini bottoms.

He didn't warm me up. But he also knew I didn't need him to. I had a bad habit of being soaked as soon as he kissed me. He thrust inside of me hard.

Fuck. I gripped the back of his neck.

He reached up, pushing the fabric of my bikini top out of the way as he palmed my breast. And somehow pulled me closer still, guiding my hips up and down his length.

The water splashed around us as he thrust into me harder. Faster.

God.

His fingers dug into the skin of my ass. "I loved the sound of that," he groaned.

For a second I didn't know what he was talking about. The splashing water? The birds cawing in the distance? But I had a feeling he meant the housewife thing. My heart started racing even faster. I didn't know how that made me feel. Mostly because I couldn't think straight when he...*oh God.*

"One day I'll make you my wife," Miller said.

I came at his words. I knew they were full of love. But they were also so damn hot. Because to me…they were forbidden. My stomach twisted into knots as I came down from my high.

I'd promised someone else my hand. It was one of those moments that hit me like a ton of bricks. I pulled Miller closer, burying my face in the side of his neck. My stomach twisted further into knots. Because I wanted to tell him I liked the sound of it too. Because I did like the sound of it.

But then I heard Matt's words echoing around me. *"Liar."*

"I love you," I whispered against Miller's wet skin. "I love you so much that sometimes it feels like it hurts."

He just held me. I think we both knew what I was thinking. Miller was always there to hold me when I was sad. Or happy. He was always there. He was my person. Why did happiness have to be so painful?

I heard Matt's words again. *"Liar."*

CHAPTER 38

1 Year Later - Sunday

I opened up the back door. "Miller, Miller come here!" The screen door banged shut as I ran back down the stairs.

"Is everything okay?" he called.

I felt bad about the alarm in his voice. I hadn't meant to scare him. But this was a very momentous occasion.

"Look!" I pointed to the first cherry tomato in my garden. It was green and tiny and barely really anything at all yet. But it was there. I'd done tons of research over the winter. I'd finally done it. I dropped to my knees in front of the elevated planter Miller had built me and squinted at the little tomato plant. "Look." I pointed to it.

He squatted down beside me. "What exactly am I looking at?"

"A future tomato." I gently touched the side of the little green circle. "We can make a lasagna with fresh tomatoes from the garden in a few weeks."

"How much do you want to bet?"

I lightly shoved his shoulder. "Don't talk to him like that. He needs support in order to grow." I started humming to my plant.

"You've completely lost it, kid."

"They like music."

"We've been over this. I'm pretty sure that's houseplants."

"Definitely not. It's all plants." *I think*. Honestly I wasn't even sure anymore. We'd had this discussion several times and I always stayed firm on my side. I quickly shook my head instead of admitting that I wasn't sure. "No, Henry loves music."

"You named it?"

"He's my first healthy plant."

"Don't tomato plants have to be replanted every year?"

"That's not the point. The point is that I'm going to fill all these planters you build with fresh veggies and herbs and everything we can possibly imagine. It's going to be amazing." I looked over at the other planters that were very much empty despite the seeds I'd planted. It was a work in progress. I'd spent hours out here trying to grow things the past couple years. But it was never a waste of time. Because I got to enjoy the view of the lake the whole time. Our backyard was beautiful.

"That does sound amazing," Miller said.

"So you'll sing to it?"

Miller laughed but didn't reply.

I always begged him to sing. We danced to music all the time but I'd never once heard him sing. Unless you counted him talk-singing me happy birthday every year. I most certainly did not count that. He swore he had a terrible singing voice. But I secretly thought that maybe his voice was as beautiful as the rest of him. And that he was keeping it hidden for no good reason at all.

"I can do you one better," he said.

I shook my head. "I doubt that."

"Close your eyes."

"You know I don't like surprises."

Miller laughed. "And like I always say…it's a good surprise. I'm not going to steal your other kidney."

I couldn't help but laugh. "Okay…" I reluctantly closed my eyes.

I heard his feet retreating. It was tempting to sneak a peek but I somehow managed to keep my eyes shut tight.

Music started lightly playing around me and then I felt Miller's hands on mine, pulling me to my feet.

"You can open your eyes," he whispered in my ear.

I slowly opened my eyes. Miller lightly touched the bottom of my chin, lifting my eyes to the trees above us. The whole sky was lit up with lights. "Oh my God." I twirled in a circle staring up at the fairy lights he'd strung between the huge trees in our backyard, extending all the way down to the dock. And the music? I looked over at the speaker on the side of the house. I wasn't sure how I hadn't noticed it before. But I'd been very distracted by my beautiful tomato.

"Congratulations on graduating," he said. "I know we couldn't do the whole cap and gown thing. I hope this makes up for it."

Was he kidding? This was so much better than walking across some dumb stage. I smiled up at him. "I can't believe you did all this."

"Do you like it?"

"I love it. Henry will like it too. The music. And extra light and…everything." I felt tears welling in my eyes. This was the most beautiful present I'd ever received. Although, that Christmas morning when he'd surprised me was at the top of the list too. "Thank you."

"Of course."

I blinked my tears away. He refused to sing. But he'd made it so we could play my plants music. And the lights? I looked back up at the sky again as he pulled me in close. We started swaying to the music. Usually I was very distracted by Miller's face but tonight I couldn't help looking up at the sky. It was like we were dancing in the stars.

I laughed as he dipped me and then pulled me in close again.

His eyes locked with mine as we swayed to the music. "There's one more thing," he said.

"What?" How could he have possibly gotten me something else? This was so perfect... My train of thought quickly stopped when Miller dropped to his knee.

"Brooklyn. You've turned my world upside down. In the best way possible. I never imagined when we first met that this would have happened. I tried to fight it. But I think you and I were written in the stars." He glanced up for a second.

I knew he was looking at the lights above us. The ones he must have spent hours setting up. Just for this occasion. Because he thought our love was written in the stars. He reached into his pocket and pulled out a ring box.

I started crying. "Miller..."

"I love you. With all my heart. Will you do me the honor of being my wife?" He opened up the ring box.

It wasn't anything like the ring Matt gave me. This one was simple. Just a thin elegant gold band with a small single diamond in the middle. It was classic. It was...it was perfect. And yet... "I can't." I took a step back from him. "I can't." It felt like I was choking. I pictured Matt's face when he'd fake proposed with a hotdog. I pictured being sprawled in the sheets with him as we talked about getting married. I pictured joking with him when I said he'd be my first husband. And he promised he'd be my *only* husband. I pictured the wedding we were planning. I pictured the future I'd imagined with him. With kids and our friends and... "I can't."

I took another step back. I wanted to turn around and run. I wanted to run as fast and as far as I could. I wanted to run away from the pain in my chest. I took another step back.

Miller stood up and put his hands on my shoulders. "Okay. That's…that's fine. You don't have to say yes. That's why it's a question." He smiled but there was so much pain in his eyes.

I dropped my face into my hands. What was I doing? Why did I want to suddenly run away from the one person I had? The one person who loved me? The one person who actually cared whether I was alive or dead? The one person who cared if I smiled and laughed every day? Miller had given me his whole heart. And I'd only given him fragments of mine. All I had to offer him were the pieces of my heart that weren't broken.

"I'm sorry," I choked.

"It's okay." He pulled me into his chest, running his hand soothingly up and down my back. "You're not ready. It's okay, Brooklyn."

But that wasn't the truth. Nothing about this was okay. And it had nothing to do with me not being ready. I was ready. I loved Miller. I was head over heels in love with that man. But I'd made a promise to Matt. Yes, I'd joked around with him about being my first husband. But I'd meant my first and only. How could I possibly accept this proposal?

But that was the whole problem…I was upset because I did want to accept. I held Miller tighter, letting my tears stain the front of his shirt.

"It's okay," Miller said again, more believably this time. "I'm happy. Right here, right now. With you. I can't imagine being any happier. I shouldn't have tried to change anything…"

"No." I took a step back from him again. Yes, I'd made promises to Matt. But I'd also promised myself to put those demons to rest. I promised myself to live in the moment. To let my past go. There were tears in my eyes again as I looked up at Miller's face.

I reached out and gently traced the scar under his eye with my index finger. I stared at the hurt in his eyes. We were an us. It was us against my dad. Us against Isabella. Us against the whole world. I just needed more time. I was trying so hard to live in the present. And being terrified of the future was the exact opposite of that. I'd be ready soon. I would be. Just not yet. I needed just a little more time. "I'm not ready to get married."

"That's okay. I'm sorry, Brooklyn. I just…"

"But I want this."

"What?"

I reached into his pocket and grabbed the ring box. "I want this. I want to be your fiancée. Do it again and this time I won't mess it up." I pushed the ring box into his chest.

He laughed. But he didn't protest at all. He got back down on one knee. "Brooklyn, one day I want to marry you. I want you to be my wife. But in the meantime, I'm promising you forever. Will you marry me one day, when you're ready? Will you be my fiancée?"

"Yes." This time my tears were happy ones. This felt less scary. This was a promise. But it gave me time.

He slid the ring onto my finger. And even though it was lighter than the one Matt had given me, it felt heavier. More important. More…everything.

This ring meant I was living. It meant I'd found love again. It meant I wasn't broken.

Miller lifted me in his arms, twirling us around.

I laughed and looked up at the stars, trying hard not to start crying again.

Because as happy as I was…this ring also meant that one day soon I'd be exactly what Matt had called me. I hadn't given Miller any new firsts yet. But when I walked down the aisle with him? I'd be exactly what Matt called me. His last words to me. *Liar.*

I closed my eyes and held Miller tight. Because I didn't care if I was a liar or not. All I cared about was that I was happy. Just like Miller had said. I was happy. Right here right now. With him. I couldn't imagine being any happier.

He set me down on my feet again and I looked up at the fairy lights. Maybe it was always me and Miller written in the stars. I was supposed to have loved and lost all along in order to find this love. A great love.

"Just tell me when you're ready," Miller said as we started swaying to the music again. "Whenever you're ready, I'll be here." His lips dropped to my neck.

He was the world's most patient man. I looped my hand behind his neck, guiding his lips to mine. I kissed him like I'd just said yes to his first proposal. I kissed him like I was ready to marry him. Because in my heart…I was. It was my head that was all messed up.

"I love you," I whispered against his lips.

"Be careful, Henry over there is getting jealous." He nodded toward my tomato plant.

I laughed. I could see the reflection of the lights in Miller's eyes. "I'll be ready soon." I searched his face. He looked happy now. The sadness in his eyes gone. I wanted to spend the rest of my life making him as happy as he made me. "I promise," I said. I didn't care that I'd be a liar soon. I'd rather lie a million times to Matt than a single time to Miller.

CHAPTER 39

1 Year Later - Friday

The fall air was crisp, but the sweat dripping down my back made it feel more like summer. I picked up my pace, the leaves crunching under my feet.

"You're trying to kill me," Miller said as he jogged beside me. "How many laps have we done?" Despite his complaining, he didn't even sound out of breath.

I'd figured out that the circumference of the little lake behind our house was a little over a mile. Over the past few years we'd naturally worn down a path around the lake with our runs. The weeds and grass turning into a dirt path that wound around the whole thing. This was one of the reasons I'd bought this property. The house itself was modest, although it had all the nicest features and updates. It was the land I loved.

I smiled over at Miller as he wiped a bead of sweat off his brow. "Four laps."

"How many are you running today?"

"As many as it takes until my legs are sore."

He groaned.

"You don't have to come with me you know."

He gave me a sideways glance. Because we both know it was better if he did come. A few weeks ago I thought I saw someone watching me in the woods. I'd been so spooked that I'd brought Miller back to the spot I'd seen him. I was worried my father had found us. That one of his men was watching our every move. But no one had been there. Thinking about it still made me shiver.

Ever since that day, I'd been having recurring night-mares of Isabella showing up here. And killing me. I pictured her hands wrapped around my throat. Or her stabbing a knife into my chest. I woke up most nights drenched in sweat, with an image of Isabella's cruel smile etched into my mind. I tried to push the images out of my head. They plagued my sleep enough. I didn't need to think about them when I was awake.

We ran in silence.

Miller seemed so comfortable in silence. But whenever he was stoically quiet, it made my mind race. Was he think-ing about getting married? I hadn't brought it up in months. I wanted to be able to say "I do" without a single thought of Matt clouding that day. I wanted to just be happy. I was close. I knew I was. But I'd always regret the day not just being about us if I rushed it. I owed that to Miller. And I'd told him as much.

As we started on our sixth lap, Miller caught me around the waist, almost knocking us both over. But he managed to lift me over his shoulder. "Nope," he said.

"What are you doing?"

He tossed me into the water.

I screamed at the top of my lungs as the cold water surrounded me.

"There's plenty more ways to get a good workout," he said, pulling me close.

"Oh yeah?" I kissed the side of his neck. I loved when Miller's skin was salty from a good workout. It reminded me of the beach house and the salty smell of the sea air.

But as he slipped inside of me, I remembered just how much better the lake was than the ocean. We had this whole place to ourselves. And could do whatever we want-ed wherever we wanted.

I looked over at the edge of the woods and for just a second I thought I saw someone.

Miller groaned as my body tensed.

I blinked and whatever I had seen or hadn't seen was gone. I closed my eyes tight and held Miller close. My head was playing tricks on me. I was safe. My lips glided across Miller's sweaty skin. I was happy. The taste of salt made me smile. I was whole.

Miller thrust inside of me harder.

God, I was so fucking whole.

CHAPTER 40

2 Years Later - Wednesday

I sat up in bed, clutching my throat. Isabella had been right there. Standing over my bed. Her hands wrapped tightly around my neck. I took another deep breath.

It was just a dream.

I tried to take another deep breath, the sweat dripping down the back of my neck.

No matter what I did over the years, the dreams wouldn't go away.

If anything they got worse. More frequent. I'd had the same dream every night this week. And I knew why. I thought I'd seen someone in the woods again. A woman this time. A woman with brunette hair.

I knew what Miller thought. That isolation was leading to paranoia. I looked down at him sleeping. He looked so peaceful when he slept. Not a single nightmare plagued his slumber.

He thought we were safe. We had been for years. There was no reason Isabella would come now. But…what if she was coming? Or what if she was already here? Or maybe she sent one of her minions to off me?

I swallowed hard. *It was just a dream.* But it was easy to be paranoid. Before we left the beach house, we were on lockdown because my dad swore Isabella thought I was alive. What if he never swayed her opinion? What if she'd been looking for me the whole time? I remembered how easily she'd killed her own dog. The way she so easily dispensed death haunted me. Everything about her haunted me.

It was just a dream. Miller was here with me. I was safe. I leaned over and kissed Miller's temple.

He groaned in his sleep.

I snuggled back into his side and closed my eyes.

But then I heard a noise from outside. I sat up with a start. And this time it wasn't just some nightmare in my head. Because Miller sat up too.

I grabbed his arm. "Did you…"

Miller put his hand over my mouth. "Shh," he whispered.

We were both quiet for a moment as we listened and heard another branch snap.

Miller lowered his mouth to my ear. "Grab the go bags." And then his hand was off me and he was climbing out of the bed. I was completely frozen. But he'd sprung into action. He opened up the closet and put in the code for the safe. I watched him pull out his handgun.

I scrambled out of bed to follow him. He'd made us pack go bags years ago, that first time I freaked out about the man in the woods. Just in case we had to leave at a moment's notice.

Just in case. Miller always seemed so calm. But I knew he must worry too. Or else there would be no need for *just in case.*

I heard another branch snap and put my hand over my mouth so I wouldn't scream. *Fucking hell, who's out there?*

I grabbed the two backpacks I kept in the closet and shoved my feet into my sneakers even though Miller was still in his boxers. If we were making a run for it, it was good I had all the stuff in the backpacks. But I knew he was more focused on what was outside than if we were actually leaving. I ran after Miller as he left the bedroom.

We crept down the hallway slowly and Miller put his hand back to stop me as he peered into the great room.

Miller turned back to me and put his finger up to his lips to remind me to stay quiet. I didn't need reminding. All I could hear was my own heartbeat in my ears. Panic rising in my chest.

I knew what it meant if there were people out there in the woods watching us. Even if Miller didn't want to believe it. Someone knew we were here. Surveilling us. Watching our every move. I could see Isabella waiting. Plotting. Figuring out the perfect way for vengeance. The best way to torture me.

"Stay here," Miller whispered.

"But…"

He put his hand on my shoulder and squeezed it. And then he left me standing alone in the hallway before I had a chance to figure out what to do. It had been years since my last panic attack. I would have thought being on the run from my dad would have made them more frequent. But Miller had a way of making me feel protected. He always had. But as soon as he left me? It was like the panic had wound its way around my chest, spreading up into my throat. I couldn't breathe.

I put my hand on the wall trying to steady myself. If someone was out there…how were we going to make a run for it?

And what if I'd been alone? We only had one car. It was like I was just sitting here. The perfect bait. Waiting. Always waiting for something to go terribly wrong.

I watched in horror as Miller lifted his gun in front of the back door.

That meant someone was on the other side. It meant he'd seen something. It meant we'd been found.

I felt my back sliding down the wall as my legs gave out. As my lungs refused to inflate with air.

The back door opened and I waited for the sound of gunshots. I tried to push myself back up, but I couldn't. Everything was quiet, except for my own heart beating. Louder and louder. I grabbed my throat as it felt like my windpipes were collapsing.

But then I heard the most beautiful sound in the world. Miller's laughter. It echoed around me, making my heart slow down. Making my lungs fill up. Making my body stop shaking.

"It's just a deer," he said as he crouched down next to me. "It's okay." He pulled me to my feet and into his arms, making all the tension and fear evaporate from my limbs. "We're okay. We're safe."

I sobbed into his chest.

"Take a deep breath, Brooklyn." He ran his hand up and down my back. "In and out. Slowly."

I listened to his words as my heart slowly stopped racing.

"We're okay."

I held on to him like he was my life raft. God, I didn't know what I'd do if anything ever happened to him. *We're okay.*

"I've got you," he said, kissing the top of my head. "It's just a deer. No one's out there."

I peered over his shoulder. The back door was still open. And I could see the deer clearly in our backyard. It was leaning over my garden…eating my tomatoes! "What is that evil deer doing?"

Miller laughed.

"It's not funny. He's eating my tomatoes! Shoot it."

"You don't mean that."

"He's killing Henry Juniors! He's a terribly behaved deer. Off with his head!"

Miller started laughing harder.

"I'm serious. Go get 'em!"

It was like Miller couldn't stop the laughter erupting from his chest. I understood. It was how the tension was draining off him. But I was livid.

"If you're not going to do it, I will." I put my hand out for his gun.

He moved it away from me. "No shooting innocent deer. You're not thinking clearly."

I glared at him. I was thinking perfectly clearly. Isabella was... *Wow. Okay, fine.* I wasn't thinking clearly. I'd just called the deer Isabella. Just because the deer was a demonic tomato killer didn't mean it was Isabella. I'd been having a nightmare about her before I woke up, and thoughts of her were just colliding in my head. It was so easy to remember the words she'd written in blood on the wall. *"You're next."* If Isabella somehow knew I was still alive, I had no doubt she'd make good on her promise.

Miller looked down at his gun. "But yeah, you should probably learn how to handle this thing. Just in case something happens to me and you need it."

I scowled at him. "Nothing's going to happen to you."

"Just in case." He held on to it tightly, like he was afraid I'd grab it and shoot the deer.

Which definitely sounded crazy. I'd never hurt an animal.

"Please, Brooklyn. It would give me peace of mind. Just in case something happens and you need to use it while I'm at work."

"Yeah, fine. But nothing is going to happen to you." I stood up on my tiptoes and kissed him. "You said it yourself. I'm not bad luck."

"No. You're not. If anything you're my good luck charm."

I smiled up at him. I liked the sound of that.

CHAPTER 41

2 Years Later - Friday

I waved at Alice from across the restaurant as I put the bakery boxes, filled with pastries and desserts, down on the hostess stand. Alice was the owner of the restaurant Miller worked at. And one of the only people in town I ever spoke to.

She quickly hurried over. "Just in time. We already have a few orders for cheesecakes."

"Sorry I was running late. It took way longer to sign everything than I thought."

She smiled. "No problem at all, Jane. Oh and I have last week's payment." She pulled out an envelope full of money from her apron and handed it to me. I always felt awkward taking money from her. I loved baking. And Miller was making enough money now after his recent promotion to head chef that we didn't really need it. But it was good to have money tucked away for a rainy day. After all, I'd just put a huge dent in my limited savings. I quickly shoved the envelope into my purse. "Does he suspect anything?" I asked.

"Not a thing. Let me go tell him you're here. He's all yours for the rest of the day."

"Thanks, Alice."

She disappeared into the kitchen.

God, I really hoped he liked his surprise. I'd pretended to still be asleep when he left for work today. So as far as he knew I'd completely forgotten his birthday. Which wasn't true. How could I possibly? I looked forward to it every year. I didn't like surprises, but Miller loved them.

And I always surprised him. I was pretty sure this would top all his other birthdays though.

Miller came out with a big smile on his face. "Are you staying for lunch today?" he asked and swept me up into his arms.

"Not exactly." I wrapped my arms behind his neck. "I'm here because you're playing hooky."

"Oh, so you did remember my birthday?" He was smiling down at me.

"Of course I remembered your birthday. It's my favorite day of the year."

He didn't care that the restaurant was crowded as he leaned down and kissed me.

"I already talked to Alice," I whispered against his lips. "Come on." I grabbed his hand. "You're coming with me."

He laughed as I pulled him out of the restaurant. He went to the driver's side door, but I stopped him.

"No way, mister. I'm on a top-secret mission. I'm driving."

Miller always drove whenever we went anywhere. I swore he didn't trust my driving. But he should have. He was the one that taught me.

He closed the driver side door behind me and then climbed into the passenger seat. "So where exactly are we going?"

"That's for me to know and for you to be surprised about." I pulled out one of his ties from when he used to work for my dad and lifted it up. "Close your eyes."

"I don't like being blindfolded, kid."

I laughed. "You'll like this. I promise."

He reluctantly closed his eyes. I tied the tie in a tight knot behind his head and my eyes trailed to his lips. I leaned over the center console and gently pressed my lips against his.

He groaned. "Okay, maybe I like being blindfolded a little bit." He grabbed my waist to try and pull me closer.

"Don't you want your surprise?"

"Is this not my surprise?" he said with a smile.

I laughed. "Nope. Well, maybe later if you want. But I need to show you something." I slid back into my seat.

Miller and I never gave each other extravagant gifts. They were more thoughtful. Or gifts that we spent time making or preparing. Like when he put the fairy lights through the trees in our backyard. Or when he made me the elevated planters. I wasn't nearly as handy as him. He loved my cooking, especially my desserts. But this was a big birthday. So I'd pulled out all the stops.

I drove slowly on the road back to our house. I knew he probably thought we were going somewhere as the surprise. That was half the fun of it. Besides, where would we go? I only felt safe at home. With his arms wrapped around me.

I pulled into our driveway and cut the engine.

He went to take the blindfold off but I caught his hand.

"Not so fast." I climbed out of the car and hurried around to his side to help him out. I slowly guided him a few feet to the right and held my breath.

He was either going to love this or hate it.

I was hoping he'd love it. I stood up on my tiptoes and kissed him again before slowly untying the blindfold.

Miller smiled down at me for a moment before his eyes drifted over to the new truck parked next to us on the driveway. And by new I mean slightly used. I don't know why I'd been worried. I just knew he'd love it.

"Who's here?" His voice was laced with concern.

And I realized immediately that I hadn't thought about this reaction. It had been a long time now since I'd seen someone in the woods watching us. My first thought was never that he'd panic that someone had found us.

"It's yours." I quickly shook my head because I wasn't explaining this right. "You always have to rent a truck when you go to the hardware store, so I thought…" my voice trailed off. *Oh my God, he hates it.*

But the concern on his face quickly disappeared.

"How did you…" he looked around. "How did you even get it here?"

"One of the employees at the dealership drove it over. I wanted to surprise you." I pulled the keys out of my purse and handed them to him. "Happy 30th birthday, Little Dicky," I said.

He laughed and looked over at me. "I'm going to ignore the last part of your sentence because you just bought me a freaking truck."

I smiled up at him. "And you haven't even seen the best part." I grabbed his hand and pulled him to the truck bed. I opened up the back to reveal the picnic blanket and basket I'd laid out for us.

Yes, we could have gone to a nearby park or something. But I felt anxious leaving our property. And for some reason I thought this would be romantic. We could pretend we were anywhere in the world back here. Like we'd just driven hundreds of miles to some romantic destination.

He grabbed my hand and helped me up into the back of the truck. He sat down and I kicked off my sandals and sat down beside him. I pulled out the sandwiches from the picnic basket. I'd made all his favorite things. And I couldn't help but smile as he took a big bite and sighed.

"This is delicious," he said.

"Almost as delicious as something the new head chef would make." I lightly tapped his thigh with my bare foot.

He laughed and caught my foot in his hand. "No, this is better." The way he was looking at me made it impossible to know if he was saying if it was my cooking that was delicious or just...*me*. He pulled my foot to bring me closer to him. And then he abandoned his sandwich and leaned over me, kissing the side of my neck.

"I was thinking about that blindfold," he said as he kissed along my jawline.

I laughed. "Oh yeah? What were you thinking about it?"

He reached into my purse. "That I'd like it a lot better on you."

He slowly wrapped it around my eyes, tying it tight in the back. The next thing I knew I was on my back, the skirt of my dress bunched around my waist.

His lips found my clit and he sucked hard.

I reached down, my fingers getting tangled in his hair. God, this felt a lot more like my birthday than his.

***

We stayed in the truck all day, watching the sun set and the stars light up the sky. Normally on nights like this we'd sit on the deck, our feet dangling in the water. Those nights were perfect. But this was even better. I never wanted to move from this spot.

My head was on Miller's lap and we were both laying there staring at the stars. His fingers absentmindedly ran through my hair.

"Do you think anyone from our past ever thinks about us still?" I asked.

His fingers stilled.

Shit. I knew where his mind had just gone. And that wasn't even what I'd meant. "I think about Kennedy sometimes," I said quickly, ending the awkward silence in the air. "And Mrs. Alcaraz. I wonder how they're doing. If Kennedy went to a fancy art school. If she pursued photography." I knew she and I fought before I left. But she'd been my best friend. I desperately hoped she was happy. That she'd found everything she wanted in life. "And I wonder if Mrs. Alcaraz still lives in the same apartment." Mrs. Alcaraz was like a surrogate mother to me. I missed her cooking and her hugs. I turned so I could face Miller.

But his eyes were still trained on the sky. "I can find out. If you want me to."

I swallowed hard. A part of me did want to know. I wanted to know all of it. Was my dad healthy now that he had my kidney? Did Isabella get what she secretly wanted and end up with Matt? Did she ever really get the help she needed or was it just a lie my dad told? Did Felix follow in his parent's footsteps after all? Was Rob still cracking jokes? Did James still frown more than he smiled? I hoped not. I hoped they were all happy. Even Matt. I hoped he wasn't plagued by thoughts of me. Although, I was certain he'd stopped thinking about me years ago. Slowly over time I thought about him less and less too. I never belonged in his world. In any of their worlds. This right here? This was me. This was where I was supposed to be. "No. It's better just believing they all lived happily ever after. Like me."

Miller propped himself up on his elbows so he could look down at me. "Is that really how you feel?"

"Yes. I wake up smiling every morning." At least when I didn't have nightmares. "And I go to bed smiling every night. And I get to spend all day with you. My very own prince charming."

He smiled. But he didn't say anything at all. I could tell what he was thinking though. I'd gotten very good at reading his silence. He reached out and lightly traced my jawline with his index finger. Tonight he was thinking about all the questions he couldn't ask me. The questions we'd stopped talking about over the years.

I'd told him that I'd tell him when I was ready. "Thank you for loving me," I said. "Even though sometimes I make it hard."

His fingers dipped down my neck, tracing my clavicle. "Loving you is easy."

Loving him was easy too. Like we just fit perfectly together. We lived in a bubble. A perfect bubble that I loved. Yes, sometimes I wondered how the people I left behind were. But I never wanted to go back. Never. "I've been thinking."

He didn't say a word.

I slowly sat up and stared at the stars. *We're written in the stars.* That's what Miller had said. I straddled him, locking my arms behind his neck.

His hands settled on my waist.

"I did some research," I said. "And…it would be really hard to get married with our fake IDs."

He nodded. I think it's what he expected. For me to tell him I wasn't ready. *Again.*

But that wasn't what I was saying. "The dead couple whose identity we took…they were married. I don't think you've ever seen my ID. But I have the same last name as you already. Thompson. Jane and George Thompson. We're already married."

"Are we?" He smiled, but it looked sad.

"Mhm."

"Jane and George are married. But we're not Jane and George Thompson. Brooklyn, I want you to take my last name."

"Won't it be weird for my last name to be Miller? Since I call you Miller?"

"Do you think it would be weird for your last name to be Miller?"

I was a Sanders. I'd thought about being a Caldwell. I'd been forced to be a Pruitt for a short time. "Brooklyn Miller. It feels more meaningful than anything else. Especially since I call you Miller."

His eyes locked with mine.

"I like the sound of it."

"You do?"

"I do." I dropped my forehead to his. "I think I'm almost ready."

He exhaled slowly and I breathed him in. I'd never felt this close to anybody. I knew that. My heart knew it. And I was pretty sure my head did too. "Do you ever still think about going to college?"

He pulled his head back so he could look at me. "I'm really happy exactly where I am. I wouldn't change a thing. Except for your last name."

I smiled down at him.

"What about you?" he asked. "Do you think of going to school?"

"No." What would I even do with a college degree? I was already doing what made me happy. I got to bake every day. I got to grow fresh vegetables in the garden. Swim in the lake in the spring and summer. Dance the night away with Miller. Curl up with him under a blanket and drink hot chocolate in the winter. My life was perfect. It truly was a fairytale. "I'm happy exactly where I am too," I said. "With you. With this life we created."

"And you're sure it wouldn't give you peace of mind to figure out what everyone you left behind is up to?"

I shook my head. "I don't want to know." I could have looked it up too. I'd been tempted a few times. But I never typed their names into Google. I never signed up for any social media accounts. I liked being a ghost online. I liked not knowing. The less I knew the better.

"Do you really think we're safe here?" I asked.

"I do. And now you have your own car. Just in case something does happen when I'm not home. I know you wanted that."

I looked over at the old car next to his new truck. Having it was a sense of security. If he took his truck to work now, I'd still be able to get away if Isabella showed up.

He cradled my face in his hands, pulling me back to the present. He was good at that. Distracting me from my wandering thoughts of the future. I needed that. I needed him.

"Happy 30th birthday, Miller."

"I wasn't super excited to turn 30. But it certainly beats the alternative. I want to grow old with you."

"You'll always be a lot older than me."

"Hey." He tickled my side in retaliation to my comment.

Which turned into a full out tickle war. And we somehow managed to knock over the picnic basket. His cake I'd painstakingly spent hours on toppled onto the front of my dress.

"Crap," I said. I went to wipe it off when he caught my hand.

"This was how I wanted to eat it anyway." He pushed my strap off my shoulder and licked some icing off the top of my breast.

I laughed. "You still have to make a wish."

He pushed my dress down, exposing my breasts. He lightly blew on my nipple, making it harden, as if he was making a wish off that instead of a candle. "I have everything I need right here."

I caught his head before he devoured more cake. "Well I'll make a wish if you won't."

"And what's your wish, gorgeous?"

I smiled. "A million more birthdays just like...*this*." I slammed some cake into his face.

He laughed and kissed me, smushing some of the cake back onto my face.

My laughter quickly turned to moans as he devoured every inch of me.

CHAPTER 42

3 Years Later - Saturday

I wandered into the spare bedroom. The one where all the moving boxes were. I only ever went in here if I was looking for something in particular to wear. But I knew there were more than just clothes in here.

I moved a few boxes, searching through the contents until I found what I was looking for. I sat down with the pictures on my lap. I didn't have much left from my time in New York. These were mostly pictures my dad had given me. Pictures I'd thought weren't true. Even though the proof was right in front of me. Matt was smiling at the camera, his arm draped around some girl I didn't recognize.

Tears pooled in my eyes, remembering how it felt to be on the opposite end of that smile. Remembering what it felt like to be his, before everything broke. But this wasn't why I was in here. I sifted through the pictures until I found what I was looking for.

After all these years, I still had it. Matt, Mason, James, and Rob were young in this picture. It was summer and they were all laughing. James had let me take it from his treehouse years ago. The same day he'd proposed to me. I laughed through my tears. How different my life would have been if I'd said yes to that. To the sad boy who frowned more than he smiled. He played it off like he was kidding. But I was pretty sure he'd been serious. His parents had wanted him to marry a Pruitt. I really hoped he'd had a better future than that. But I wasn't looking at this picture because of James.

I wiped the tears from my eyes as I stared at all four boys. I loved one. The other three I had thought were my friends. I'd told Matt I wanted four kids. I wanted four boys so that they could be like the boys smiling in this picture. The best of friends. Were the four of them friends now? My dad had made it seem like they reconnected. I hoped that they had. I wanted all four of them to be as happy as they were as children on a summer's day by the pool.

I'd dreamed of that future.

And in a weird, twisted way, I'd kept my promises to Matt. Miller and I hadn't walked down the aisle yet. It was impossible to do it as ourselves. But ever since his 30th birthday, we'd acted like a married couple. Hell, we'd been acting like a married couple for a lot longer than that. Even though I hadn't said 'I do' I'd been acting like I had. Not acting. That wasn't the right word. Because I wasn't acting. I loved Miller with my whole heart.

But I'd only ever given Miller what I'd given Matt. My body. My heart. A promise of the future.

I'd promised Matt all my firsts. And I hadn't given any new ones to Miller.

Until now.

I'd missed my period.

Not just once.

I'd missed it two months in a row.

I knew I was pregnant. I hadn't taken a test, but I could feel myself changing. I was certainly more emotional.

I wiped the tears away from my cheeks as I stared down at the Caldwell and Hunter brothers. That was the future I thought I wanted. I was crying partially because I was sad. But I was crying because I was happy too. I was so blissfully happy.

I'd broken a promise to Matt now. This was a first. Probably the biggest first of all. My first child. And I was…relieved. I was excited. I hadn't thought much at all about getting pregnant. But now that I was? I wanted it. I wanted this baby. I wanted Miller's baby.

Matt had probably had a million firsts with someone new. I touched his smiling face in the picture. I hoped he was happy with whoever he was with. I hoped he was having those summers surrounded by children like we'd dreamed of together.

I put my hand on my stomach. It was like breaking this first broke some kind of wall in my heart. Miller was going to have the rest of my firsts. He was my future. Our baby was our future.

I put the picture back in the box and closed the lid. Now I just had to figure out a way to tell him.

CHAPTER 43

2 Weeks Later - Saturday - Christmas

I pressed the side of my face against Miller's chest as we slow danced in the kitchen to Christmas music. I wasn't scared to tell him. We'd never talked much about kids, but I knew he'd be a great dad. This would change things though. And he always said he was happy. That he wouldn't change a thing about our lives. This changed everything.

Tears rolled down my cheeks. *Stupid hormones.*

"What's going through that head of yours?" He cupped my face in his hands. Brushing away my tears with his thumbs. He looked concerned. But he had nothing to be concerned about.

"Today's been perfect."

"Then why are you crying?" He brushed more tears away. "You love Christmas."

"No, I love Christmases with you."

He smiled, but it didn't quite reach his eyes. "Just tell me, kid. Get it off your chest. It's okay."

What did he think I was going to say? "Now *I* want to know what *you're* thinking."

"I'm thinking you've been pulling away from me the past few weeks. This is your favorite time of year but you've been so…sad."

"I'm not sad."

"You're crying." He wiped more of my tears away.

These were happy tears. I was so happy I felt like I was going to burst. But he thought I was slipping away from him. He couldn't be farther from the truth. I was just nervous. I hoped he wanted this as much as I did. "I have one more present for you," I said.

"Whatever it is, I don't want it." He pulled me in close, capturing me against his chest.

I laughed. "I promise you'll want it. I mean, I think you'll want it. I hope you do."

"Seriously, you're freaking me out." He looked down at me. "Are you thinking about going back to New York?"

"What? No." I shook my head. "Not at all. The opposite, if anything."

He lowered his eyebrows.

"Give me a second to grab your present."

He reluctantly let go of me, like he thought I was already slipping away.

It was true. I'd been emotional the past few weeks. But this was a big step for me. A huge step. I was finally ready to make it with him. I was ready for our future.

I went to our bedroom and grabbed the small box in the drawer I'd hidden it in.

Miller was sitting on the couch when I walked back into the room. He was leaning forward, his elbows on his knees as he stared at the fire. I wasn't sure how it was even possible, but the shadows that danced across his face made him even more handsome.

I stopped right in front of him and cleared my throat. "I'm in love with you," I said, staring down at him.

"I'm in love with you too, kid."

I smiled and tucked a loose strand of hair behind my ear. I'd practiced this speech in my head dozens of times. But my stomach was filled with butterflies and somehow them flapping around messed with the plans in my brain. I shook my head, like I could clear it of my nerves. "I…" my voice trailed off. *Screw the plan.* I handed him the box. "Open it."

He pressed his lips together, like he wanted to say something. But instead of speaking, he slowly unwrapped the paper and took off the lid.

There were two rings inside. One that would fit me. And one that I hoped would fit him.

"We can't really get married legally. But that doesn't mean we can't get married."

He looked up at me.

"What matters is what's in our hearts. And my heart aches for you. I love you and only you. I'm sorry it's taken me forever to figure this out…" I got down on one knee. "Richard Miller…will you marry me?"

There were tears in his eyes as he pulled me into his laps. His lips crashed against mine. And as happy as I was that this probably meant 'yes,' I needed him to know exactly what he was agreeing to.

I put my hand on his chest. "There's something you should probably know."

"Kiss me, Brooklyn."

I smiled as he tried to kiss me again, but I pulled back. "There is one contingency to this marriage."

"The answer is yes, to whatever it is." He kissed me again.

I laughed. "Miller, I'm serious."

"Okay." His eyes searched mine. "What is it?"

"We have to get married tonight. Because this is a shotgun situation."

His eyes slowly traveled to my belly. "What?"

"I'm pregnant. I took the test this week."

"You're pregnant?"

"Yes." I held my breath waiting for his reaction.

"You're pregnant?" he asked again.

My heart started racing. I was good at reading him, but right now I had no idea what he was thinking. "I think I'm a few months along."

He placed his hand on my stomach. "You're pregnant." This time it wasn't a question. And a smile spread across his face. "You're pregnant!" He stood up, pulling me with him, twirling me around.

I laughed as I moved my legs around his waist. "We're having a baby."

The tears were back in his eyes. "I'm going to be a dad."

This joy in his voice brought tears into my eyes too. "Yes."

He kissed me and this time I let him. I wasn't sure why I'd been nervous. Miller and I were in this together. We'd made roots in this town. This was our home. And we were going to be a family.

"We should probably make this thing official," I said.

"I'm more than ready to consummate our marriage." His hands slid to my ass.

I laughed and slowly unwound myself from him. "No. Well, yes. But come with me first." I grabbed the box of rings and pulled him to the back door.

One of my presents to him had been a pair of matching flannel pajamas for us. We'd changed into them right away this morning and we were both still wearing them. I knew we looked ridiculous as we stuffed our feet into boots and grabbed our winter coats before heading outside.

I hadn't realized it, but it had started snowing. Light flurries danced around us. I plugged in the fairy lights, lighting up the snow falling from the sky. It was magical. It was perfect.

I didn't have any more words planned. So I just pulled Miller into the middle of our backyard and spoke from the heart. "I'm sorry it took me so long to be ready for this. But it was always you. I've always loved you. Do you promise all the marriage things that I can't remember right now?" I said and lifted up his ring out of the box.

He smiled down at me. "I do."

I slid the ring onto his finger.

He grabbed my ring from the box. "I will spend my whole life loving you, Brooklyn. The life we created here together is better than anything in my wildest dreams. Us against the world." He put his hand on my stomach. "The three of us against the world."

I couldn't help the tears streaming down my cheeks. The wind blew sending flurries dancing between us. And I had the strangest sensation that this was all a dream. Because my life had never felt this good. My life had been riddled with so much heartache up until this point. But I felt whole now. Like none of those bad things had happened. As long as Miller was beside me. I could spend a lifetime of happiness with this man.

He smiled down at me. "Brooklyn, do you promise all the marriage things that I can't remember right now?"

I laughed. "A million times yes. I do."

He slid the simple band onto my finger, right next to the engagement ring that had sat there alone for far too long. We stood there in our pajamas, both smiling so hard it hurt. And even though we weren't dressed for a wedding, it felt as momentous as a real one. And as beautiful. I looked up at the lights in the sky and the snow falling harder around us. This was perfect. I couldn't imagine a more beautiful wedding.

"We're going to be a family I said," looping my arms behind his neck.

"We already are a family." He leaned down and kissed me. He kissed me like I was his whole world. And I knew I kissed him back the same. Miller was my whole world. He had been for years.

I'd broken two firsts now. Two firsts I'd promised to Matt. But it didn't hurt. I barely even remembered what Matt had sounded like when he'd called me a liar.

And I wasn't a liar. I was allowed to be happy. I was allowed to live my life. And this was the life I wanted. Miller was who I wanted it with.

CHAPTER 44

3 Months Later - Saturday

"Hey, Alice," I said as I balanced the bakery boxes in my arms. I set them down on the hostess stand.

"I'm so glad you came back," she said. "You rushed off so fast earlier, I thought something was wrong. I guess you just forgot the boxes in the car?"

My hands froze. "What?"

"When you came in a few minutes ago. I asked you where the boxes were and you hurried off without responding."

My heart started racing. "I wasn't here a few minutes ago."

"Of course you were. I saw you with my own eyes, Jane. Although, you were wearing different clothes." She frowned. "Weren't you just in high heels?"

High heels? It was like I could hear the click of them echoing around me, like I was back at Empire High dreading the sound. I hated to admit it, but there was only one person who could pull off looking like me. Someone who shared my DNA. And someone who I'd only ever seen in heels. Even at private family dinners. I turned around, like I could feel Isabella's eyes on me.

"Is everything alright?" Alice asked.

"Yes. I just…is Mil…" I cleared my throat. "Is George here?"

"Yeah, one second, I'll go get him."

As she walked away I hurried outside and looked both ways. I swore I saw a black SUV speeding down the street.

Or maybe it was just a normal car. I blinked and it was gone. Maybe it hadn't been there at all.

Miller rushed out of the restaurant. He spotted me standing on the sidewalk, staring at nothing at all. But I felt it in my bones. I'd felt her eyes on me. Isabella was here. She knew where we were.

"What's wrong?" Miller said as he put his hand on my shoulder. "Alice said you seemed disoriented. How about we sit down." He tried to lower me to sit on the curb but I pulled back.

"It's her. She's here."

"Hey, take a deep breath for me."

"I'm not having a panic attack! And I'm not disoriented. She's here."

"Who's here? Brooklyn, look at me." He grabbed both sides of my face. "What are you talking about?"

"Isabella."

He lowered his eyebrows.

"I came into the restaurant and Alice said I'd just been in. And that I'd rushed off. I only just came in. It has to be…" my voice trailed off. "She found us." Now I was pretty sure I was having a panic attack. "We need to go. We need to get out of here."

But Miller didn't move.

"We have to go!"

Miller looked over at a couple that was walking into the restaurant, who were blatantly staring back at us. "There's security footage," Miller whispered as he turned back to me. "How about you come inside. We'll watch it together."

"Why don't you believe me?"

"I do believe you. But I don't want to uproot our whole lives unless you're 100% sure. Did you actually see Isabella?"

"No…but…"

"Let's just look at the tapes."

"Miller who else could it possibly be? Alice thought it was me. Isabella must have been dressed up like me. She must have…"

"Brooklyn." Miller put his hand on my stomach that was getting bigger by the day. "I've pictured our whole lives here. The three of us. I don't want to start over again. We have good jobs. We're doing well here. Please, just take a deep breath and we can look at the security tapes."

Miller had never seen someone watching us from the woods. He'd only ever heard my recounting of it. And he hadn't felt the chill run down my back when I felt Isabella's eyes on me. "I'm not crazy."

"I never said you were. I'm just saying that I love it here. I want to raise my family here at the lake house. Please, Brooklyn. Just take a deep breath."

I wasn't crazy. But I knew my hormones sometimes made me feel that way.

"I've always protected you," he said. "Let me keep protecting you. Don't you trust me?"

I breathed in slowly and exhaled even slower. "Of course I trust you."

"We'll figure out if it was her." He grabbed my hand. "Come with me."

I walked with him back into the restaurant.

He started talking to Alice. Telling her that I hadn't been in earlier.

Alice shook her head and laughed. "Yeah, as soon as I saw the surprised look on your face, I knew I must have made a mistake. I was slammed with tables this afternoon. I must not have gotten a good look at the girl."

"Did you see what car she was driving?" I asked.

"I'm afraid not."

"Do you mind if we look at the security footage?" Miller asked. "Just to see if we recognize her? It may have been family from out of town."

"Of course. My office is unlocked."

"Thanks, Alice." He guided us into her office. Instead of going to the computer on Alice's desk he went over to the corner and lifted up this secret cubby thing. There was another computer hidden behind the wooden façade.

I stared at Miller and then back at the screen.

He typed in a password and the security footage came up.

I looked back at him. "How did you know the password?" Alice hadn't just told him. How did he even know to use this hidden computer?

"Because I set it up."

"What?"

"I have security cameras everywhere, Brooklyn. I figured you knew that. Do you really think I'd let you stay home all day without surveillance?" He clicked a few buttons and then there was a video of the girl that looked like me walking into the restaurant.

But for just a minute I was a little more concerned about the surveillance comment. "You have cameras in our house?"

"No, outside the house."

"Miller, it's not your job to watch me all the time anymore."

"I don't watch you." He turned to me. "I'm busy all day here. But yeah, I have an alarm on my phone that will go off if there's any motion outside our place."

"So when I go outside to garden…"

"I get an alert, yes."

"And you click through and see that it's just me in the garden."

He sighed. "I don't understand the issue here."

"I just told you the issue. It's not your job to watch me anymore."

He ran his hand down his face. "I'm not watching you. I'm protecting you and our kid. And I'd set up most of this before you even came back."

"You put up all these cameras before I moved in?"

"Do you think you're the only one freaked out about Mr. Pruitt finding us? I used to lie awake at night holding a gun in my hand. The woods make terribly creepy noises in the middle of the night. I kept thinking he'd found me. I was pretty sure I was going crazy without you."

I knew the noises that the woods made well. I remembered how spooked we'd both been when the deer had woken us up. But it was the last part of what he said that hit me1 the hardest. That he was going crazy without me. I'd felt that same way without him.

"So yes, I set up cameras to make sure I was safe. And then when you came? I set up a few more. He said he'd kill me if I touched you, Brooklyn. What would he do to me now? You're pregnant with my kid."

I swallowed hard. "I'd hope that he wouldn't hurt the father of my child."

Miller shook his head. "You're giving him grace he doesn't deserve."

I'd had a lot of time to think about what my father had done to me. I thought about it more than ever now that I was pregnant. Now that I was about to have a kid of my own. My dad swore he thought I'd agreed to the kidney thing. I'd seen the tears in his eyes. I'd seen how grateful he'd been. He'd made a mistake.

But I still resented him. I felt exploited. He made me feel weak. And used. When he kept me a prisoner it twisted things even more. Was he trying to keep me safe from

Isabella? Or keeping me safe for himself, just in case he needed me again. I liked to think it was the first one. That he was scared of Isabella too. I hated my father. But now I wasn't as sure that he was the monster I'd made him out to be in my youth. Or maybe Miller was right. That I was giving him grace he didn't deserve. That the years apart from him had made me forget who he truly was. Time played tricks on me sometimes. Making me remember the good instead of the bad.

Miller looked over his shoulder at the open door of Alice's office. "We can discuss this more at home. Let's see if it was Isabella, okay?"

I didn't know what to say anymore. Honestly, I was relieved he had cameras set up. But why hadn't he told me until now? He knew before we had two cars that I was nervous being home alone. He'd even taught me how to use a gun instead of just telling me there were cameras. 'I figured you knew' didn't seem like a good excuse to me. But he was right. We didn't want Alice to overhear us.

Miller rewound the footage and paused it.

"It's so blurry."

He zoomed in a bit more but it didn't help.

I looked over at him and he was squinting at the screen. "Do you really think that's her? Why would she dress up as you?"

"Because she's a crazy person."

He switched to a different still, but it was equally blurry. "But why would she come here after all these years?"

"I don't know." It had been twelve years since I'd died. Twelve years and no word about anything from the life I left behind. Nothing from Isabella. Nothing from my dad. "What if my dad found us? And Isabella somehow figured it out? Saw something she wasn't supposed to see?"

"We've been careful. This is pretty much the only place we come."

"And she showed up here. The one place we've slipped." I stared at the picture again. It had been a long time since I'd seen Isabella. Would I even recognize her now? Even if the picture wasn't blurry?

"You heard what Alice said, though. That she realized it wasn't you. She was just slammed. She didn't even get a good look at her." He pulled out his phone. "And if she knew where we lived and had gone to the house, I'd have an alert by now."

I took a deep breath. "You really think it was a false alarm?"

"I hope so."

Me too. Now that I'd had a few minutes to calm down, Miller's words made sense. I didn't want to move again. I didn't want to start over. I put my hand on my stomach. This was where I pictured raising our kid. I wanted to give our baby the life we'd lived here. Long summer nights and lazy winter days. I wanted all of it.

"Stay here today. We'll go home together after my shift ends. You can sit in a booth and…"

"Can I help you cook?" The last thing I wanted to do was sit around being nervous.

He smiled. "Of course." He pulled me into his chest. "It's going to be okay."

It was easy to believe him when his arms were around me.

***

Miller had checked every inch of our home. We'd taken a walk around the lake, searching the perimeter of the woods for anything amiss. And then he'd checked the house for a second time. There was…nothing.

He handed me a cup of hot chocolate and joined me on the couch, lifting up the blanket to drape it over both of our laps.

I blew on the top of the mug. I'd had all day to calm down. All day to think about the blurry face in the surveillance footage. There was no reason why Isabella would suddenly think I was alive. And no reason why she'd dress like me. Or dye her hair to be blonde like mine. None of it made any sense. Isabella thought I was dead. She was out there somewhere living her life. I wasn't on her mind anymore. Surely I didn't haunt her dreams the way she'd haunted mine.

I took a sip of the hot chocolate, letting it warm my cold bones. "Why'd you think I knew about the cameras?"

"Because it's my responsibility to protect you, kid."

"You're missing a key word there. *Was*. It *was* your responsibility to protect me."

"No. It was my *job* to protect you when I didn't know you. It's my *responsibility* to protect you now. As your husband. As the father of our child. As the love of your life."

I didn't need the hot chocolate to warm my heart. He'd already done it. "You really think we're safe?"

"I would never put your life in jeopardy ever again, Brooklyn." He put his hand on my stomach.

I loved when he did that. Like his love radiated through to the baby growing inside of me. We'd decided we didn't want to know if it was a boy or a girl. That it would be a surprise we'd wait for. But I had a feeling it was a boy. And I prayed to God it came out looking exactly like Miller.

I took another sip of hot chocolate, and his words finally registered in my head. "Wait. What do you mean *again*?"

"At homecoming. When Isabella…"

I laughed. "You're joking. You can't possibly still blame yourself for that. Isabella injected you with something and locked you in the closet. That wasn't your fault."

"I left my post because I was pissed. I walked out of the ballroom of that stupid hotel because I needed air. If I hadn't left…"

"Trust me, I would have left too. If I'd seen you dancing with a bunch of other girls."

He laughed. "I would never."

I set my hot chocolate down on the coffee table and straddled him. "Never huh? You only want to dance with me for the rest of your life?"

"Us against the world, Brooklyn."

I leaned down and kissed him. I kept thinking that one day he might push me away as my belly swelled more. That he might be repulsed by the sight of me. But that never happened. If anything, he loved me more.

CHAPTER 45

3 Months Later - Sunday

Miller rowed the boat out slowly as if he was worried I might burst.

"He's not coming today," I said. I propped my bare feet up on one of the benches. Everything hurt. Miller was not at all excited about the idea of bare feet on the wooden rowboat. But I swore if I tried to put on shoes I'd cry. Besides, the summer heat was finally here. I was unbearably hot. And my stomach was unbearably large, despite the fact that my son wasn't due for another month.

"You keep saying 'he.' I swear we're having a girl."

"I don't think so." I put my hand over the edge of the boat, letting my fingertips glide over the water.

Miller rowed a little farther until we were in the middle of our small lake. I loved coming out here. When all I could really hear was the water. I closed my eyes. It reminded me of the beach house. It reminded me of falling in love with Miller.

I put my hand on my stomach when I felt a kick. "Henry's kicking again."

Miller groaned. "We're not naming our kid after a tomato plant."

"But…"

"You've named every single one of your plants Henry. Or Henry Junior. Or Henry VIII, which I'm not fond of at all. It's not happening."

"Henry is a really good name. Our Henry won't kill all his wives. Besides, all my Henrys live now."

"The baby is healthy. You have nothing to worry about." He reached over and placed his hand on my stomach. Henry kicked him immediately.

"He's trying to tell you to stop trying to rename him," I said.

Miller smiled and removed his hand from my stomach. "You really want to name our kid after a tomato plant?"

"Yes. Like I said…all my plants live now. I want Henry to have a long and healthy life." Despite what Miller always told me, sometimes I still worried I was back luck. I didn't want that to extend to my child. I needed him alive and healthy. I couldn't wait to meet him. I already protected him fiercely. Especially his rightful name.

"Not all of your plants live," Miller said. "How would you feel if a deer bit Henry's head off?"

I put my arm protectively around my stomach. "Nunca."

Miller raised his eyebrow at me. "He's not a plant. He's a baby."

I looked down at my stomach. Of course Miller had a point. But I'd been calling the baby Henry in my mind for months now. He felt like a Henry to me. And I liked watching him grow just like I liked watching my plants grow. "Wait." I looked back up at Miller. "You just said *he*. Does that mean you finally agree we're having a boy?"

Miller laughed. "No. It's definitely a girl. Which makes this conversation moot. What do you think about Chloe?"

I'd already vetoed a bunch of Miller's names. But I actually liked that one. I looked down at my stomach. "There's just one problem with that suggestion. Henry is a boy. Not a girl."

"You're impossible."

I laughed. "Henry is the stubborn one, not me."

"Sure." He smiled back at me. The same smile he always gave me. He still looked at me like I was the most beautiful girl he'd ever seen. Even when I was as big as a whale.

I felt my cheeks flush as I looked out over the water. "I really do like the name Chloe."

"Me too. And if this one isn't a girl, maybe the next one will be."

I turned back to face him. "How are you already thinking about Henry #2 when Henry #1 hasn't arrived yet?"

He laughed. "No way are we naming both our kids Henry."

I loved that Miller thought about the future. A future with me. "We could fill this whole little boat with Henrys."

"We will continue this very important discussion when you're being more reasonable."

I laughed.

"Are you and Henry hungry?" Miller asked. He opened up the lid of the picnic basket. This time he'd packed it. And I had no idea what was inside.

"Always."

He laughed. "I have just the thing." He pulled out a bowl filled to the brim with watermelon.

"You're my favorite human," I said and grabbed the bowl from him. I'd been craving watermelon during this pregnancy like crazy. During the winter that was not a great thing, because it was impossible to find. But now? I grabbed a fork and took a bite. Holy, juicy, watermelon goodness.

"Fuck, Brooklyn."

"What?" I stared down at the front of his swim trunks that were visibly tenting. I smiled to myself and then looked back up at him.

"You're doing that moaning thing again."

I laughed. "I am not."

"You are too. Ever since you started showing." He put his hand on my protruding tummy. "You make the most sexual noises when you eat. Especially when you're eating watermelon."

"I do not." We'd been over this before. I was most certainly not moaning when I ate watermelon.

"Yes. You do."

"I do not." Fine, maybe I knew I was moaning. And maybe I really liked his reaction to it. But it was completely involuntary. Watermelon just did something to me. So did the sight of Miller getting aroused. I craved watermelon while I was pregnant. But I craved him most of all. My hormones were insane. If I could have stayed in bed for the past few months getting railed by him, I would have dropped everything in a heartbeat.

But I had no idea why he was turned on. I was huge and I'd been running around barefoot like a barbarian for months.

I forgot about everything else as he leaned forward and kissed me. I buried my fingers in his hair.

"I love you," he said, kissing my chin, my throat, between my breasts. He kept going lower and kissed the top of my stomach, but he was looking right at me. "You're so beautiful."

I swallowed hard. "Stop making fun of me."

"I'm not." He kissed my stomach again. "You're gorgeous." He kissed me lower, pulling down the front of my bikini bottoms. I hadn't gotten any new bathing suits. So I just had a huge pregnant tummy sticking out of a bikini that should have been sexy but was most certainly not. And yet…he was looking at me like he desired me. He lowered his head more, disappearing from my view beneath my stomach.

But I felt his warm breath where I was dying for him to touch me.

"Beautiful," he whispered and then ran his tongue slowly along my clit.

Jesus.

His tongue was slow. His lips slower. Like he knew he was driving me insane.

And I was too overheated for this. Too turned on. Too impatient. I needed his cock inside of me. I thought about it all the time. Foreplay be damned. I didn't need it.

"Please. Miller," I groaned.

"Brooklyn." He kissed the inside of my thigh.

No! He was going the wrong way! I shifted, trying to push him back so I could get on top of him. But I was a lot bigger than I normally was. And the weight made the boat tilt to the side. A lot. So much so that it tipped and we toppled off the side.

I laughed as I came up for air. The water was freezing but it felt amazing. I started laughing harder. "I'm so big I knocked over the whole boat."

"It's not a cruise ship," Miller said with a laugh. "It's a small rowboat."

"Still."

We both treaded water as we stared at each other.

"I don't think it was your weight that cause the boat to tip. It was definitely your insatiable appetite."

"No! My watermelon!" I was about to swim back over to the boat to see if I could salvage anything, but Miller caught my ankle, pulling me back toward him.

"I didn't mean for watermelon. But I'll get you more later." He put his hands under my ass, lifting me up to the surface so I was floating. "I meant your sexual appetite."

I tried to move but he shifted his hand to my waist so I'd stay still. "Float. I promise it'll make you feel better."

I sighed and let the sun hit my face and stomach. I wasn't good at floating. But for some reason I had no trouble today. Maybe having a pregnant belly made it easier or something. Either way, Miller was right. This felt amazing. My knees hurt from the extra weight. My feet were swollen. Hell, everything hurt. But floating here made me feel so much better.

"Relax," Miller whispered.

He didn't have to tell me. I was already relaxed.

But then I felt his fingers push the fabric between my legs to the side. "Relax," he whispered again. "Let me take care of you."

God, how was I supposed to relax when he…*fuck*.

His thumb traced slow circles around my clit before he slipped it inside of me.

I swore I would have started to sink, but he put his free hand back on my ass, lifting me back to the surface.

"Relax." His hot breath in my ear was driving me almost as wild as his thumb.

"Miller…"

"Sh." His teeth gently bit down on my earlobe. "You're so fucking sexy like this."

I wasn't. I couldn't possibly be. But his thumb was driving me too insane to care. Tracing slow circles inside of me.

I swore it felt like I was floating on clouds. I didn't feel uncomfortable because of my pregnant belly. All I felt was the coolness of the water, Miller's hot breath as he licked behind my ear, and his thumb. God, his hands were almost as amazing as his mouth.

"Relax," he whispered again, his teeth digging into my earlobe until it almost hurt.

He started moving his thumb slowly in and out of me, spreading my juices across my clit.

"Come for me, gorgeous. Just like this." His thumb lazily slipped back inside of me.

It was the slowest torture. This warm feeling spreading in my stomach. His fingers splayed across my ass cheeks as he thrust his thumb all the way inside of me.

I felt myself clenching around him.

He groaned into my ear, like this was the sexiest thing he'd ever witnessed. And I hadn't even touched him. But I was certainly about to. As soon as the stars in my eyes disappeared. And I could catch my breath.

My butt started sinking back down. "My turn," I said and tried to turn toward him, reaching for his erection.

He pushed my ass back up. "Just float, Brooklyn."

"But…"

"Trust me, I'll let you suck my cock later." He kissed the side of my jaw. "But right now, just relax."

I laughed and stared up at the clouds. This truly was amazing. But I think he was underestimating just how badly I wanted his cock in the back of my throat. I'd just cum and yet I was so horny I could scream.

"Relax," he whispered.

"Only if you do that thing again."

He pushed the fabric to the side and started the slow torture all over again.

God, I was going to give him the best blowjob ever later.

CHAPTER 46

1 Month Later - Sunday

I stared down at the little bundle of blue in my arms. I still couldn't believe he was finally here.

Miller was stretched out on the hospital bed beside me, fast asleep. He'd stayed up all night trying to get our son to stop crying so I could get some rest. But I wasn't tired anyway. I just wanted to hold my baby boy.

They'd both fallen asleep about an hour ago. And I kept looking back and forth between their sleeping faces. This little guy was a spitting image of his father.

Miller moaned and slowly opened his eyes. "How are we doing?"

"Good." I reached down and lightly ran my fingers through Miller's hair. "He's sleeping."

"And do we have a name yet?"

I'd insisted for months that I wanted to call him Henry. But Miller remained adamant that he didn't want to name our son after a tomato. He had a few names picked out. And the longer I stared at our son, the more I realized Miller was right. This little boy was so much better than a tomato plant. He'd quickly stolen half my heart. The other half was still with Miller.

"Yeah, I think we finally have a name," I said.

Miller reached his hand up, cradling my face. "I'm okay with Henry. If that's really what you want. You know that."

Even with all his protests, I did know that. Miller always just wanted me to be happy. And that included letting me pick our child's name. But…this was *our* baby. And our baby wasn't one of many Henrys.

"No," I said. "I like the one you picked out. It suits him." I looked back down at our son.

Miller didn't move. "Which name?" He reached up, grabbing my chin so I'd look back down at him.

"Which one was your favorite again?" I was teasing him. I knew what his favorite was. And it was my favorite now too.

"Jacob."

I nodded. "Jacob. I think that's his name, don't you?"

"Yeah?"

"Jacob Miller sounds perfect. Doesn't it?"

Miller nodded. "You're perfect."

"Only because I didn't name our son after my tomato plants."

"That would have been weird."

"Well I've only ever loved them and you." *And Matt.* I blinked, the thought of Matt hitting me like a slap in the face. I swallowed hard, trying to push away the image of his face in my head. I cleared my throat. "And as much as I love you, I wasn't going to name our son Richard."

Miller laughed and sat up. "I wouldn't have wanted that either." He put his arms out so I could let him hold Jacob.

He pulled him against his chest. "We don't need another Little Dicky running around."

I laughed. "No we do not. One Little Dicky is plenty." I yawned.

"Come here." Miller put his arm out so I could nestle into his side.

I rested my head against his shoulder.

"Look at what we made."

I looked up at Miller instead of at Jacob. "I love you."

He looked down at me. "I love you."

I blinked the tears out of my eyes. "If something ever happens to me, you'll keep him safe, right?"

"What are you talking about? Nothing's going to happen to you."

I blinked faster. "She'll eventually find me," I said. I looked down at our son. Isabella would find me one day. She'd kill me. I'd always had nightmares about it. But they'd been worse recently. Like I could feel her wrath all around me. Like I could feel her anger. What bothered me the most about it was that it made it seem like I was connected to her somehow. Like maybe this bond we had as sisters somehow made me know she'd lost her mind again.

Miller was quiet for a moment. "I need to tell you something. And I need you to promise not to be upset."

"Let me guess. You installed cameras all over the hospital?" I looked back up at him.

"No. But you don't have to worry about Isabella anymore. She's...dead."

"What? How? How do you even know that?"

"That day we thought she showed up at the restaurant? I set up a Google alert for her name. To keep an eye on her. To make sure she was nowhere near us. I didn't tell you about it, because I remembered you'd told me you just wanted to picture everyone from our past living happily ever after. I figured keeping tabs on her went against that. I'm sorry, I should have told you ages ago."

"I never wanted Isabella to live happily ever though." I swallowed hard, the guilt catching weird in my throat. "I wanted her to die."

Miller was quiet.

"I worry sometimes. That I'm just like her."

"What? No." Miller pulled me closer to him. "She was crazy, Brooklyn. You're not crazy. You're kind and passionate and lovely."

"Then why aren't I sad that my half-sister is dead?"

"Does it help if you know that I'm relieved too?"

I took a deep breath. "A little. How…how did she die?" I doubted it was kidney failure. Surely my dad would have stolen some rando's kidney for his daughter if that was the case.

"She fell out of a window in a hospital."

A chill ran down my spine as I sat in my hospital bed. "Like…a mental hospital?"

"No. A normal hospital. I don't know all the specifics, but the article I read made it seem as though she kind of lost it when her marriage to James started falling apart…"

"James?"

Miller was silent.

"James Hunter? He married her?"

"Yeah."

Oh, James. I put my hand over my mouth. I'd always hoped he'd go down a better path than that. Like he'd wake up from the fog of drugs and booze. Like he'd make a choice for himself. It broke my heart that he hadn't. That he'd married that monster. And it broke my heart more, remembering him proposing to me. Remembering Rob saying James had to marry a Pruitt. *James.*

I'd left New York behind for a reason. Because my dad had painted a picture for me…of everyone being better off without me. Matt being happy. The Untouchables being friends again. Kennedy and Felix possibly becoming more than friends.

I hadn't believed it at first. I hadn't wanted to believe it. But I saw the pictures. And then I saw it for myself. The image of Matt in that pool with the brunette girl would always be seared into my brain.

They were all supposed to be better off. So why the hell had James married Isabella? Where were his friends when he needed them? Were they not speaking again? Were they still not friends? My stomach twisted into knots. I was so disappointed that James had married Isabella. Knowing everything she did to me. But I was more disappointed in Matt, Mason, and Rob. They were supposed to have his back. They were supposed to care more than that. It felt like my heart was breaking in two.

"I…" my voice trailed off. Maybe a few years ago, I may have been filled with doubt. Over whether I made the right choice. But it wasn't my responsibility for anyone else to have a happily ever after. I only had control over my own life. And I couldn't think about what James was going through. Or anyone else. Sometimes I was bad at putting myself first. But it was really easy for me to put Miller first. To put our baby first. "I don't want to know any more."

"Okay."

I swallowed hard. I needed to believe they were all better off without me. Because I was better off without them.

I looked down at Jacob. Isabella was dead. Which meant he was safe. We were safe. *Almost*. I tucked Jacob's blanket a little more snuggly. "Is my father still alive?"

"Yes."

I nodded. And I did a terrible thing as I snuggled back into Miller's side. As I looked down at the newborn life, I wished my father would die too. That Miller, Jacob, and I would be safe forever. That my past would never catch up to me.

I needed to believe that. Because I didn't want to leave my son too early. Like my mom had left me. Like my uncle had left me.

I needed to be here for him.

CHAPTER 47

6 Months Later - Wednesday

I held Jacob to my chest as I stared out at the frozen lake. I had this sense of dread in my chest. And I had no idea why. But I'd felt it with my mom. With my uncle. Like time was ticking down too quickly and I didn't know how to stop it.

I heard the crunch of snow behind me. And even though I felt like something terrible was about to happen, I didn't turn around. Because time had only just started ticking down in my head. And I knew it was just Miller walking up behind me on the dock. We were safe. *For now.*

Miller wrapped his arms around me, kissing the side of my neck. "How are my two favorite people in the world today?"

I sighed, leaning into Miller. "Worried."

Even though he was behind me, I could sense his frown.

"I think we need to move."

He held me tighter. "Brooklyn, we've been over this. Isabella's not out there anymore."

I knew that. And yet…why was I still nervous? "I can't stop thinking about my dad. And how he said he'd kill you if you ever touched me again."

"Like this?" He swept my hair to the side and kissed my neck.

I laughed and turned to him. "I'm serious. I can't lose you. We both need to be here for Jacob."

Miller leaned down, kissing Jacob's forehead. And then his fingers disappeared into my hair as he drew my temple to his lips, kissing it. "I know you're worried, kid. I also know you haven't been getting much sleep lately. Why don't you let me take Jacob and you can take a nap before dinner."

"It's not because I'm tired, Miller. I feel this sense of doom in my chest."

He pulled me closer as if he could warm the feeling from my heart.

"I think if we move…"

"Our life is here. And it's perfect."

"I know. It's almost…too perfect."

He kissed my forehead again. "There's no such thing as too perfect. I want to raise all our kids here. I want us to grow old here together."

I wanted that too. Desperately. But to me it didn't matter where we were as long as we were together.

A snowflake hit the tip of my nose and I looked up at the sky. Flurries were suddenly dancing around us.

"Remember our first winter here together? When we were out on the lake? And I almost fell through? You saved me. But every day…it feels like I'm falling through that ice all over again."

"I swear on my life, that I will never let anything bad happen to you. To either of you. Please, Brooklyn. I'm begging you to let this go. I'm begging you to just be happy."

"I am happy."

"Worrying every day isn't being happy."

I swallowed hard. I didn't know what it was, but I did worry more now. It felt like the weight of the world was on my shoulders. When really it was just the weight of Jacob in my arms. I needed to protect him. I needed to protect all of us.

"If anything ever happens to any of us…it'll be my fault. Because my dad…"

"No. If anything ever happens to any of us, it'll be my fault. Okay? Because I'm the one protecting you. Not the other way around, kid."

I tried to blink the tears in my eyes away.

"Remember when you used to get those panic attacks all the time?" He touched the side of my face. "You learned to breathe through them. I know everything feels heavy right now. But I'm here to help you carry that burden." He lifted Jacob out of my arms. "I need you back, Brooklyn. I need you to breathe through this."

Tears started welling in my eyes. I knew he thought I had postpartum depression. I didn't think that was it. I think I just had a lifetime of being scared. But…maybe he was right. "I'm scared all the time."

"I know." He pulled me in close. "Okay. I think you're right. Maybe we need some time away from here. Maybe we should go somewhere sunnier for a bit. I have a few vacation weeks saved up."

"Thank you." I knew he didn't want to leave. But I already felt relieved.

CHAPTER 48

1 Week Later - Thursday

I picked up my pace as I ran down the beach. Ever since Jacob had been born, Miller and I had stopped running together, since one of us always needed to be with the baby. I missed him by my side.

I missed him *period*.

Every day that passed here, I felt more like myself. I felt like me again. And I realized just how much Miller was right. I'd been pushing him away. I'd been anxious. It had been hard to get out of bed for a few months. I was worried all the time. But it was all in my head.

I had everything I could possibly want in my life. And I'd let fears of the future creep up on me. I'd vowed to live in the present. I didn't want to miss out on today because I was so worried about tomorrow. And I did trust Miller to keep us safe.

I paused on the beach, placing my hands on my knees. God, I'd needed this. I breathed in the familiar smell of salty air. I'd needed this so badly. It was like the sun on my skin was exactly what I'd needed to wake up again.

I didn't want to be running away from my family. Suddenly even the distance on the beach felt like too much. I needed to run back to them. I turned around and ran faster back toward the little house we were renting.

I smiled as I saw them in the distance. They were sitting on a blanket under an umbrella. Miller was reading something and it looked like Jacob was fast asleep. I sprinted up the sand and launched myself into Miller's arms, knocking him backward into the sand.

"Hey," Miller said with a smile, even though I'd probably just knocked the wind out of him and definitely gotten his book sandy.

"Hey."

His fingers wandered into my hair. "You look happy."

"I'm so happy."

His eyes dropped to my lips. "I think we should stay here."

I laughed. "I was just about to tell you that I'm ready to go home."

He drew his eyebrows together. "You weren't happy there anymore. I really think we should stay. I want to stay."

His cheeks were rosy from the sun. And he was staring at me with that same love in his eyes. Love that stretched years.

"I have an idea," I said.

He stayed quiet.

"How about once a year we come back to the beach for vacation?"

"Or we could stay…"

"No. I love our home. I want to raise Jacob and all our children there." I looked over at Jacob who was sleeping under the umbrella.

Miller rolled us over in the sand, pinning me below him. "All our children, huh?"

My skin was sweaty from my run and I knew my back was now covered in sand. It reminded me of that time, years ago, when Miller had rolled around in the sand, completely covering himself. He was ridiculous. He was the love of my life. "Yes, all our children."

"Were you thinking about making one right now?"

I laughed as he pressed his weight down on me. "We're on a public beach. And Jacob is right there."

Miller looked over at our son. "He's sleeping."

I laughed and put my hand on his chest. "Take me home, Miller. I want to go home."

"You are my home." He dropped his forehead to mine. "I really am okay with staying. I'm addicted to your smiles, kid."

"I'm okay. It was like you said. I just needed some air."

He placed a kiss against my lips. We were on a secluded beach in the middle of the day. And Jacob was asleep. I breathed in Miller's exhales as I wrapped my legs around his waist. Maybe I hadn't needed air at all. Maybe I'd just needed to let him in again. Because his exhales were sweeter than the salty air.

CHAPTER 49

6 Months Later - Thursday

Jacob sat on the kitchen counter as I finished the last batch of cupcakes.

"Jacob, no," I said with a laugh as I grabbed him off the counter. He was used to being my little taste tester, but these had to wait. "Those are your birthday cupcakes. We have to wait till Daddy is home."

"Daddy!"

"Yes, sweet boy." I placed him back on the counter. "Be good."

He crawled toward the cupcakes again.

I laughed and picked him back up. I didn't want to wait either. "How about we go surprise Daddy at work?"

"Daddy!" Jacob yelled.

I peppered his face with kisses and he laughed. "Come on, let's go get him to come home. We have a birthday to celebrate. Someone's turning one!"

"Me."

"Yes, you." I kissed the tip of his head. "Let's go get dressed."

"No." The way he said 'no' always broke my heart. He dragged out the "o" forever. And he put so much sadness and passion behind it. Like he was always about to cry when he said it. But it was also somehow the most adorable thing I'd ever heard.

"Noooo," he said again. He did *not* like clothes.

I blamed myself. I'd run around barefoot almost the whole time I was pregnant with him. I was pretty sure that somehow transferred to him. He only liked wearing a diaper. And 'liked' was probably too strong a term. Because he'd learned to take them off and loved running around naked the most.

It took me forever to wrassle him into a pair of shorts and a t-shirt. And I abandoned the idea of shoes after he accidentally flung one at my face. I'd just hold him.

We pulled up to the restaurant and I turned around to look at Jacob.

He'd somehow managed to take off his shirt even though he was securely in his car seat.

"How did you take that off?" I asked.

He pressed his lips together.

Jacob never lied to me. But he liked to withhold the truth. "Sweet boy, you have to wear clothes when we leave the house."

"No."

I laughed. "Well it is your birthday."

He smiled at me.

That smile melted my heart. I climbed out of the car and pulled him out of his car seat. At least he was still wearing his shorts. Luckily Alice didn't have one of those "No shirt, no shoes, no service," signs. Because Jacob was not following the rules.

I carried him into the restaurant.

Alice smiled when she saw us.

"He was very impatient for his birthday festivities to start," I said.

"I bet." Alice booped him on the nose. "You're getting so big. How old are you now?"

Jacob lifted up one finger.

"One?"

He nodded and then ducked his head under my arm. Jacob had stranger danger. Even for people he'd met countless times. And I loved that about him. He was shy and thoughtful and careful. Just like he needed to be. Maybe he wouldn't have to be one day. But right now I was relieved that he was careful.

"Is there any way I could steal George away a little early?"

"If you brought some of those mini scones I think I can arrange that."

"Done. They're in the car." It was a silly barter. She knew I was bringing them.

Miller emerged from the back. He'd probably heard us talking.

"Daddy!" Jacob reached out for him.

"Champ, where is your shirt? And your shoes?" He lifted Jacob out of my arms.

"No," Jacob said.

Miller laughed and balanced him on his hip. "We've talked about this. You have to wear clothes in public."

"No."

He laughed. "You're lucky it's your birthday."

Jacob smiled and held up his finger.

"You're one? How did you get so old?" Miller tickled his side.

Jacob went into a fit of laughter.

"Let me go grab the boxes," I said.

"I've got them," Miller said. He headed out to my car and brought back in the bakery boxes, somehow balancing them and Jacob. And Jacob was also suddenly wearing a shirt.

I had no idea how Miller did it. I swore it had taken me half an hour to get that shirt on Jacob. And Jacob didn't even look upset about it now. Miller was so good with him.

"Are you excited for your birthday, champ?" Miller said.

"Yes. Cuppycakes!"

Miller kissed the top of his head. "I'll be home in a few hours, okay?"

"Go ahead," Alice said. "It's a big day. You only turn one, once, right Jacob?"

Jacob nodded his head before hiding under Miller's arm.

We tried to get Jacob to wave goodbye to Alice but he was very happy in his hiding spot.

When we got home, Jacob immediately took his shirt off. Then his shorts. I caught him at the last second so he couldn't undo his diaper.

"Sweet boy, please keep that on."

He kept his hands on the waistband.

"Jacob."

"My birthday."

I laughed and looked up at Miller. "Were you a nudist when you were little too?"

"Me? I thought he got it from you."

I sighed. "Yeah. I think maybe he did."

Jacob unstrapped one side.

I mean…it was his birthday.

He unstrapped the other side and his diaper slid to the floor. He squealed in delight and started shaking his hips. "Dance. Dance!"

He'd quickly picked up on our tradition of dancing when we cooked dinner together. Sometimes he'd sit on the counter and clap as Miller and I danced. Other times he'd want to join in. Maybe he got the nudity thing from me. But he got this from both of us.

I grabbed one of his hands and Miller grabbed the other and we all started dancing. The three of us danced around the room, mimicking Jacob's stellar dance moves. I wasn't sure how long we danced, but eventually Jacob stopped. And he scrunched his mouth up.

Oh no. I knew that face. He was about to...

"Bathroom emergency," Miller said and grabbed Jacob under the arms. He sprinted toward the bathroom and I hoped they made it in time.

I laughed to myself as I picked up Jacob's discarded clothes. I knew it was dinner time, but Jacob had been so excited for cupcakes all day. I put icing on the rest of the cupcakes and plopped a candle in one. From other bathroom emergencies, I knew Jacob got embarrassed. He was a very private little person. This would cheer him up.

I lit the candle as I heard his little feet running back into the room.

He stopped right in front of me. "Oopsies." He blinked up at me with his big brown eyes. They were rimmed with red and I knew he'd been crying.

"It's okay, sweet boy. Oopsies happen." Although, maybe a little less for children who wore clothes. I leaned down and lifted him up, letting him sit in his preferred place...the middle of the kitchen counter. "Do you know what makes oopsies better? Birthday cupcakes!"

"Cuppycakes!" He tried to reach out and grab the one that was lit.

"We have to sing. And then we can all blow out the candle together, okay?"

His eyes grew round as he stared at the flame, but he nodded.

Miller wrapped his arms around me. He did that half singing, mostly talking thing. But I didn't think Jacob even noticed.

"Make a wish, champ," he said.

"Wishies?"

We blew on wishies all the time outside. Jacob loved to watch the pieces of the flower blow around in the wind like snowflakes.

I nodded. "Wish for anything you want."

Jacob scrunched his face to the side. And then he leaned forward.

I didn't want him to get too close to the flame. So Miller and I leaned forward at the same time. And we all blew out the candle together.

It wasn't my birthday. But I'd snuck in a wish anyway. For endless days like this with my boys.

I snuck a glance at Miller. He was smiling down at me. I was pretty sure he'd snuck in a similar wish too.

CHAPTER 50

4 Months Later - Wednesday - Thanksgiving

"Jacob, if you want to go outside, you have to put on a shirt and your sneakers."

"No."

"Sweet boy, you'll freeze your toesies." I grabbed his little foot.

"No."

I laughed. "Yes you will." I looked over at Miller for his help. But when I saw him, I completely lost my train of thought. He was dressed like he was about to go for a run around the lake. Gym shorts without a shirt. I'm pretty sure my heart skipped a beat every time I saw him with his shirt off. But my eyes narrowed at his bare feet. "Miller, what are you doing?"

"It's not that cold out yet, kid," he said and kissed my cheek. "Besides, we're gonna get overheated."

"Doing what exactly?"

"Footie!" Jacob yelled and held up a brand new football.

"Football," Miller corrected and ruffled Jacob's hair. "Starting new Thanksgiving traditions."

"Yes. Footie," Jacob said.

I turned back to Miller. The two of them had become obsessed with watching football every Sunday. And even though Jacob claimed he loved it, there was no way he had any idea what was happening. And he was certainly too young to play. "No."

"Now you sound like Jacob," Miller said with a laugh. "Come on. Don't give me that look. You're invited too." He started backing up slowly toward the door.

"Both of you need shoes," I said.

"Nope. Come on, you don't want to miss out."

I looked down at my own bare feet. Yeah, I was a hypocrite. I shook my head but laughed. Miller had me just where he wanted me. "But the turkey will be ready in half an hour," I said.

"I'm a good cook now. I won't forget the turkey."

"You will too forget the turkey."

But Miller had already reached the door. And I certainly didn't want to miss out. I ran out after them into the chilly fall air.

The ground was cold, just like I expected. But after we started running around it didn't feel that cold anymore.

Miller tossed the football at Jacob.

Jacob dodged it. He was not great at catching the football yet. I was happy that he was scared of the ball. I hadn't had great experience with football players. The thought hit me like a brick.

It was Thanksgiving. And I hadn't thought about Matt until just now. Thanksgivings were usually the hardest on me, remembering my fight with him. But honestly? I barely remembered our fight. I barely remembered the way his voice sounded. I could barely picture his face. And I couldn't even remember the last time that he'd interrupted my thoughts.

I watched as Miller pretended to tackle Jacob.

Jacob squealed at the top of his lungs as they rolled into the grass.

It was easy to forget the past when your present made your heart so full. I laughed and ran over to my family.

Miller sat up, pulling Jacob into his lap. "Okay, champ. Do you want to be on my team or Mommy's?" He tossed me the ball and I caught it.

Jacob pointed at Miller.

"Hey, no teaming up against me," I said. I tossed the ball back at Miller, who caught it with one hand.

Miller smiled at me and then looked back down at our son. "See those two trees over there?"

Jacob nodded.

"That's the endzone we're running to. And between the garden and that tree is the endzone Mommy's running to."

Jacob nodded.

"You ready?"

"Yessie." Jacob climbed off his lap.

Miller handed him the ball and then whispered something in his ear.

Jacob giggled and then started running as fast as he could with the ball.

"Hey!" I called after him. "You didn't say hike!"

Jacob ran through the trees.

And even though my husband and son were a bunch of cheaters, I cheered at the top of my lungs. "Touchdown!"

Jacob threw the ball on the ground and started to dance.

I smiled over at Miller.

He smiled back and pushed himself off the ground. He grabbed my hand and pulled me toward the fake endzone and we all started dancing together.

"Mommy," Jacob said and handed me the ball.

Miller took a step toward me.

No way were they the only ones scoring touchdowns today. I started sprinting in the opposite direction. Before I was even a quarter of the way to my endzone, Miller grabbed me around the waist.

I thought he was going to tackle me into the grass, but instead he lifted me over his shoulder and sprinted toward the opposite endzone.

"Ah!" My weight shifted, my hands moving to his ass.

I heard him chuckle.

"Miller you're cheating!" I slapped his butt. "Put me down!"

"Go, Daddy go!" Jacob cheered.

Miller ran past the two trees and started dancing. "Touchdown!"

"That is not a touchdown!" I slapped his butt again, but I couldn't stop laughing. "Put me down!"

"Safety!" Jacob yelled.

Miller laughed. "Did he just say safety? I can't believe he knows that. I swear we're raising a little genius baby."

"I'm pretty sure he said salad," I said. But it was kind of hard to tell because I was upside down and a little distracted.

"No, I swear he said safety. I'm telling you…boy genius!" Miller slowly put me down on my feet, but then pulled me into his chest.

"Genius or not, you're a dirty cheater," I said. I was smiling so hard it hurt.

Instead of responding, he kissed me. And then dipped me low as if it was all still part of his touchdown celebration dance.

"Ewie," Jacob said.

I looked over at Jacob. And he was no longer wearing shorts. "Sweet boy, where are your shorts?"

He shrugged his little shoulders.

What was I going to do with him? Last time his shorts disappeared I found them floating in the lake a few days later. I didn't think he'd had enough time to run over there but…I also rarely ever saw him taking off his clothes. They usually just disappeared. Maybe he was a little boy genius.

He ran over to us. Miller leaned down so Jacob could launch himself into his arms. I took advantage of Miller's distraction to grab the ball and earn myself a touchdown too.

***

We'd put Jacob to bed and we'd been lying on the couch, my head in Miller's lap. My stomach was still so full from our Thanksgiving dinner. I was pretty sure neither of us could move. I was definitely in a food coma.

Miller's fingers ran through my hair.

I looked up at him. Today had been amazing. Perfect, really. But football? I was fine that they watched it together. But I didn't want my son playing it. "Miller?"

He looked down at me.

"Maybe we can start playing soccer together or something instead of football?" I asked.

He continued running his fingers through my hair. "I thought it might be fun. A new Thanksgiving tradition for the three of us."

"It was fun. I just…" I swallowed hard. "I don't want Jacob to play football. Maybe you could teach him soccer? Or baseball?" I honestly couldn't imagine ever sitting in the stands at a football game ever again. There were too many memories. And I didn't want to think of any of them.

Miller pulled his eyebrows together.

"Just like…any other sport. I mean, why football?" Miller knew that Matt used to play. He'd been to games with me. He knew all of it.

Miller cleared his throat. "I used to watch football with my dad every Sunday."

Oh. Miller never talked about his family. It was almost as if they didn't exist. "Yeah?"

"Yeah." He suddenly sounded so sad. He looked away from me, staring at something on the mantle. "And he'd play with me on Thanksgiving every year. At least, until I was a teenager. It's one of my only good memories of him."

Oh, Miller. I could feel tears welling in my eyes. I turned to see what he was looking at on the mantle. I was pretty sure he was staring at the picture of my mom and me dancing in our kitchen all those years ago. He'd adopted all my traditions. Every single one. And we'd created so many new ones together. I swallowed hard. The least I could do was accept this one of his. This had nothing to do with Matt. This had nothing to do with my past. This was about Miller and him holding on to one good memory of his father. We didn't even know if his dad was alive or dead. But this could keep those good memories alive for Miller and our son.

I sat up and straddled him on the couch. "Okay."

He raised his eyebrow. "Okay?"

I nodded. "Just…don't let him get any concussions or anything."

"I would never let anything bad happen to Jacob."

He didn't need to say that, I knew it. "It's weird. We've been together for so long, but I can still learn new things about you." I kissed the tip of his nose.

He slid his hand to my neck so I couldn't move away. "Want to know something else?"

I nodded.

"You've never looked more beautiful than you do right now."

I smiled down at him. "You're full of crap, Miller. I ate my weight in turkey. I can barely move."

"You moved on top of me."

I laughed. "Fair point."

"You know what would be even more fun than football on Thanksgiving?"

"No." I couldn't stop smiling because his smile was infectious. "What would be more fun?"

"Let's make another baby."

"Hmm." I locked my hands behind his back. "Another one, huh?"

"Or five."

I laughed. I wanted to fill our house with children. I wanted all of it. "You better take me to the bedroom then, Miller." Because Jacob was as good at escaping from his crib as he was at taking off his clothes. And if he caught us going at it one more time I was worried he'd be permanently scarred.

CHAPTER 51

1 Year Later - Wednesday - Christmas

I loved Christmas. But this one felt heavy. I watched Jacob open his presents with the biggest smile on his face. Three years ago, I'd surprised Miller by telling him I was pregnant. We'd said our vows outside in the snow. It was perfect. It was so freaking perfect. We'd created this amazing little human who I loved with all my heart. I knew how blessed we were.

But today everything hurt. Yes, I had everything I'd ever wanted. I had a family that loved me as much as I loved them. And yet…I couldn't stop blinking away the tears in my eyes. I excused myself after the last present was opened and headed outside before I started full-on crying. I didn't want to ruin today like I'd been ruining all our days recently. I just needed a minute.

It was cold out and there were clouds in the sky threatening snow, but no snow came. It was like the universe somehow knew snow was only for good moods.

I wandered down to the dock and sat down, my boots dangling over the side.

I closed my eyes and pictured the lake in the summer. All of us laughing out there in the boat.

I felt Miller's presence before I heard his feet on the dock. He sat down beside me and I kept my eyes closed tight. If I didn't open them, maybe I wouldn't cry.

"Brooklyn." He grabbed my hand, and his was still warm from the fire inside. "I need you to know that I have everything I need right here, kid."

I let my head fall to his chest. "I know that's not true."

"I swear it is."

I opened my eyes and the tears rolled down my cheeks. "What if something is wrong with me?" I touched my stomach. A habit I needed to stop now that there was no longer a baby growing inside.

"Nothing is wrong with you. Hey, look at me." He grabbed the bottom of my chin and tilted my face up to his. "Brooklyn, nothing is wrong with you. You're perfect."

We both knew that wasn't true. If nothing was wrong, I wouldn't have woken up last month with the sheets covered in blood. I wouldn't have had a miscarriage if I was perfect.

"Whatever you're thinking, stop it." He put his hand on the side of my head. "These things happen."

"I was already picturing what he'd be like."

Miller smiled, but it was the saddest smile I'd ever seen in my life. A few months ago, this would have been when he'd argue that the baby was going to be a girl, not a boy. But now…it would never be anything. Because my body was broken.

"We can try again," he said. "When you're ready."

I shook my head. "I don't want to try again. I want *him*."

"I know." He ran his thumbs beneath his eyes, doing his best to erase my tears. "I did too."

I knew this wasn't just hard on me. That he was experiencing the loss too. But it felt like my heart had been ripped out. I'd been so happy for so long, I'd forgotten how much life could hurt.

"We're going to get through this," Miller said. "Together."

I nodded and put my head back against his chest. It just hurt. Every inch of my body. Everything hurt. Miller wanted a big family. I thought I did too. But… "What if I'm not strong enough to try again?"

"Are you kidding? You're the strongest person I know." He kissed the top of my head and ran his hand up and down my back. "And I meant what I said. I have everything I need right here."

He was making my heart hurt even more. "We both know that isn't true."

"Yes it is. I wanted a life with you. The good, the bad, the ups and downs. Don't you remember what I said to you three years ago when I finally made you my wife?"

It felt like the first time I'd smiled in months. "Remind me again."

He shifted so that I could see his face.

"I will spend my whole life loving you, Brooklyn. The life we created here together is better than anything in my wildest dreams. Us against the world." He put his hand on the side of my face. "The three of us against the world."

"You swear you mean it? Even if it's always just the three of us?"

"I swear I mean every word." He leaned down and kissed me. He didn't care that my lips were salty from my tears. He just wanted to erase the pain.

I crawled onto his lap and stared into his eyes. "I think I need it to be just the three of us for a while, okay? Because my heart hurts so damn much."

"Mine too. I also think maybe we can take our vacation a little early this year." He reached into his pocket and pulled out a piece of paper with a travel itinerary.

"You already booked our beach trip?" He always knew how to turn my frowns into smiles.

He grabbed my hand and kissed where my wedding and engagement rings sat. "I know how to make my wife happy."

I smiled down at him. "Yes you do." I dropped my forehead to his. Being in his arms made everything hurt a little less.

CHAPTER 52

Friday

Jacob started laughing.

I put my book down on the beach blanket and stared at Jacob and Miller practicing football in the sand. I smiled to myself as Jacob threw the ball a few feet right onto the ground.

"Good job, champ," Miller said and picked it up. "You almost got it right to me!" He tossed the ball back to Jacob and crouched down. "Let's try that again." He put his hands out for Jacob to throw them in.

This time when Jacob threw it, Miller was close enough to the ground to catch it. "You did it!" Miller cheered.

"Yessie!" Jacob started doing his signature touchdown dance. Which was him shaking his little hips.

"Mommy!" Jacob yelled and raced toward me. "I did it!" He launched himself into my arms, getting sand all over me. But I didn't even care. He was my little sugar-coated doughnut and I loved him to pieces.

"I saw." I held him tight. "It was a perfect throw." I started attacking him with kisses.

He giggled as he wriggled in my arms. "Jump! Jump!"

I knew exactly what he wanted. I grabbed one of his hands as I slowly stood up, and Miller grabbed his other hand. We all ran down to the water together.

Every time a wave came we lifted him up so he could pretend he was jumping them. It was his favorite thing in the world. Well, this and football. And I'd keep doing this until my arm ached because his smiles made me smile.

I looked over at Miller. And I was very aware that he was smiling over at me instead of down at our son.

And I have no idea why, but I could feel myself blushing. How could he still make me blush after all these years?

***

"Wake up," Miller whispered. "I have a surprise for you."

"Miller, you know I don't like surprises." But I could already feel myself smiling as I sat up in bed.

"Oh, I think you'll like this one. I got the monitor so we don't have to worry." He held up the baby monitor. "I just need you to come with me." He put his hand out for me.

"Shouldn't I change?"

"No. You look amazing just the way you are."

I smiled and slid my hand into his. I loved that whatever he had planned didn't require me to change into something fancy. Or put on many clothes in general. I had gone to bed in one of his old t-shirts.

I held his hand as he guided me out of the beach house and down the stairs of the deck.

The sand was cold now. But I knew I didn't need to hop along on it for very long because I could see our destination in the distance.

Miller had strung lights between two beach umbrellas and there was a blanket underneath them. It was like a little piece of our backyard at the lake house had been plopped down in the middle of the beach. But it also reminded me of the little blanket fort he'd made me one of those first nights, years ago, at the beach house when I swore I needed to be outside.

"Happy anniversary, a few days late," Miller said when we reached the blanket.

I smiled up at him. "Happy anniversary. This is a little different than saying 'I do' in the snow."

"Just as perfect."

I smiled and looked out at the water. I'd fought so hard not to fall in love with Miller years ago at the beach house. But it had taken me a few months and a beach in California to make me realize that I'd already fallen. A spot just like this, hundreds of miles away from here.

"May I have this dance?" Miller asked. He stepped away from me and then put his hand out.

There wasn't any music. But I'd never pass up a dance with the most handsome man I knew. "Always."

He pulled me back in close and we swayed to the sounds of the waves crashing.

"We're going to be okay," I said, wrapping my arms around his waist and smiling up at him.

"I know." He kissed my forehead.

We both stared out at the water as we slow danced. I knew better than anyone else that loss eventually faded into a dull ache. Which eventually faded to a blurry memory. We were definitely going to be okay eventually. Even if my heart still hurt right now. If I'd learned any-thing about a life with Miller, it was that he always made everything better. He knew exactly how to cheer me up. And a summer sun in the middle of winter to chase away the cold. Ever since we'd stepped foot on the beach I couldn't help but smile. But this? Right here with him? I could already feel my heart healing.

"And before I forget," he said and smiled down at me. "We have champagne. And midnight snacks."

I laughed. "I thought we gave up midnight snacks?"

"Not on our anniversary."

"Oh, of course." I laughed as he pulled me down onto the blanket. After giving birth to Jacob I'd stopped eating late night ice cream as I tried to lose the extra weight. But sometimes everyone needed a little late night ice cream. And Miller didn't disappoint, because he pulled out a container of mint chocolate chip from the cooler.

"I love you," I said. "More than you could possibly know."

He handed me the whole container and I laughed. "I love you too, kid."

I stuck my tongue out at him.

"Keep doing that and I'll have to retaliate." He popped the bottle of champagne and poured me a glass.

"And how will you retaliate?" I took a sip of champagne and smiled. I loved how cozy and fancy this seemed at the same time.

"Oh I can think of a few ways."

The way he said it made me swallow hard. Miller was always patient with me. But especially the past couple of months. I was grieving for what we lost. And even though I didn't think I was pulling away from him, I think I always tended to do that when I was hurting. Like somehow I was protecting him from hurting too. And it had been a while since we'd had sex. "A few ways?"

He smiled, but the humor didn't quite reach his eyes. All I could see was desire. He'd gotten sexier over the years, if that was even possible. And I knew I hadn't. I had stretch marks on my stomach and I was pretty sure my butt was twice the size it used to be. But he always looked at me like that. Like he couldn't get enough. And I didn't want to be grieving tonight. I just wanted…him.

"I'm ready for your retaliation, good sir," I said.

"You are, huh?" He put his glass down and leaned over me, not caring that my glass fell over in the sand.

I hitched my legs around his waist. There was something about Miller and the way we fit together. Like we were always meant to be. I felt like I was home when I was with him. And I felt so loved I could just burst. "I've missed you," I said and buried my fingers into his hair.

"I've been right here." He kissed the side of my neck as he pushed my t-shirt up. "I'll always be right here." He kissed my stomach, not caring about my stretch marks. "Always, Brooklyn." He slowly pulled my panties down my legs.

And I tried not to cry out when his lips found my clit and his fingers slid inside me.

God I'd missed his mouth. And his fingers. I pulled him closer as his tongue swirled around me, his fingers driving me insane.

"Shit, Miller, the lights." I was staring up at the twinkling fairy lights above us. Which lit us up on the beach.

He reached over and switched them off, shrouding us in darkness.

I blinked and stared up at the stars in the sky. Or maybe it was just stars in my eyes because he'd just started doing that thing with his tongue that I loved…*fuck*. I came embarrassingly fast. Or at least it would have been embarrassing if Miller wasn't so damn happy with himself. I could feel his smile against my skin.

I propped myself up on my elbows so I could see him. "Oh and you don't think I can make you cum just as fast?"

He kissed the inside of my thigh. "No." He kissed the inside of my other thigh. "No, I don't."

"Challenge accepted." I pushed him back, straddling him. Somehow we'd wandered off the blanket, but I didn't even care. I'd dreamed of having sex with him on the beach years ago. And it was crazy that we'd never done it.

All those runs we went on together…I should have just tackled him. I should have made him mine right away. Why had I waited so many years to say "I do"? I loved this man. I loved him so much and being here with the salt in the air and the sand on my skin reminded me just how much we really were always meant to be.

If I hadn't just accepted a challenge to try to make him cum as fast as possible, I would have made love to him in the sand. But…I was never one to back down from a challenge. I was going to give him the blowjob to end all blowjobs. I pushed down his shorts and boxers, wrapping my hand around his length. He was already impossibly hard.

I shifted, the cold sand against my knees sending a chill down my spine, as I placed my lips against his tip.

Miller's sharp exhale was all I needed to spur me on. I wrapped my lips around him and he buried his fingers in my hair.

I moved my head, taking him all the way to the back of my throat.

"Jesus," he groaned.

I bobbed my head up and down faster, pressing my lips harder against him. I swore I was seconds away from making him cum when his fingers tightened in my hair, pulling me back.

"You win," he said before I could protest that he was cheating. "But I don't want to come in your mouth." He grabbed my waist and flipped me over, my back hitting the cold sand. He thrust himself inside of me.

God. I gripped his shoulders.

"Do you have any idea how many times I dreamed of having you just like this?" His breath was hot on my neck.

"Probably as many times as I have."

He groaned. "I never imagined you'd really choose me."

His words would have broken my heart if I wasn't so consumed by the feeling of him inside of me. "Miller…"

"My wife." He kissed the side of my neck. "My heart." He kissed between my breasts. "My home." He kissed my chest where my heart was pounding. "You're mine."

"I'm yours." My fingers dug into his back. I was his. And I was pretty sure I would have always come to my senses and chosen him. He was my person.

He slammed into me harder.

God, I loved this man. He moved faster, a relentless pace that was making it hard to think about anything but him. Each thrust made me feel more like myself. Like he was piecing me back together again. I'd needed this so badly.

"I loved chasing you down the beach, Brooklyn." His hand slid to my ass.

I moaned, the change of angle hitting me in all the right places.

"I would have chased you forever."

"No need for chasing," I said. "My heart was already yours. You knew it all along." As much as I tried to fight it…I couldn't. I'd loved Miller at that beach house. I'd always loved him.

His thumb brushed against my clit. "You really lost this challenge, because I'm going to make you come again before…"

"Hey! I don't think so." I wrapped my legs around his waist, pulling him closer.

He groaned.

I lifted my hips, matching each thrust. "Please, Miller." *God.* "I need you. I need this."

He groaned again, his cock pulsing inside of me.

My fingers dug into his back as I clenched around him. I held his body to mine as I came, my toes curling into the sand.

We were both panting, our chests pressed together.

I grabbed his face so I could stare at him in the moonlight. All the good and bad had led me here. To this moment. And as hard as the bad times had been, I'd never change this moment for anything. I looked up at the stars. "We were written in the stars," I whispered. "You and me."

"The three of us," he said, rolling us over so we could both look up at the starry sky.

I rested my head against his chest. *The three of us.* I smiled listening to his steady heartbeat. I was okay with being three.

CHAPTER 53

6 Months Later - Saturday

I leaned against the doorjamb and watched Miller read Jacob a bedtime story, the smile on my face growing by the second.

"And the cow goes…"

"Moo!" Jacob said.

Miller smiled and turned the page of Jacob's favorite book. "And the pig goes…

"Oink!"

"And the monster goes…"

"The monster?" Jacob sat up in bed and grabbed the top of the book to tilt it down. "Daddy that's not a monster. That's a duck."

"But what noise does a monster make?"

"A scary one?"

"It goes…rawr!" Miller tickled Jacob's side.

Jacob started laughing, flailing around in the sheets.

"Hey, you two," I said. "You're supposed to be getting ready for bed."

Miller patted the bed next to me. "We were waiting for you."

"Mhm." I shook my head, but I was smiling. I ran over to the bed and jumped on it.

Miller laughed as I ducked under his arm. He pulled me in close, placing a kiss on my cheek. This was my favorite place to be.

I leaned over and tickled Jacob too, sending him into another fit of laughter, before leaning back against Miller's shoulder. "Now, where were we?"

"That part about monsters," Miller said.

"Of course. And what noise does a monster make?" I asked.

Jacob smiled. And then he "rawred" at the top of his lungs.

I rawred back.

And so did Miller.

And somehow we all started jumping on the bed rawring.

I tumbled down, grabbing Jacob with me. "Little monster, it's time for bed."

"But, Mommy…"

"Even monsters need sleep."

He yawned. "Even monsters?"

"Yes, sweet boy."

"I want to grow up and be a monster," Jacob said. "Can I go to school for that?"

The thought of Jacob going to school made my heart race. I glanced at Miller and then back down at Jacob. "Hmm." I kissed his forehead. "We'll have to see. For now, let's finish your book."

Miller sat down on the opposite side of Jacob. He tucked Jacob in like a sausage so he couldn't move and then cleared his throat. "And the duck goes…"

"Quack," Jacob said.

"And the lion goes…"

"Roar," Jacob said with a yawn.

"And the turkey goes…"

"Gobble gobble…" Jacob started snoring.

I smiled down at him and then looked back up at Miller. I knew he could see the worry in my eyes.

He leaned down and kissed Jacob's forehead before climbing off the bed slowly, doing his best not to wake Jacob. I followed his lead, tiptoeing out into the hall.

I took one more look at our adorable little guy before softly closing the door. I sighed and turned around, pressing my hands to Miller's chest. "School? We can't send him to school." I'd been teaching him by myself. He could already say his alphabet and he could count pretty high.

"Hey." Miller reached down and smoothed my furrowed brow with his thumb. "He's only three. We have two more years to worry about that."

"But…"

"Right now, let's just enjoy ourselves. In our little bubble." He pulled me in close.

"He should be socializing though, right? What if I keep him here too long and he doesn't know how to make friends?"

"Kids know how to make friends. It's fine."

"What if we do send him and he starts stripping in class?"

Miller laughed. "Well that would just be hilarious…"

"Miller!" I pressed my lips together. "I'm a terrible mother, aren't I?"

"What? No." He cupped the side of my face in his hand. "Not in a million years."

"He's scared of everyone he comes across and he doesn't like clothes."

"I don't like clothes either. And honestly, you're wearing a little too many for my taste."

"Miller I'm being serious…"

"Me too." He leaned down and hoisted me over his shoulder.

I laughed as he carried me to our bedroom. "You're impossible, you know."

"You're worrying about nothing. Jacob's an adorable kid. When we think it's safe to send him to school he'll make tons of friends. With or without clothes." He lightly slapped my butt.

"He has to wear clothes if he goes to school."

"Then he'll probably choose not to go. Win win."

I laughed as Miller threw me down on our bed. But my laughter died in my throat as Miller peeled off his shirt.

"Okay, fine, maybe clothes are a little overrated."

"Rawr."

I laughed as he stalked toward me. "What are you doing?"

He rawred again.

I squealed as he reached for my ankle. I pushed myself up on my knees and crawled along the bed as he rawred again.

I tossed a pillow at him and jumped off the bed as he lunged for me.

He chased me around the room, prowling after me. God, how was he so sexy even when he was being ridiculously silly?

I was completely out of breath as he caged me in against the door. "You caught me," I said, panting. "What are you going to do to me now?"

"I'm going to eat you."

It was such a classic monster response. I would have tried to run again, but he dropped to his knees, pushing my shorts and panties down.

Oh. *Eat me.* He lifted one of my thighs over my shoulder. *Oh God.* Miller was ridiculously good at erasing my worries. He slowly swirled his tongue around inside of me. *Yes. Just like that.*

CHAPTER 54

1 Year Later - Friday

"I can't believe our little boy is four. How did that happen?"

"I can't believe it either." Miller wrapped his arms around me from behind, resting his head on my shoulder.

We stared down at the lake where Jacob was fighting an imaginary foe with a sword. Well, actually a stick. But he swore it was a sword.

"Daddy, Daddy!" Jacob ran up to us. "Cowboys and Indians!"

"You got it, champ." Miller took out two imaginary guns from his waistband. "Best get on yer way, son."

Jacob loved watching old movies with Miller. And I think he felt some kind of comradery with how Native Americans were depicted. Mostly because they didn't wear shirts. Jacob was convinced he was an Indian.

Jacob put his hand to his mouth and tapped it repeatedly, chanting, "Oh, oh, oh, oh." It sounded like an Indian war cry. Which meant he was about to attack.

Miller took a step back like it was terrifying. "I said get!" He held out one of his fake guns.

Jacob pulled back one of his arms and shot fake arrows at Miller.

"I'm hit!" Miller said, grabbing his chest. "No! Save yourself, woman!" He looked over at me.

I laughed as Miller collapsed on the ground with a flourish.

Jacob started chanting again. Dancing around with his fake bow and arrow.

Miller opened one eye and then closed it again.

"Daddy!" Jacob said and jumped on top of Miller.

"Oomph."

"You're a knight now. Get up."

Miller opened his eyes. He reached out beside him and grabbed at the air. "I dropped my sword."

I heard the timer beeping inside. Jacob's cupcakes were ready.

***

Miller was giving Jacob a bath. The cute little dude had gotten cuppycakes pretty much everywhere. I smiled to myself. If I could have made a wish on his birthday candles, I would have wished that he'd call cupcakes cuppycakes for a little while longer. He was growing up too fast. Really…how was he already four?

There was another wish I'd make though. I sat down on the bathroom floor and closed my eyes instead of glancing at the pregnancy test too early.

Months and months of negative tests were starting to weigh on me. What if there really was something wrong with me?

I'd take back the cupcake wish if it meant I could get pregnant again. I wanted to give Jacob a sister. Or a brother. Desperately. And if I had another kid, I wouldn't feel so bad about not letting Jacob go to school next year. He'd get to socialize with his sibling. Hopefully siblings plural. But that was jumping the gun a bit. I couldn't seem to get pregnant with one more kid, let alone two or three.

I closed my eyes tighter. *Please.* I wasn't even sure who I was begging. But I kept saying *please* in my head over and over again.

There was a knock on the bathroom door. I opened my eyes as Miller popped his head in.

"I can't look," I said, avoiding glancing down at the test.

Miller grabbed the stick from my hand and then sat down next to me on the bathroom floor.

He looked down. He was good at hiding his emotions about this. I think he wanted to make sure I didn't feel bad that I couldn't give him another child. Even though it was breaking me in two regardless. We'd wanted a big family.

He finally looked up at me and smiled. But the smile didn't reach his eyes.

And I already knew what he was going to say.

"Just the three of us for a little longer."

It was the sweetest way he could possibly put it. But I felt myself deflating.

"Don't," he said, pulling me into his side. "Don't be upset about something that isn't in your control." He kissed my temple, holding me tight.

It was easy to melt into him, letting him take away some of my pain. "Maybe next month," I said, even though I wasn't sure I believed the words.

"Maybe. And look on the bright side. It means you can have a glass of wine tonight."

I smiled up at him. "That's true."

"And that you can eat sushi for at least another month."

I laughed. "You know I don't like sushi."

"Well, now you have another month to try some new varieties. I really think if you tried it again…"

"I promise you I don't like it."

"You're very unadventurous."

"Really? If I recall correctly, I escaped from a mob boss, lived on my own for months barely scraping by because I wanted to see the Pacific Ocean, and shagged my bodyguard. I even know how to use a gun. I'm very adventurous."

"I stand corrected." Miller pushed himself up off the floor and put his hand out for me. "Come on my adventurous wife. I know just what you need."

"And what is it that I need?"

"I'm going to need you to trust me on that one." He put his hand closer to me.

Of course I trusted him. I put my hand in his and let him help me to my feet.

He led me past Jacob's bedroom. Jacob was fast asleep. He'd had a busy birthday. I bet he'd fallen asleep as soon as his head hit the pillow.

Miller led me down the hall, through the great room, and out the back door.

"Where are we going?" I said with a laugh as we walked through the grass. God I loved the summer. There was something magical about walking barefoot in the grass.

We walked onto the dock and he led me to the very end.

"Okay," he said. "Do your thing."

"What thing?" Did he want me to jump in or something?

"Your thing."

I laughed. "I have no idea what you're talking about."

"Scream, kid. Scream it all out."

I hadn't done that in ages. I remember screaming at the top of my lungs at the beach house when I was frustrated. I knew he'd seen me do it. Or at least heard me do it. I smiled over at him.

"Come on, we'll do it together," he said and squeezed my hand.

"Won't someone hear us?" The night was quiet, except for the hum of cicadas in the trees. I always thought my screams at the beach got swept up with the crashing waves.

Instead of responding, he turned to the water and screamed at the top of his lungs.

I smiled and then turned to the lake. And I screamed at the top of my lungs too. I screamed for the baby we lost. I screamed for the dozens of wasted pregnancy tests. I screamed out my frustrations. I screamed so loudly that my throat hurt.

I was panting when I was done, my chest rising and falling fast. "Wow that felt good."

"You know what else would feel good?"

"What?"

He shoved me off the deck and into the cold water before I had a chance to register what was happening. "What the hell?!" I yelled when I came up for air. I splashed water at him.

He jumped into the lake beside me. "I thought a late-night swim might be fun."

"You're ridiculous."

"It's a shame that you think so. Because you're stuck with me."

I laughed and wrapped my legs around his waist. "Oh, I happen to love ridiculous things."

"Is that so?"

"Yes." I kissed the tip of his nose.

He smiled and held me tight. He was right. This did feel good.

CHAPTER 55

3 Months Later - Thursday

Jacob barged into our room and jumped on our bed. "I'm hungry," he said and nestled in between us. "I want pancakes."

"Sweet boy, it's too early," I said with a yawn.

"No. The sun is out."

I blinked and turned toward the window. The sun was streaming fiercely through the blinds. I glanced at the clock on my nightstand and it was blinking. *Shit*. I sat up and lightly shook Miller. "Miller, the storm must have knocked out the power."

He groaned in his sleep, somehow having not been woken up by Jacob running in and jumping on him. "What?" he yawned.

"The storm last night." I reached over him and grabbed his watch off the nightstand. "It's past 8!" *Shit*. There was no way I'd be able to have all the baked goods ready for my normal noon drop off. I was hours behind my schedule.

"Crap," he said and sat up.

"Daddy said a bad word!" Jacob said.

"Yeah, don't say that word," Miller said and ruffled Jacob's hair. "I gotta run. I'm late for work."

This was not a good start to the day. We were going to double piss off Alice, first with Miller coming in late and then me dropping off the desserts really late this afternoon. "I should have been half done baking for the day by now." I scrambled out of bed.

Miller was already pulling on a pair of jeans and a t-shirt.

"I'm hungry," Jacob said again. "Can I go to work with Daddy today? I want *his* pancakes."

I was going to be frantic the rest of the morning trying to bake at twice my usual speed, which of course wasn't possible. If Jacob wanted to sit around the kitchen at the restaurant for hours instead of stealing cookies from me, that was fine. "Yeah, you can go with Daddy."

"Yay!" He jumped off the bed and ran toward the door.

"You have to wear a shirt!" I yelled after him.

Miller laughed.

"Will you tell Alice I'm running a bit late today?"

"No problem." Miller gave me a quick kiss and we both hurried out of the bedroom.

I turned on the oven and started pulling out ingredients from the fridge and pantry. I'd been planning on trying a new recipe today, but I'd have to push that off.

I watched as Jacob opened the front door, shirtless.

"Jacob, your shirt!"

He held up a shirt that was balled up in his fist. "I have it."

"I need you to put that on."

"No."

"Listen to your mother, champ," Miller said and joined Jacob at the front door. He turned back to me. "Your car is blocking me in, Brooklyn."

Shoot. "I'll move it. One sec." I placed a bag of flour down on the counter a little too hard and a billow of flour burst into the air, covering my face. I coughed and waved my hand through the air.

I didn't even see Miller as he grabbed me around the waist. "It's okay, I'll move your car," he said, pulling me close. "You look adorable when you're covered in flour."

I laughed because I knew that couldn't possibly be true.

He pushed some of my hair out of my face and kissed me.

"Miller, there's no time for kissing! You're already late," I said, but I couldn't help but smile when his lips met mine again.

"Alice won't care."

I hated being late for things, but honestly Miller was right. We'd had late starts to our days before. Like a few months ago when Jacob caught that nasty cold.

Miller gave me one last kiss and then grabbed the keys to my car off the key hook. "I'll move your car. But I need your help wrassling Jacob into his shirt if he's gonna come with me."

"No," Jacob said again.

I laughed because it was all I could do. The stress of the morning had been moments away from making me crack. But Miller was always able to easily remind me to calm down. I couldn't even remember the last time I'd had a panic attack. And it certainly wasn't worth it over delivering cookies an hour late.

Miller laughed too as Jacob threw his shirt on the ground and sprinted outside.

"That little menace," I said.

"So much like his mother."

"I'm wearing a shirt."

"If I recall correctly, you weren't last night."

I lightly swatted at his butt before he started backing away.

"Think you can get him in his shirt in under thirty seconds?" Miller asked.

"Oh, challenge accepted." I grabbed the shirt off the ground and ran outside.

Jacob was doing his Indian war cry as he jumped around the front yard. Which meant this was not going to be easy.

"Sweet boy, let's get you into this shirt."

He ran farther into the yard, away from the driveway. "But I'm an Indian today."

"No you are not."

"Yes I am." He started his war cry again. "Oh, oh, oh, oh."

Miller was already getting into my car to move it. I did not have much time to succeed at this challenge. Ten seconds at the most.

"Oh, oh, oh, oh," Jacob chanted as he danced around.

I laughed and knelt down in front of Jacob. "I'll make a deal with you. Let me put this shirt on you, but as soon as you get in the car you can take it off, okay?" I was not past bribery here. I probably only had five seconds…

"But I don't want to, Mommy."

Four seconds.

"Sweet boy…"

Three seconds.

"No," he said.

Two seconds.

"You can have extra dessert tonight."

One second.

Jacob's eyes grew round. "Deal. Extra cuppycakes." He put his arms above his head.

"That's my boy." But before I even lifted his shirt, the earth shook as a huge boom echoed around us. The blast threw me and Jacob to the ground.

All I could hear was a loud ringing in my ears. And I couldn't see anything. *What the hell was that?!* I wiped the dirt out of my eyes and looked to make sure Jacob was okay. He was crying, but I couldn't hear him through the ringing in my ears.

"Jacob!" I wasn't sure if I was yelling or not, but he didn't register my words.

I blinked again and cradled his face in my hands. Even though he was crying he looked unharmed. We'd fallen in the soft grass. My eyes scanned the rest of him. I didn't see a single scratch on him, but he wasn't making eye contact with me.

"Jacob!" I said again trying to make sure he was okay.

And then I smelled it. *Smoke.* And I saw the reflection in Jacob's eyes. He wasn't looking at me because he was looking at what was behind me. *Fire.*

I turned to look over my shoulder.

No.

"No!" I yelled, but still heard nothing but the ringing in my ears.

My car was engulfed in flames. The same car that Miller had just sat down in. Smoke and debris everywhere.

"Miller," I choked. "Miller!" I screamed at the top of my lungs, while still holding on to Jacob.

Oh God, oh God, oh God.

There was another loud blast that somehow made it through the ringing in my ears as the roof of the car peeled back.

"Miller!" I didn't know how I got to the car. I didn't remember letting go of Jacob. Or running over here. But I was reaching out for the door handle, I could feel the heat on my skin before I even made contact with the handle. And still I reached out. "Miller!" But before I could wrap my hand around the handle, the door fell off its hinges.

The smoldering air escaped the car and threw me back, my elbows skidding across the pavement.

The smell of blood swirled around with the smoke and dust.

"Miller." I wasn't screaming anymore. All I could see were flames. I didn't see my husband. I couldn't see my husband. "Miller," I sobbed. "Miller." The car blurred in front of me. "Miller." All I could see were flames. The heat on my face. The smell of burning. The smell of death. "Miller."

I pushed myself up and ran back to the car. I saw Miller through the flames then. Or…what was left of him. Slumped over the steering wheel.

No. All I could smell now was the burnt flesh. It was like I could taste it in my mouth. *Death.* The smell of death all around me, suffocating me.

I tried to reach into the car but twisted metal and debris were in the way. "Miller!"

He didn't move. He didn't respond at all. And I knew there was nothing left in him to respond. He wasn't there. I felt it in my bones. He wasn't with me anymore. He was gone.

No. My tears burned my eyes and I tried to reach into the car again.

My forearm hit one of the bent pieces of metal and it scorched my skin.

I screamed and for the first time I could hear myself through the ringing in my ears. Broken sobs ripped through my chest. "Miller!" I screamed. *No.*

He couldn't be gone. He couldn't. I needed him. "Miller."

I needed him.

"Miller," I choked.

I don't know how I ended up on the ground again. But I knew I was kneeling there, because Jacob grabbed both sides of my face, his little hands spreading my tears on my cheeks. His tear-stained eyes finding mine. "Mommy," he said in an eerily calm voice. "Go bags."

Go bags. Oh God. Oh God.

My father had found us.

He'd made good on his promise.

Miller was never supposed to touch me.

I screamed at the top of my lungs. Like I'd screamed on the beach all those times. Like I'd screamed a few months ago when I couldn't get pregnant. But I screamed louder.

Because this felt worse than losing my mom.

Worse than losing my uncle.

Worse than losing my life back in New York.

This was losing everything.

My heart.

My soul.

My home.

I'd lost loved ones before. And it always felt like my heart was breaking. But this time was different. This time my heart was burning. Like my chest was on fire. Scorched, never to beat again. No pieces to put back together. It was gone. A piece of me died in that car with Miller.

But it was like I could hear Miller's voice in my ear.

Run.

Run, kid.

So I grabbed Jacob, holding him as tightly to me as I could, and I ran.

CHAPTER 56

Thursday

Miller had been teaching Jacob about our go bags for as long as I could remember. That if something scary ever happened, we were supposed to grab them and run as fast as possible. Jacob had approached the situation exactly like Miller had taught him to. Where I'd been screaming and crying uncontrollably, Jacob had remained stoic and calm. My little boy was so brave. So much braver than me.

My hand shook as I put in the code for the safe. I pulled out the gun and slipped it into my bag. I lifted Jacob into my arms and started running to the front door.

"No," Jacob said as I grabbed Miller's keys off the key hook. He pointed out the back door toward the woods.

God, he was right. My car had had a bomb in it. Maybe Miller's truck did too. And I wondered what on earth Miller had taught our son. Because this was beyond a "scary situation." It was like he knew exactly how to act in this particular situation. But this wasn't the time or place to ask him about it. He'd reminded me of the danger we were in. And I was pretty sure that he'd saved us.

Jacob remained eerily calm as we ran through the woods and hotwired a neighbor's car. But as soon as I buckled him into the backseat, it was like a dam broke.

All the training Miller had given him ended as soon as he felt like we were in the clear. His tears bubbled over and he started crying louder than me. "Daddy!" he wailed. "I want Daddy!"

I winced as I sped down the highway. Jacob had seen it. He'd seen what I'd seen. He knew Miller was gone. And

I needed to comfort him. But I felt like I was burning too. Like my whole body was on fire. "We're going to be okay," I said, even though I didn't believe the words out of my own mouth. I wasn't okay. I'd never be okay again.

"Daddy!" Jacob sobbed, making my heart feel even more scorched.

I didn't know where we were going. But I had to get the hell away from here.

Miller was dead.

I'd fled the scene.

I'd stolen a car.

I had a fake ID in my go bag.

I was so fucked. And I needed to get away from here to protect my son. I'd do anything to protect him. I reached behind me while still looking at the road and put my hand on Jacob's knee.

My other hand shook on the steering wheel.

My vision blurred with tears. I tried my best to blink them away.

But I kept driving.

All I could hear was Jacob sobbing. All I could smell was the stench of burnt flesh that was stuck in my nose.

God, I can't do this. I can't do this without Miller. I tried to push away the thought, but it was true. I couldn't do life without him.

But then I felt Jacob wrap his little hand around mine and hold on.

It gave me the strength to keep driving.

We still had each other.

I'd get us somewhere safe.

CHAPTER 57

2 Weeks Later - Friday

I'd rented the tiniest place I could find at the beach. One - so that I could keep my eyes on the one entrance at all times. And two - because one bed meant I wouldn't have to explain to Jacob why I needed to snuggle up to him all night.

But tonight we were sitting on the beach under the stars. Because this was where I felt closest to Miller.

We were written in the stars.

I blinked away the tears as I stared up at the sky. How many nights had we sat on the beach just like this? And even more nights at the lake. He was here with me. And I knew if I closed my eyes I could imagine that he was. But I'd done that enough times over the past couple weeks to know how much it hurt when I opened my eyes again.

"I miss Daddy," Jacob said.

I turned to him. I'd thought he was sleeping. "I miss Daddy too."

"I want to go home."

Me too, sweet boy. But that wasn't an option. I'd fled the scene of a crime. I knew the cops were probably looking for me. And even if they weren't...my father had found us. We weren't safe there.

And the longer I had to think about it...the more questions I had. It was *my* car that had blown up. So...was my father trying to kill me? Or had his target been Miller? Or had he been hoping to off both of us?

Jacob's bottom lip started to tremble.

He'd been so brave on the day of the explosion. And he'd been brave several days ago when I tried to explain death to him. I wasn't sure he really understood. But he'd stopped asking for his daddy. And started saying he missed him instead. So maybe he understood better than I realized. "You know that your daddy is always with us though. No matter what."

"Noooo."

God, if my heart wasn't already broken, that drawn out 'No' would have done it. "Of course he is. He's in the stars." I looked up at the sky. The sight that made me feel closest to Miller. I smiled to myself, remembering I used to look for the stars in the sky in NYC too. Because they reminded me of the home I'd left behind.

"Which one is he?"

That was a good question. My eyes searched the sky, landing on the North Star. "See that big bright one?"

"The brightest one?"

"Yes. That's Daddy."

"Oh." He was quiet for a moment. "He's big."

"Well, he was the tallest man you knew, right?"

"Yessie." Jacob smiled but there were tears in his eyes.

"Come here." I opened up my arms so he could snuggle in next to me.

I held him as he cried himself to sleep. I couldn't do anything to make it better. But I could get even.

"I'm going to make it right, okay?" I ran my fingers through his hair. I knew I was running out of time. My husband had been murdered and I'd fled. I'd stolen a car. I had a fake ID. I had a gun registered to that fake ID.

If a cop pulled me over I'd go to jail for a really long time.

I was sure my picture was being slowly spread to every police station in the country.

I heard a clock ticking down in my head.

I had a plan on how to get us out of the country. But there was something I had to take care of first. I'd never be able to look Jacob in the eye if I didn't do this. I knew it was risky, but I had no choice. And it meant I needed a backup plan, just in case something happened to me. There was only one person I trusted with my son. Kennedy's mom, Mrs. Alcaraz. She'd been like a second mother to me. She'd keep Jacob safe. Just in case I couldn't.

And it just so happened that I needed to go to New York either way.

The city I swore I'd never go back to.

I stared up into the starry sky.

I'll make it right, Miller.

CHAPTER 58

Saturday - Present Day

Jacob was fast asleep in my arms as I walked down the hall. He was heavy. But the gun in the waistband of my jeans felt heavier.

Tonight everything would change.

I'd never be able to go back.

I swallowed hard and stopped outside my uncle's old apartment. Someone new probably lived there now. If I'd had any idea how short my time was going to be there, I would have tried to spend more time with my uncle. I would have tried to be better behaved. I would have done so many things differently.

I turned away. Thinking of all my regrets wasn't why I was here. I kissed Jacob's forehead and he stirred in his sleep. He made this adorable little moaning noise.

And I almost changed my plan. Looking down at his sweet face made me want to rethink everything.

But I couldn't live with myself if I didn't do this. I couldn't. As hard as it was to risk everything…I had to do this.

Please still live here, Mrs. Alcaraz. I walked down the hall and knocked on her door. I tried to breathe slowly, settling my nerves. *Please be here.*

I heard the muffled sound of someone saying "puta mierda" and smiled. I still had no idea what that meant. All I knew was that it was something bad. And I knew exactly who was on the other side of the door. I knew exactly how shocked she was to see me after all these years. And I'd kind of guessed she'd call me that.

The door opened and it was like I was transported back in time. Knocking on the door when I was back in high school. I couldn't help but smile through all the pain of the last couple weeks.

Kennedy was standing there. Staring at me like she was looking at a ghost. Which made sense. She thought I'd died 16 years ago. And even though she looked shocked…I could tell she was happy. She looked like the Kennedy I knew when I first met her. Before everything broke. Before I messed everything up. There was a reason I'd stayed away this whole time. Because I knew that everyone was better off without me.

"Brooklyn?" her voice wavered.

I didn't even hesitate. God, I'd been dying to talk to her for 16 years. Dying to let her know I was out there. And it was so fucking good to see my best friend. I threw my arms around her. Or…one arm. Because I was still holding Jacob. I didn't care if she was happier without me in her life. I'd missed her. I'd missed her so freaking much.

For a second she just stood there frozen. And then she started to cry and she hugged me back.

"You're alive." It didn't sound like she believed her own words. "What the hell?" She took a step back from me. Looked back at my son. Back at me. "Seriously, what the hell is going on? Where have you been all these years?"

"I'm really sorry. For everything. I've spent half a lifetime wishing I could fix what happened between us. And I wish I had more time to explain but…I have to go." *Before I chicken out.*

"Wait, what?"

I wanted to ask her a million questions. Was she still with Felix? Was that why she looked happy? Had everything turned out the way she wanted? But I didn't have time to catch up. And it would just make leaving harder. "Is your mom here?"

Kennedy nodded.

I could tell she was in shock. And as much as I wished I could sit and talk to her for hours, I didn't have time. I walked over to the couch and lay Jacob down. Tears formed in my eyes as I leaned over and kissed his forehead. *I love you. So much, sweet boy. I'm doing this for you. For us.* I pushed his hair off his forehead. And I said a silent prayer that everything would go according to plan and I'd be back in an hour. This wasn't goodbye. It couldn't be. He needed me. I'd come back and we'd disappear for good this time. The two of us against the world.

I wiped the tears out of my eyes and knocked on Mrs. Alcaraz' bedroom door.

"Mi amor, please stop questioning a good thing…" Mrs. Alcaraz's words stopped as soon as she saw me. "Ay dios mío. Mi amor." She grabbed both sides of my face. "You're alive."

God, she still smelled like empanadas and home. I was seconds away from falling apart. Seconds away from staying. But I'd be putting them all in danger. I needed to finish what I should have finished years ago.

I pulled the envelope out of my pocket. I'd written down everything. What had happened years ago. What I was about to do. All of it. I'd arranged for Mrs. Alcaraz to be Jacob's guardian just in case something happened to me. All she had to do was call my lawyer and sign the papers. My will was rock solid. My father wouldn't be stealing Jacob away like he'd stolen me. Not that I was worried about that happening after tonight.

"I'm going to be back in an hour. But if…if I don't come back…" my voice cracked. I couldn't think like that. But I had to think like that because of my son. I had to think of everything to protect him. "If I don't come back, I need you to take care of my baby," I said.

"What?"

I gestured to Jacob on the couch. "It's all in here," I said and handed her the envelope. "If I don't come back, read it. It explains everything. But he likes watching football on Sundays. And don't always make him wear a shirt. He hates them. Just keep my baby safe. Please." I grabbed Mrs. Alcaraz' hands. "Please."

She just nodded. "Of course."

"You can't leave," Kennedy said. "You just got here. You can't." There were tears in her eyes again.

I'm so sorry. For everything. "Don't tell a soul I was here. No one can know. Not until it's safe."

"When will we know it's safe?" Kennedy asked.

"When I come back. Or…when you read the note in an hour." I gave her another hug. "You've always been my best friend. Always, Kennedy. And I really am so sorry about everything."

"I'm sorry too," she said. "I'm so fucking sorry, Brooklyn."

I closed my eyes. "And if I don't come back, make sure Jacob knows how much I love him. And that I did it for him." I quickly stepped back before I completely lost it.

I took one last look at Jacob and it felt like my heart was breaking. I wasn't ready. I needed one more minute. Just to make sure he'd be okay if I didn't come back. I needed him to be okay. And he was scared of strangers. I didn't want him to freak out. I crouched down in front of him on the couch and lightly shook his shoulder. "Jacob, wake up."

He moaned in his sleep.

I shook his shoulder again and he slowly opened his eyes. "Mommy." His eyes darted to Mrs. Alcaraz and then he tried to duck under my arms.

"Sweet boy, I have to run out for a bit. But these are Mommy's friends and they're going to be right here with you while I'm gone."

"Nooo." He kept trying to hide.

I blinked fast so I wouldn't cry. "I'll be back. I promise." I didn't want to lie. I wanted it to be true.

"Hey, Jacob," Kennedy said and sat down beside me. She always knew when I needed her. And right now I really needed her. She smiled at me and then down at my son.

Jacob blinked at her.

"It's nice to meet you," she said. "I heard you like football."

He pressed his little lips together as he stared at her.

"She's my best friend," I said. "And she's going to be right here until I get back, okay?"

His eyelids were growing heavy again. "Footie," he mumbled. If he was calm enough to fall asleep knowing there were strangers watching him, he'd be calm enough waking up too. He had to be. He had to be my brave little man. I watched his eyes close and his breathing slow.

I glanced over at Kennedy who was staring down at my son. She reached out and pushed his bangs out of his face. "He looks like you," she whispered.

No. He looked like his father. I blinked faster, barely keeping my tears at bay. Jacob would be safe here if the next few hours didn't go as planned. Kennedy and Mrs. Alcaraz would make sure of it. I leaned down and kissed his forehead. *I love you. I love you so much.* I closed my eyes tight and breathed him in. I needed his strength. *I'm doing this for you, sweet boy. For your father. For our family.* I stood up and turned away without looking back. It felt like my heart was on fire again as I ran down the rickety stairs and climbed into a taxi.

I stared out the window at the cars zipping past. I hated it here. The air smelled rotten. There were too many people. It was stifling.

Breathe in. Breathe out.

The last thing I needed right now was to have a panic attack.

The cab pulled to a stop outside my dad's apartment building.

The doorman let me in and I ducked my head and hurried past him. I slammed the door closed button on the elevator before he could realize I wasn't a resident. The doors slowly slid closed and I breathed a sigh of relief. This place definitely didn't have the best security in the city anymore. I would have said it was my lucky day, but I didn't have lucky days. My days were all hell because of my father.

He'd ruined everything.

He'd ruined my whole fucking life.

The elevator slowed to a stop on his floor. I stepped off. I remembered the last time I'd been here. The morning after Thanksgiving.

My father stole my kidney.

He never cared.

I'd forgiven him for stealing my kidney. But I'd never forgive him for killing my husband. I told him what would happen if he ever came after Miller. I'd fucking told him.

I said he'd be dead to me. Buried in the grave next to my fake one. I meant it metaphorically back then. I didn't mean it metaphorically anymore.

Jacob had been eerily calm following Miller's instructions after the explosion. I was eerily calm now. Because really, I'd been planning this for a long time. I'd gone over it a million times in my head over the past 16 years.

I took a deep breath and knocked on my father's door.

I thought I'd be scared.

I thought I might change my mind.

But now that I was here, I wasn't second guessing a thing. Because I'd been debating one question over the past 16 years - Had my father ever really loved me? I knew the answer now.

No.

He'd told my mom to abort me.

Never.

He only got close to me to steal my kidney.

Nunca.

He'd killed my fucking husband.

I pulled my gun out of my waistband and held it up in front of me. It was time for Richard Pruitt to take his last breath.

WHAT'S NEXT?

Brooklyn is back in the same city as Matt! But what will she do now that she's back?

Find out in Book 6, coming in 2022.

While you wait, see what Matt was thinking when he first met Brooklyn back in high school.

To get your free copy of Matt's point-of-view, go to:

www.ivysmoak.com/ehr-pb

A NOTE FROM IVY

This was not how book 5 was supposed to go. I expected to write a very small amount about Brooklyn's life during the past 16 years. Just to catch everyone up. But when I started writing it…I couldn't stop. I couldn't cut Miller's time with her short. Because to me, their life was happiness in this amazing little bubble. My husband Ryan and I live in a little bubble just like Miller and Brooklyn did. And I think I saw us in them. And I didn't want it to end. I actually couldn't write the words The End. Because I knew they'd break me.

This book means everything to me. Probably more than any other I've ever written.

I found myself again in this book. It was the most selfish book I've ever written. Because I wrote it for myself. Because I needed it. I wrote this story right from my heart.

I've always loved Miller. And I had this idea in my head that in another lifetime, he and Brooklyn would have wound up together forever. Happy and in love in each other's arms forever and always. I needed to tell Miller's story. Because he deserved it. He deserved a lifetime of happiness, and it kills me that I could only give him 16 years. Because 16 years will never be enough.

I wish I could say I was numb writing this book. But I felt all those emotions too. This book devastated me.

And if you're feeling that right now too…know you're not alone. I want to climb back into the middle of this book and just stay there with this happy little family of three.

I'm crying writing this note, just remembering this feeling of panic in my throat as Miller's story came to an end. I hate writing that word. End. But Miller will live forever in this book. And I'm going to go read the middle again as he and Brooklyn danced around the kitchen in bliss, never knowing that their time would be cut short.

But as hard as it is for me to keep going…Brooklyn's story isn't over yet. I don't have to write The End for her. And things are about to get really messy.

Look out New York City. Brooklyn is back.

Ivy Smoak
Wilmington, DE
www.ivysmoak.com

ABOUT THE AUTHOR

Ivy Smoak is the USA Today and Wallstreet Journal best-selling author of *The Hunted Series*. Her books have sold over 3 million copies worldwide.

When she's not writing, you can find Ivy binge watching too many TV shows, taking long walks, playing outside, and generally refusing to act like an adult. She lives with her husband in Delaware.

Facebook: IvySmoakAuthor
Instagram: @IvySmoakAuthor
Goodreads: IvySmoak

Recommend *Runaway* for your next book club!

Book club questions available at:
www.ivysmoak.com/bookclub

CPSIA information can be obtained
at www.ICGtesting.com
Printed in the USA
LVHW051229040322
712556LV00008B/999

9 781942 381389